THE ALPHA KING AND HIS HUMAN MATE

Copyright May 2019 ©

Melisa Bigler

Dedicated to my biggest fan, my mother, Raola Lee. Thank you for reading all my books several times, and then some.

Other books by Melisa Bigler
The Profiler
The Princess Lottery
The Medicine Lark
Luna in Disguise
Blue Eyed Thief

All books available on Amazon.com

"I want to be the King in your story,
I want to know who you are,
I want your heart to beat for me."
DERMOT KENNEDY

"Me, a human, being a wolf's mate, that's rich. I know why
you're here. You're here to get girls for your harems. Well, I can
tell you, Mr. Tall, Dark, and Handsome, I won't be a part of
that, so you can count me out." Jillian said, starting to walk
away. But he reached out and grabbed her hand, sending a
thousand volts through her. She looked down at his hand and
then at him. "Would you kindly let me go before I scream?"

Chapter 1

It was Jillian's first day at a new high school, again. She hated being the new kid, everyone would gossip about her, trying to find her flaws, and then she would make a few friends and a few enemies. She just wished that her family would quit moving so much; it was really annoying trying to make new friends every place they went, then to get torn away from her friends once again when her dad found new work. It was getting old. She was glad it was the last few months of her senior year and that she wouldn't have to deal with moving to a new high school anymore.

Jillian got dressed that morning, putting on jeans and a t-shirt, her typical style of dress, and hoped that she might make some new friends this late in the school year. It was the beginning of March, and her dad had decided that they had to move again just the week before. Jillian was getting ready to graduate, so why now? But Jillian's parents had insisted that they move; her dad had actually looked worried as they packed their things as if something terrible was going to happen if they didn't move. So, after some protesting, Jillian finally gave in, and so here they were in some little town, although Jillian had to admit, it was a pretty town. Especially the vast mansion that sat on the hill overlooking the town. She wondered who lived there; they were obviously rich, and why live here of all the places? In the middle of nowhere, really, it was. The closest city was an hour away. She wondered if she would ever meet whoever lived in the mansion, but she didn't care for now. All Jillian cared about was graduating, catching up on work she knew she had missed, and hoping that she would survive school until the middle of June.

Jillian's parents were already at work, no surprise, off on a new dig. Her father was a paleontologist who dug up fossils and bones, unlike an archeologist who dug up ancient civilizations.

Jillian was used to having her parents head to work before she got up, and she usually didn't see them until dark, so she made herself some breakfast and then headed to school. She walked since the school was nearby. Jillian smiled as she walked, nodding at the neighbors who were out watering their lawns or sending their kids off on the school bus. Jillian hoped that it would be a good place to live, and she really hoped that she would find a boyfriend. She had made friends with boys at her other schools, but they hadn't wanted to get serious with her, mostly because she wouldn't sleep with them. Jillian was not that type of girl. The only problem was, she only had a little over two months of school left. Would she be able to make any friends at all, let alone a boyfriend?

A few minutes later, she walked up to the typical-looking high school. It was on a dead-end street and looked like it took up quite a bit of property. She could see a football stadium on one side of the school and tennis courts on the other side.

Jillian headed up the school's stairs, hoping to be ignored by the students ahead of her, but of course, they all looked at her, the new girl. A few girls snickered as she walked by, but she was used to it. She noticed then as she headed inside that most of the girls were dressed slutty, and she thought, 'great, I'm going to school with a bunch of Ho's.'

Jillian sighed as she walked into the office, then stopped at the secretary's desk. The lady behind the desk was busy painting her nails; she must have had quite an exciting job. She was also dressed like a Ho in an extremely low cut and revealing top, along with a tight mini skirt. The sad thing about it was that she had to have been older than Jillian's parents. Her gray hair was peeking through what looked like a bad dye job. Jillian wasn't sure if her hair was supposed to be blonde, black, or skunk, maybe? Jillian was kind of disgusted at the woman's outfit, besides the awful hair. Who dressed like that when you were her age, really?

The woman finally looked up and smiled a fake smile. "Can I help you?"

"I'm the new student, Jillian Everett; I need my class schedule."

"Oh, of course," the woman said, gingerly picking up a piece of paper next to her so she wouldn't ruin her freshly painted nails. She handed it to Jillian. "Your first class is down the hall, on the left, in the middle. Your locker assignment and combination are on there also."

"Um, thanks," Jillian said and walked out, looking at her schedule. At least she had classes that she liked, no math because she didn't need it, but English, Science, P.E., and the other two classes were electives, which were French and Dutch oven cooking. Those were the classes she looked forward to taking; Jillian just hoped she wouldn't be too far behind, especially in French, since it was only her first year of taking that class.

As Jillian walked down the hall, she tried to ignore the looks being given her by the other students. She heard the whispers, "New girl, feel sorry for her."

Why would they feel sorry for her? Was it because she was a new student starting in the middle of the year? She didn't worry about it, though, as she walked into her classroom and headed to the teacher. He was a nice-looking man, with blonde hair and light blue eyes. He watched her as she walked in.

"Ahh, a new student, welcome, Miss?"

"Jillian Everett," Jillian supplied.

"Yes, Jillian, I'm Mr. Flynn. Unfortunately, you'll need to sit up here in the corner because I have assigned seats, and that's the only one available."

Jillian shrugged and headed to the seat as the other students filed in. "New girl," she heard among the whispers, "she's sitting in Kathy's seat, poor Kathy," came the giggles.

Jillian tried to ignore them but wondered what they were talking about.

"Class, we have a new student, Jillian Everett," Mr. Flynn said.

Jillian waved her hand half-heartedly; some of the kids snickered. She wasn't about to stand up and see them giggling at her.

"Make her feel welcome," the teacher said, "but not too welcome, and you know what I mean," he growled. Did he just growl? Jillian looked up to see the teacher's eyes go black for a second. Okay, that was weird. She had to be imagining things.

The students nodded at him as he walked around. "I have a new reading assignment for you."

Everyone groaned in feigned agony.

"Twilight," he chuckled.

The students burst into laughter.

"I know it's a teenage werewolf, vampire thing, but I want you to read it and dissect it for me. Why was there a love triangle? I want some in-depth essays written about this book."

He then handed out paperback copies of the book. The students were still snickering.

"This is so fake," one of the boys laughed, "I mean, really, a human falling in love with a vampire and a werewolf? Who dreams up such things? Everyone knows werewolves are superior."

The other students laughed along with him. Was Jillian missing out on something? Or did that kid just prefer werewolves? Not that she blamed him. Jacob *was* a lot better looking than Edward, at least in the movies.

The teacher handed Jillian the book. "Don't mind them; they're just goofy teens."

"Oh yeah, the new girl is in for a rude awakening," one of the guys hollered.

"Les, shut up," the teacher growled again. The boy nodded. "Sorry, sir, just saying."

"Rude awakening? Oh, but enlighten me," Jillian said, turning in her seat to glare at the boy that had spoken.

He grinned at her and shrugged, making some students snicker again.

"Les, like I said, knock it off. You're all going to treat Jillian with respect, right?" Mr. Flynn said, glaring at all the students.

The class nodded, even though some were still smirking at her.

Okay, what kind of school had she gotten herself into? They all acted like they held some sort of secret, and the girls were dressed like they were going out for a night on the corner. This school was bizarre, Jillian decided.

The students started to read as Jillian looked around. She noticed that all the boys were very handsome and very well built. As if all of them could play linebackers on a football team, and the girls, gorgeous. Jillian felt totally out of place in her t-shirt and jeans and her plain looks. One of the boys caught her perusing the students, and he winked at her. She just shook her head at him and opened her book to read. She had read Twilight several times before and knew the book almost word for word, but writing an in-depth essay would be interesting.

It didn't seem too long after that the bell rang, dismissing the students. Jillian waited until the others had left before she headed to the door. "Jillian, good luck out there," Mr. Flynn said. She shrugged and walked out, ignoring the looks from the students. They were probably staring at her because she wasn't dressed like a skank.

In her next class, another introduction, more snickering. Jillian should be used to it, though; after all, she had been in new schools almost every year since she could remember. She just always kept her head down and tried to blend in, but how could you blend in when all the girls were dressed slutty, and you were the only one who wasn't? She didn't even own clothes like the rest of the girls did, and didn't want to, ever.

P.E. rolled around, and the girls finally changed into t-shirts and shorts, but the shorts were really short, most of them showing off butt cheeks. Jillian couldn't believe that they would dress like that for gym class, too, unbelievable. The boys, of course, ogled the girls, but the girls ignored the boys, and Jillian wondered why? Jillian hoped that one would flirt with her, but even the boys ignored her. It was the most bizarre thing she had ever seen. The students were hanging out in their little cliques, and every once in a while, they would look at Jillian and laugh. She sighed and wondered if she could talk her mom into letting her be homeschooled for the last few months. She wasn't sure she could handle being laughed at for two months straight.

The P.E. teacher let Jillian sit out for the first day since she didn't have gym clothes but was told to buy some in town. Would she even be able to find something modest in town? If all they sold were prostitute clothes, she might have to talk her parents into letting her borrow the car and go into the city.

Jillian was glad when it was finally lunch. She had packed a sandwich because she wasn't sure if any hot lunch was served. The students filed in and got their lunches in the line, and Jillian noticed there seemed to be a different kind of buzz going on in the lunchroom. The girls were grooming themselves and making sure their cleavage showed, besides hiking up their skirts just a bit higher. Many girls had mirrors out, checking their makeup, and Jillian wondered what was going on.

She heard a huff beside her and looked to see a girl sitting by her. She looked normal, as in, she didn't have the skank look. She had blonde hair and light blue eyes, and a pleasant-looking face. "Hey, I'm Kimberly, and you must be the new girl, Jillian."

"How did you guess?" Jillian said dryly.

"Well, considering that you are the only one, besides me, not dressed like a prostitute, it's kind of hard not to notice."

Jillian grinned. Kimberly was dressed in jeans and a hoodie. She liked her instantly because she *wasn't* dressed like a Ho.

"So, why aren't you dressed like them?" Jillian asked her.

"Because I don't have to worry about being chosen."

"Chosen?" Jillian asked, confused.

"Oh, sorry new girl, you don't know, do you," Kimberly said. "You are all normal and stuff. Come on, let's go outside. I can enlighten you as to why the girls dress that way."

"O-kay," Jillian said, grabbing her lunch and following Kimberly out the door. Everyone ignored them as they left. The girls were too busy looking at themselves in their compact mirrors.

"It would be nice if I wasn't talked about and laughed at," Jillian sighed as they sat at a table outside under some trees.

"Yeah, I hear you," Kimberly nodded as if that had happened to her before.

"So, spill it, why are the girls dressed like prostitutes, but not you?" Jillian asked her.

"Do you really want to know? It is going to be a shock. But I can tell you, you know, rip off the Band-Aid all at once," Kimberly grinned.

"Sure, throw it at me." I mean, what could she possibly say? Nothing really ever surprised Jillian.

"Are you sure? Maybe I should wait a bit; you know, a few weeks perhaps to see what happens. Maybe then everyone will ignore you. All the girls care about is themselves anyway."

Kimberly looked like she was having an internal battle with herself.

"Is it really that bad? The girls aren't training to be prostitutes, are they?" Jillian asked.

Kimberly laughed. "You are actually closer than you think."

"What? That's disgusting."

"I know, but that's not the main reason why they dress that way. It's kind of complicated."

"So, they are kind of training to be prostitutes, but kind of not. That makes no sense."

Kimberly sighed. "I really don't know if I should tell you. You will freak out, and with it being your first day here, well," she paused. "My mate not like it if I do tell you."

"Mate?" Jillian asked, confused.

"Soulmate," Kimberly shrugged.

"Soulmate? How old are you?"

"18."

"You are too young to be talking about soulmates and true love, aren't you? I mean, I'm 18 and haven't even had a boyfriend."

Kimberly laughed. "You'll understand one day. I am sure you will find a guy that will knock you off your feet too."

"You are seriously in love, aren't you," Jillian said, watching Kimberly.

"Oh yes. Ruben is incredible. He is such a sweet guy and treats me like a queen."

"That sounds so cheesy but sweet too," Jillian commented, making Kimberly laugh again. "So, are you going to tell me what is going on?"

"Fine, but you are going to freak."

"I am all about freaky things. So pull off the Band-Aid already. I'm not a patient girl."

"Those girls want to be chosen by the Alpha King," Kimberly admitted.

"The whosit?" Jillian asked, confused.

"The Alpha King, you know, werewolf?"

Okay, so maybe something could shock her. Jillian busted out laughing.

"Ha, that is very funny. All of you must have been reading way too many teen novels."

She looked at Kimberly, but she was not smiling.

"You *are* kidding, right?" Jillian asked her.

"I'm not," Kimberly said, watching Jillian to see if she would freak out.

"Okay, should I start freaking out right now?" Jillian joked, but her voice was shaky.

"You can; no one will notice," Kimberly shrugged, "since all the other girls are inside waiting for the Alpha King."

"So, the girls dress slutty to be his prostitutes?"

Kimberly chuckled. "Some of them, but mostly they want to be his mate. When they hit 18, he knows. Don't ask me how he knows, but then he is the King, and so he comes to the school to look for his mate."

"Are all of those girls 18?" Jillian asked her.

"No, only a very few, but if he doesn't find his mate, and the girl doesn't find her mate here at the school when she turns 18, he sends them away to find their mate in another pack or to be a part of someone's harem."

"Yuck, that is sick if they are put into a harem."

"I know, tell me about it," Kimberly shuddered. "Good thing I don't have to worry about being a Ho."

"Sounds like a very crappy thing to do to those girls," Jillian agreed.

"It is, but most of the girls that are sent away have found their mates. Not here, but elsewhere."

"Do the girls want to be in a harem if they aren't mated?" Jillian asked, shaking her head in disbelief.

"Oh, yeah, they are treated like royalty. They are given whatever they want, as long as they satisfy whoever they are given to."

"Does the king have a harem?" Jillian asked her.

"I don't think so, but I have heard rumors that the girls who aren't placed in harems hang around the palace until they are."

"So, technically, he has a harem."

"Yes, I guess, technically he does."

Jillian shuddered. "So, he comes here once a week?"

"Yes, more so now, since more girls are turning 18."

"Remind me to hide when he does."

Kimberly chuckled. "You're safe."

"Why is that?"

"You're human, and he needs a werewolf for a mate."

"So you're saying, every girl in the school is a werewolf?" Jillian shouted in shock, jumping up.

"Woah, settle it down, friend," Kimberly said, putting an arm on Jillian. "Yes, everyone, but you, guys included. Now take a deep breath; it's okay."

Jillian was pale as she collapsed back onto the bench. "I'm so screwed. Why of all the places would my parents put me in a school full of werewolves?"

"They probably didn't know."

"Isn't there another high school I could go to?" Jillian whispered.

"In the city, but it's over an hour away. Besides, as I told you, you are safe. You'll be ignored because you aren't a wolf, and that's a good thing, trust me."

"I hope so," Jillian said, her hands shaking as she picked up her sandwich again, but then she set it back down. She didn't feel so hungry anymore. She couldn't wrap her mind around what Kimberly had told her. Werewolves? Was that even possible?

"So, I'm very freaked out right now," Jillian said, trying not to feel sick.

"I know, it's a shock, but don't think about it. Just pretend we are all normal people."

"How? You just admitted you get all furry."

Kimberly laughed. "Yes, we do, but it will be okay, I promise."

"What happens if all of you turn into wolves and I get attacked?"

"You won't get attacked. None of us are like that."

"So, when do you get all furry?" Jillian asked, still wondering if Kimberly was telling the truth.

"Whenever we want to, I suppose."

"So it's not with the full moon?"

"No," Kimberly laughed. "That's just a myth, and before you ask, a werewolf can't bite someone else and make them a werewolf. We are born that way."

"So, I should be safe then."

"Yes, very," Kimberly assured. "You have nothing to worry about, okay? As I said, pretend we are just normal people."

"Except for the Ho look?" Jillian asked, making Kimberly laugh.

"Yes, that."

"Do the girls dress like that every day?" Jillian then asked.

"No, only on Monday's, when the King comes."

"Oh, thank goodness. So, I will only stand out once a week," Jillian said weakly.

"Yes, this is true," Kimberly laughed again.

"And you act so normal," Jillian admitted.

Kimberly shrugged. "Yes, as normal as I can be."

Kimberly's eyes lit up then as one of the boys headed to her. He stopped and kissed her. "Hey, love, making friends with the new girl I see?" he chuckled.

"Yep. Ruben, meet Jillian, Jillian, meet Ruben."

"So, you are a werewolf too," Jillian said, noticing how tall and built he was.

"I see that Kimberly spilled our secret," he chuckled. "And yes, I am."

"So, what makes you so special? Kimberly flirts with you, but the other girls don't flirt with the other boys?" Jillian asked him.

Ruben laughed. "I'm Kim's mate. We are meant for each other. No other wolf can touch her, or I can kill them, and that includes the Alpha King."

"Oh," Jillian said. "and how did you know we were out here?"

He pointed to his head. "Kim and I can mind link. I know where she is at all times, and I know when she needs me."

"Oh, that's kind of cool, I guess, but don't you ever get any private time?"

Kimberly laughed. "Yes, we do. We can block each other out if we want."

"But not often," her mate growled.

Kimberly just punched his arm in response, a massive grin on her face.

"You two are pretty nice, for werewolves. I can't believe you *are* werewolves. I feel like I should totally be flipping out now or waking up from one of my bad dreams," Jillian said.

Kimberly laughed. "You aren't in a bad dream, girl. Get used to it; besides, after today, all the girls will go back to being their normal witchy selves and will dress better."

"Do they know I am human?" Jillian asked Kimberly.

"Oh yeah," Ruben nodded. "You smell different than a wolf."

"Like what?" Jillian asked, smelling her armpits. "I thought I put on deodorant today."

Kimberly busted out laughing. "Not like that, silly. All of us have a unique scent, and that is what attracts our mates to us."

"So, me, being human, what do I smell like?" Jillian asked.

"You smell different than a normal human," Ruben told her. "For some reason, you smell older like you are an old soul, but a good soul, don't get me wrong," he said, as Jillian glared at him. "You smell like cinnamon, chocolate, and something else; I can't put my finger on it."

"Her mate will know what it is when he meets her," Kimberly said.

"Hey, human here, I won't get a mate," Jillian pointed out.

Kimberly laughed. "Sorry, my bad. Interestingly, you have a unique smell; it is kind of cool, though."

"Thanks, I think," Jillian replied, wondering how come she smelled like cinnamon and chocolate. She knew that her shampoo and body wash didn't smell like that at all.

"So, what happens when you find your mate?" Jillian asked curiously.

"You calm down," Ruben grinned, "at least the guys do. Our mates mellow us out."

"Interesting, so the unmated males are out of control then?"

"Something like that," Ruben nodded. "They want to chase all the unmated females."

"So, a school full of testosterone, lovely," Jillian frowned, making the couple laugh.

"They'll leave you alone," Ruben said. "They only want female wolves."

"So, no chance of finding a boyfriend here then," Jillian huffed. She was kind of disappointed, sure that she would find a man at last.

"Nope, sorry about that," Ruben laughed. "But don't worry, I'm sure one day some nice human guy will snag you up."

"Gee, thanks," Jillian sighed, throwing her sandwich back into the bag and wadding it up.

"Wait, you don't want to be a mate to a werewolf, do you?" Ruben asked her.

"No, of course not, that would be weird, especially if he could go all furry, and I couldn't."

"You could always ask him for a ride," Kimberly snickered.

"You mean like a pack mule?" Jillian laughed. "I'm sure he would love that. "Honey, let me put a saddle on you so you can take me to school."

Ruben snorted.

"Just don't wear spurs," Kimberly said. She started laughing so hard that tears were running down her face.

"Yeah, ouch," Jillian grinned. "Don't want to kick him in the wrong places."

"Oh boy, I can tell we're going to be the best of friends," Kimberly said, wiping at her eyes.

"I agree," Jillian smiled at her, glad to have met Kimberly on her first day of school.

The bell rang then signaling the end of lunch.

"Can I walk you to class?" Ruben asked Kimberly then.

"Jillian, what is your next class?" Kimberly asked her.

"Umm, French."

"Good, we are in the same class. Ruben can walk us there."

"I would like that; maybe people won't stare at me so much if they see I have a friend. How is French anyway? I kind of suck at it, especially since it is my first year."

"Don't worry about it; the teacher is really laid back. I'm sure that she can help you catch up."

"Good," Jillian sighed.

Ruben then looked around as they headed back to the school. "That's strange."

"What is?" Jillian asked.

"Usually, the King and his entourage are here by now. Lunch is almost over. I wonder what the holdup is. There will be some disappointed girls today," Ruben commented.

"I, for one, am glad he didn't come," Jillian told them. "Then I don't have to see them throwing themselves at him like I'm sure they do."

Kimberly laughed. "They do that."

"By the way, I heard someone mention that I was in Kathy's seat this morning. Who was Kathy? And should I be worried?"

Ruben smirked. "She was the last girl who was chosen for someone's mate or harem. Not sure where she went."

Jillian shuddered. "That's just so wrong if she went to a harem. Why throw your life away like that? Who would want someone who has been used?"

Ruben threw back his head and laughed. "That's an excellent question, Jillian." He was still laughing as they headed back to the school, no Alpha King in sight.

Chapter 2

At the palace, the Alpha King paced. He was supposed to go to the high school today, but he didn't feel up to it. He knew no girls had turned 18, and the other girls could wait. He didn't want to go and look for harem girls, even though the other Alpha's liked it when he sent some their way. He needed to stop sending them girls. He didn't know why he had started that anyway, but he supposed it helped keep the other packs from starting a war with him by keeping the unmated Alpha's happy. Something wasn't right, though. It was almost a feeling of jealousy and then a sense of anger. He didn't like to feel that way. The door opened suddenly.

"Alpha, the girls are waiting for you at the school," the man said.

"Not today, Beta. They'll have to wait another week."

The Beta looked surprised. "Edric? Are you all right?"

Edric shook his head. "I don't feel right today; something is off."

"Maybe we need to start *you* a harem," the Beta grinned.

Edric shook his head. "I'm sick of girls, Warren."

Warren looked even more surprised. "You love women, I thought," he said, closing the door behind him as he stepped into the room.

"I liked looking at them, but not so much anymore. Now they're just a nuisance."

"It makes me wonder about you," Warren teased him. "You usually love having all those girls hanging around the palace. So, tell me, why the change of heart today? The girls are going to be disappointed. You show up like clockwork every week for the last year, so what's different now?" Warren asked.

"I don't know, but something is just off, and no, a girl will not help me right now," he sighed.

"Are you sure? There are some beauties there."

"No, because that's just that much more money spent on some girl, that's going to end up in someone's harem. I'm sick of them, Warren. I'm sick of them being in my home and watching them walk around with almost nothing on, flaunting themselves and trying to throw themselves at me. Even though I send them off to someone else, they still want me. They're not my mate, and I want them out of here."

Warren laughed. "You used to love that, though, when they threw themselves at you."

"Not anymore. Those girls disgust me. I'm thinking of telling the other packs if they want girls for their harems, they can come and get them, themselves."

Warren nodded. "I might have an idea of what your problem is."

"What?"

"You haven't found your mate yet, and your wolf is getting restless. Perhaps your mate is nearby, and your wolf can sense her."

"I doubt it," Edric scoffed. "Where would she be? Not at that stupid high school; there hasn't been a new student there for ages."

"Until today," Warren replied.

Edric glared at him. "Well, why didn't you say so?"

"Because she's human."

"Oh," Edric sighed, making his wolf growl. "That's too bad. You got my hopes up."

His wolf growled again. "*Be quiet, Raul,*" he told his wolf.

"*What if the human is our mate?*" his wolf responded.

"*Wolves do not mate with humans, ever.*"

"I take it you are arguing with your wolf?" Warren grinned.

"Yes, he thinks he is funny. He thinks that maybe the human is our mate."

Warren laughed. "Yeah, that *is* a good one."

"I know, right?" Edric shook his head. He stood. "I need to vent some frustration. Let's go to the training center."

Warren nodded, and the men headed out the door and to the extensive training center the king had set up for his men. He had them train in case any of the other packs attacked; he didn't want to take any chances. He only had his Beta and Omega besides his guards who lived on the property, but he ensured the other wolves that lived close by had access to the facility.

The rest of Jillian's day wasn't so bad, as long as she ignored the whispers. "Human," she heard amid giggles and smirks. So, they knew she was human, and they knew that she knew about them, but whatever.

Kimberly had been right about the French teacher; she was laid back and gave Jillian a book to help her study her French. Jillian's last class was the best, though. The teacher in that class threw Jillian right into cooking her first dutch oven dish, a cobbler, which turned out well. Even her teacher complimented her, telling her that she cooked better than most of the students in the class. Jillian stuck her tongue out at the students, making the boys chuckle. The girls just rolled their eyes at her and snickered.

When school finally ended, Kimberly and Ruben walked up to Jillian as she headed out the door.

"Where do you live? We can just give you a ride home," Ruben told her.

"Just down the street, I can walk, and don't you turn into wolves so you can get home faster?"

Kimberly laughed. "No, silly. There are too many humans around who would freak out if they saw huge wolves running the streets. So, we drive, just like you would."

"Okay, too bad, I would have told you to giddyap."

Kimberly snorted with laughter. "Good one."

"I know, right?" Jillian grinned. She was kind of disappointed, though; it would have been kind of cool to see them shift into wolves.

"See you tomorrow then," Kimberly told her.

"Yep, same boring day, same boring school."

"Terribly boring," Kimberly agreed, hugged Jillian, and then she and Ruben headed to their car.

Jillian wondered as she headed home from school if she would survive the two months with all those wolves and why was she taking the whole werewolf thing so well? Maybe because in the back of her mind, being in a school of werewolves was rather exciting. Jillian just had to make sure her parents didn't find out about the werewolves, or they would have to move again; Jillian was sure of that.

Her parents were still at work when she got home. They expected Jillian to have dinner ready for them when they arrived, so she pulled out what she would need for dinner, then headed to her room to do homework. Her first day of school and tons of homework. Jillian sighed as she sat down at her desk in her room, wondering how her parents could put her in such a school. She pulled out some paper from her notebook to start on her essay and cussed as the paper sliced right across her finger. Jillian watched, though, as her finger healed instantly. She smiled. That was one cool thing about her body; she could heal like nothing else. When she was younger, she had told one of her classmates, which had been a mistake, because she had been teased and called a liar, so now she hid it. If she got hurt, no one ever knew. Her parents just figured that she never got hurt, if only they knew. Jillian returned to her homework, wondering how the actual werewolves would write about a fake story. It was too bad that they only mated with other wolves. It would be kind of cool to have a wolf for a mate, but then again, maybe not, especially if they shed or had fleas. Jillian snickered. She cracked herself up sometimes.

Jillian heard her parents walk in after nine that night. She had made dinner and ended up putting most of it in the fridge for her parents to warm up later.

She heard someone walk up the stairs, and a knock sounded on her door.

"Come in."

Her mom walked in, covered in dust. "Hey sweetie, how was your first day of school."

"Interesting," Jillian said.

"Did you make some friends?"

"I did."

"Oh, good. We have some great news. Your father found some bones this afternoon, they look to be Jurassic age, and they look like huge wolf bones, probably a Sabretooth," she grinned. "On our first day of the dig too. Your father is quite excited."

After finding out what she had that day, Jillian wasn't sure that those bones were that old. She wondered if they were digging up old werewolf bones, but she wouldn't say anything because it's not like her parents would believe her.

"That's cool, mom. Sabretooth, huh?"

"Well, maybe not quite Sabretooth. They do have long canines, though, longer than a normal wolf."

"Interesting," Jillian responded.

"Maybe this weekend, you can come to the dig site."

"Okay, mom, that'd be great," Jillian said unenthusiastically. That was the last thing she wanted to do.

Her mom laughed. "I know, it seems so boring to you, but it's rather exciting," she gushed.

"Whatever, mom," Jillian shrugged and yawned.

"I know you are tired, sweetie. We'll see you tomorrow, okay?"

Jillian nodded and watched her mom walk out and close the door.

She just hoped that her parents weren't digging up something they shouldn't be, but she was afraid they were doing just that.

Chapter 3

The following day, the Alpha King was pacing the halls as one of the harem girls strolled up to him wearing nothing but a bikini. She wrapped her arms around him. "Your Highness," she purred. "Might I be of service? You look so down."

He frowned down at her and pushed her away. "Go put some clothes on," he muttered.

"But sire, you like us to dress like this," she pouted.

"Not anymore. You know you girls aren't here for me; you are here until the other packs send for you. Now get out of my sight," he frowned at her, "and tomorrow, all of you are out of here."

"Yes, sire," she muttered and headed away, swinging her hips as she went. She looked back to see if he was watching, but he was headed down a different hallway.

"Alpha," Warren stopped him as he went into his office, "we have a problem."

The two went inside and closed the door.

"Warren, what's wrong?"

"The paleontologists. They have dug up the burial ground from the last war."

The King growled in anger. "How did that happen? That land is guarded!" he yelled.

"They got special permission from someone," Warren said.

"How far down are they?"

"Just uncovering the first wolves, sire."

"Go stop it immediately. I do not want that disturbed. I don't care by what means, but get it stopped. Offer them money, whatever, just get them off that land, and make sure the wolves are reburied."

"Yes, Alpha." Warren walked out of the door, closing it behind him. Edric pinched his nose, feeling another headache coming on. They were getting to be more frequent.

"*You need your mate*," his wolf reminded him.

"*I can't find her,*" Edric muttered back.

"*She has to be close by; why else would you be hurting?*" his wolf pointed out. "*Maybe Warren lied about the new girl being human. Maybe he just wanted her for himself.*"

Edric chuckled. "*I doubt that. He is loyal to me, Raul. He would not lie.*"

"*I think we should go check anyway,*" his wolf said.

"*If it will shut you up,*" Edric said.

His wolf chuckled. "*You wish.*"

Jillian knew her parents were already at work when she got up for school, so she hurried and got ready for the day, putting on another t-shirt and jeans, and after grabbing a quick breakfast, she headed out the door.

When she reached the school, she noticed with relief that the girls were dressed normal, well, mostly. Some of them still wore skanky clothes, but everyone was in jeans and a regular shirt for the most part. The boys seemed relieved also, and the girls were actually flirting with them today. Jillian thought it interesting that the boys got ignored once a week, and then the girls flirted with them for the rest of the week. That was just wrong. Jillian felt bad for the guys. She wondered if they were sick of how they were treated, she would be.

The girls still snickered at her as she walked down the hall to her first class, but as usual, she ignored them.

"Hey girl, want to hang out after school?" Kimberly asked her, walking up to her.

"Sure, why not? My parents aren't home until late anyway."

"So what do they do for a living, something cool, I am sure."

"They're paleontologists."

"That *is* cool, so are they the ones who dig up dinosaur bones or humans?"

"You know the difference?" Jillian was shocked.

"Yeah, it was something I was interested in for a little while, but not now."

"They are into the dinosaur thing, but yesterday they dug up some bones that I think might be some of your ancestors."

"Really?"

"Yeah, my mom said that they were big with long canines."

"I bet they are," Kimberly frowned. "I bet the Alpha King will love that if he finds out your parents are digging up our ancestors."

Jillian chuckled. "Yep, I am sure he will be."

"So, do you move around a lot?" Kim asked her as they stopped outside Jillian's classroom.

"Yep, we move every year for my dad's work; it's been really annoying."

"I bet. It's probably hard to make friends."

"You have no idea. I am just glad this is my senior year, and I don't have to move if I don't want to."

"I hear you," she smiled as the first bell rang. "See you at lunch," Kimberly then said and wandered off.

Edric was working in his office when his phone rang. "What's going on, Warren? Why didn't you mind link?" he asked his Beta.

"Too long of a conversation," Warren said. "Look, these people have all the right permits; there was no bribery going on. I can't kick them off the land unless we have proof saying it is privately owned."

Edric growled, as did his wolf. His headache was getting worse. "Fine, I will dig up the papers and come down there myself."

"Yes, Alpha, you had better move it along. They have the first skeleton removed."

"I will hurry," he assured. He hung up, frustrated. He could not have some humans digging up his ancestors. He opened his filing cabinet and started to sort through the papers, finally finding what he needed almost an hour later. "Ha!" he said triumphantly.

"*Are you going to the school today after you clear up this mess?*" his wolf asked.

"*Not unless we can get those people off our land before school is over.*"

"*Then let's get going,*" his wolf said.

"*I don't know why you think our mate is there.*"

"*Why else would you be so ornery,*" Raul chuckled.

Jillian's parents were a bit surprised when a limo and two dark SUVs pulled up to the dig site. They had already been halted with their progress when some guy had shown up claiming they were digging on private property. But he didn't have proof that he owned it, so he had left, promising to return with the paperwork proving it was private land. They were just getting back to work when the limo pulled in, and a large man got out.

He exuded power as he headed to them, and he looked angry.

He walked over to them, holding up a piece of paper. "You need to stop your digging. This is private property."

Jillian's dad hopped out of the hole, not intimidated by the man, even though he towered over him. "Who says?"

"I do. I am Edric Ventin, and this is my land."

Jillian's dad hated it when people like him acted like a God or something. Rich men always seemed to be like that, and he looked rich. He also looked like Jillian's dad should know him, but he was not one of those who worshiped men like him or was in awe of them.

"Can I see your proof?" Jillian's dad asked.

Edric handed over the paper, and Jillian's dad read it. He then whistled, making everyone stop their work.

"This man has proof that this is his land; we need to get off of it."

He then looked up at Edric. "We do apologize, sir. We had no idea. But someone permitted us to dig here."

"Do you know who?" Edric asked him.

"No, sir, we just got a letter from the city saying they had work for me, so here I am."

"I will find out who it is and have a word with him," Edric growled. "Now, if you wouldn't mind putting the bones back in the ground and burying the site back up, it would be appreciated."

"All right," Jillian's father sighed. He looked at his wife. "I hope there are more digging sites around. I hate to uproot Jillian on her second day of school."

Edric's heart leaped at the name, but why? This must be the human girl's parents. Why would her name cause excitement in him? His wolf chuckled. "*I am telling you, she is our mate.*"

"*She is not,*" Edric argued. He shook Jillian's dad's hand. "Thank you, sir, you will be compensated for your work," Edric promised, "and I will try and find you another dig site."

"That would be really kind of you, sir," Jillian's mom stepped up to him. She was a petite woman but very lovely. She looked young, except for the few gray hairs in her brown hair. "I don't want to have to pull our daughter out of school so soon. We have already moved too many times," she smiled at Edric, "it would be nice if she could make some friends and stay here for a while."

Edric nodded. "I will see what I can do," he assured them.

Edric then looked at two of his guards. "Let them get back to work; make sure everything is covered up before they leave." He then turned to Jillian's dad. "I will be in touch with you sir, if I could get your name and phone number."

"My name is Henry Everett, and this is my wife, Nadine," he said, hugging her to him. He was suddenly a little protective of his wife, but it didn't help that she was checking Edric out.

Edric nodded as Henry handed over his business card to Edric. "If you could find us more work, we would appreciate it."

"I will try, Henry," Edric assured him.

"Thank you, sir," Henry said, and then nodding at his team, they headed back into the hole to bury the remains.

Edric and Warren both sighed as the team threw dirt back on the site.

"Let's go see if we can find out who gave them permission, shall we?" Edric told Warren.

Warren nodded, but Edric's wolf growled.

"We are going to the school, remember?"

"No, we are not; I have important work to do."

"Do you want your headache to go away? Our mate is nearby; I can feel it."

"Fine, if it will shut you up," Edric growled, making his wolf chuckle.

He looked at Warren as they got into the limo. "My wolf thinks our mate is at the school. I don't believe it, but I will appease him by going, and then I am going to find out who let those people dig up my land."

Warren nodded. "Whatever you say, Alpha. I think your wolf is nuts, though."

Raul growled in response.

"He did not like that," Edric pointed out to Warren, who only chuckled.

Chapter 4

The Alpha King headed to the school. Wouldn't everyone be surprised, Edric grinned as he got out of the limo with Warren and two of his guards. He was glad he was coming in unannounced. He was sick of all the girls dressing like prostitutes, hoping he would choose one of them. As they headed into the school, Edric's wolf perked up and began to sniff. "*She is here,*" he said, urging Edric to hurry to the cafeteria where the students were eating lunch.

As the men walked in, all conversation stopped. Every eye was on the Alpha King. The King was here? Today? Not one of the girls was dressed to entertain him. The girls all started to groom themselves, but he was not watching any of them, he only saw one girl, and she was absolutely stunning, what he could see of her. She had a curvaceous body, beautiful brown, curly hair that went past her shoulders, and her scent hit him like a ton of bricks. It was chocolate, cinnamon, and orange.

"*Mate,*" his wolf growled.

Jillian was wondering why the cafeteria was suddenly deathly quiet.

"The Alpha King," Kimberly whispered, wondering why he was there. Jillian glanced up and saw the most handsome man she had ever seen in her life. He was tall and muscular, with dark hair and the greenest eyes she had ever seen, and he was looking right at her.

She blushed and ducked her head.

"Why is he here?" Jillian whispered.

"I don't know, but he is headed this way," Ruben said.

"Jillian Everett," she heard.

Jillian looked up. The man was towering over her. How did he know her name?

"You are mine," he said. She was absolutely gorgeous up close, and she had the bluest eyes he had ever seen. His wolf was pleased. Here was their mate.

Ruben's mouth hung open. "Sire, you do know she is a human, right?"

Warren chuckled beside him. "I told him that also."

Jillian was still watching the king. "Did I just hear you right?"

"Yes, my lady, you are my mate," he said, making everyone in the cafeteria gasp.

Jillian began to laugh. "Oh, that is a good one. Me, a human, being a wolf's mate. That is rich." She then stood and poked his chest. "I know why you are here. You are here to get girls for your harems. Well, I can tell you, Mr. Tall, Dark and Handsome," making his wolf chuckle, and Edric grin at her feistiness, "I will not be part of that, so you can count me out."

She then started to walk away, but he reached out and grabbed her hand. She gasped as a thousand volts ran through her. She looked down at his hand and then at him. "Would you kindly let me go before I scream?"

Edric chuckled. "Who, pray tell, would come to your rescue? Everyone here is a wolf."

"I don't care, but it would make me feel better."

He chuckled again. "Jillian, please, I am not here to make you a part of the harem. As a matter of fact, as of today, they are gone. They are being sent to the other packs, and I am not finding any more. If the packs want girls, they can come and get them themselves."

The girls gasped around him, and some began to cry. Edric ignored them. He had finally found his mate, and his wolf was very happy.

Jillian tore her hand from his. "That's too bad for them; I am sure all those girls were looking forward to sleeping with you or your men. Well, guess what, I won't. I am not that kind of girl, and the likes of you will not use me," she hissed. "Now, if you would kindly leave or choose some other slut, but you can't have me. Thanks, but no thanks." Jillian then walked away, everyone staring after her in awe or horror.

Edric headed out the door after her, making the girls angry. How dare he choose a human over them. Their Luna, a human? Impossible.

Jillian was fuming as she headed out the door. How dare that arrogant man tell her that she was his mate. Alpha King, right. He did exude power, great power. She could feel it oozing off of him, but she was human. So what if when he had touched her that she felt her body come alive. She scoffed again. It was ridiculous. She didn't care if he was extraordinarily handsome or well built or drool-worthy; she was not his. *But,"* her inner voice said, *"weren't you just talking about having a wolf for a mate?"*

"Jillian," she heard. She turned around to see the supposed King headed to her, his entourage absent.

"Where are your guards, your Highness?" she spit out.

"I don't need them. I want to talk to you alone."

"I have nothing to say to you."

"I want you to come home with me," he told her.

"No. You will not use me, and I will not be one of your girls. I have heard of your reputation. Who knows what kind of disease you have from sleeping with all those skanks," Jillian snarled. Why was she so angry with him? It wasn't like she knew him, plus she was probably being disrespectful, but she really didn't care. *'But you want to get to know him,'* her inner voice said to her. She shoved it back down. She would not ever want to get to know him, no matter how good-looking he was.

"For your information, I do not sleep with them, and I assure you, I am clean of diseases," the king frowned.

"I seriously don't care," Jillian replied. "Go back to your little palace, or wherever you live, I will not be a part of it, ever."

She stomped away. Edric admired her backside as she walked away.

"Go after her," his wolf said.

"*I won't. She needs to cool down.*"

"*Go after her,*" his wolf said again. Edric could feel his wolf taking over. "*Raul, no.*"

"*If you don't, I will,*" his wolf said, and the Alpha felt his bones cracking and his canines lengthening as he turned into his wolf and raced after his mate.

Jillian was ticked off. How dare some arrogant man tell her what to do. She knew she was not his so-called mate. Who believed in that crap anyway? Seriously? Even if Kimberly had told her about it, she didn't have proof of any of it. She hadn't seen anyone become a wolf.

She suddenly was confronted by an enormous light gray wolf with a white face and incredible green eyes. He was almost as tall as she was. He whimpered at her. Okay, so maybe what Kimberly had said *was* true. Werewolves did exist.

She rolled her eyes at him, making him chuckle. He nudged her with his nose.

"No, wolf boy, I don't care if you do look handsome as a wolf. I am not giving in to you. You are that same guy, right?" she asked, looking him in the eyes.

He nodded.

"Yeah, look at me talking to a dog," Jillian sighed. "Sorry, but no, even if it is cool that you can change into a wolf."

The wolf chuckled again, nudging her hand with his head.

"No, I am not petting you either," she replied, "even if your fur looks nice and soft," she said.

The wolf laid down by Jillian's side and put his head under her hand. Even laying down, she didn't have to bend down to pet him. She felt his fur. It *was* really soft. She found herself rubbing his head, making the wolf smile. He nudged her hand, wanting more.

"No, you are going to be nothing but trouble," she said, shaking her head, making him laugh again.

She began to walk away, and the wolf whimpered.

"No, I am sorry, but no. I will not be a part of your harem or whatever you call it."

"Jillian," she heard from behind her then. She ignored him. Had he changed back into a human already?

He caught up with her, grabbing her hand, sending sparks through her. So he had changed back, and he was totally nude. She blushed, making him chuckle.

"This is all yours if you come home with me," he said.

"No, and no," she said, looking away. "Just leave me be. I will not be in your bed now, or ever, got it?" she said and walked away, after yanking her hand free from his.

Warren was headed to them, eyeing his king, who was naked and following the girl.

"Need some clothes, Alpha?" Warren smirked.

"If you would, Beta," Edric responded. "I seem to be intimidating the girl with my sexiness."

"You wish," she scoffed. "I've seen bigger."

Warren busted out laughing as he handed over some clothes he had snagged from the limo. Edric's mouth hung open. He could not believe she would talk to him like that, not her King and mate. He quickly dressed and caught up with Jillian, stopping her again by grabbing her arm, a frown on his face. "Do not tell me you have seen a man naked," he growled at her. His wolf was furious. His mate should not be looking at other men.

"Oh please, go growl somewhere else," she said. "You see naked women every day, so don't even go there."

He frowned again. She was right. He really needed to get rid of those girls.

"I promise you; the girls are gone as of today. The only naked body I want to see is yours," he said.

"In your dreams," she replied, heading back to the school.

"Jillian, do not walk away from me," he said.

"Or what, your Highness?" she mock bowed at him, "You will throw me in the dungeon? Go back to your harem, king, and leave me be."

He had had enough. His mate would not disrespect him. Edric walked over to Jillian, picked her up, threw her over his shoulder, and walking to the limo, he threw her inside, kicking and screaming.

Jillian opened the other door as he scooted in and was ready to leap out, but he reached over her, slammed the door, and locked it. "You are not leaving; you are mine."

"I am not yours," she hissed. "You can go to hell."

He smirked. "I've already been there, love."

She tried to unlock the door but to no avail.

"Let me out," she ground out.

"No. You are going home with me."

"You can't just kidnap me. My parents will wonder where I am," she pointed out.

"Yes, your parents," he said as Warren started the car and pulled out to the road. "I met your parents today."

She paled. "What did you do to them?"

"I did nothing to them, although they were digging on my land," he said, "and digging up my relatives, without my permission."

"I don't think they knew," she told him.

"They didn't. I informed them. They were quite gracious, unlike their daughter," he growled.

"You kidnapped me, jerk; what do you expect me to do? Bow at your feet?"

"I wouldn't mind," he smirked at her.

"Ass," he said, making him chuckle. "Let me go."

"No, never, and if you don't stay, I am going to press charges against your parents for trespassing and have them thrown in jail."

She paled. "You wouldn't."

"Watch me. I am tired of this. Either you come willingly, or they pay; what is your choice?"

Tears started down her face. "I will come, jerk. If only to save them."

"Good girl," he said, but he felt terrible seeing her tears. How else would he get her to come home, though? His wolf whimpered. He wanted to comfort his mate.

She turned to the window, tears running down her face. She was headed to a life of hell and couldn't do a thing about it.

The rest of the ride was silent, and when they pulled up to the palace, the doors were opened, and a nice-looking man helped Jillian out. He saw her tears and looked at his Alpha. He shook his head at the man.

"Luna, welcome," the man said, bowing to her.

She looked at the man, and more tears ran down her face, but she didn't say a word.

"Let me show you to your room," he told her.

Jillian ignored Edric as he came up to her to put a hand on her waist, but she shook him off and followed the man, her shoulders slumped in defeat.

Edric frowned. He did not like to see his mate so sad, but he could not have her fighting him. She would have to learn that she was his.

"I will be in my office," he told Warren and headed to his office after watching Jillian head up the stairs, her head down and crying.

One of the harem girls sauntered up to Edric, clad in a bra and lacy underwear. Jillian had also noticed her when she came in, making her cry harder. She was about to become one of them.

The man put a gentle hand on Jillian's arm as he showed her to her room on the second floor. He opened a door for her. "Your room adjoins the kings. If you need anything, let me know, okay?" he said.

She nodded, and as soon as the man left, she locked her door and the adjoining door and, throwing herself onto the bed, she sobbed.

How could he do this to her? Why would he kidnap her? She was just a human, not some wolf. She wasn't unique by any means.

"*Are you sure?*" her inner voice asked her.

"Shut up," Jillian told herself.

Edric could feel his mate's sorrow as she cried, and his wolf whimpered again. Edric growled at the harem girl. "I thought I told you girls to put some clothes on, now get out of my sight. In a few hours, all of you are being shipped out of here."

The girl whimpered as she walked away, feeling his anger.

"*Go to your mate, apologize to her,*" his wolf told him.

"*I will, but not now. She needs to cool down, and I can't let her treat me with disrespect. She is the Luna. I don't want the others disrespecting me because she does. I will not tolerate it.*"

"*She is scared, though,*" his wolf said.

"*I am sure she is. But she will get used to it here.*"

"*What of her parents?*"

"*I will call them,*" Edric replied. "*They will need to know.*"

"*You aren't going to tell them that you are her mate, though?*"

"*No. They wouldn't know anything about mates.*"

He sat down at the desk and pulled out Jillian's father's number from his pocket.

He answered. "Hello, Henry speaking."

"Henry, this is Edric."

"Oh, hello, sir. The site is almost cleaned up."

"Good to hear. Listen, I need to discuss something with you."

"Oh? Did you find me more work?"

"Well, no, not exactly, but I did find your daughter."

"My daughter?" he gasped. "Is she okay?"

"She is fine. I assure you, Mr. Everett. "*Really fine,*" his wolf snickered. "I saw her at school today when I went to visit. She has a strong personality, your daughter," Edric said, ignoring the comment his wolf had made, even though he agreed.

Henry chuckled. "Tell me something I don't know. So is she still at school?"

"Actually, no, I invited her to come and stay with me."

"Why would you do that?" Henry asked.

"Because I have taken a liking to her."

"Wait, you kidnapped my daughter?" Henry roared.

"That is a strong word, kidnapped," Edric said. "I offered for her to come and stay."

"And did she say yes?"

"Well," Edric hesitated.

"I take that as a no. I suggest, sir that you let her go, now."

"She was meant to be mine; she will be my queen."

Henry scoffed. "So you think you are her king?"

"Did you not see a palace when you moved here?"

"Yes, but I thought it to be a tourist destination or some rich man's house."

"I am that rich man, Henry, and a King."

Her father swore. "If you do not let her go, I will call the cops."

"The cops work for me, Mr. Everett. Now listen to me and listen well. If you try and take her back, I will have you arrested for trespassing on my property and digging up what was not yours. Do you understand me?"

"Promise me you won't kill her," Henry whispered. "She is my only child."

"She is in good hands, Mr. Everett, no harm will befall your daughter, and I will let you come visit her soon, okay?"

"Aren't you a little old for her?" Henry then asked.

"I am only 25; I am not that old."

"But why would you do this?" Henry asked again. "What did I do wrong that you would kidnap my daughter?"

"As I said, I have taken a liking to her."

Henry sighed heavily. "I will do anything to get her back. What do you want? I don't have that much money, but I will give it to you if that is what you want."

"No, I do not need any money. I want your daughter."

"Why would you kidnap her, though? Any normal man would ask her out on a date, yes?"

Edric shrugged. "Yes, I suppose I should have done that. But I was not sure she would say yes, seeing as I am older than her."

"So, your answer was to kidnap her. This is just wrong, sir, and you know it."

"I will take good care of her, I promise."

"What of her things?"

"I will send someone to get her things so she can feel more at home here."

"I don't understand why you are doing this. Are you some kind of child predator?"

"I assure you, Mr. Everett, I am not a predator."

"Can I speak with her?"

"Not right now, no. I will allow her to call you tonight."

"You had better not lay a hand on her head Edric, or I will have *your* head, king or not," her father growled out.

"She is safe here, Henry," Edric assured him. "Now, if you will excuse me, I have things to do."

"Hopefully, not my daughter."

"Not yet," Edric chuckled and then hung up, knowing that would tick him off. He couldn't help saying that Jillian's dad was making him mad.

He headed out of his office, where Warren stood, waiting for his Alpha.

"So, how did the call go?" he smirked.

"He couldn't refuse me. She is mine now."

"You know she is going to fight this."

"So be it, but she is mine Warren, and she is going to have to get used to it."

"You could have asked her out instead of kidnapping her."

"I know, but my wolf was getting impatient, and that was the only thing I could think of."

"She is human, Edric. That was not the way to go about wooing your mate. You know she is going to hate you now."

Edric sighed. "You are right; I suppose I was rather hasty."

"You think?" Warren chuckled. "Good luck in trying to get her to stay."

Edric sighed as he headed up the stairs to see his mate. What he had done had been rather rash. Maybe he should tell her that she could go home but had to promise not to date anyone because she was his. But would that work? He knocked on her door, feeling like the Beast in the Beauty and the Beast story. Would she forgive him and see past his rough exterior?

There was no answer as he knocked again. That would not stop him. He headed into his room and then to the adjoining door. It was locked. "The little minx," he chuckled. Good thing he had a key. He went to his dresser, pulled out the key, walked to the door, and opened it. He walked in, and not seeing her in the bedroom, he headed to the bathroom and cussed. Jillian was on the floor, a broken mirror next to her, a piece of glass in her hand, and both of her arms were covered in blood.

"Jillian, why?" Edric asked, his wolf whimpering to see his mate hurt. Edric knelt by her, pulling her to him while she cried.

"Why would you try and kill yourself?" he asked softly. "I don't want to be one of your sex slaves," she whispered, pushing herself away from him.

"You will never be a slave; you are my mate," he assured her and then stood up to grab towels and bandages. He then mind-linked

Warren. "*I need your help. She tried to slit her wrists. I need some pain killers and some cream for her wounds.*"

"*Yes, Alpha,*" came the response.

Warren appeared in the room moments later; he also came through the adjoining door. He knelt by Jillian. "Luna, you do know if you kill yourself, your Alpha will die also," Warren pointed out.

She snorted. "No, he won't. I've read enough stories to know that he won't die unless he has marked me, which is never going to happen."

"If you were marked, I could heal you with my touch," Edric told her.

"It's never going to happen," she hissed out. He frowned as she said that.

"Fine, this will hurt, but you will heal in a few days," he told her, ignoring her outburst.

He wiped the blood away, ready to put medicine on her when he paused. "Jillian, I thought you cut yourself."

She chuckled dryly. "Yeah, about that. I can hurt myself as much as I want, and look at me," she sighed. "I heal really fast."

Warren exchanged a glance with Edric.

"Jillian, you heal as fast as a werewolf. Are you a werewolf?" Edric asked her.

She laughed rudely. "Oh, hell no. I think I would know it if I was."

It hurt Edric and his wolf to see the hatred in Jillian's eyes and for her to talk like that to him.

"Please do not try and hurt yourself again, Luna," Edric said. "It hurts me when you do so," he said gently.

She glared at him. "No, it doesn't, you lie. Just leave, okay? I would rather you left me alone and let me go." She began to cry again.

"Why are you determined to kill yourself?" he asked her.

"Because I would rather die than be here with you and your harem."

Edric flinched at Jillian's words. He stood then, angry. He had had enough of her sass, and he was known for having a short fuse.

"I am glad you cleared that up, Jillian, I was going to get rid of the harem, but perhaps I will keep them now since you don't want to be mine," he wanted to smirk, but then he saw her pale face.

"Have a good afternoon, mate," he growled and left the room, slamming the door behind him.

"Will he actually go sleep with one of them?" Jillian whispered to Warren.

"No. He has saved himself for his mate, you," Warren said.

"I feel sorry for those girls," Jillian said and stood up with Warren's help. Then she headed into the bedroom and sat on the bed.

Warren cleaned up the mess on the floor and then left the room, shaking his head. He wondered if Edric and Jillian would ever work things out. It would be better for both of them if they did.

Warren frowned when he walked down into the hall to see the Alpha pushing away one of the harem girls who only had a pair of underwear on.

"Get out of my sight," he growled at her.

"But sire, you love me, I thought," the girl said.

"No, leave. I don't need you or any of you stupid girls," he growled out.

"But sire," she whimpered.

"Leave now!" he shouted at her.

She sashayed away. Edric glared at Warren. "What do you want?"

"Just came to say that the Luna is resting," he smirked. "If I didn't know any better, I would think she is getting under your skin, and what happened to you getting rid of the sluts? You know she won't be happy if she runs into one of them."

"Right now, I really don't care," he growled, walking into his office and slamming the door.

Warren just shook his head and headed away.

In his office, Edric sat down, running his fingers through his hair. "I swear she is going to drive me nuts," Edric said.

"*You did kidnap her,*" Raul pointed out.

"*That's because she is mine, and she wouldn't have come with me if I hadn't made her.*"

"*So you tick off your Luna, who then, in turn, tries to kill herself.*"

"*Yes, and how did she heal so fast? She is not a wolf. I can't sense one in her.*"

"*She is obviously special.*"

"*I know, but how? Her parents are human.*"

"*Interesting, but you need to apologize to her again.*"

"*I will after she calms down.*"

"*Good luck with that,*" Raul chuckled.

"*I know. I have a feisty Luna on my hands, that is for sure.*"

Jillian cried herself to sleep but was awoken when a knock sounded on her door later. "Dinner," she heard, but she ignored it. She would show the king. She would not eat, and she would stay in her room. Maybe if she were nothing but skin and bones, he would leave her alone, forget all about her, and let her go. Since she couldn't kill herself with objects, maybe she could starve herself. Then he would think she looked disgusting and get rid of her. But that little voice in her head said, "*Now, why would you want to do that?*"

Jillian snuggled under the covers even more. She hadn't changed from her bloodied clothes, and she didn't care if she ruined the sheets. She was so ticked off. How dare the Alpha kidnap her and tell her she was his. It was ridiculous. Who cared if she felt amazing when he touched her. That whole mate thing was ridiculous, and she was going to prove it. Jillian would either escape or starve herself, and then the Alpha could shove it.

It was dark outside when she heard the adjoining door open. She feigned sleep as she felt the bed sink by her. She felt her hair brushed back from her face and heard a heavy sigh. "I am sorry," she heard

Edric whisper, "but I can't let you go. I will die if you leave; you have to understand that."

She tried not to sigh under his touch. It was comforting, but she would not admit to it. She would not give into him, no matter how good his touch made her feel.

Jillian heard Edric get back up, and the door was closed again. She sighed in relief that he was gone and fell back asleep.

The following day she heard a key in the lock of her door and heard someone walk in, then they sat on the bed by her. "Oh dear, what has he done?" she heard a feminine voice say.

Jillian's eyes opened to see a woman who looked to be in her 30's, sitting by her.

"Luna, how are you feeling today?"

"How am I supposed to feel? That jerk out there kidnapped me, and I am no Luna. I don't want to be a Luna. So don't call me that," Jillian said angrily. She was still incredibly ticked off.

The woman chuckled, ignoring her outburst. "I am Carla. I am the Alpha's aunt. I heard you were here, and he told me to help you. He didn't tell me you were human, though."

"So?" Jillian grumbled. "I didn't ask to be his stupid mate if that is what I am. Personally, I think I am here for his harem, and I don't want to be part of that," she shuddered.

Carla shook her head. "No, sweet Jillian, you will never be a part of a harem. The Alpha already claimed you. I am quite surprised, though, that he has not gotten rid of them. He was supposed to ship them off yesterday."

Jillian sighed. "See? He obviously is keeping them around to add me to them."

"You do not need to worry about those girls. They are just playthings."

"I don't want to be one of his playthings," Jillian whispered.

"You will never be a plaything. You are his Luna, and he will treat you with respect. Don't worry, I will make sure they leave, even if I have to kick them out myself."

"Does he care for any of them?" Jillian asked her.

"No, of course not. He has been saving himself for you."

"Ha, I don't believe it for a minute."

"Believe it. Even though those girls have been here, he has tried to distance himself from them."

"Then why are they here? Why can't the other Alpha's come and get them? Why am I here? I am not his Luna," Jillian said adamantly. "I can't be. I am a human, not a wolf. Why can't he choose someone else, like one of his sluts? Besides, I have been here for less than a day. Why would he think I would fall in love with him? He kidnapped me. Would you fall in love with someone if they kidnapped you?" Jillian asked her.

"If they were my mate, then I suppose so," Carla shrugged.

"But I'm not; I can't be Carla. I am just normal. Look at me; I am not special."

"The Alpha can't just choose someone else. When you find your mate, that is it. You will not find someone else. If your mate dies, then you die, if you have marked each other, that is," she shrugged.

"Do you have a mate? Not that I really care, but do you?" Jillian asked.

"Yes. My husband is the Omega. He helps run the household."

"Are you happy?"

"Of course."

"Probably because you weren't kidnapped and forced here against your will."

"You are one angry Luna; I will give you that," Carla said, "but you need to forgive him. He saw you, knew you were his mate, and you defied him, so he had to do something drastic." Carla then pushed Jillian to the huge and opulent bathroom. "I am sorry, Luna, but this is your home now."

Jillian started to cry again. "Will I never get to see my parents again?"

"Yes. The Alpha does feel bad for what he did and is going to talk to your parents about coming and seeing you every day," Carla assured her. "Now dry those eyes. Let's get you bathed and dressed. I will have some breakfast sent up to you, okay?"

Jillian nodded, not that she would eat it, even though her stomach grumbled.

Carla smiled. "I can hear that you are hungry. Take a bath; there are clothes in your closet. Your things should be here later today."

"He is having my things brought here?"

"Yes, the Alpha is having all your belongings brought here."

Jillian started to cry again. "So, I truly am a prisoner," she whispered in defeat.

"No, you are not a prisoner. You are the Luna, and you will be a fine Luna. Don't worry, you will get used to being here, and I am sure that you can go and visit your home as much as you want, okay?"

"Are you sure? The Alpha acted like I could never leave," Jillian said.

"Yes, but he is a man. He's not thinking straight right now. All he knows is that you are his mate, and he doesn't want to let you go. He has been searching for you for a very long time."

"It's not like I would be going that far. I literally live down the street," Jillian pointed out.

"True, but would you want to come back here if he let you go home?"

"No, but do you blame me? The jerk didn't even ask if I wanted to come here. He just threw me into his car and brought me here. If it were any normal person, he would have asked me, but no. Do you see why I am mad, Carla?"

"Yes, and I do understand. But as I said, I think once the Alpha gets used to having you as his mate, he will let you have some freedoms, okay?"

Jillian sighed. "What of school?"

"I am sure you can continue your studies."

"Do my parents even know I am here?"

"They do. The Alpha called them yesterday."

"Can I call them?"

"Of course, but let's get you cleaned up and eating something first, okay?"

"Fine," Jillian grumbled. She was not happy, but at least she would be able to talk to her parents and perhaps go home to see them.

Carla started the water for her and then left the room. Jillian sighed and stripped from her dirty clothes. She found some bath salts and put them into the tub, along with some oils, and sank into the tub, sighing as her aches started to dissipate. She soaked for a while, and then deciding she had better get out before she fell asleep, she stepped from the tub, grabbed a large towel, and wrapping herself in it, she headed to the closet. She heard the door open, and thinking it was just Carla bringing in breakfast, she let the towel drop so she could get some clothes on.

She heard an intake of breath and turned to see the Alpha eyeing her hungrily. She shrieked and slammed the closet door in his face. "Don't you knock?" she screamed.

She heard him chuckle. "It is my palace, so no. You are quite lovely, by the way."

She reopened the door a few minutes later, dressed in shorts and a t-shirt. "I'm sure I don't compare to your harlots," she hissed at him, her face bright red.

He pulled her into his arms. "No, you are much sexier." He then laid a scorching kiss on her lips.

She gasped. His kiss was the best thing she had ever had in her life, as fireworks exploded in her. She would never admit that she enjoyed it, though, and she struggled against him.

He finally released her, and she stepped back, wanting to slap his arrogant face. But she was not sure if he would hit her back. He had shown his anger already and wasn't sure how violent the Alpha could become.

Edric could see the anger on Jillian's face, but he knew she had enjoyed their kiss and knew one thing for sure, it was the best kiss he had ever had in his life. Talk about fireworks. He knew for a certain that she was his Luna, even if she denied it.

He smirked at her.

"Get out," she hissed.

"No, this is my room."

"Then I shall leave," she said, walking around him.

He grabbed her arm, pulling her to him. She struggled against him. "Let me go."

"No, you are mine, and I will never let you go."

"I will never be yours," she glared at him.

"One day," he promised.

"Leave," she demanded.

He grinned and, bowing to her, he walked out, just as Carla appeared with some food.

"What did you do to the poor girl?" she huffed at him.

"Nothing, just kissing my mate," he chuckled.

Carla shook her head, setting the food on the small table in the sitting area.

She saw Jillian's tears.

"Did he hurt you?" she asked Jillian.

"No, he was just acting like a jerk."

"He just wants you to give in to him; you are his mate. Want to eat?"

"I'm not hungry," Jillian muttered.

"Well, I will leave it here if you want it," Carla said, then left the room.

Down in his office, Edric had to calm down. His mate was incredible. Her body was perfect, and he could not wait to claim her. He sighed, calming his hormones. One day he promised himself, but not until she was ready. He would not force himself on her. He was not like that.

Jillian sat on her bed for a bit, trying to calm herself. She really needed to quit being so angry, but the Alpha brought it out in her. She did like his kiss, though; for her first kiss, it was incredible. She would never tell him that it was her first kiss, though he didn't need to know that she had never had a boyfriend.

Feeling suddenly cooped up and wanting to explore, she headed out of her door, down the hall, and down the stairs. She frowned when she saw one of the harlot's sauntering through the hall, with only a pair of lace underwear on.

She saw Jillian and smirked. "Oh, look, another Harem girl."

"I will never be a slut like you," Jillian ground out.

"Are you sure? The Alpha likes his women," she grinned, "and one day, you will enjoy walking around like this, showing off your assets. The men, especially the Alpha, love it."

Jillian paled. Over her dead body. She would not be one of the harlots.

"Never," Jillian said. She hurried outside, ticked off, only to run into Warren.

He stopped her, hugging her. "What's wrong, Luna?" he asked, seeing her tears.

"One of those harlots, she was telling me I would be naked like her and like it, and that the Alpha likes it when they run around like that," she sobbed.

"Enough!" she heard a roar behind her and felt herself yanked away from Warren. "Do not touch my Luna," Edric growled at his Beta.

The Beta exposed his neck to his Alpha, showing him his allegiance. "I am sorry, Alpha, she ran into me, and then she said she had run into one of the girls," he frowned at his Alpha.

"I heard," the Alpha frowned. "Round up all of them. I want them locked in their rooms until they are picked up."

Warren nodded and hurried inside. Edric tucked an arm about Jillian, who was still crying. He knew he was the cause of it. He should have gotten rid of the girls before bringing his Luna home. He could see the hurt he was causing her, and his wolf whimpered.

"I am sorry, Luna, they will not be here soon," he assured her as he led her to his gardens. She stayed silent, only wiping at her tears.

He looked down at her, his heart feeling sad at seeing her tears. "I am truly sorry," he said again.

"Do you like it?" Jillian asked him.

"Like what?"

"When they run around without clothes."

"I used to," he said, making her wince, and making him feel awful. He stopped her and, taking her face in his hand, he looked into her eyes. "I used to," he said, "I don't anymore. I haven't for a long time."

"Then why are they still here?" she whispered, not knowing why she was so angry and jealous. It wasn't like she loved the Alpha. She despised him, right? Jillian stepped away from him. "You said you would get rid of them yesterday, and you didn't, and they are still wandering the halls practically naked," she whispered. "I am sorry, but I don't trust you."

She then walked away, leaving his wolf whimpering in pain. Edric started after her, but his wolf stopped him. "*Let her be, Edric. She is hurting, and I don't blame her. Those girls should have been gone a long time ago."*

"I don't need to hear it from you, too," Edric told his wolf.

"Your Luna will never trust you. You are an idiot, Edric."

Edric felt like his guts were tied in a knot because his wolf was right. She would never trust him, but he would try until his dying day to earn her trust.

Edric shifted into his wolf and headed into the woods, howling. Echoing howls followed. The other wolves could feel their Alpha hurting and wondered why.

Jillian headed back inside. She had seen the Alpha run by her in his wolf form. She wasn't sure she would get used to it and hoped she didn't have to. All she wanted was to go home, and hopefully, the Alpha would let her.

Chapter 5

Jillian sighed and wandered the grounds for a bit, and then headed back inside again. She frowned when she headed inside. Warren had a hold on a girl who was scantily clad. "I told you, Jessy, get to your room; you are out of here today."

"No. I will not listen to you. You are not the Alpha. He is the only one who tells me what to do and where to do it," she smirked at him, and then seeing Jillian standing there, she grinned at her. "Well, well, another girl, but I am his favorite; you will never have him; he is mine, and mine alone."

Jillian had heard enough. She ran back outside. She couldn't stay there; there was no way. She ran to the palace gates and pushed the button to open the gates. It started to open, so she snuck through and began to run. She couldn't handle being there. She would rather die than be held prisoner and be second place to a slut.

She heard someone chasing her and started running faster, but she was no match as the Alpha caught up with her. He was still in wolf form. He made her stop and started to push her back with his nose.

"No, I am not going back. I will not play second to that hussy in there," she seethed in anger.

The Alpha chuckled, and she punched him in the nose, making him whimper.

"It is not funny, Alpha. Your prostitute in there said she was yours."

The Alpha growled in anger.

"Sure, get angry with me, I don't care, but I am not staying," Jillian said, tears in her eyes.

The wolf whimpered and pushed his head under her hand.

"No, leave me alone, okay? Go back to your girl; she said she wants you and that you want her, that you are hers alone."

She felt him grasp her arm in his jaw. He was gentle with her as he began to tug her back to the palace. She stood still. "No, don't you understand? I don't want this. I can't do this," Jillian cried. "Can't you just leave me alone?"

He refused to let her go, tugging on her even more.

"No, Alpha, I will never be yours," she whispered, looking behind her longingly. "I want to go home," she whispered.

He shook his head at her.

"Yes," she said, removing her arm from his mouth. "I am not yours, Alpha. Go back to your slut."

She then turned to walk away, but he was blocking her path, and he was human and naked.

She flushed bright red. "Will you stop doing that?" she hissed, making him chuckle.

She turned away, not wanting to admire his physique. He was well built in all the right places.

"I would stop running around like this if you would listen to me," the Alpha told her, grasping her hand in his. She closed her eyes and refused to open them.

"Jillian, look at me," he said, hiding a chuckle. He knew his nudity bothered her. But he had seen the admiration in her eyes for a split second before she had closed her eyes.

"Look at me, Jillian."

"No, not until you have clothes on."

He chuckled. "I do not have clothes with me; you will have to wait until I get back to the palace."

"No," she said. "I will wait here until you get dressed."

"I don't think so, you little minx. You are not running away again. You are mine, remember?"

"And so is every slut in there," she whispered, tears falling out from under her eyelids.

He kissed the tears away, leaving sparks behind. "They are being dealt with, I promise. Now come back with me."

Jillian shook her head still. "No, I won't. I still don't believe you," she said.

"What can I do to make you trust me?" he pleaded with her.

She kept her eyes closed and turned away. He turned her back to him, pressing her to him. Jillian gasped as she felt Edric's hard body against her. He chuckled as he kissed her ear and then her neck. She would not enjoy it. "*Are you sure?*" that little voice said to her.

"Tell me, Jillian, what can I do to earn your trust?" Edric whispered as he turned her around and kissed her softly, sending incredible sparks shooting through her.

"Nothing," she said, pulling away.

"Why? Open your eyes and tell me why."

"No," she said.

"Very well," he sighed, and she suddenly found herself in his arms. He began to walk back to the palace with her.

"Put me down," she said.

"No. You refuse to open your eyes and look at me to answer me, so I am taking you back to the palace."

A tear escaped down her cheek as a heaviness settled into her chest.

Edric wanted to wipe it away, but he was carrying her. She was extremely light, and he really enjoyed the feel of her in his arms. One day she would be in his arms willingly.

Jillian felt herself being carried up the stairs, and then she was deposited on her feet.

She heard a door close, and she opened her eyes to see herself in her room again. She sighed. She had been so close to escaping. She wondered how he had known she was leaving? Had Warren told him? Or had he seen her? It didn't matter; she was a prisoner again.

The door opened a moment later, and Carla walked in with a tray of food. "I see you didn't eat breakfast; here is lunch," she said, setting it on the nightstand and taking the uneaten breakfast. "By the way, the Alpha said you could call your parents if you wanted."

"He did?" Jillian whispered, hopefully.

Carla smiled at her. "Yes, he did."

She then walked out, leaving Jillian alone.

Jillian walked to the phone on the nightstand and picked it up. There was a dial tone. She dialed her parent's number.

"Hello?" her mom said.

"Mom," Jillian cried.

"Oh, Jillian," her mom started to cry. "Henry, it's Jillian," she said.

The other line was picked up. "Are you okay, sweetheart?" her father asked her. "I am so sorry about all of this; I swear I will come and rescue you; I just need to figure out how."

"The King told me he would arrest you if you interfered," Jillian cried.

"Oh, honey, don't cry," her mother said. "We will get you out of there, I promise. Somehow, someway, we will, even if he does arrest us."

"Mom, Dad, I love you," Jillian sobbed.

"We love you too, sweetie," her mother said. "Take care of yourself, and do not let that man touch you."

"Don't worry, he will never touch me," Jillian assured them.

"Good girl. Keep in touch with us," her father said. "We will come up with a plan to get you out; believe me, we will."

"I believe you," Jillian whispered.

"Do you think we could come and see you?" Jillian's mother asked then.

"I was told that you could," Jillian replied.

"Good, we will be over as soon as we can," her father said. "Even if I have to beat down the doors."

Jillian smiled. "Thanks, dad. I love you."

"We love you," her father said, and then they hung up.

Jillian was mad. She was going to give the Alpha a piece of her mind, and if he didn't let her go or let her parents come and visit her, there would be hell to pay. She stomped down the stairs and walked down the hall, hoping that she could find the Alpha's office.

Seeing one of the harem girls standing in the hall, she shoved her aside, making her hit the wall, and tore open the office door. How she knew Edric was in there, she wasn't sure, but she did. Jessy was trying desperately to kiss Edric as he sat in his chair, she on his lap. She was only in a t-shirt and bikini bottom and had her arms were wrapped around Edric. He was trying to push her off, but she was clinging to him desperately.

"How could you!" Jillian said, and walking over to Jessy, she punched her, sending her sailing off of Edric's lap to hit the floor, and then she slapped Edric as hard as she could, snapping his head back. He was in shock. No one had ever hit him that hard before.

"That is for breaking your promise in not getting rid of your sluts," and then she slapped him again, "and that is for keeping me here without my permission."

She then burst into tears and raced out the door.

Warren saw the whole thing and smirked. He had told the Alpha to get rid of those girls.

Edric stood, power emanating from him. Warren and Jessy cowered under his glare.

"Warren get Jessy out of here, now, before I kill her. I am going after my mate."

Warren nodded and picked Jessy off the floor. She held her nose, which seemed broken, bruises forming on her face. Warren smirked.

"I warned you to stay in your room," he said and hauled her out the door as the Alpha went after his mate.

Jillian was out the gates and far down the road when Edric caught up with her. He stayed in human form; he didn't want to embarrass her again.

Edric halted her progress by grabbing her arm. Jillian glared up at him, an intense hatred in her eyes. He whimpered, as did his wolf.

"Luna, let me explain," he said.

"No, let me go, you filth. Don't ever touch me again. You are just as I thought. You promised me, Edric, you promised," she sobbed.

Tears formed in his eyes as he gathered her into his arms. "I am so sorry, my love, it was not what you thought. I was trying to get her to leave; she didn't want to; she was trying to appeal to my hormones."

Jillian glared at him. "I didn't see you protesting."

"I was trying to push her off my lap when you busted in the door."

"That is no excuse. You let her kiss you. You could have stopped her; you are stronger than her. You could have," Jillian cried softly, her heart breaking for some reason. Why was she feeling that way? She hated the man.

"I tried, my love; she caught me by surprise."

"I don't believe it," Jillian said. She then glared at him, the hurt strong in her eyes. "You haven't gotten rid of those girls, and you are blackmailing me to stay here. I hate you."

He swallowed. He felt the lowest of low. "You are my mate. I can't live without you," he told her.

She pushed him away. "That is the biggest lie I have ever heard," she hissed at him. "You are just fine without me. Go back to your lover; she can be your mate. I will never be your mate, ever."

"Jillian," he begged, glad she didn't know the words to reject him.

"Let me go," she cried. " Just let me go. I will never be yours. I hate you," she said again, making him wince.

"Love," he said, trying to pull her back to him.

"No, let me be," she said, backing away from him, but Jillian suddenly went pale and collapsed.

Edric caught her before she hit the ground. "Jillian," he whispered as he ran back to the palace with her unconscious body.

Warren met him at the door. "Get Emerson. There is something wrong," Edric told his Beta. Emerson was the pack doctor.

As Edric walked quickly to Jillian's room, Warren hurried away. Edric then laid Jillian gently onto her bed. She was not waking up, her face was pale, and she was sweating.

Emerson walked into the room then, his mate, Carla, on his heels. "What happened, Alpha?"

"I don't know. One minute she was yelling at me, and the next, she collapsed."

Emerson pulled out his stethoscope and listened to Jillian's heart.

"Her heart sounds fine, as does her breathing. Did you hurt her?" Edric growled. "Of course not; I would never hurt my mate."

"Only break her heart," Carla glared at him. "We know what happened with Jessy and what you did to her parents. The poor girl has a broken heart. How could you treat her like that?" she accused him. "Your poor Luna," she cooed, putting a cold rag on Jillian's forehead that Warren had handed over.

Carla then spied the food on the nightstand. She frowned. "Emerson, I think I know why she passed out."

"Oh?" he asked, looking at his mate.

"I don't think she has eaten since yesterday sometime. She never touched dinner last night, nor her breakfast or lunch. Her blood sugar must have dropped."

Emerson nodded. "You are probably right." He pulled out a glucose meter from his medical kit and pricked Jillian's finger. She didn't even flinch.

He frowned when he saw the number. "Her blood sugar is 50. Those numbers are bordering on a heart attack if we don't get some food in her. Carla, go to my office and get some saline. I'll get her started on an I.V. to get her hydrated. Then we'll see if we can get her to wake up so we can feed her."

"If she doesn't wake up?" Edric asked, his face pale.

"Then she will die," Emerson stated.

Carla came back with the saline, and then Emerson looked at Edric. "Go to the kitchen and find some sugar, honey, preferably, so I can stick it on her tongue. She needs it to bring her blood sugar back up, and then Warren, go find some other sweets, like cookies or something she can eat when she wakes up."

The men nodded and hurried out the door to find the food.

"He does care for her, Carla," Emerson told his mate as he poked the needle into Jillian's arm. She startled and woke up, but just for a moment, then she closed her eyes again as he hooked up the saline.

"If he cared for her, he wouldn't be making out with one of the sluts, or holding her against her will," Carla pointed out as Emerson got the saline going.

"I know, and it will take some time for her to trust him. He has been alone too long and has done some foolish things. But I can see that he loves her. They will both come around, it might take time, but it will happen."

"Hopefully, before they kill each other," Carla said.

"Hopefully," Emerson agreed as Edric walked back in with a bottle of honey and a spoon.

"Put some honey on your finger and put it in her mouth," Emerson told Edric.

"I don't know Emerson; she might try to bite it off," he grimaced.

"You'll just have to trust that she doesn't, won't you," Emerson grinned.

Edric did as he was told, put some honey on his finger, and prying open Jillian's mouth, he stuck his finger in.

Jillian tasted something sweet in her mouth and sucked on it, earning a slight moan from Edric. It was turning him on, having her suck on his finger. He just hoped the others hadn't heard it, but then he saw Emerson smirk before he looked away.

Jillian opened her eyes as Edric removed his finger.

"I have cookies," Warren said, walking in, waving a package.

"Good, hand them over. I should have had you grab some apple juice too," Emerson said.

"I'll go get some," he replied, handing Edric the cookies and leaving again.

"Jillian, we need you to eat some sugar; you need your blood sugar raised," Emerson told her.

She nodded weakly.

"Good girl. You had us worried. We don't like seeing our Luna unconscious."

"I am no Luna," she whispered.

"You are and will always be," Carla told her.

"I will never make a good Luna. I don't like your Alpha."

Edric flinched.

"True, he is a jerk sometimes, but you will learn to like him. He *can* be nice," Carla assured her.

"But what of the other girls?" Jillian asked, ignoring Edric.

"They are gone," Warren said, handing over some apple juice. "I kicked them out personally, every single one of them. They are headed home to their families or to another pack."

"Promise?"

"I promise, and they will never come back; you have our word. Right, Alpha?" Warren said.

"Yes, they are gone for good, Luna," he assured her, watching her drink her juice and nibble on a cookie. Her color was returning, which he was grateful for.

"Promise me you will eat from now on?" Emerson asked Jillian.

"I'll try," she whispered, still ignoring Edric, making his wolf whimper again.

"Can I talk to my Luna?" Edric asked his friends.

They nodded. Carla looked at Jillian and then at Edric. "Both of you, be nice; I will bring you some food in a minute," she added and then left the room.

Edric sat down on the bed, taking Jillian's hand. She didn't flinch or pull away, for which he was grateful.

She was still extremely ticked off at him and wanted to yank her hand away, but she didn't want to admit, his touch comforted her.

"Jillian," he began, "I am sorry for the things I have said, and more importantly, for the things I have done. I know I keep promising things and then not doing what I promised. I understand if you don't want to forgive me, I deserve it, and I deserved it when you hit me," he said, rubbing his jaw.

She was watching him as he talked to her. He did look genuinely repentant, but was he? It was Warren who finally threw out the garbage, not him.

"I'm not sure you are sorry. You keep apologizing, and then I keep finding you doing something stupid. I don't think I believe you."

"I know, and I don't blame you," he sighed. "I kept saying I would get rid of those girls, and I didn't. I truly apologize for my stupidity. But as Warren said, they are gone. Can you give me a second chance?" he asked her, watching her, hoping to see any hint of forgiveness. Her blue eyes were sparkling with tears as she said, "One month."

"What?" Edric asked.

"One month. I give you one month to get your crap together. To forget about those girls and to keep your promises. If I am supposed to be your Luna, I don't want to hear about or see any more sluts in here and no more arguing. If we can stand each other after that, I will stay. If not, I will leave and go home, understood?"

"It's a deal." He then leaned down to her. "Can we seal it with a kiss?"

"How about a handshake."

He nodded, disappointed. "Fine," he said, shaking her hand. "But if we are to work things out, then I have to be allowed to kiss you. Others will wonder why I am not kissing my Luna if they see us together."

"But no one is in here to witness that, are they."

He frowned. "True, but what if someone does walk in, and I am shaking your hand? How would that look? Me, shaking the hand of my Luna."

She sighed. "Fine," acting like it was torture when she was actually looking forward to his kiss.

He chuckled. "You know you don't have to make this so hard on yourself."

"You know, you don't have to look so smug," she retaliated.

He leaned down and kissed her softly.

She sighed, trying not to enjoy it too much. He pulled away, a smirk on his face, knowing she had enjoyed the kiss just as much as he had.

"See, that wasn't so bad now, was it?" he asked her.

"It could have been worse," she shrugged.

"You are something else, Luna," he chuckled, kissed her cheek, and stood. "Eat, and rest today. Tomorrow, I would like for you to go back to school."

"You do?"

"Of course. I decided it would be good for you. You need to finish your senior year, and if you would like, you may take college classes online."

"I can't afford college."

"I will pay for it. Is there something that interests you?"

"Yes, but it's not worth pursuing."

"Why not?"

"Because my dad said so."

"What is it, Jillian?"

"Nothing," she shrugged.

"I will get it out of you later," he promised.

"If you think so."

"I know so. Don't dare me; I have my ways of making you talk."

She just rolled her eyes at him. "Whatever."

"Jillian," he warned. "I am your Alpha and mate. It is not respectful to roll your eyes at me."

She sighed. "Fine, would you rather I flip you off?"

His wolf chuckled. "*She is a feisty one.*"

"No, and don't even think of it," he said, and shaking his head, he left the room. She was tempted to flip him off as he left, but she was worried he would turn around and see her doing it.

Carla brought in a plate of food then, pulled out a lap tray from under the bed, and placed it on Jillian's lap. "Eat; you need it."

"Thanks, Carla."

"Anytime, Luna."

"Edric wants me to go back to school tomorrow."

"Good. You can't stay locked in the palace forever."

"Do I have clothes to wear?"

"Your clothes are in your closet. Your parents didn't have time to drop them off. Edric found them another digging site right out of town. So Edric had two of the pack go and get your clothes."

"What about my pictures and things?"

"Everything is in boxes in your closet; you can sort through them if you want."

"Thanks again, Carla."

"Anytime. Now eat up and change. If you need anything, just holler, okay?"

Jillian nodded and watched as Carla walked out, closing the door behind her. She could see them becoming friends. Even though Jillian had only known her for a day, she was beginning to like Carla.

Chapter 6

Excited to go through her things, Jillian devoured her lunch, then headed to the closet to change. She spied all of her clothes hanging up and grabbed a hoodie and some jeans, slipped them on, and then sat on the floor and opened a box. She smiled as she saw her photos. She would start by hanging those up. She was grateful that someone had brought her everything from her room and the storage closet in the hallway of her house. Her parents must have told the men where her things were. She picked up the box and put it onto her bed, then looked around at the walls. A few paintings were hanging up, but she didn't like them. They were boring modern ones. She hated contemporary art; it was so ugly. She stood on the bed and pulled a picture down, and then the other one on the east wall. She set them next to the door to hang somewhere else. Jillian then opened the French doors that led to a balcony. She walked out and smiled. Would it be so bad to live in a luxurious palace with a swimming pool and the best food she had ever eaten, plus having people at your beck and call?

Maybe she would stay, just for a few days, to see how the Alpha acted. He did act repentant, but was he really? Was she nuts for wanting to stay and see how he treated her? He was being nice to her, and he was incredibly gorgeous. Would it be so bad to let him pamper her and kiss her? His kisses were incredible, unlike anything she could have ever imagined.

She stepped back into her room, leaving the doors open, and walked to the phone. She picked it up, not sure what number to dial. So she hit 0. It rang once. "Yes, Luna?" came the response. It was Emerson.

"Um, Emerson, I wanted to hang up some pictures. Can I get some command strips or some thumbtacks or something?"

"I'll see what we have and bring you some, okay?"

"Thanks, Emerson."

"No problem Luna," he said and hung up.

Jillian laid her pictures out on her bed. She had several of her and her parents from their many trips around the world. She had to admit that even though she had been in several different schools, she had a background that no one else had. She had been to Egypt, Germany, Mexico, Australia, Russia, the Bahamas, the Virgin Islands, and Africa. She still needed to add South America to her list. She wanted to go there, and to France of course. France was such a romantic place; at least she had heard it was. She picked up each picture, smiling at the memories.

A knock sounded on her door.

"Come in," Jillian said.

The door opened, and Emerson walked in with a couple of packages. "I found both thumbtacks and command strips," he said, handing them to her, and then stopped when he saw all of her photos.

"Wow. You have been to a lot of places, even the Kremlin?"

"I have."

"How was it? I have always wanted to visit."

"Go during the middle of summer. The winters are killer," she grinned.

"So I have heard." He then picked up each photo. "These are amazing, Jillian. I am jealous of you right now," he chuckled.

"My parents took me everywhere. I haven't been to South America, and I would like to go there. I also would like to go to Paris."

"Paris is overrated," he said, picking up a photo she had taken in the Virgin Islands. She was standing in front of a sailboat, a look of pure bliss on her face.

"You look happy here," he stated.

"Why is Paris overrated?" Jillian asked, ignoring his statement.

"Oh, I have been there a few times on pack business. It is too touristy. On every street corner is someone selling some type of souvenir, and you should see the base of the Eiffel Tower. You can barely make it through there without someone trying to sell you some trinket."

"I would still like to go, though, just to say I have."

"Perhaps next time I go on pack business, you can go with me."

"I would like that a lot," she grinned, hugging him.

"Ahem, why are you hugging my husband?" Carla asked as she walked into the room, but she was smiling.

"He said he would take me to Paris next time he went," Jillian grinned.

"It is boring," Carla shrugged. "Too many tourists."

"That's what Emerson said, but I still want to go."

"Look at these photos, love," Emerson said, pointing at the pictures lined up on the bed.

"Wow," Carla said, picking some of them up. "You have been everywhere."

"Not quite," Jillian said as she pulled out some command strips and put them on the back of the photos.

Emerson and Carla watched her. "You look happier," Carla said.

"I am trying to be positive about my situation," Jillian shrugged.

"What was your favorite place to visit?" Emerson asked as he helped her with the strips, and then the three began to hang photos around the room. Jillian made sure they were in chronological order as they hung them.

"My favorite place," Jillian mused as she hung up the photos. "I would have to say, Germany. It is wonderful. I loved touring the castles, and the Christmas Markets were really awesome."

"I would love to go to Germany," Carla sighed, "especially when they have Oktoberfest."

"It's boring," Jillian said.

"Only because you can't drink," Carla grinned at her.

"True, but I don't ever want to drink either. That stuff smells nasty."

"I heard German beer is incredible, though," Carla said, "and besides, werewolves don't get drunk."

"That is so not fair," Jillian said.

"You are not getting drunk around me, young lady," Edric teased as he walked in the door. "What's going on? I've been trying to mind link you, Emerson."

"Oh, sorry, Alpha. We got talking about Jillian's travels. She has traveled all over the world, and we were a bit jealous."

He pointed to all of the photos on the wall. Edric stepped up and admired them. He had to admit, his Luna looked happy in the pictures, and he suddenly felt awful for ripping her from her parents.

"What did you need me for, Alpha?" Emerson asked him.

"Oh, it can wait." He then looked at Jillian. "How would you like to have your parents over for dinner?"

Her eyes got teary. "Really?"

"Really."

"I would love that; thank you, Alpha," she said and hugged him.

He hugged her back, loving how she felt in his arms. She seemed a bit happier after they had talked, and he was glad.

She stepped back and smiled up at him. "Can I call them?"

"Of course," he smiled down at her.

Emerson and Carla glanced at each other. *"I think someone is falling for her, mate."* Carla thought.

"He loves her, that is for sure; you can see it in his face."

"I will finish hanging these for you," Emerson told Jillian. She wondered what they had said to each other as she watched them. They looked smug.

"Thanks, Emerson," she smiled, and walking to the phone, she picked it up and dialed her parent's number.

Her mother answered. "Hello?"

"Hi, mom."

"Oh, sweetheart, how are you? Is that man treating you well? Last time we talked, you were miserable."

"I am okay, mom. Edric and I have come to an agreement."

"Oh?"

"Yes. I told him I would give him a month, and if I don't like it here after that time, I get to come home."

"Good for you," her mom said.

"So, I was wondering if you and dad would like to come to dinner tonight."

"He will allow it?"

"Yes, mom."

"I would like that. That way, we can see how he is treating you."

Jillian was watching Edric as she talked. He could hear her conversation and winked at her, making her blush.

"He is treating me better, mom."

"Good, and sure, we can come. We are at a new dig site. The King was nice enough to compensate us for the last dig and set us up with this one. Tell him thank you," she added.

"I will."

"What time do you want us for dinner?"

"How about seven? Then you can go home and clean up."

"Okay, dear, see you then."

Jillian hung up, a smile on her face. She then walked up to Edric and kissed his cheek. "Thank you."

"You are welcome," he smiled softly at her.

"All done," Emerson told her, standing back to admire their handiwork. He had finished hanging the photos.

"I like it; it makes me feel more at home," Jillian said.

She then walked into her closet and pulled out another box. Edric followed her and carried it to the bed for her. She opened it and pulled out some paintings.

"These are incredible," Edric said, helping her pull them out. "Who painted these?"

"I did," she whispered.

He looked at her in surprise. "You did? These are truly amazing," he whispered.

Emerson and Carla stepped forward to look at the paintings. They were of places Jillian had been. But she had never thought herself good enough to show them to anyone. She had wanted to hang one or two in her room, though.

"You have quite a talent," Emerson grinned. "These are of the places you have visited?"

"Yes," she blushed. "It was something to do when my parents were at work, and I was home after school with nothing to do. I didn't think they were that good, but I wanted to hang a few of them up in my room."

"Choose which ones you want in here," Edric told her. "I would like to hang a few of your paintings in my room, if that is okay, and some in the dining hall."

"You would?" Jillian blushed again.

"Of course. You have some talent Luna," he smiled softly at her. "Perhaps you should pursue a degree in art."

"My parents told me not to, that it was pointless, I would never make any money painting, and that I would be broke my entire life." "They were wrong," Edric stated. "You are an incredible artist, and I could see you making a lot of money, not that you need to. Would you like me to buy you some paints and canvas so you can paint while you are here?"

"I would like that, but I don't have anywhere to paint," Jillian said, pointing to the room.

"I have just the spot," he said, "follow me."

She nodded and walked out to the hall with him. Emerson and Carla grinning at each other.

"Maybe they can work things out after all," Carla said.

"Yes, perhaps they will," Emerson agreed. "It would be good for both of them."

Jillian followed Edric to the back door, and he opened it. "I don't have on shoes," she told him.

"No problem," he stated and swept her into his arms.

She gasped, and he chuckled. "I can go get some shoes, you know," she protested.

"But why? I enjoy carrying my Luna."

"At least you have clothes on this time," she muttered, making him chuckle.

"Admit you liked it when I was carrying you without clothes," he teased, making her blush.

"That's what I thought," he laughed. He walked down a graveled path that ran past the pool, through some hedges, and into an incredible garden. In the middle of the garden was a small cottage. He walked to it, set Jillian on her feet, and then opened the door to the cottage. "I need to have it dusted, but this place would be perfect. My mother used to paint also," he smiled fondly at the memory. "My father built this place for her. It was quiet, and she could paint undisturbed."

He walked inside, Jillian following. Jillian smiled as she looked around. It was just a single room, and all the walls were windows. There was a couch covered in a dust cloth, a chair, along with a stool, and an easel, all of them covered to protect them from dust and mold.

"I will have some of the pack come clean this up today, and then you can have this place. Just let me know what supplies you need."

He then looked at Jillian. She had tears in her eyes.

"Are you okay?" he asked her softly.

She nodded and wiped her tears away. "Yes, this is just so incredible, thank you," she whispered. She was so happy that she kissed him.

He smiled against her lips. "If things like this make you happy, I will have to do it more often," he whispered, and crushing her to him, he kissed her passionately.

She moaned against his lips. It felt too good to kiss him. But why? She had been so ticked off him just a few hours before. "*Because you are his mate*," came that little voice. She gripped his shoulders, desperate for his kisses. They were driving her crazy. They were so full of passion and something else, love perhaps? Or was it just lust? She didn't care. All she knew was that she could not get enough.

He pulled away a few moments later, grinning down at her, but held her to him. She could hear his heart beating hard. "You are going to drive me crazy, woman," he whispered into her hair. "We need to stop before I have my way with you on the couch."

She sighed but stayed in his arms for a moment, loving having his arms about her. Perhaps she had been wrong about the Alpha. He was showing that he cared for her, and since she was being kind to him, he seemed happier.

"What does it mean to be marked?" she asked him then.

He looked down at her, surprised. "I have to bite you. If I mark you, everyone knows you are mine. It is quite intimate; it is like becoming engaged in a way. No one else can touch you, or I can kill them."

"Oh."

"Would you like me to mark you?" he asked softly.

She swallowed. "Will it hurt?"

"Only for a moment."

"Will I be able to read your thoughts?"

"I don't know. Where you are human, probably not; we probably won't have that connection."

"Okay."

"Are you disappointed?"

"Not really. I don't want you in my head," she grinned up at him.

"Why, because of all the dirty things you think about me?" he teased her.

"Are you kidding? Definitely not. I didn't want you in there in case I decided to escape."

He frowned.

"I'm kidding, Alpha. I won't escape as long as you treat me well, and with those sluts gone, I think we can get along."

He walked to the couch and pulled the cover off, and had her sit; then, he sat by her. "Are you sure you want this? After all, we have known each other for only a few days. For me, that seems an eternity because I love you; you are my mate. I fell in love with you the moment I laid eyes on you, but how about you? I don't want to mark you and have you regret it. This is a big step, Jillian. Just yesterday, you hated me; what has changed your mind?"

Jillian sighed. "I don't know. I did hate you, loathed you, actually, but since our talk, I don't know, I feel a connection to you, is that weird?"

"No, not at all. That is the mate bond."

"Why am I feeling like this?" Jillian then asked.

"Like what, my love?" Edric asked.

"I can't describe it. I'm not a wolf, but I feel this pull towards you as if I can't be alone or my heart would shatter."

Edric nodded. "As I said, it is the mate bond. I am surprised that you feel it as a human, but I am very pleased. Now you know how I feel."

"I've only known you for a couple of days."

"Yes, but as mates, it doesn't matter how long you have known each other; all that matters is that you are together."

"I don't know if I like feeling like this," Jillian admitted.

"Why?" Edric frowned. "I know you haven't been happy with me, but why would you fight the pull?"

Jillian sighed. "I have never had a boyfriend. I have never been kissed, and then you show up out of the blue, claim I am your mate, and it's kind of scary."

Edric put his hand under Jillian's chin so that she would look at him.

"It is meant to be my love. I know it is scary, but I will be gentle with you, and we will take our time getting to know each other, okay? I will not do anything unless you ask me to."

"Okay," she said.

"I am okay if you have your parents come and visit every day if you would like," he then added.

"May I go home?"

"Do you want to go home?" he asked, dreading her answer.

"I do, but I kind of like the bed here. It's much nicer than mine, and the food is delicious. My mom's not that great of a cook," Jillian admitted, making Edric chuckle.

"Is that the only reasons why you want to stay?"

"Maybe I kind of think you are handsome too."

"So you *are* going to stay?" he asked hopefully.

"I suppose I am, as long as you keep doing things like this," she said, pointing around the room.

He chuckled. "So, if I spoil you, you will fall in love with me?"

She shook her head. "Oh, no, Alpha. That's not how it works. You don't need to buy me things. That would only make me upset. No, I want things like this," she pointed to the room, "and time together, and kindness. Then yes, I think I could like you more."

"Not love me?" he asked, feeling disappointed.

She touched his face, and he took her hand, kissing it.

"I can grow to love you," she said. "Since I am not a wolf, I don't know how strong our bond will be, but I want to make it work if you do."

"That is my wish, Luna. I want to be yours, and you mine, for eternity."

She sighed then, "I hope we live that long."

"Why do you say that?"

She shook her head. "It's nothing."

"Jillian, what is going on?" he could see the worry on her face.

"I have dreams," she admitted.

"Dreams?"

"Yes, and most of the time, they come true."

He was intrigued. She could heal fast, and her dreams came true? He knew of another like that. He would have to give him a call.

"Did you have one of these dreams recently?" he asked her softly, rubbing her hands as he held them.

She nodded.

"Can you tell me about it?"

"It's not important," she said softly.

"When did you have this dream?" he asked her, concerned.

"Last night."

That was weird because he had been in his room and hadn't heard her cry out. Was her dream really that bad? And if it had been, why didn't she want to tell him about it? It made him curious.

"I am just wondering if you mark me that I might be able to reach out to you if I need help," she said.

"I'm not sure if it would work, love, but I can get you a cell phone if it doesn't work, okay?"

"I suppose that would do," Jillian nodded.

"Do you really want me to mark you?" he asked then, his teeth elongating, his wolf wanting to get it over with. He wanted his mate, and now.

"I am willing to try if you are," he told her.

"*I am too,*" his wolf agreed, happy.

"I will mark you, but I cannot guarantee the results, okay? I do know that no other wolf can touch you, though, and that will be a great comfort to me."

He sniffed her neck, relishing in her incredible scent. Jillian shuddered. "Don't be scared," Edric said, feeling a great deal of satisfaction that she wanted him to mark her because he wanted the same thing. He wanted to make her his.

"Ready?" he whispered, holding her to him.

"Ready," she whispered. Why she wanted him to mark her when they had only known each other for a few days was beyond her, but she needed to be marked for some reason. She felt like her life would not be the same if he didn't.

"I love you," he whispered as he bit into her neck.

She gasped but held onto him. It felt good. It wasn't as painful as she thought it would be, and the emotions that filled her were intense.

He groaned as he pulled away, feeling an instant connection with his Luna. He wasn't sure if Jillian felt it, though. He hoped she did. His love for her instantly grew a thousandfold. He kissed her wound, making her moan softly. He pulled back and smiled at her.

"Did it hurt?"

"No, it felt good," she admitted. It had made her want to do something she knew she was not ready for.

Raul growled in satisfaction. "*Mate,*" he said.

Edric kissed Jillian and then pulled her to her feet. "Come, we had better head back before I have my way with you," he said.

"Hmm, as tempting as that is, I think we had better wait for that step. I am not ready for that."

His wolf howled in anticipation.

"Did you just howl?" she grinned at him.

"My wolf is very happy," Edric grinned.

"And you?" she asked shyly.

"Very happy," he said, kissing her and then picked her back up into his arms. "You are mine now, and for always."

She just hoped that she hadn't made a mistake in letting him mark her. But she felt good and felt more connected to him as if she could feel his love radiating to her. She leaned her head against his chest, making him smile, and held her closer. He was a very happy Alpha right now, and he hoped that Jillian was happy too. He would do anything for her, his Luna.

Chapter 7

Edric carried Jillian back to the house and deposited her into the kitchen. Emerson was there. "Come into the dining room," he grinned.

Edric took Jillian's hand in his, glad she didn't pull away, and they headed into the dining hall.

"Like it?" Warren asked, climbing down from a ladder. "We thought all of your paintings should be displayed."

Carla walked to them then, a few nails in her hands. She gasped, then looked at Edric, who was grinning foolishly. "You didn't."

"I did," he smirked.

"Emerson, come here," Carla said.

He walked over to Jillian, and Carla pointed to Jillian's neck. "Really. You marked her already?" he asked in surprise.

"I did."

"With her permission?" Carla asked.

"Yes," Edric smiled, pulling Jillian to him.

"Wow, that was fast; why the change of heart?" she asked Jillian.

"It was his charm, his kisses, his hotness, and the fact that he has given me his mother's studio to paint in."

Carla smiled. "I think it is more than that. I think you are falling for the Alpha. His hotness, as you put it," she chuckled, making the men grin.

Jillian blushed.

"It's okay, Luna, that is what you are supposed to do," she grinned and then kissed Jillian's cheek. "Congratulations."

"How does that work with a human anyway," Emerson asked, touching Jillian's neck and making Edric growl in anger.

"Well, you obviously know when someone touches your woman."

"Do not touch her again," Edric growled in anger.

"It's okay, Edric," Jillian said.

"No one can touch you, mated or not," Edric growled, "or I have the right to kill them."

"You are not going to kill your Omega, so settle it down, Mister," Jillian said, holding him back from Emerson.

"He issued a challenge," Edric spit out.

"No, he did not. He was curious, now stop it." She then kissed him.

He growled, pulling her to him tightly.

"Perhaps we should leave," Carla chuckled, and the two of them walked out, Warren following them.

"Quit being jealous," Jillian told Edric.

"You are mine," he growled.

"Yes, you pointed that out."

"How would you feel if I touched another girl?" he asked her.

"You already have, many times," Jillian pointed out.

"That was before I marked you. Now you are marked, if I touched or kissed a girl, you would feel extreme anger, and you would have the right to kill them."

Jillian smirked at him. "Because I would do that. I might slap her about and send her packing to somewhere really cold and no clothes," making Edric chuckle, "but I won't kill someone, as long as *you* don't let them kiss you," she pointed out.

"Same goes to you," he said. "No touching or kissing other men."

"Like I would," she said, "I have his Hotness to kiss."

"You think I am hot, do you?" he smirked at her. "Well, duh," she grinned, then stood on her tiptoes and put her lips really close to his, "but don't let it go to your head," she teased, then took off running.

His wolf took it as a challenge, and he instantly shifted and headed after her. She was laughing hard as she ran out the door and to the front lawn; she couldn't catch her breath, and then an enormous wolf pushed her over. She giggled as he licked her face.

"Yuck, dog slobber," she said, wiping her face and making him chuckle. He licked her face again. "Get off me, you furry beast," she said, pushing on him.

He chuckled again and laid down by her.

She began to rub his side, making him groan, but it came out like a purr.

She laughed. "You like your stomach rubbed? I wonder if you do as a human, too," she teased, making him nip her hair. She pushed him away but continued to rub her hands through his soft fur. He settled next to her as she stroked his fur. "Do you like being a wolf?" she asked him.

He nodded.

"Do you wish I was one?"

He nodded again.

"Yeah, it's too bad I am all human," she sighed, making him grin at her. She scratched his head and then his belly, trying to ignore the boy parts hanging down. She blushed as she saw them and scrambled to her feet. He knew what she had seen, and it made him laugh. She was indeed too innocent.

She headed back inside, him on her heels, staying in his wolf form so as not to embarrass her. Although he knew she liked how he looked.

He headed to his room to change, and Jillian headed to find Carla and Emerson. They were back in the dining hall.

"I apologize for making the Alpha mad," Emerson told Jillian.

"He'll get over it," she grinned. "Thank you for helping to hang my paintings."

"Anytime, they are incredible. Would you like me to buy you some more art supplies?"

"I will take her after school tomorrow," Edric said, walking in, dressed.

"How am I getting to school anyway?" Jillian asked.

"My limo," Edric said.

"Like that won't be embarrassing."

Edric chuckled. "Everyone will just know you are mine; what is wrong with that?"

"It's just like when your parents take you to school, is all," she said.

"Do I look like your father?" he growled, pulling her close to him.

"No," she breathed out.

"I didn't think so," he chuckled. "I will take you and pick you up."

"Yes, dad," she teased, making him reach for her again, but she had escaped his grasp. He growled at her.

"Don't go all wolf on me again," she warned, making Emerson and Carla grin.

"I thought you liked rubbing my fur," Edric teased her, making her blush.

He laughed.

"I think they'll be just fine," Emerson said, kissing his wife's cheek.

"Better than okay," she smiled.

"Dinner will be ready in an hour," said a voice from behind them.

"Thanks, Den," Edric told the man who was standing there. Jillian turned to look at him.

He bowed to her. "Luna, it is a pleasure," he said. "I heard your parents are coming for dinner. Is there anything that you would like me to cook?"

"I'm not picky," she shrugged, "but I could go for a nice steak."

He smiled and looked at Edric.

He nodded. "Yes, a steak sounds nice, thanks, Den."

"Yes, sir," he said and headed from the room.

"I think I am going to go change for dinner if that is okay," Jillian said.

"Need some help?" Edric grinned.

"Get a room, you two," Carla teased.

"We have one, but she won't let me in," Edric chuckled, making Emerson and Carla laugh.

Jillian shook her head. "I think I can manage on my own, thanks," she said and headed to her room.

She went into her closet, finding a dark blue cocktail dress. It looked a bit mature for her, but she wanted to look suitable for the Alpha. After all, he was treating her well and had spoiled her that day. She left her hair down, though. She didn't want her parents seeing her mark and wondering if it was a weird hickey. Jillian's mark was already healed and had left a silver mark in the shape of a crescent moon on her. It was beautiful. After a quick shower and putting on makeup, her dress, and matching heels, Jillian headed out the door where Edric was waiting for her.

He looked her up and down, making her blush. He growled hungrily at her, and stepping forward, he laid a heart-stopping kiss on her.

"You look incredible," he murmured, kissing her neck where he had marked her. He looked at her mark and smiled. "A true Luna."

"Why do you say that?" she asked him.

"Your mark is in the shape of the moon. Luna means moon. You are mine, my Luna." He then kissed her, putting his arms around her bare back. He growled in her ear. "You know, I am not a very patient man, and if you keep dressing like that, you might find yourself in my bed sooner than later."

"Later," she gasped out as he kissed her neck and then her lips.

"Is that a promise?" he growled in her ear.

"If you keep kissing me like that, it will be," she whispered.

He chuckled. "Hmm, perhaps we should skip dinner," he said.

She swallowed and stepped back. "We had better head to dinner," she whispered. "My parents are probably here."

"Yes, we had better," he growled, eyeing her hungrily, "and you are dessert."

She shuddered against him, making him chuckle.

He kept an arm about her waist, and they headed down to dinner. Her parents were already seated but jumped up and hugged Jillian as they walked in.

"You look beautiful," her mother said.

"I see that your paintings are hung up in here," her father said. "That's nice. I hope you aren't planning on doing that for a living, though. I know that is what you want, but it doesn't make money."

Edric frowned as Jillian's father talked.

"Actually, Henry," Edric interrupted. "I have an art gallery in the city, and I am going to display your daughter's work there. I think she could sell every one of them."

Jillian smiled at Edric. "You will?"

"I will," he promised her, pulling her close to him. "Your work is astounding, and I want everyone to see it."

"You care for my daughter," Jillian's father accused.

"I do, sir, very much, and after she graduates high school, I plan on marrying her."

Jillian gasped and looked up at him. All she saw was love and great promises in his eyes.

"Well, that was fast," her mother replied, "but if you are happy, Jillian, you have my blessing."

"She does not have mine," her father replied angrily. "She probably has Stockholm Syndrome, where the captive falls in love with the captor."

Jillian frowned at her father. "Dad, I think I know the difference. Edric has been kind, and I kind of like him."

"I kind of like you too," Edric smiled at her as he pulled her chair out for her so she could sit.

"This is not a Disney fairy tale," her father frowned. "You can't just fall in love with someone you met less than a week ago."

"You can if they are your mate," Edric pointed out.

"Mate, right," he scoffed. "That is a bunch of bogus. There are no such things as soulmates. I love my wife, but I don't think we are soulmates," he said, looking at her.

Nadine was frowning. "Henry, shut your mouth," she warned him.

"No, I will not. This is a bunch of bull crap. He has our daughter hoodwinked, and I will not have it. I want to bring her home with us."

"You already have your answer, Henry; she said she was staying," Edric told him. If Henry were a wolf, Edric would challenge him. He didn't like how he was treating Jillian. Henry glared at Edric.

"He probably only wants you for his plaything," Jillian's father muttered.

Jillian flushed. "I admit, that is what I also thought, father, especially when I was brought here against my will. But I have changed my mind. I like it here."

"I don't like that you are staying here."

"Now, dear, she is just down the street from us," Nadine said. "Besides, she seems happy. I can tell."

"I still don't like it," Henry grumbled.

"Dad, I am 18; I can make my own decisions," Jillian said.

"Yes, you are 18, but that doesn't mean you are ready for this," he replied.

"Shall we eat?" Edric asked, changing the subject. "I think your daughter's mind is made up."

Henry sighed. "Very well, but if he mistreats you, Jillian, heads will roll."

"Yes, I know," Jillian replied as the door opened, and six people came in, each with a plate of salad. They placed them in front of everyone and left the room.

Jillian looked at her salad. Cucumbers, she hated cucumbers. She put them to the side.

Edric saw what she was doing and chuckled.

"You don't like cucumbers?" he whispered to her.

"I can't stand them," she admitted.

"You should have said something; Den would have left them off," he told her.

"That's okay; I took them off."

"Next time, if you don't like something, let the cooks know; you are my Luna after all," he whispered to her. "You can be catered to, and I will make sure of it."

She blushed. "Thank you."

"Lovely," Jillian's mother said as she picked up her fork.

Edric dug into his salad, watching those at his table. Emerson struck up a conversation with Jillian's father about paleontology, and Carla started talking about the fun places to shop in town to Jillian's mother.

Edric then looked at Jillian, who was listening to everyone visit. She had a smile on her face.

He squeezed her hand under the table, and she squeezed back.

"It's nice seeing my parents getting along with Carla and Emerson," Jillian told him.

Edric nodded. "Yes, it is nice, and I hope that your parents realize that you are here because I love you."

She smiled up at him. "I think I am falling for you also," she admitted to him. How could someone fall for someone so fast? Was she indeed his mate? She had only known him for a few days.

"I am glad," he said, kissing her cheek.

The dinner was delicious. After the salad came a cold fruit soup, steak cooked to perfection, red potatoes with seasoning, and fresh green beans from the garden. For dessert, Den had made Flambé, which he lit on fire in front of them. Jillian was impressed. She enjoyed the dinner, and Edric invited everyone to the sitting room for a nightcap. Her parents shook their heads. "We don't drink, and neither does Jillian," her father glared at her.

"She has not been drinking, I assure you, Henry," Edric grinned. "I also have tea, coffee, and hot chocolate," he told them.

They agreed, and everyone headed to the sitting room at the front of the palace in a large room next to the front door.

Emerson poured tea for Jillian and her mom, coffee for himself, and Jillian's father. Edric shook his head. "I am fine."

"Yes, you are," Jillian whispered to him.

He grinned foolishly. "Glad you think so," he whispered back.

The couples visited about travels, and Jillian sat on the couch by Edric, laying her head on his chest. He took her cup, set it aside, and tucked her against him. She felt herself growing sleepy, and soon she was asleep.

Edric could feel Jillian relax, and he smiled down at her as he saw that she was asleep. He tucked his arms under her and stood. "I am taking Jillian to bed; I will be right back," he stated and walked out of the room with her. Edric looked down at Jillian as he carried her up the stairs. She was so gorgeous and seemed content. He was so glad she was his. He laid her onto her bed, took off her shoes, then pulled the covers over her. He watched her for a moment, feeling such an intense love for her. He kissed her forehead and closed the door behind him softly, then he headed back down the stairs to see that Jillian's parents were headed out for the night.

"Thank you for coming," he shook Henry's hand and hugged Nadine. "I know Jillian was happy to see you, and you can come and visit whenever you like."

"Yes, your Highness," Nadine smiled up at him. "I cannot believe that my daughter is falling for such a handsome man and royalty at that. We had high hopes for her, but this is even higher than imagined."

Edric chuckled. "So, are you feeling better about me keeping your daughter here?"

"Yes, I can see that she is happy."

"She makes me happy also," Edric replied, seeing them out the door.

Henry looked at Edric. "Treat her well."

"I will, Henry, don't worry."

"Good, I hate to have to come and shoot you if you mistreat her."

Edric chuckled. "I hope it never comes to that."

"Tell me, if you are a king, why are you here, in this town?" Henry then asked Edric.

"It is kind of a long story," Edric replied. "One that I will tell you one day, but not right now."

"Does anyone else know you are a king?" Henry asked.

"Yes, several people do."

"Interesting," Henry said, and tucking an arm about Nadine's waist, they headed to their car. Edric watched them drive away and then headed back inside. Warren and Emerson were there, along with his two most trusted guards, Orson and Wes. They followed him into his office, and he closed the door.

"As you know, I marked my Luna today," Edric told them.

They all nodded. "Which means her life will be in greater danger. I want her protected without it looking like she is being protected."

The men nodded.

"Good. Gentlemen, I am tired and headed to bed. I will see you tomorrow. Orson, Wes, you know your duties."

"Yes, sire," they both said and headed out the door behind him; Warren headed to his room and Emerson to his.

As Emerson closed the door behind him, Carla was waiting for him in bed. She smiled at him. "Our Alpha is happy."

"Extremely."

"That's good. He has needed a mate for too long."

"I agree, and Jillian will be a good match for him; keep him in his place."

"You had better believe it. I can't see her letting him get away with anything."

"Which is just what he needs," Emerson told her as he climbed into bed by her.

"I just hope that she will love him as much as he does her," Carla said as she drifted off to sleep.

"I am sure that she will," Emerson grinned, kissed her cheek, and fell asleep.

Edric went to his room but walked into Jillian's to check on her first. She looked like she was sleeping okay, her face peaceful as she slept. He was tempted to climb in beside her, but he didn't want her to be angry with him in the morning, so he went back to his room, promising himself that one day soon, she would willingly have him in her bed, and that would be a perfect day.

"*A very perfect day,*" Raul agreed.

Chapter 8

Jillian was not sure what time it was when she woke up, but she felt uncomfortable. She realized why when she found her dress was hiked up past her thighs in bed.

She got up, stripped off the dress, put on a long t-shirt, and headed back to bed, setting her alarm so that she could get up for school.

Jillian fell right back asleep and didn't wake up until her alarm went off. She hurriedly got up, showered and dressed in jeans and a nice shirt, and then grabbed her backpack off the floor. She wondered how behind she was in schoolwork. She hoped Edric had dismissed her for a few days so she wouldn't be marked absent with no call in.

Carla brought her breakfast into her.

"I'm glad to see you are ready. Alpha is ready to take you to school when you are ready to go."

"He is really taking me?" Jillian frowned.

Carla grinned. "Yes, and don't argue about it. He is just watching out for his Luna," she pointed out and left the room.

Jillian hurriedly ate the waffle, chased it down with orange juice, and headed down the stairs. Edric was visiting with Emerson by the front door, waiting for her. They both nodded at her, then Edric stepped up to her and kissed her softly. She didn't think she would get used to having attention from such an amazing-looking man, and his kisses were enough to make her want to pass out; they were so incredible.

"Good morning Luna," Emerson said. "Ready for school?"

"Hopefully," Jillian said, stepping back from Edric. "I just hope that I am not treated like I was before."

Edric frowned. "People were not nice to you?"

"I'm never a popular one," Jillian shrugged, "and who knows how it will be now that you marked me."

"Now you are my Luna; they have to treat you with respect," Edric told her as he put an arm about her waist and headed outside with her. "If not, I will know, and they will regret it."

"Will they know who I am? I am human, after all."

"You are human, but they will see your mark, and they will respect you. Don't worry, Luna; I am close by if you need me," he said, kissing her and helping her into the limo.

He slid in beside her, and Emerson climbed into the driver's seat.

"We'll be back to get you when school gets out," Edric assured her.

Jillian nodded as Edric held her hand until they pulled up to the school. Students were walking in but stopped when they saw the limo.

Edric got out, making the girls grin, and head towards him, but they stopped when he pulled Jillian from the car and, putting his arms around her, he laid a searing kiss on her lips.

She pulled away, her face bright red. "Thanks for embarrassing me," she muttered.

"Just letting everyone know you are mine," he chuckled. "See you after school."

He climbed back into the limo, and it pulled away.

"Jillian!" Kimberly shouted, running up to her and hugging her friend tightly. "I thought you were gone for good, yet here you are." She stepped back to eye her friend and then gasped. "No way," she whispered, touching Jillian's mark. "He marked you as his Luna," she said reverently.

"Luna," Jillian heard the murmur, and then she saw the students who were outside, bare their necks to her, swearing their loyalty to her.

"Well, I'll be," Ruben chuckled as he headed to them. "A Luna, it is about time, and our friend Jillian at that," and then he hugged her.

"Um, Ruben, that's not a good idea," Jillian said, backing away.

"Why not? Can't I hug my friend?"

"Not if you don't want to be pummeled," Jillian said, as suddenly the limo came back, roaring to a stop, and Edric hopped out, looking ready to kill. He knew another male had touched his Luna, and he was furious.

He headed to Ruben, his eyes black, his teeth elongated, but Jillian stepped in front of him.

"Edric, he was hugging me as a friend."

"He knows not to touch my Luna, or he pays with his life," Edric growled.

"Edric, Ruben is mated; you don't have to worry about him," Jillian pointed out, pulling Kimberly forward. "See? This is his mate Kimberly, so just chill."

Edric growled and stepped back. "You are lucky, wolf," he growled at him. "If you were not mated, I would have your head."

A crowd had gathered, all of them fascinated that the Alpha would protect his human Luna so fiercely.

"I told you he would go all wolf," Jillian smiled at her friends. She then kissed Edric. "We are fine; I promise no one else will touch me. They hate me anyway."

"They had better not hate their Luna," he said, glaring at the students. They all exposed their necks to him. Even Jillian felt like she needed to, she could feel the power rolling off of him, but she didn't expose her neck. She kissed him again. "Go, you have better things to do."

He nodded. "Behave," he told her, and then getting back into the limo, he left once again.

"Well, I've been told," Ruben chuckled as they headed into the school, the other students following.

"So, what have I missed?" Jillian asked them as she headed to her first class.

"Not much. The girls are behaving better, and two have found their mates," Kimberly shrugged.

"Are the girls disappointed that the Alpha is off the market?" Jillian asked.

"Very disappointed, but they will get over it."

"Good, they had better," Jillian said.

"You act like a Luna," Kimberly grinned as Jillian stopped outside her classroom.

"What do you mean?"

"You exude power, for a human, I can feel it, and you look happy even."

"It must be the mark," Jillian shrugged.

"That and you are in love," Kimberly stated.

"I don't think so."

Kimberly laughed. "Whatever, girl, you have it bad. But that's okay; the Alpha is one hot specimen," she pointed out.

"And here we thought I would be safe because I was human," Jillian laughed.

"I know," Kimberly smiled. "Who would have thought?"

Jillian hugged her friend then. "See you for lunch?"

"Of course, see you later," she said as Jillian walked into her class.

Mr. Flynn was getting ready for class when Jillian walked in. He stopped and exposed his neck to her. "Luna," he said.

"Mr. Flynn," she replied, finding her seat.

"Have you started your essay?" he asked her. "I know you are Luna, but you still have homework."

"No, I haven't started it, but I will this weekend."

"Good. It is due in two weeks unless you are going on the trip to France?"

"Trip to France?"

"The French class goes every year. I think they are going next week; you will have to ask your teacher."

"Oh, I don't know if I can, not where it is that soon. I don't have the money."

Her teacher chuckled. "I am sure it can be arranged for you to go. If the Alpha will let you."

"I will ask him," she said as the rest of the class filed in. All of them nodded to her in respect. What a change a few days made and she kind of liked it.

Jillian's next class was the same. All of the students nodded at her with respect.

When lunch came around, and she walked into the lunchroom, all talking stopped, and every student and teacher stood and exposed their necks to her. Jillian blushed as they did so and nodded at them. They then sat down, and she went to get her lunch.

She stood at the back of the line, but the students pushed her to the front. "Luna always eats first," she was told.

"Oh," she whispered, feeling embarrassed.

She got her food and then headed to her table, only to find it had been moved to the head of the lunchroom. She felt even more embarrassed as she sat down.

Ruben was chuckling as he walked up to her with his lunch. "Can we join you?" he asked her, making her sigh with relief.

"Of course," she said as he and Kimberly sat down. "I am so embarrassed," she admitted.

"Why?" Kimberly grinned. "You are our Luna now. We have to treat you with the utmost respect, and if we don't, the Alpha will not be happy," she stated.

"It's not like he is going to know if one of them is mean to me," Jillian said.

"He will," Ruben assured her. "Once you are marked, he can feel all of your emotions. He will know when you are angry or hurt or scared."

"Oh, great," Jillian snorted, making the couple laugh.

"Do you have the mind link?" Kimberly asked curiously.

"No. I guess it doesn't work on humans."

"You are lucky," Kimberly laughed. "At least you don't have to worry about him reading your every thought unless you learn to block him out," she said, looking at Ruben.

He shrugged. "Hey, sometimes it comes in handy. You don't need to hear every dirty thought I have in my head about you," he grinned.

"Are you sure?" Kimberly teased.

"TMI, you two," Jillian said, making gagging noises.

The two of them laughed. "You just wait," Kimberly said.

"Whatever," Jillian said. "So, what is this I hear about a trip to France with the French class?"

"Oh," Kimberly grinned. "The French class takes a trip every year. We usually go during spring break, which is next week, by the way," she said, "and we spend two weeks there, learning the culture."

"Have you been?" Jillian asked her.

"No, but I am this year. I can afford it since both of us work."

"Are you going, Ruben?" Jillian asked him.

"No, I can't handle culture," he snickered, "and I do not speak French."

Kimberly punched his arm. "He hates art museums. I told him to come for the food, but he said no."

"We can't afford for both of us to go anyway," Ruben shrugged.

"Oh, yeah, I bet it is pricey. I probably can't go either since it is next week, and I don't have that kind of money. Plus, getting my parents' permission."

Kimberly snickered.

"What?" Jillian asked.

"You don't have to ask your parents' permission; you are the Luna, remember? You do need to ask the Alpha, though."

"I don't know if he could afford to send me, though," Jillian shrugged.

Ruben guffawed. "You have no idea, do you?"

"Idea about what?"

"The Alpha is very wealthy, Luna. I am pretty sure he could afford to send you," he snickered.

"Oh," Jillian blushed. "I guess he would be. He does own a palace."

"It's okay, friend, you are new to this whole thing," Kimberly said, putting an arm around Jillian. "Let's just say he makes Bill Gates look like a pauper."

"Oh," Jillian said. "How did he get to be so rich?"

"Inheritance," Ruben told her, "and all the businesses he owns."

"He owns businesses?"

Kimberly shook her head. "For a Luna, you do not know much about your Alpha," she teased.

"I have known him less than a week," Jillian pointed out, "and it's not like I was going to discuss finances with him."

"True," Kimberly grinned. "So, ask for permission. I bet he will let you go. We can share a room."

"That would be awesome. I have always wanted to visit France."

"All you need is a permission slip," Kimberly snickered.

Ruben grinned. "Yes, a permission slip from the Alpha," he chuckled.

"I think I could finagle it," Jillian grinned.

"I'm sure you could," Ruben grinned at her, waggling his eyebrows up and down.

Jillian blushed, and Kimberly smacked him. "Quit embarrassing the poor girl," she teased.

"Luna?" she heard from behind her.

She turned to see a guy about her age. "I was wondering if you could help me with something."

"Oh?"

"Yes, I was wondering what you had to do to become a Luna. Were you one of his harem girls?" he grinned meanly at her.

Jillian gasped.

Ruben jumped to his feet. "Apologize now."

"No. She's not a Luna. She's human. I will never support her."

"Apologize, or I will make sure the Alpha knows about this," Ruben growled, his canines lengthening.

"Whatever," the guy scoffed. "She's human; she can't mind link with him. Even if she tells him when she gets home, he's not going to believe her; I mean, come on, look at her," he scoffed. "She is nothing but a low-down, worthless piece of garbage. I will never respect her. You will never have my loyalty," he growled at her, making Jillian tear up. She shouldn't let someone get to her like that. She was the Luna, wasn't she?

"*Alpha, you need to come to the school and quickly,*" Ruben mind linked with him.

Edric was going over some books at the palace when he felt his Luna's sadness; then, he heard Ruben.

"*What's going on, Ruben?*"

"*One of the students is humiliating the Luna in front of the student body.*"

"*I will be right there.*"

He looked at Orson and Wes. "Come on; I need backup. My Luna is in distress."

They nodded, and all three shifted into their wolves.

Emerson walked in. "I'll follow in the car, with clothes, don't need you showing off your Hotness to the ladies," he chuckled.

Edric ignored him and ran out the door, his guards following.

Ruben was growling at the kid who was threatening Jillian. "Back down, Jarem."

"No way, she is worthless. Did you sleep with the Alpha to make him yours?" he chuckled meanly. "I mean, come on. Look at you; you are pitiful, you can't even stand up for yourself, and you aren't even that pretty; some of those harem girls were a lot more beautiful than you."

Jillian gritted her teeth. She had had enough and was just about to tell him off when she heard a loud growl. Every head bowed as the Alpha stormed into the cafeteria, Orson and Wes on his heels.

"Jarem Hinckley," the Alpha growled.

Jarem turned, feeling a great power wash over him. He fell to his knees as the Alpha towered over him. "How dare you disrespect my Luna."

"I was just having fun," Jarem whimpered.

"You were not," the Alpha fumed. "You were disrespecting my Luna, and when you disrespect her, you disrespect me, and I will not tolerate it."

"But, I was just,"

"No, don't even say it. It does not matter if she is human. She is still your Luna."

"Yes, Alpha," he muttered.

"What?" the Alpha growled, a wave of power pushing out from him, making everyone whimper in pain, except for Jillian. She just sat and watched the Alpha, glad he was there to protect her. She could tell he was incredibly ticked, but she didn't care. Jarem deserved it.

"I promise I will never disrespect her again," Jarem croaked out.

"No, you will not. As for punishment, you are banned from the pack for a month."

He paled. "But Alpha," he whimpered, still feeling the Alpha's power pushing on him.

"No, I told you, I will not tolerate disrespect," Edric growled.

Jillian wanted to step in, but she didn't dare. She would let him deal with the wolf. She didn't want to make the Alpha look weak in front of everyone if she stopped his punishment.

"Luna?" the Alpha said, looking at her, his face softening. "I will leave it up to you. Do you want him punished?" He had noticed that she wanted to say something.

"I do want him punished, but not banishment," she said with a smirk.

"Oh, and what do you have in mind?" he asked her, seeing the devilish twinkle in her eye. "*Oh, this should be good*," Raul chuckled.

"I think that he should work in the palace horse stables for a month, shoveling crap, since he treated me like crap." She stood and glared at Jarem. He flinched. She looked ready to tear him apart. For a human, she looked powerful.

Edric smirked. His Luna was taking him down a notch, and he was proud of her.

"Very well. Jarem, you will start in the horse stalls today after school, for one month, every day. If you complain about it or slack off, I will banish you, understood?"

"Yes, Alpha," Jarem said, exposing his neck to the king.

"Good, and don't let me hear of any more disrespect from any of you," he growled, eyeing all of them.

They nodded, feeling the power coming from him still. He relaxed, and everyone breathed a sigh of relief as the pressure was released.

"Very well, then." He then looked at Jillian. "Are you okay?"

"I am, thank you," she said softly.

Edric pulled Jillian into his arms, then kissed her in front of everyone.

She blushed and pulled away, making him chuckle. "I like making you blush," he grinned and then walked out.

"Well, that wasn't embarrassing," Jillian said, sitting back down with her friends so they could finish their lunch.

"Sorry, Luna, I mind linked him," Ruben told her. "I knew he would not want you to be disrespected like that."

"I wonder how he got here so fast?" Jillian mused as she watched Jarem slink out of the lunchroom, but not before glaring at her. She glared back.

"The Alpha shifted," Ruben said. "That would put him here in moments."

"At least he dressed before he came in here," Jillian said, making Kimberly laugh.

"I take it he has shifted in front of you?"

Jillian nodded, embarrassed. "Yes, and he laughs about it. He thinks I want to see that."

"And don't you?" Kimberly asked, laughing as Jillian turned bright red.

"Maybe?" she squeaked, making Kimberly laugh even harder, Ruben joining in.

The bell rang, then signaling lunch was over.

"Oh, I forgot to ask Edric about the trip," Jillian said as she and Kimberly headed to French.

"That's okay; you can ask when you get home. You'll need a permission slip anyway."

"That's true," Jillian said as they walked into class. The students and teacher nodded at her.

As soon as class started, the teacher said, "Class, our trip is next week; I hope you are practicing your French." She then looked at Jillian. "You have permission from the Alpha, and he is paying for your way," she told her.

"How?" Jillian asked.

The teacher pointed to her head. "Of course," Jillian said, shaking her head. "That would be nice to do, sometimes," she admitted.

They went over what to expect on their trip for the rest of class time. Both girls looked starry-eyed as they left the class.

"This is going to be incredible," Kimberly sighed.

"I know," Jillian agreed. "We are going to have so much fun. I am so glad you are my friend Kim and that we can room together; otherwise, I probably wouldn't go."

"I'm glad we are friends too, Luna," she winked as she headed to her next class.

Chapter 9

The rest of the school day went by much better, and Jillian was grinning as she climbed into the limo after school. Edric pulled her to him and laid a scorching kiss on her lips.

"How was school?" he asked.

"Good. Thanks for coming earlier."

"You are welcome and thank you for not interfering. I don't want to look weak in front of anyone."

"I kind of figured, and thank you for letting me have a say in his punishment."

"I have to admit; it is much harsher than what I had in mind," Edric chuckled. "Did he give you any problems after I left?"

"Jarem glared at me, but that was it."

"He glared at you?" Edric growled.

"Yes, but it's not a big deal."

"It is a big deal. That is just as disrespectful. I will have a word with him," he growled.

"It's okay, Edric, really," Jillian protested.

"No, it is not," he said.

"It is," she promised, and pushing the button to roll up the window separating Emerson from them, she climbed onto his lap and kissed him soundly.

"You know, woman, if you tease me like that, I might take you here in the car," he growled in her ear.

She gasped, her face heated, and tried to scramble off of his lap, but he held her tight, nuzzling her neck and kissing her senseless.

He finally set her down when they pulled through the gates. He grinned down at her. "Perhaps when we have a longer ride one of these days, I will have to show you the art of lovemaking in a car," he teased.

She blushed, making him laugh. He kissed her cheek. "I know you want to," he murmured in her ear.

She opened the door and escaped, making him laugh harder.

She ran to her room, trying to calm her heart. Yes, she wanted him badly, but she would wait. She had to make sure that he loved her, and she loved him before she took that step. Besides, she had known him for only a week. She didn't want to take that step quite yet, even though it was tempting.

The next day, Edric took her to school once again, and once again, he laid a scorching kiss on Jillian's lips in front of everyone. She just shook her head at him.

"You are mine, remember that," he told her.

"How could I forget," she laughed, then headed into school. He watched her as she walked inside.

"*You need to mate with her,*" his wolf said, "*then she will truly be yours.*"

"*I don't think she is ready.*"

"*Make her ready. She loves your kisses; I am sure you could think of some way to seduce her.*"

Edric just chuckled. "*You are worse than I am, Raul.*"

"*She's our mate; what do you expect?*"

Jillian's school day was good; even lunch was better. Jarem wasn't there, and she was grateful. The other students just ignored her after nodding at her, which she was also thankful for.

When Edric picked her up from school, she was smiling.

"You look happy," he said, kissing her as he put her into the limo and climbed in after her.

"I am."

"Did something happen?"

"No, just excited about my trip next week. Our French teacher keeps talking about it."

"It's going to be boring," Emerson teased her from the front seat.

"Whatever, Emerson, you are just jealous."

"I am so not jealous. I told you I went there already, and it's not that great."

Jillian looked at Edric. "You are okay with me going to Paris?"

"I am; I think you will be okay. Just make sure you stay with your class and not wander on your own."

"I'll be gone for two weeks."

"I know, and it will kill me," he sighed.

She punched him in the arm.

"What was that for?"

Emerson laughed.

"You will not die without me, you big bully."

"Only because we haven't mated yet," he whispered in her ear, making her blush once again.

"In your dreams, Mister."

"Oh, I do have good dreams about you, but I sure wish they would come true, you know, as yours do?" he teased her. "How have your dreams been lately anyway?"

"Okay," she shrugged. Jillian didn't want to tell Edric that she had dreamt of a plane crash just the night before. She didn't want to worry him.

Emerson pulled into the drive and opened the door for his Alpha and Luna; he then headed to the trunk, grabbed a few bags, and handed them to Jillian. "Edric bought these for you."

"What are they?" Jillian asked, looking into the bags. Inside were paints, brushes, and canvases.

"You bought me these?" she asked, tears in her eyes.

"Yes, love, I knew you wanted them."

"Thank you," she said, dropping the bags and kissing him.

He chuckled. "You are welcome, my Luna. Want me to take them to the studio? It is all cleaned up for you, by the way."

"It is?"

"It is."

"I want to go and see it," she told him.

"Very well, come on," he said, leading her through the house and to the cottage, carrying the bags.

She opened the door and walked in, smiling. The place had been scrubbed clean, and it looked beautiful. She then noticed a few paintings of flowers on two easels.

"Were those your mother's?" Jillian asked him as he set the bags on the floor.

"They were. The only ones I could find. She gave most of them away."

"She was excellent," Jillian said, reverently touching one.

"She was, but I think you are better," Edric admitted.

"Thank you, Edric, that means a lot to me," she smiled at him. "Your mother must have been a kind soul. I can see it in her paintings."

"Yes, she was a good mother," he said curtly, closing the subject, and she wondered why. But she wouldn't ask him. The subject must have been touchy.

"Do you care if I paint until dinner is ready?"

"That is fine, love. I have some work to catch up on." He kissed her and then headed out the door.

She sighed and looked around. She would be very happy in the studio.

She set out her paints and brushes then put a canvas on an easel, knowing just what she wanted to paint, and so she got to work after finding an apron to protect her clothes.

She was smiling when she headed into dinner. Edric was visiting with Warren when she walked in. Edric walked to her and wiped her nose, showing a blue smudge on his finger. "I see you enjoyed yourself," he chuckled.

"I did, thank you," she said, kissing him.

"I was just discussing with Warren about cleaning up the art gallery and getting it ready to open for you."

Jillian smiled. "That's nice. Thank you, both of you."

Warren nodded.

"Join us for dinner, Beta," Edric told him.

"Yes, Alpha," he nodded and sat down. Emerson and Carla soon joined them.

"So, how is the painting going?" Emerson asked Jillian as they began to eat.

"Good, thank you."

"I'll have to come and check out what you are painting," he said.

"Not until I am finished," she responded. "It's a work in progress."

"Very well, Luna," he grinned at her. He then turned to Carla. "Jillian is going to Paris next week."

"Really. You're going with your French class, huh?"

"Yep."

"I am sure you will have a better time there than we did. You will get to visit museums and art galleries. We were only there on pack business, so it was boring."

"So, you said."

"Jillian, I hope you have your passport up to date?" Edric asked her.

"Of course. With my parents traveling as much as we did, they made sure it never expired."

"I wonder why they moved so much," he mused.

"My dad's job."

"Yes, but didn't you move every year? You would think there would be some dig sites that would last longer than that."

"You are right; he never did get to finish a dig. But as soon as the school year ended, we moved."

"Interesting," Edric said, wondering why they would do that. Did they have a particular reason?

"It was hard making friends, moving so much," Jillian admitted, "but I don't have to worry about that anymore. I have finally found my permanent home."

"You plan on staying then?" Carla asked her.

"You had better believe she is staying," Edric frowned.

Jillian grinned. "Don't get your panties in a knot, Edric; I will stay."

Everyone laughed at what she said.

"I will have you know, I do not wear panties," Edric replied, "usually, I don't wear anything."

Jillian blushed bright red.

"Edric, embarrass the poor girl, why don't you," Carla grinned.

"Well, my appetite is ruined," Emerson replied.

Jillian laughed at that. "I know, right? Like I needed to know that. TMI Edric, TMI."

Even Edric's guards, standing by the door, were snickering.

Edric leaned over and whispered in her ear. "I can show you later if you want."

She blushed again, making him chuckle.

"Edric, seriously, leave the poor girl alone," Carla said. "Jillian, maybe you need to lock your door tonight."

"Good idea," Jillian replied.

"Hey, don't give her any ideas," Edric protested.

"Too late," Jillian grinned.

After dinner, it was getting dark, so Jillian couldn't paint. After kissing Jillian soundly, she headed to her room instead, while Edric headed to his office.

"Leave your door unlocked," he told her.

"You wish," she laughed, but she did.

He checked on her later, and she was sound asleep, uncovered. He tamped down his hormones because she was only in a long t-shirt that was riding up her thighs. He gently covered her up, and after kissing her cheek, he headed to his room.

The rest of the week went by quickly. Jillian spent her afternoons painting, and that Sunday afternoon before dinner, she packed, and after she did so, she called her mom.

"I know you always wanted to go," her mother said. "I am happy for you. Have fun."

"I will, mother, love you."

"Love you, my girl; I am glad you are happy there."

"I am," Jillian assured her.

"I hope he is treating you well."

"Very well."

"Good. Your father is still worried about him."

"I know, mom, but I am okay, really. He has been nothing but a gentleman."

She then felt warm breath on her ear and turned to see Edric. He started nibbling on her ear, making her hold in a gasp because it felt good.

"Be safe, daughter of mine, and call when you get back."

"I will," Jillian promised, hanging up and turning to Edric, who had a devilish grin on his face.

"You are in so much trouble," she said, pushing his chest.

"Oh really, how much trouble," he asked, picking Jillian up and making her wrap her arms around his neck and her legs about his waist.

"A lot," she gasped out as he kissed her neck where he had marked her. She shuddered because it felt good.

"Hmm, sounds good," he chuckled, carrying her to her bed, and laying her down.

"Oh no, you don't, Mister," Jillian said, scrambling to get up.

He pushed her back down, undoing her jeans.

"Edric, I am warning you," Jillian gasped out as he leisurely slid her jeans down her legs.

"I'm just helping you get ready for dinner," he teased as he kissed her legs.

"Edric, not now. You know I'm not ready."

"I know, love," he said, kissing her again. "I just need to tease you a bit, let you know what you are missing out on," he said, then he kissed her mouth. "I will let you get ready, but you know Jillian, my wolf is getting impatient."

"So?"

"I just don't know how much longer I can control him."

"Are you talking about him, or you?" she asked.

"Both," he said, laid an incredible kiss on her lips, and then left the room so she could get dressed for dinner.

He would be the death of her if she didn't give in to him. It was getting to be too tempting. Just the night before, Edric had walked into Jillian's room without his shirt on, so he could tuck her into bed. She had eyed him hungrily, checking out his eight pack. "Like what you see? It's all yours if you want it," he said seductively, kissing her until she couldn't think straight.

"No, no, not right now," she had said, and he nodded, walking out. She knew he was disappointed, but she just wasn't ready, was she?

She had a hard time eating dinner because every time she looked at Edric, he watched her with lust in his eyes. She wanted so badly to give in. Would it be so bad if she did? She knew she couldn't hold out much longer. He was driving her nuts.

They finally finished dinner, and she excused herself to her room. She took a quick shower then climbed into bed, only wearing a long t-shirt and nothing else. She hoped that he would come and tuck her in, but she waited and waited and was just about asleep when she felt him lay next to her. She felt feathery kisses on her ear and then her neck. She sighed. He pulled her closer, putting his arm across her waist, trapping her against him. His wolf smiled. He could sense Jillian was ready. "I love you, Luna," Edric whispered to her. She turned to look at him; his eyes were dark. He kissed her. "I want you, Jillian."

"I want you," she admitted and then got lost in his kisses.

When she awoke the following day, she felt a warm arm wrapped across her waist. She smiled. She had finally given in to the Alpha, and she was glad she had. She felt whole now, as if she had been missing out on something. She sighed in contentment. She was happy and in love.

Chapter 10

Her alarm went off a few minutes later, and she moved to get up.

"Don't go," Edric muttered next to her.

"I have a flight to catch," she reminded him.

"Cancel it," he muttered, pulling her on top of him.

"Edric," she said. "I have to get dressed."

"Not yet," he said.

She couldn't resist him as he kissed her all over. She had to hurry a bit later so that she wouldn't miss her flight.

Edric was dressed when she came out of the bathroom, wrapped only in a towel. He eyed her lustily again.

"Don't even start," she said, "I have got to get ready," she said.

"Then you shouldn't come out of the bathroom in only a towel," he growled, kissing her and trying to peel the towel off of her.

She laughed and smacked his hands. "Stop, or I will be late."

"Fine," he pouted. "No flirting with the men over there," he told her. "You are mine, in every sense of the word," he told her, yanking her to him, making her squeal.

"Don't worry, they would never compare to your lovemaking skills," she teased him.

"I don't even want you to go there," he warned her.

She smiled up at him, kissing him. "You are my one and only, Alpha," she assured him, kissed him, then hurried to grab her clothes for the day. She then headed out the door, Edric on her heels, watching her hind end as she walked down the stairs. He smiled. He was a happy and content man.

"Well, don't you two look refreshed," Emerson teased, making Jillian blush bright red.

Edric chuckled. "I feel refreshed."

Emerson grinned as he took Jillian's luggage out to the limo.

"Be safe," Edric told her.

"I will be," she promised, kissed him, and then headed out the door.

Edric stood in the door, watching Emerson drive away, and sighed. If he hadn't been in love before, he was now head over heels. He couldn't wait until she got home again. He sighed; two whole weeks, he could survive, right?

Emerson helped Jillian with her luggage at the airport, and then after wishing her a good trip, he headed back to the palace. He was grinning. His Alpha and Luna were deeply in love, and he was glad; it was about time his Alpha had someone to love.

Chapter 11

Most of her class was waiting when Jillian walked into the airport. "Just three more students," her teacher said, and a few minutes later, they were all gathered at the gate.

"This is going to be incredible," Kimberly smiled, dancing a little dance.

"Yes, it will be," Jillian agreed as they headed to the ticket agent to hand over their boarding passes. Jillian tried to ignore the bad feeling she had had when she had her dream the other day. It wasn't going to be her plane; she would be all right; she was sure of it. But then again, she never dreamt of when she was about to get hurt, only others.

It was a straight flight to Paris, no layovers, so it would be hours of being on the plane. Jillian was glad she brought some books in her carry-on so she wouldn't be bored.

The flight was full; they weren't the only ones headed to Paris. The plane was noisy as everyone got loaded, and then the stewardesses showed the usual safety stuff, how to use the oxygen masks, etc. Just a few minutes later, they were taxiing down the runway. Jillian looked out the window as they went faster and faster down the runway. The plane shuddered for a moment and then shot up into the sky.

"I hate the takeoff," Kimberly muttered. She was gripping the seat tightly.

Jillian chuckled. "It's okay, Kim, I'm right here," but then she heard a boom and gasped, as suddenly the plane began to drop rapidly backward, tail down. The two girls screamed, along with everyone else.

"We're going to die!" Kimberly screamed in terror.

Jillian closed her eyes as the plane hit tail first and exploded on impact.

"Edric!" Jillian screamed as she put her hand out to protect Kimberly.

Edric heard Jillian's cry as he felt a significant pain tear through his thigh and his gut. He was standing in his office and collapsed to the ground, Warren running to his side. "Alpha," he said worriedly.

"Jillian," he moaned, "her plane," he whispered, his face extremely pale.

Warren frowned and helped Edric up, and the two men raced out the door. Emerson was waiting for them, as were Wes and Orson.

"Jillian's plane crashed," Edric said, his face pale, his leg felt like it was on fire, along with his torso.

Emerson helped Edric into the limo, Warren and Edric's two guards hopping in beside him. Emerson hit the gas.

"Do you think she is dead?" Warren asked his Alpha.

"I don't know, I don't think so," Edric moaned. He couldn't lose his Luna when he had just found her.

When they reached the airport, they raced past security and to the gate, no one stopping them because everyone was watching in horror out the window at the plane, which was in flames.

The men stared in horror as several ambulances pulled up to the plane, along with firefighters who began to put out the fire.

"I have to get to her," the Alpha ground out, and not caring about the police around the plane, or anyone else, he ran to the plane, his men following.

They stopped short as they saw the EMTs pulling burnt bodies from the plane, all of them dead.

"No, she is alive, I can feel it," the Alpha moaned in agony as he hurried forward.

The paramedics looked up at the Alpha as he hurried forward. "My Luna, she is in there," he gasped out.

"We will find her, Alpha," one of the men said as they hurried back onto the plane, which was just smoldering now.

"We have two alive!" came the word, and the Alpha watched as the paramedics gently carried two women off the plane, both of them scorched, bruised, and bloodied.

"Jillian," Edric moaned and hurried forward to her. The paramedic set her gently onto a stretcher.

"Is one of these girls your Luna, Alpha?" the paramedic asked.

"Yes, and her friend," Edric choked out.

"They are severely hurt, but because they were in the middle of the plane, they survived. There are only a few others that are alive," he said, shaking his head sadly.

"The pilot?"

"He and the co-pilot are dead; everyone is but the seven who were sitting in the middle," he shook his head sadly. "What a loss." He then hooked an I.V. up to Jillian, but she didn't stir.

Tears ran down Edric's face as he kissed her. She didn't look good. Even though he knew she could heal, he wasn't sure she would make it through. She was severely injured. "I want to ride with her," he told the paramedic.

The man nodded. "Of course, Alpha."

The paramedic loaded Jillian into the ambulance, Kimberly into another, and the four others who lived were loaded into other ambulances.

The Alpha howled in pain, the other wolves joining him. He couldn't lose his love; he just couldn't. He hopped into the ambulance, mind linking his men to meet him at the hospital. The men hurried to the limo to do as asked, as Edric sat at Jillian's side in the ambulance, watching the heart monitor beep. He squeezed her hand, but she didn't respond.

As soon as the ambulance arrived at the hospital, Jillian was ushered into the E.R. The doctor took one look at her and told the nurses to prep her for surgery. Edric sat down in the waiting room and called Jillian's parents, letting them know what had happened. They immediately left their dig and headed to the hospital.

Nadine hugged Edric as soon as she walked in. She had been crying. "How is she?"

"She is still in surgery."

"Will she be okay?"

"I'm not sure, but I am hoping so," Edric said worriedly.

It seemed like ages when a doctor finally came into the waiting room.

"Alpha, a word?" he asked.

Edric nodded and followed the doctor into a consulting room.

"How is she?" Edric asked.

"She will live. She has some busted ribs, a punctured lung, and a chunk taken from her thigh that is going to require extensive surgeries."

"I wish she were a wolf so that she could heal faster," he whispered. He didn't know the extent of Jillian's healing powers. He figured they were nothing like a wolf's.

"We will do all that we can," the doctor assured him, "She seems like a fighter."

"Can I go see her?"

"Once we put her into ICU. She is in recovery right now," he said and headed away. "I'll have a nurse inform you when she has been moved."

Edric felt anger, elation, and pain, all at once. He was angry that his Luna was gravely injured. He was elated she would live, and he felt pain because she was in pain. He could feel it. Even though she wasn't awake, he could feel how injured she was. Even though Jillian was human, she was mated to an Alpha, and he could feel anything she could.

He headed back to the waiting room. Jillian's parents hopped up. "How is she?"

"She has some serious injuries, but she will live," Edric said.

"What are her injuries?" Henry asked.

"Punctured lung, broken ribs, and a hole in her thigh."

Her mother began to cry, and Henry hugged her. "It's okay, love; she will be okay."

Ruben ran into the room then and stopped when he saw the Alpha. "How are they?" he asked, tears in his eyes.

"The Luna will live; I am not sure about your mate," he told Ruben.

"She will be okay," another doctor said, walking into the room. "She is healing nicely. She was injured, but from what I understand, the Luna helped protect her," the doctor shook his head, "when the Luna was the one who needed saving." He looked at the Alpha. "You have a fearless Luna. She will be respected and loved, especially after everyone learns of her heroics."

"Why would she do that?" Warren shook his head. "She is human; she could die."

"Because she is a Luna," Edric whispered. "That is what Luna's do; they protect others at the cost of their own lives."

"That sounds like our daughter," Jillian's mom said, "she always was selfless." She didn't seem bothered that everyone was calling her daughter Luna.

A nurse walked into the waiting room then. "Alpha, your Luna is in I.C.U." she was smiling.

"That was fast," Edric replied. The doctor had only told him moments ago that she was in recovery.

"Can we come and see our daughter?" Henry asked.

The nurse looked at the Alpha.

"Let me go see her, and then I will be back to get you," Edric told him.

Henry nodded and sat down by his wife, impatient, to see how his daughter was doing.

The Alpha hurried after the nurse and to the I.C.U. She led him to a room that was all windows so the nurses could keep an eye on their patients. A nurse sitting outside the room at a desk jumped to her feet and bowed her head. "Alpha," she smiled. "Come in, you are going to be pleased," the nurse said, and walked into the small room, the other nurse following.

Edric swallowed as he saw his love hooked up to all kinds of machines, her face extremely bruised.

"Look at this," the nurse said, pulling back the gown but leaving enough of it to cover Jillian without exposing her. There was a huge bandage on her left thigh, but the nurse pulled it back. "In surgery, this was a gaping hole. Big enough for a baseball to fit into it," she said, making Edric wince.

"But look at it now," she said, pointing at it. Edric gasped. The wound was closed up; there was only a large pink spot where new skin had formed.

"Amazing, right?" the nurse said. "I am sure if we do another x-ray on her, her ribs will be healed."

He watched in fascination as the bruises started disappearing from Jillian's face.

"Amazing," Edric said, "and she's human."

"But, she is your Luna, and you are her mate; that is why she is healing so fast," the nurse told him.

Edric was pleased, but he knew that it wasn't because of him that she was healing; that was all Jillian.

The nurse walked out but returned moments later with a portable ultrasound. She lifted Jillian's gown and ran the machine over her stomach. Her stomach was deep purple, but Edric watched as the bruises started to lessen.

"Absolutely incredible," he whispered.

"Just as I thought. Her ribs are healed, as is her lung," the nurse whispered. "You can't even tell that she had severe internal injuries.

See here, Alpha? This is where her ribs were broken," the nurse pointed out, but there was only a thin line, and then there was none. "Incredible," the nurse grinned. "Dr. Hess will want to know his patient is healing at such a fast rate." She put Jillian's gown back down, then took the machine out.

"Will she wake up soon?" Edric asked the other nurse.

"I don't know, Alpha, but with the way she is healing, I am sure it won't be long," she smiled and left the room.

Edric leaned down and kissed Jillian's cheek. She didn't stir. "I love you, my Luna; you are amazing, you know that? Even I don't heal that fast."

Dr. Hess walked back in moments later with the primary nurse, and she showed him the results. He shook his head, hardly believing it himself. "Well, I'll be. You have one special Luna, Alpha," he said. "I have never seen a human heal like this before." He looked to the nurse. "At her rate of recovery, we should be able to move her to a room first thing in the morning."

"When do you think she will wake up?" Edric asked the doctor.

"I don't know Alpha, be patient; her body had some serious, life-threatening injuries. I am truly amazed that the crash didn't kill her. If I didn't know any better, I would think she was a wolf too," he said, shaking his head. He then left the room, as did the nurse. Edric kissed his Luna once more and then went to get Jillian's parents. He would not tell them how quickly she was healing, they would not understand, but he would tell Emerson and Warren they would be interested in the news.

The nurse took Jillian's parents back with her, while Edric shared the news with his Beta, Emerson, and Carla, who had shown up a few minutes before.

"She is a true Luna," Carla whispered.

They then heard sobbing. They looked to see a family huddled together, crying.

Edric walked over to them, kneeling by them.

The man looked up and bowed his head. "Alpha."

"Was one of your children on the plane?" he asked him.

"Yes," the woman sobbed. "She burned up at the back of the plane when it hit the ground. We thought, we thought," she cried.

"We thought she would be okay, being a wolf, they told us that she was one of the seven who had miraculously lived, but then we were just informed that she wasn't and that she burned up at the back of the plane with the others," the father cried.

"I am sorry," Edric said, putting a hand on the man's shoulder. "I am truly sorry."

"Why are you here?" the man then asked Edric softly.

"My Luna was in that plane crash, too," he whispered.

The wife gasped. "Oh no, Alpha, we are so sorry."

He nodded. "She will be okay. I am sorry for your loss, though. If I can help with funeral expenses, let me know," he said.

"Thank you," the man said sadly. "We appreciate it."

Edric nodded and stood. He patted the man's shoulder one more time and headed back to his friends.

"Poor family," Carla said, wiping her eyes.

"There were only seven survivors," Warren informed the Alpha, "including your Luna. Those that lived were in the middle of the plane. When it landed, it did so on its tail. It exploded when it hit, from what we understand."

"More than likely, the fuel tanks exploded," Emerson said.

"Probably," Edric frowned. "I just don't understand how the passengers in the front and the back, even the pilot and co-pilot, were killed, but not those seven in the middle."

"So if Jillian had sat anywhere else," Carla whispered.

"She would have died," Emerson finished.

Edric collapsed into a chair. He was one lucky son of a gun to have his Luna still. He bolted upright then and cussed.

"What is it, Alpha?" Warren asked.

"Something Jillian said the other day," he frowned.

"What?" Emerson asked.

"She said she has bad dreams, that most of them come true."

"So, do you think that she dreamt of the plane crash?" Carla asked.

"I don't know. But if she had, wouldn't she have not gone or let me know?" Edric frowned.

Emerson said, "I have heard of seers running in the werewolf family, but never in a human, but from the sounds of it, she could be a seer."

"Unbelievable," Warren said, shaking his head. "And you felt her pain when they crashed."

"Because they are mated," Emerson replied. "Even though she is human, Edric can still feel her pain and emotions."

"Interesting," Carla mused.

"Are you sure she isn't a wolf?" Warren asked him.

"I don't think so. Her parents aren't wolves; I'm sure it doesn't even run in her family."

"Can you mind link with her?" Emerson asked him.

"No, not at all; it's as if there is just a wall there."

"That's interesting," Emerson replied.

Jillian's parents walked back into the waiting room then, her mother wiping away her tears.

"She looks so peaceful. You can't even tell she is injured," she sniffled. "She looks only like she is sleeping."

"She'll be okay, but she will need to stay for a few weeks so she can heal; that's what the nurse said," Henry sighed.

Edric glanced at Warren and Emerson, and Warren both smiled. "Yes, she will need time," Edric said, looking at Jillian's parents.

They all sat down to visit and decided that they had better head home as it got late. They all needed sleep. They would not be any good to Jillian if they were dead on their feet. Edric went to Jillian's room before he left and kissed her softly. Her bruises were gone. She didn't awaken as he kissed her, but a slight smile appeared on her face. He sighed as he left the room, forever grateful that she was alive.

Edric collapsed into Jillian's bed after he got home, pulling her pillow to him, smelling her scent on it. Tears were on his face as he fell asleep.

Jillian moaned in her sleep. She was having such a horrible dream of a crash and fire, but then Jillian had put her hand out to help Kimberly and had watched in fascination as blue sparks had flown from her hand, and those around her that looked on the verge of death had miraculously been saved. Jillian was startled awake and looked around her. She was hooked up to several machines. Maybe it wasn't a dream. She had been hurt. She closed her eyes as tears leaked down her face, remembering the plane falling, the screams from everyone, and the pain. The pain had been excruciating, but she realized that she wasn't in pain now. She was a little sore and exhausted, but that was it. Had she healed that fast? She usually did heal fast, and she wondered how injured she had been. Her injuries couldn't have been that bad to recover so quickly, right? She wondered if anyone had survived besides her. Jillian knew that she had tried to save Kim; had she been able to? The tears started again, and that was how the Alpha found her, in her room, with tears coursing down her face.

The nurse was right behind him and rushed to Jillian's side. "She must be in pain."

"No," Jillian whispered.

Edric walked to her side and collapsed onto his knees beside her. "My love," he said, tears in his eyes. "I thought I had lost you," he said.

She wiped his tears. "Did others live?" she whispered.

"Seven, including you."

"Kimberly?"

"She is going home today, thanks to you," the nurse smiled at Jillian. "You saved her life."

"I didn't want her to die; she is my friend."

"She would have been okay, love," Edric said, kissing her hand. "You are the human, not her. Her wolf would have healed her anyway."

"But how did the others die? Most of them were werewolves," Jillian pointed out.

He smiled sadly at her, proud of her for being so concerned about her classmates.

"The impact and the fire were too great for their bodies to handle."

"Oh," she said, more tears streaming down her face.

"Are you in pain, Luna?" the nurse asked in concern.

"No, just tired and a little sore. How injured was I?"

"You were severely injured when you were pulled off the plane, and now you are healed. Your bruises are gone, your broken ribs and punctured lung healed. There was a gaping hole in your thigh, and all that is there now is a pink scar," Edric shook his head in wonder.

"Oh, wow," Jillian whispered. So she had been injured more severely than she had thought.

The nurse checked her vitals, and then she left the room, a smile on her face.

Jillian pulled Edric to her and kissed him, tears on her face again.

He kissed her back and then picked her up, careful not to pull out the tubes running into her; he set her onto his lap and held her, letting her cry.

"I am so sorry that this happened," he said, kissing her tears. "I am also eternally grateful you lived. I would die without you, you know. I heard you call my name, and then I felt your pain when the plane crashed," he said, shaking his head. "It was excruciating, and I can't even imagine what you were going through."

"How did you hear me, and how did you feel my pain?"

"I am sure it because we are mated; that is all I can figure out. You are also healing incredibly fast, and I am so grateful you will be okay."

She snuggled against him.

"I love you, Luna," he whispered to her.

"I love you," she whispered back, grateful that she would be okay and that he was there with her.

Her parents came back that afternoon to check on her. She was in a regular room then, and they sat by her side with the Alpha, telling him stories of her growing up while she rested.

She was tired and kept her eyes closed as her parents talked. Edric had told her she needed to fake being more injured than she was for her parent's sake, so she just feigned sleep; it was the easiest thing to do.

"Jillian told me that you moved a lot while she was growing up," Edric said as he watched Jillian rest. Her color looked good, and her vitals were good.

"My job," Henry nodded. "I had to move wherever there was work."

"Oh? I heard that you moved even before your work was done."

Henry frowned. "Well, yes. You see, we moved every time Jillian's school year ended."

"But why? Why not let her stay and make friends?"

"That was the thing. We knew that if she stayed that she might end up with a boy, and we didn't want her hanging with the wrong crowd."

"So you uprooted your daughter so she wouldn't meet a boy or hang out with the wrong people? That's not right," Edric growled.

"It was what was best for her," Henry shrugged.

"You had better not plan on moving again."

"We won't. Besides, she graduates soon, and she can decide what she wants to do from there."

"Why did you move here in the middle of the school year?" Edric asked him.

Henry flushed. "Well, it's a long story."

"I'm all ears."

"It's not something I want to discuss right now. Let's just say a good friend of ours found out something about Jillian that made us move."

"What?"

"I can't tell you. But it wasn't good. He was worried for her safety."

"I see. Was she hanging out with the wrong crowd then?" Edric frowned.

"Something like that," Henry shrugged.

Edric knew he was lying, but he wasn't sure why. He *could* see Jillian causing a stir wherever she went, though.

Jillian tried not to frown as she listened. What were her parents hiding from Edric? She knew her dad was lying about something, but what?

Chapter 12

Jillian heard her parents leave a while later, she was not even sure what time it was, but she was kind of relieved. She had a hard time with her mother crying and grasping her hand all the time. "I love you, sweet girl," she kept saying.

It seemed that she felt herself being lifted and held by the Alpha only minutes later. She cuddled against him, and he chuckled. She then felt herself being laid onto a much more comfortable bed, and then she was covered up with a warm blanket. She fell into a deep sleep after that until she started having another nightmare.

She screamed out and felt an arm tighten about her. "Shh, love, I'm right here," Edric said.

She rolled over and opened her eyes. Edric was looking at her in concern.

He wiped a tear off her face. "What is wrong, love?" he asked softly.

"I had another dream," she whispered.

"Want to talk about it?"

"Some people were out on a big yacht, a huge storm came up, and they all went overboard and drowned," she whispered.

"Was it anyone you knew?" he asked her.

"Some girls from school, I don't really know them, but I don't want them to die," she whispered.

"Hm," he frowned. He then looked at her. "Jillian, will you tell me about the dream you had before the airplane crashed?"

She shuddered, and he gathered her into his arms. She then looked at him. "Why are you in my bed?"

He chuckled. "I had the nurses put you in a bigger bed so I could be here with you," he shrugged.

"Really."

"Yes, really," he grinned.

"That's not awkward," she stated, making him chuckle.

"Your dream," he insisted.

"It was just as it happened, the plane crash," she said, "but I wasn't in that dream. There were others that I didn't know, so I figured that I would be okay. I dreamt that it suddenly dived backward as soon as the plane took off. I had no idea it would be my plane, or I wouldn't have gone," she shuddered, "and I would have had you or someone warn the others. I didn't know Edric," she cried. "I could have saved everyone, but they all died because I didn't say anything."

"It is not your fault, my love," he said, kissing her softly. "You didn't know."

"What of the others who lived?" she whispered. "Are they okay?"

He nodded. "Yes, they are all healing nicely. We figured that because of where the seven of you were sitting, that is why you were saved."

Jillian nodded, but she knew that wasn't why they had all lived. She had saved them. She wouldn't tell him, though, because it was still strange to her, blue sparks flying from her hands to heal the others.

"I am going to call the school and see if any of the girls have a yacht and if they are planning on an excursion soon," Edric said. "We don't need any more deaths."

"You believe me?" Jillian whispered.

"Of course, love. I am just trying to figure out why you are having these dreams."

"Maybe something is wrong with my head," she muttered.

He chuckled, and leaning over, he kissed her softly. "No, my love, you are definitely all there." He kissed her once again, "Plus, I have good news; the doctor said you are healed. I will take you home tomorrow if that is okay."

"For being healed, I have been so tired; why?"

"Because healing takes a lot out of someone, and you healed even faster than I do, which is quite amazing. You are amazing, my Luna."

"It's because I have you as my mate," she smiled at him.

"Yes, I am sure that is it," he chuckled. "I'll send a nurse in with some light food for you, and I'll come and check on you later, okay?"

She nodded, and he left the room after kissing her.

She then got to look around the room. It was pretty opulent for a hospital room. It looked like a very nice bedroom, except for all the medical equipment. She also noticed she was in pajamas and not a hospital gown and wondered who had changed her and how she had been so out of it that they were able to do so.

Jillian's door opened a few minutes later, and Ruben walked in with Kimberly. She squealed with delight when she saw Jillian was awake. She threw herself at Jillian, hugging her tightly, and then she began to cry.

"I am so glad you are alive," Kimberly cried. She then sat down on the bed by Jillian. "You saved me," she whispered.

"I know, and you are welcome."

"I can't believe you would save me at the cost of almost killing you," Kimberly pointed out. "I would have been okay, but you are human."

"I didn't think about that," Jillian shrugged, "but I am glad I saved you."

"I am, too," Ruben smiled at her. "I owe you everything for saving my mate."

Kimberly hugged her again. "You look good for being so injured."

"Something about being a Luna," Jillian shrugged. "I heal fast, just like you guys do."

"Woah," Ruben said, shaking his head. "That is crazy."

"I know, I agree. But I don't mind not having to be hooked up to all kinds of contraptions," Jillian said, pointing to the single saline drip in her arm.

"So, it looks like you got the best suite in the house," Kimberly teased her.

"Yes, I noticed. I wonder why I am in here?"

"I am sure the Alpha insisted," Ruben told her. "This is his room if he gets injured enough to warrant a hospital visit."

Jillian paled at his comment.

"Not that he has been in here, for a long, long time," Ruben backtracked, seeing her face.

"So, the Alpha has his own room?" Jillian asked in shock.

"Well, duh, he does own the hospital," Kimberly said.

"Of course he does," Jillian muttered.

Kimberly laughed. "Just saying, the man has some money, honey. Has he bought you anything?" she winked.

Jillian rolled her eyes at her friend. "No, well, except for artist supplies."

"Art supplies? You paint?" Kimberly asked.

"Yes, and he has this incredible studio that he set me up in that was his mom's, so I can paint when I want," Jillian smiled.

"Oh, honey, you have it bad," Kimberly laughed.

"What?"

"You love the Alpha," she winked.

"Is it that obvious?" Jillian blushed.

"Just a bit," Ruben grinned. "It's okay, Jillian; you *are* supposed to love your mate."

The nurse walked in, then with a tray and set it on Jillian's lap. "Here's some broth, Jell-O, and apple juice. The doctor wants you to start with liquids. If you can handle it, then we can feed you something soft this evening, okay?"

"Yippee," Jillian said sarcastically.

Kimberly snickered as the nurse left the room.

"I hate Jell-O," Jillian muttered. She set the tray next to her on a nightstand. "Eat up if you two want it."

"Um, yuck," Kimberly laughed.

The door opened again, and the Alpha walked in. He was frowning. Warren and Emerson were behind him.

"Can I speak with the Luna?" Edric asked Ruben and Kimberly.

"Sure," Kimberly said. She hugged Jillian. "Call me when you get home, we can hang out, and I'll make sure you get your homework from school."

"Yeah, homework," Jillian muttered, making Ruben grin.

"Get better, Luna," he said and headed out with Kimberly, closing the door behind them.

"About that dream," Edric started.

But the door opened again, and her parents walked in. Her mother gasped when she saw that Jillian was awake.

"Jillian," she cried, running to her daughter to hug her. "You look so much better," she said, wiping at her tears. "Edric said you would take weeks to heal."

"I have good doctors', mom," Jillian assured her.

"You look like you weren't even hurt," her father commented.

"That's because all of my injuries are internal," Jillian shrugged. If only they knew that she was totally healed, but she wasn't about to, that was for sure.

"But you don't seem to be in pain," her mother said.

"Good drugs," Jillian shrugged, making Edric grin.

"When do you think she will be able to come home?" her father asked Edric.

"You mean to my home? Soon," he said.

"Oh, yes, I forget that you have her as your prisoner," he muttered.

Warren and Emerson glanced at the Alpha, who shrugged.

"I am not a prisoner, father. I felt like I was at first, but Edric has been very kind, you know that. You have seen that Edric treats me well."

"Are you sure? He lets you take this trip, and then you get severely injured."

"That was not his doing, dad; why would you even say that?" Jillian replied angrily.

Warren began to cough. "Sorry," he choked out. "I need to go get a drink." He then walked out, Emerson following him, but not before winking at Jillian. The two men would leave them alone to discuss things.

"I'm just saying, if he cared for you, he would have gone with you, and perhaps he could have prevented you from getting hurt," Jillian's father said.

"And how would that have happened, father? He would have been just as injured, if not more so."

He sighed. "I am sorry, Jillian, I just am worried about you; you seem to care for the King."

"Yes, father. I do care for Edric."

"You have known him for what, almost three weeks now?"

"How long have I been in the hospital?" she asked Edric.

"For a few days."

"It's been a few weeks then," Jillian agreed.

"When can she go home, do you think, Edric?" her mother asked.

"I was actually planning on taking her home tomorrow so she would be more comfortable in her own bed."

"But it's probably not wise to move her with her injuries," her father stated.

"I have a doctor that is going to look after her," Edric promised.

"But isn't this room like home?" her mother asked, "I mean, look at this place. It looks more incredible than any hospital room I have seen."

"That's because it is the King's room, mom. Would you expect him to have less?"

"Oh, of course," she flushed. "My daughter in love with a King, that will take some getting used to."

Jillian yawned then. "I'm sorry, I'm tired and in pain. Edric, could you see if I could get some pain meds?" she asked him. She didn't really need them, but she wanted her parents to leave. She wasn't in the mood to argue.

He nodded and headed out the door.

"Oh honey, I am sorry," her mom said, hugging her. "I am just glad you are going to be okay. It is sad for all those other families who lost their loved ones. What no one can figure out is how the plane ended up crashing and exploding."

"I am sure they will look into it, mom," Jillian assured her.

"Yes, I am sure they will, and I am glad your friend is okay."

"I am too."

"We will come and visit you tomorrow unless you are at the palace," her father said, hugging her softly.

"You are welcome to come and see her there," Edric assured them as he walked back into the room. "The nurse will be here in a minute," he winked at her.

Jillian's mother kissed her cheek. "We will see you tomorrow, sweetie."

"Bye, mom, dad," Jillian said and watched them walk out.

As soon as they left, Warren and Emerson walked back in, but no nurse.

"Are you not well, love? We can talk about this later," Edric told her, watching her in concern.

"No, I am okay. It is just hard faking being injured," she shrugged, "and I was tired of my dad arguing with me."

He chuckled. "So, about your dream."

"Edric told us about your dreams," Warren said, pulling up a chair for Edric and then for him and Emerson.

"I feel like I am being judged," Jillian said, watching the men.

Edric chuckled. "No, my love, just wondering about how that lovely head of yours can come up with things that are going to happen."

"So, you found out the girls *are* going to be on a yacht?"

"I did. They were supposed to be leaving this afternoon. They are inviting a whole bunch of friends to party on the boat. I called the boat owner and warned him of the impending storm. He said he would let the girls know."

"I hope that helps," Jillian said.

"I hope so too," he smiled at her, watching her curiously.

"What?"

"Just trying to figure you out," he said.

"Oh gee, thanks, I am a specimen now."

Emerson and Warren laughed.

"No, my love. You are an anomaly. I would like to look into your family history and see if there is a history of seers."

"You think I am a seer? I've never heard of such a thing. It sounds as unbelievable as a werewolf."

That made the men laugh.

"Why would you think I am a seer?"

"Because you dream of things, and they come true."

"But that doesn't mean anything."

"It does," he assured her. "If you are a seer, that means you are one of a kind, and it might put your life in danger if anyone finds out."

"Why?"

"Because people would want you to protect them from events happening."

"Oh. That makes sense, but I'm not about to tell anyone, and I am sure none of you will."

"No, we won't," Edric looked at his men, who nodded. She yawned, and he saw how tired she looked. He stood up, then leaned over and kissed her. "Get some rest, love; I will be back later." He then spied her uneaten food. "And eat your Jell-O," he teased.

She growled at him, making him chuckle. "Now, don't go all wolf on me," he grinned.

"You wish," she replied.

"I do, my love, I really do," he grinned, walking out the door, his men on his heels.

Chapter 13

Jillian's parents came to revisit her that evening, and they were extremely wet. They were laughing, though.

"It is pouring rain out there," her dad laughed as water dripped on the floor from his clothes.

"I can see that," Jillian grinned. "I am sure there are towels around here somewhere."

He nodded and started looking for towels in the bathroom as her mom pulled a bag out from under her jacket. "I know how hospital food is," she grinned, handing it over to Jillian. Inside was a hamburger and fries, and amazingly the bag was dry.

"Oh, mom, you love me," she grinned, pulling out a French fry. It was still warm.

Her mom smiled at Jillian as she was handed a towel to dry off.

"I can't believe anyone would want to be out in this storm," her father said, drying his hair with the towel and then his pants.

"Why were you?" Jillian asked.

"Your mother insisted we go get you some food," he said, looking at his wife.

"I saw the stuff they were serving you, and I know how much you love Jell-O," she teased her daughter.

"You two are the best," Jillian sighed, feeling much better with the food in her stomach.

Once her parents were as dry as they could get, and Jillian's mom had put the towels over the shower in the bathroom, they came to sit down.

"Thanks, mom and dad, for being here for me," Jillian smiled.

"You are welcome, dear," her mother said. "We've been so worried about you; how are you feeling?"

"Better mom, thanks."

"You are looking better. I've been so worried about you," she whispered, tears in her eyes. "When they first brought you in, and the doctors were telling us what had happened, I was so scared we would lose you."

"I was in a lot of pain," Jillian admitted, "but the pain meds help," she lied. She hadn't been on anything since the first day she had been there.

"Have you been able to shower?" her mom asked her.

"Yes, the nurse came in earlier and helped me," Jillian told her.

"Oh, good. I know I always feel better after a nice warm bath or shower."

"How long has it been raining?" Jillian asked then. Her room had a window, but the blinds had been closed all day, and she hadn't gotten up to open them.

"Since early this afternoon," her father told her. "It's been coming down in torrents. I am sure there has been some flooding. I don't think we have had this much rain in months."

"I just hope it doesn't wash out our dig," her mother sighed.

"I hope the men covered the dig as I asked them to," her father said.

The door opened then, and Edric walked in. He looked distraught.

"Edric?" Jillian frowned. She knew he didn't have good news.

Emerson and Warren walked in a moment later; they also looked worried.

"What's going on?" Jillian asked them.

"Some of your classmates decided to have a yacht party this afternoon, despite being warned of the impending storm," Edric ground out. "The Coast Guard is trying to battle the storm to try and find them. The yacht capsized."

Jillian gasped, as did her parents. The girls hadn't listened to Edric's warning; they had gone out on the boat anyway.

"Why would they do that?" Jillian's mom asked. "Especially if they saw the storm moving in."

"I do not know," Edric shook his head. "But I don't think they are going to find anyone in this storm. I am sorry, Jillian."

"I am too," she whispered sadly.

"How many people were on board?" Jillian's dad asked.

"Twenty," Edric ground out.

His phone buzzed then. "Yeah."

He listened for a moment, his face grim. "Yes, I understand," he then hung up.

"The coast guard is coming back to shore. The storm is getting worse, and they don't want to lose their lives also."

Jillian closed her eyes, tears running down her face. More of her classmates were gone, all because they wouldn't listen.

She felt a hand on her cheek. She opened her eyes to see Edric. "I am sorry, love," he said. He then wiped at her tears.

"I am too," she whispered. "Even though I didn't know them, I am sorry."

Edric kissed her softly and whispered, "It's not your fault; we tried to warn them."

"I still feel guilty," she whispered back.

"Don't," he shook his head. "Don't ever feel guilty about something out of your control."

She nodded but still felt sick to her stomach.

He kissed her again and then looked at Jillian's parents. "Can I give you two a ride home? My limo is probably parked closer than your car."

"That would be nice," Jillian's mom said, "but what about our car?"

"I will have Warren bring it to you when it quits raining," he assured them.

He then looked at his men. "Emerson, will you take them home?"

"Yes, sire," he nodded.

Jillian's mom hugged Jillian. "I am sorry about your classmates dear."

"I am also," Jillian said.

Her father hugged her. "We will see you tomorrow."

"Thanks, dad. Love you both."

"We love you," Jillian's mom smiled, and the two of them started to head to the door, but not before Jillian's dad turned to Edric. "Be nice to my daughter."

"I always am, sir," Edric assured him.

"Good, or I will have your head," he warned and then walked out, Emerson following.

Edric pulled up a chair by Jillian, as did Warren.

"Why didn't they listen?" Jillian asked Edric.

"I do not know love. I called the parents of the girl who was hosting the party. When I told them I heard she was having a party on the yacht, and there was a huge storm brewing, as their Alpha, I was concerned for the safety of her and her friends; he assured me he would talk to her. So, either he did tell them, and she didn't listen, or he forgot to tell them," Edric said.

"So many lives," Jillian whispered.

"Yes, needlessly lost," Edric agreed.

"First the plane, then this," she sighed. "I wonder why the plane crashed."

Edric frowned. "About that. One of the investigators called me."

"Oh?"

"He claimed it was engine failure, but I'm not so sure, especially when the plane exploded on impact. Which brings me to another thing," he said, watching her. "I walked out to the crash site today, now that the fire is out. The whole plane was destroyed and just a shell but the seats you were in. How you and the other six survived was beyond me. All of you should have died."

Jillian gasped.

"Not that I wanted you to die," he assured her, "but there is no explanation as to why you and a few others lived. The pilots died; everyone else died. I just don't get it," he shook his head.

"It's because she is a Luna," Warren pointed out.

"But that doesn't explain why her friend Kimberly and five others across the aisle lived."

Warren shrugged. "Will we ever know?" he asked.

"Probably not," Edric replied, watching Jillian.

Edric leaned over and caught her chin in his fingers. "Quit feeling guilty, love; you are not responsible."

"But I feel like I am responsible."

"You are not at all."

"I just wish I had known it was our plane that was going to crash; I would have said something."

"You didn't know," he replied, kissing her. He then pulled back. "I saw your parents snuck in food," he teased, changing the subject.

She blushed. "I hate hospital food."

"You were only on that diet because your stomach hasn't had anything for a few days. They didn't want you regretting eating something," he pointed out.

"I haven't so far," Jillian told him.

"I hope not." He then looked over at the forgotten tray of food from lunch. "Still haven't eaten your Jell-O," he smirked.

"If you even try to feed me that, you are out of my bed for a year, Alpha," she warned him.

Warren chuckled.

"Okay, I surrender," Edric chuckled. "No Jell-O."

"Wise choice," she replied.

"I know who has you wrapped around her finger," Warren laughed.

"Shut up, Beta," Edric growled, but he had a grin on his face.

Edric then leaned over and kissed Jillian soundly. "Get some rest. I will see you in the morning; then, I am taking you home."

"Yes, Alpha."

He raised an eyebrow at her, and she just smiled innocently at him.

Emerson walked in then, ready to take his Alpha home.

Edric kissed Jillian once more, shaking his head at her sass, then he, Emerson, and Warren headed out the door.

Jillian sighed as she settled down for the night. Her poor classmates, she felt awful. Why would they not listen to their Alpha? Just in the matter of a few days, over sixty students had died, and she could have stopped it. She had tried to stop the second accident, but they hadn't listened. Tears leaked down her face as she thought about them, and she wondered if she could have saved the whole plane. She had saved the ones closest to her, but what of the others? If only she had tried.

The door opened again, and Edric walked back in. He had felt Jillian's sorrow, and after sending his men home, he decided to stay the night, Orson and Wes stationed outside the door for their protection.

"Scoot over," he told her.

"Why are you back?"

"I could feel your sadness, and I didn't want to leave you alone."

She started to cry. He laid on the bed by her and gathered her into his arms.

"Shh, love, it will be okay."

"No, it won't be," she sobbed. "I could have saved them all, Edric, and because of me, they all died."

"No, my love, it is not your fault; I already told you that. It will never be your fault."

"But," she protested.

"No, Jillian, you saved your friend, and you tried to save those kids on the yacht, but they didn't listen. That is not your fault. You can't cure stupidity."

Jillian snickered, glad he could make her feel better.

He tucked her head against his shoulder.

"Try and get some sleep, my Luna; I am right here."

She nodded, and snuggling against his nice warm body, she sighed.

He kissed her head. "I love you, Jillian, with all of my soul; I hope you know that."

She didn't hear him, because she was asleep.

Chapter 14

Edric's phone rang early that morning, and he grabbed it off the nightstand, answering it quickly, hoping not to disturb Jillian, but she stirred as he answered.

"Alpha, we have bad news."

"Spit it out, soldier." It was one of the Coast Guard.

"We couldn't find any bodies. The storm last night must have swept them all away."

"What about the boat?"

"Underwater, sir. We are sending in a dive team to see if there are any bodies on board."

"Keep me updated."

"Yes, sir," the man said and hung up.

"I'm sorry," Jillian whispered.

"It is not your fault Jillian, I just wish someone had listened," he sighed.

She nodded sadly, and he kissed her lips. He could see the deep sorrow in her eyes and knew that she would be an excellent Luna. She cared deeply for people.

"I want to take you home today if that is okay."

"Okay, I am ready," she said, kissing him.

"It is fascinating how quickly you healed," Edric told her, "if I didn't know any better, I would think you were part wolf."

"Yes, I am sure you are disappointed that I'm not."

He kissed her, making her toes curl. "I will never be disappointed in you, my love," he promised. "Come on, let's get you up and dressed. I'll let the men know we are ready to go home."

"Do I get normal food?" she asked, making him laugh.

"Of course, love, whatever you want, like lots of Jell-O," he teased, and then he got hit with a pillow.

He pulled her to him and tickled her. "Okay, okay," she gasped out. "I surrender."

"Oh really," he whispered against her lips, kissing her softly.

"Not here, Alpha," she said, pushing him away, "we wouldn't want to embarrass ourselves."

He grinned. "I wouldn't be embarrassed at all."

"I don't want anyone looking at your sexy bod, though, except me," she told him.

"You think I am sexy, do you?" he asked, pulling her in for another hot kiss.

She sighed against him; she sure loved his kisses. She could stay in his arms all day she decided, but then a knock sounded on the door.

Edric pulled away. "Come in," he said.

Emerson walked in and raised an eyebrow, a smirk on his lips.

"We are ready to go whenever you are Alpha."

"Give us a few, Emerson."

"Yes, Alpha," he chuckled and closed the door behind him

"Now, where were we," Edric said, pulling Jillian on top of him.

She laughed. "Not right now, Mister; we don't need anyone hearing us."

"You don't want them to hear my wild lovemaking skills?" he teased.

She blushed, and he laughed, kissing her. "Very well, love, I'll save it for later."

He pushed her off of him gently. She headed to the bathroom, where clothes were waiting for her. She showered and dressed and then walked out.

Edric was on the phone, a frown on his face. "It can't be changed?" he was asking someone.

"Fine, but it had better be short."

He hung up and pulled Jillian to him, laying a kiss on her lips. "I have a meeting that I have to go to; one of the Alpha's in the city over wants to discuss better protection for his pack."

"Oh, okay."

"I won't be gone long. Why don't you call your friend and see if she wants to go shopping? I can drop you off at the mall on my way to my meeting."

"What day is it?" she asked him.

"Saturday," he told her.

"Wow, I've been in here six days," she whispered, shaking her head.

"Yes, love."

"You want me to go shopping?"

"Yes, pick out anything you want."

"Anything?" she asked cheekily.

"Anything within reason," he chuckled. "No new sports car or a million-dollar diamond necklace."

"Sure, spoil my fun," she smiled at him.

He knew she would never do that anyway.

He pulled out a credit card and handed it to her. "I suggest you go and get you a cell phone also. Since I can't communicate with you here," he said, pointing to his head, "I would like to know where you are if you need me."

She nodded, agreeing. He handed her his phone. "Call your friend; I'll meet you out by the nurse's desk in a few. I need to go and sign your release papers." He kissed her, then left the room.

Jillian dialed her friend's number.

"Hello?"

"Hi, Kim."

"Hey Jillian, I mean Luna," she said. "How are you doing?"

"I'm okay; as a matter of fact, I am being released to go home, but Edric has a meeting in the city. He was wondering if I wanted to take you shopping while he is in his meeting."

"Of course, girl. That sounds awesome. Are you up to it?"

"Of course, are you?"

"You had better believe it."

"Sweet. Meet me in an hour in front of the mall."

"Okay, see you then, my friend and Luna," Kimberly said, then hung up.

Jillian headed into the hall, a smile on her face. It would be nice to hang out with her friend.

"Ready, love?" Edric asked her.

"Yes," she told him.

He tucked an arm about her waist, his guards taking up position behind him. Warren and Emerson were also there and fell into step behind the guards.

All the wolves in the hospital hall that saw them bowed their heads in loyalty to her and their Alpha.

Jillian nodded back. It would be difficult getting used to that. Edric nodded at all of them, glad they showed respect to their Luna.

Edric helped her into the limo; then, he climbed in along with his two guards. Emerson drove with Warren sitting by him.

"Luna, I have not properly introduced my guards," Edric told her. "This is Orson and Wes."

"A pleasure," she nodded at them.

"The pleasure is all ours," Orson said to her. "We are glad that our Alpha has found such a caring and kind mate."

"Thank you."

"I am sending Orson and Wes to the mall with you," Edric told Jillian.

"But why?"

"Because you are the Luna, and I don't trust anyone," he pointed out.

"You think someone would try and hurt me?"

"I would not put it past anyone, especially if they were trying to get to me," he told her.

"Oh, I didn't think of that," she said as she kissed him. "Thank you for thinking of my safety."

"You are welcome."

"What about you? Don't you need guards?"

"I will be fine. I'm not too worried about today." He exchanged a glance with his guards, who nodded. Jillian hated that she couldn't mind link with him. If only she were like him.

"I invited your parents over to dinner tonight," Edric then told her. "I wanted a welcoming home dinner for you."

"Oh, that's sweet of you," Jillian smiled at him. He smiled softly at her, loving how her smiles lit up her face. He loved making her happy.

Jillian then sat there and studied the guards.

They were both tall and well-built men. One had blonde hair, the other strawberry blonde hair, and both had blue eyes.

"Are you brothers?" Jillian asked them.

Wes nodded. "We are."

"Have you always been Edric's guards?"

"For about five years," Orson replied.

"How come I rarely see you?"

"Because we like to follow at a distance. We don't want anyone knowing we are there, but if something happens, then we can step in to help."

"Oh. So you have been following Edric the whole time I have known him?"

"For the most part," Orson said. "Not to the school, but everywhere else."

"Oh. Do you like your jobs?"

"Luna, why are you asking them that?" Edric said, smiling at her. "You know they are going to answer yes in front of me." The men grinned. Orson nodded. "Yes, we do like our jobs, Luna," he winked.

She laughed, making Edric shake his head.

Almost an hour later, they pulled up to the mall. Edric's phone rang just as they did, and Jillian spotted Kimberly waiting on the stairs to the entrance.

"Edric," he answered. "Yes, we will be there in 10."

He hung up and then kissed Jillian. "Have fun," he told her.

She nodded and got out of the limo, the two guards following.

She met Kimberly on the steps, who hugged her.

"Looking good, girl. So who are the hunks?" she teased.

The men ignored her.

"My guards. Well, actually, the Alpha's guards, but he is loaning them to me today."

Orson laughed but hid it with a cough.

"Hmm, too bad I am mated; they are handsome," Kimberly teased the men, who both flushed.

"Enough out of you, Missy," Jillian said, grabbing her friend's arm. "Speaking of mates, where is yours?"

"I told him I was going shopping with you; he opted to stay home," she grinned. "He brought me and dropped me off, so if I could get a ride home with you?"

"Of course," Jillian nodded.

"We need to go to the phone store first; Edric thinks I need a phone since I can't mind link like the rest of you," Jillian told Kimberly.

"Sure, no problem," Kimberly shrugged.

Almost an hour later, she was set with her new phone, and then the two girls went into a clothing store.

The two men stayed outside, taking up sentry positions.

"Why are they staying out there?" Kimberly asked Jillian; they had stayed outside the phone store also.

"Who knows, but I think they are drawing more attention to us," Jillian pointed out as people walked by, checking out the burly men and wondering why they were guarding the store.

"They probably think someone famous is in here," Kimberly laughed.

"Yes, we are so famous," Jillian smiled.

"You are to me," Kimberly said, throwing her arms about her friend, hugging her tight, and crying. "You saved my life; I will never be able to repay you."

"I don't expect it," Jillian told her, wiping at her own tears. "You are my friend, my only friend, and I didn't want you to die."

"But you almost did," Kimberly whispered, "all because you wanted to save me."

"What can I say? You are worth saving," Jillian told her. "I just feel so awful about the others who died and then the yacht yesterday that sank in the storm."

"Oh yeah. I heard about it on the news this morning and that we lost even more classmates," Kimberly said sadly.

"I feel awful. Almost sixty students dead in the last week," Jillian whispered. "It's almost as if something is going on."

"You don't think someone wants us dead, do you?" Kimberly gasped.

"I don't know. I just hope that no one else dies," Jillian sighed. "Now enough with the morbid, we are supposed to be shopping, right?"

Kimberly nodded. "Right." She held up a cute pink top. "What about something like this, for you? I think we need to update that wardrobe of yours, besides t-shirts and jeans," she teased.

"I have dresses," Jillian pointed out.

"Sure, but do you have cute skirts and blouses?"

"No, I guess not."

"Well then, let us shop," Kimberly grinned.

Two hours later, the girls went to the food court to eat and then to a few more shops. Just as they finished, Orson approached her.

"The Alpha is on his way back to the mall, and we are wondering if you girls were finished?"

"Yes, I think we are done," Jillian nodded. She was tired. She probably wasn't totally up to par anyway. She had just gotten out of the hospital that morning, after all.

The girls loaded with bags, the four of them headed to the mall doors. They walked out and headed down the stairs to wait for the limo to pull up.

As Jillian walked down the stairs, a man walked up the stairs. He nodded at Jillian, and then he suddenly grabbed her around the neck and pointed a gun at her head.

"Tell your guards to back off, or you die," he growled in her ear.

"No, I am not going to tell them to back off," she hissed at him, feeling scared but knowing the men would protect her. "I would rather them kill you."

"Let her go, now," Orson threatened, stepping in front of the man, a gun pointed at the man's head.

"No. The Luna is mine, and if you two try to stop me, she dies," he pointed out. He started to drag Jillian down the stairs, her arms still full of bags.

She dropped the bags right in front of the guy's feet, making him stumble, but he righted himself and hit Jillian in the head with his gun, making her cry out in pain.

"Do that again, and you die right here," he told her, his gun jammed into her ribs.

Jillian could feel blood trickling down the side of her head where he had hit her. She was amazed she hadn't passed out.

"Why do you want me?" she whispered.

"Because your Alpha owes me," he chuckled but then growled in surprise as she suddenly fell. He stumbled and tried to pick her back up, but Orson let off a shot and hit the man in the center of his head. He fell on top of Jillian just as the limo pulled up.

Edric jumped out of the car and up the stairs.

"What the hell happened?" he growled, moving the dead man off of his Luna. He didn't even look at the dead man's face to see if it was someone he knew. Jillian's shirt was covered in blood, and he cussed.

"He was trying to kidnap her," Wes ground out, kneeling by Jillian.

"Luna," Edric whispered.

She opened her eyes. "Edric," she sighed.

"Where are you hurt?" he asked her.

"He pistol-whipped me," she said.

He nodded and picked her up into his arms. "Orson, Wes, clean up this mess; I am taking her to the hospital."

The men nodded, and Edric scooted back into the limo, Kimberly beside him.

"I am coming too; that is my best friend," she stated.

"Gun it, Emerson," Edric told him.

"What happened back there?" Edric asked Jillian softly as he checked her head.

She gasped in pain, but the pain was soon gone, and she relaxed against him.

"I don't know. We were coming out of the mall, he was coming up the stairs and suddenly grabbed me, putting a gun to my head. He told me that you owed him, so he was going to take me," she whispered.

"Crap," Edric said. "Warren, call Wes, have him take a photo of the guy, and send it to my phone. I want to see who would try and kidnap my Luna. I didn't even look at him."

"Yes, Alpha," he said, pulling out his cell phone.

"We don't need the hospital," Jillian said, sitting up in Edric's arm. "I feel better."

"You are wounded, Luna; you need to be checked out."

"But I feel okay now," she said.

He looked at her head, brushing her hair aside where she had been hit.

He frowned. "The cut on your head is gone."

"I know. I told you I feel okay."

"I should still have you looked at," he said, "you might have re-injured yourself when that guy fell on you."

"Yes, Alpha," she sighed, not wanting to argue and feeling tired.

"I just can't keep you out of trouble," he noted.

"I know, whatever shall we do about it?" she teased.

"Lock you in my tower, perhaps?" he grinned.

"Don't you dare," she warned.

His phone pinged then, and he looked at it. He swore and swore again.

"Alpha, what's wrong?" Warren asked him, seeing the grave look on his face.

"Kelson," was all he said.

"Not good," Emerson replied. Warren looked worried.

"Who is that?" Jillian asked him.

"My old Beta."

"Your old Beta?"

"Yes."

"Why?"

"Because he wanted to be Alpha, and he almost killed me for the position."

"Oh. So why is he still alive?"

"Because I was stupid and let him live on the promise, he would never show his face around me again."

"Now, he is dead," Jillian whispered.

"Yes, and good riddance," he growled. "But what the hell was he doing trying to kidnap you?"

"That is the question of the hour," Warren answered, "and how did he know where Jillian was and that she is your Luna?"

Chapter 15

Emerson pulled up to the hospital's emergency entrance, and two nurses walked out with a stretcher between them. Edric helped Jillian out and made her lay on the stretcher, then he, Warren, and Kimberly followed as Emerson headed to park the limo.

The nurses put Jillian into a room, and Dr. Hess walked in, shaking his head. "Didn't we just discharge you this morning, Luna?"

Jillian shrugged. "You did, but I decided to have a bit more fun before I headed home."

Edric shook his head at Jillian's witty remark.

Dr. Hess looked at Jillian's head and her eyes for signs of a concussion. "This is remarkable young lady. You look healed already."

"I am. But the Alpha wanted to make sure I didn't reinjure myself from the accident a few days ago."

He nodded. "I'll take you to x-ray then," and he and the nurses pushed Jillian out of the room and down the hall to x-ray.

Emerson joined the others in the room while they waited to see how Jillian was.

Edric looked to his men.

"*I can't believe Kelson tried to kill my Luna,*" he mind linked them. He didn't want Kimberly listening in.

"*Why?*" Emerson asked. "*And how did he know that you were mated?*"

"*How did he know she was there? And he called her Luna,*" Edric frowned.

"*We had better look and see what he has been up to,*" Warren replied. "*He might have formed his own pack.*"

Edric growled. "*He had better not have. Or I will personally kill all of them.*"

"*We'll help,*" Emerson told him. "*Especially if they were given instructions to come after the Luna.*"

"*She will need more protection,*" Warren stated.

"*Yes, she will. I just hope that he was acting alone,*" Edric frowned.

"*I guess we will find out,*" Emerson replied.

Jillian walked into the room then, Dr. Hess behind her. She was a mess with blood on her shirt and head. Emerson held up a bag for her. "I have your stuff here." Wes had thrown the bags into the trunk before they had left the mall.

"Thanks, Emerson, you are a lifesaver," Jillian told him.

"She's fine," Dr. Hess said. "Her old injuries are okay, and her head injury is fine. She seems to have healed already, which is very curious to me. I am wondering if she does have wolf blood in her. Do you care if I take a sample?" he asked Jillian. "I can test it to see if you do."

She shrugged. "Sure, that's fine."

He nodded. "Depending on what is going on, we should have results in a few minutes."

After he left, Jillian took her bag of clothes into the bathroom and changed, then washed the blood off of her head. Feeling much better and looking better, she walked out of the bathroom. The doctor was back with the empty vials.

"We'll wait out in the waiting room," Warren told Edric and took the others with him, leaving Edric behind.

Jillian sat on the bed as the nurse drew some blood.

"We'll be back in a few minutes with these," the doctor said.

Edric sat by Jillian and pulled her into his arms, kissing her. "I am glad you are okay, love."

"I am also. I am so glad you sent Orson and Wes with me, or I would have been kidnapped or killed."

"I just can't understand why he would want you and how he found out about you?"

"Do you think he was acting alone?" Jillian asked.

"I don't know, but I will check into it," he promised. "Maybe I will have to send guards with you to school, just to keep you out of trouble," he teased.

"It's not my fault you have a Luna who likes attention," Jillian grinned at him.

"If you needed attention, you could have asked me," he chuckled, kissing her again.

She snuggled against him, glad he cared for her.

Dr. Hess walked in a few minutes later, a grin on his face.

"Well, I take it you have good news," Edric said.

"I found something; her blood is definitely not normal human blood; I'll have to run some more tests on that, but that is not why I am grinning," he said.

"Oh, what is it, Doc?" Edric asked.

"Your Luna is pregnant."

"What?" Edric said, jumping up. "Are you sure?"

"Very sure," he said. "She's a little over a week along."

Edric looked at Jillian, who looked pale.

"My love, you are pregnant," he said, a massive grin on his face. He kissed her, then kissed her stomach. "I am going to be a dad," he whispered reverently.

"I'll leave you two. You are fit to go home, Luna, and I will get back to you on the other results. Congrats, by the way," he said, walking out.

Edric pulled Jillian to her feet. "How do you feel, love?"

"In shock," she admitted. "I can't believe I am pregnant."

"Well, considering we haven't been using protection," he pointed out.

"Did you want me to get pregnant?" she asked him.

"I didn't really think about it," he shrugged, "but I am thrilled that you are. I can't wait until you have my pup. I have always wanted to be a father."

"How would the doctor be able to tell I was pregnant already?"

"The blood tests," Edric smiled. "Come on, let's go tell the others the good news."

Chapter 16

Jillian stopped Edric before they left the room. "Edric, I would rather not tell anyone right now."

"Why? It is great news."

"Yes, but how would my parents react if they found out, and I am not technically married?"

He stopped. "You are right, I suppose. We should have a proper wedding before you start to show; we don't need tongues wagging if you have a belly on you," he chuckled, thrilled about the news.

"Let's wait a month. I don't want my parents thinking we got married too quickly, that I *do* have Stockholm Syndrome," she teased.

He chuckled. "Okay, one month, but they will wonder about you when you have the baby before we have been married six months."

"Six months?"

"Yes, pups are born earlier than human babies unless you have a human," he mused. "I guess we shall see, huh?"

She nodded. "I just hope that I can carry him or her to full term without a miscarriage."

"Oh, why do you say that?"

"My mom miscarried a lot; that is why she only had me," Jillian shrugged. "At least that is what she told me."

"Well, we shall just have to make sure you take it easy so that you don't miscarry," he told her.

"I can still go to school, though, can't I?"

"I don't know why not."

"Thank you," Jillian said, then yawned. "I'm suddenly tired. Can we go home?"

He nodded as they headed to the waiting room.

"So?" Warren asked. "What's going on?"

"Not sure," Edric shrugged. "The Doc can't figure out Jillian's blood. He is going to run some tests and get back with us."

"So, she's not truly human after all," Emerson teased. "Should have known."

"I wouldn't mind having another werewolf friend," Kimberly smiled.

"I'm not sure I'm a wolf," Jillian told her. "He just said my blood was different."

"Hmm, what could it be then?" Emerson asked. "I wonder if the doc would let me look at the blood sample."

"You could ask him," Edric replied, "but I need to get my Luna home, she has had a long day, and I need to call her parents and cancel dinner." He could tell Jillian was exhausted. He was sure it was because her body was trying to heal, and now she was pregnant, she would be a lot more tired.

Jillian was glad he was going to call her parents, she wasn't up to seeing them, and she didn't want them to know what had happened. They would insist on her moving back home, but she didn't want that. She liked where she was now.

Once in the limo, Edric called Jillian's mom.

"Mrs. Everett? This is Edric, look I called to cancel dinner. Jillian isn't feeling up to it right now. Can we make it another day?"

"Sure," she replied. "Just call and let us know. How is she doing, by the way?"

He looked down at Jillian, who was fast asleep, leaning against him.

"She's asleep right now. She is recovering nicely, though. It will just take some time."

"I am glad she has you," Nadine admitted. "You are good to her, I can tell."

"Yes, ma'am. She is my life now. I will take good care of your daughter."

"Good. Have her call me when she wakes up."

"I will." He hung up then and looked at Kimberly. "Is Ruben meeting you at the mall? Or are we taking you home?"

"At the mall, in a few minutes. I let him know what happened, so he is on his way to get me. You still have to go get your guards anyway, right?"

"I do. I will wait there until Ruben shows up. I don't want anything happening to you."

"I will be okay. It was your Luna that man was after, not me. He totally ignored me."

"I just can't figure out how he knew who she was," Edric said, shaking his head as they pulled up outside the mall.

Orson and Wes were with the police; the steps had been taped off to keep people away. A few people had gathered, wondering what was going on. The body was gone, but there was blood on the stairs. Wes opened the door and peeked his head in. "The police want to question Jillian."

"She's asleep," Edric told him. "Have them come by in a few hours."

Wes nodded and turned to the policeman next to him and told him. The officer nodded and stuck his head in the limo. "Alpha," he acknowledged. "We need some witness statements."

"I was there," Kimberly said. "I can tell you what happened."

The man nodded. "Will you step out so I can get your statement?"

She nodded, and he helped her out.

Jillian heard them and opened her eyes. She yawned. "I can talk to them also," she said.

"They can come and sit in here," Edric told her. "I don't want anyone hurting you again."

The door opened then, and an officer climbed in with a paper and clipboard. Alpha had mind-linked him that Jillian was awake. Warren stepped out to give them privacy.

"Luna," the man said, looking uncomfortable being around her and the Alpha. "I need your statement if you would."

He handed over the clipboard and a pen.

She wrote down what she could then handed it back. The officer had a frown on his face. Edric had been warning him that there might be more rogues, and he wasn't happy. He hated rogues. They were bad news.

"Luna, were they any indicators that the man wanted to kidnap you?" the officer asked her.

"I think that was what he was trying to do. It was as if he was waiting for me. I didn't see him in the mall, but when we walked out of the mall, he was at the bottom of the stairs, and then he headed to me. I just figured it was some guy going inside. He nodded at me, ignoring that my guards were behind me and suddenly grabbed me, pointing a gun to my head."

Edric growled. Jillian hadn't told him what had happened. All he knew was that Kelson wanted her.

"Then what happened?"

"He warned my guards to back off, or he would kill me right there."

"He didn't indicate that he wanted to take you?"

"All he said was that I was his, then tried to drag me away."

"Interesting," the man said, writing in a notebook. "Then what happened?"

"I dropped my bags, hoping that he would let me go. He tripped on them, and it made him mad, so he hit me in the head with his gun."

Edric growled again. If Orson hadn't killed him, he would have. But he wouldn't have been so merciful. He would have torn him to pieces.

"So, then what?" the officer asked.

"I screamed in pain, he told me to be quiet, or he would kill me right then, and then he started dragging me down the stairs again. I knew that if he took me, I would die, so I pretended to faint. As soon as I dropped to the ground, Orson shot and killed him."

The officer frowned and looked at Edric, who shook his head. The man nodded. He wanted to ask some more personal questions, but Edric wouldn't allow it. "Very well, then. That is all I need for now. Hopefully, he was the only one. I will get back with you, Alpha, if we can find out what this guy was doing here."

Edric nodded. "Thank you."

The man nodded and got out of the car, taking the statement with him.

Ruben arrived then and frowned when he saw the police tape, and his frown deepened as he saw that Kimberly was talking to an officer. He was angry when he realized how close he had been to losing his mate also.

He opened the limo door and stuck his head in. "How is your Luna?" he asked Edric.

Edric looked down at Jillian, who was tucked against him.

"I'm okay, Ruben," Jillian told him.

"You seem to be a magnet for trouble," Ruben pointed out to her.

"That she is," Edric agreed.

"I am not," Jillian argued.

Kimberly stepped up to Ruben then. He turned and, pulling her into his arms, he kissed her. "I am ready to go. I gave them my statement," she told him.

"Are you okay?" he asked her, looking her over.

"I am fine. The guy didn't want me. He ignored me; he only had eyes for the Luna."

Ruben then ducked his head back into the limo. "Good luck, Alpha, and you, Jillian, try and stay out of trouble?" he chuckled, then closed the door.

Wes climbed in after Ruben and Kimberly left. "I think we are about done here. Orson is making sure all the evidence is collected, then we should be able to go." He looked at Jillian. "Luna, how are you doing?"

"I'm okay Wes, thanks to you and Orson, you both saved my life."

"Anything for you, Luna; I am glad that we were here today."

Edric nodded. He had had a bad feeling, leaving Jillian on her own, and he was glad he hadn't, or she would be dead, and more than likely Kimberly also.

"Kelson sure hit her hard," Wes frowned. "I'm just glad he didn't shoot her. I don't know why he was here. It took me a moment to recognize him. I don't know why he would want the Luna unless he wanted revenge for getting his butt kicked."

"I am sure that is what it was for. I am glad he is dead, saves me from killing him. I would have ripped him to pieces if Orson hadn't shot him. Thank you, both of you," Edric growled.

"That's our job, Alpha," Wes replied.

Orson slipped into the limo, then Warren with him. "The cops are finishing up, but we can go. They will stop by if they have any more questions," Orson told the Alpha.

Edric nodded as Emerson pulled out to the street. "We need to find out what he was up to and if he was in league with someone else," Edric told his men. "I need to know if we are safe or if Jillian's life is still in danger."

Edric looked down at his Luna and smiled softly. She was asleep again. He mind linked his men. "*She didn't want me to tell you, but she is pregnant. She's not far along. That was one reason the doctor wanted to talk to us alone. I am telling you, men, because I want her protected even more now. I don't want her to lose this baby, and I don't want her life in more danger if someone finds out she is pregnant.*"

"*We will protect her, Alpha,*" Orson vowed.

"That is all I ask. I want our baby to live," he said, smiling softly. *"I'm going to be a father."*

"What will her parents say?" Warren asked.

"We aren't telling them, not until we are properly married. Jillian wants a wedding next month. Emerson, if you and Carla could work with Jillian in getting things arranged for that. Let her have free reign. I am not too worried about her going overboard," he chuckled.

"Will do," Emerson said. *"Carla is going to be excited. She loves weddings."*

They pulled up to the palace a few minutes later, and Orson got out, took Jillian from Edric, then handed her back to him once he was out. Carla met them as they headed inside.

"How is she?"

"Exhausted. I am letting her sleep. If the cops show up later with more questions and she is still sleeping, don't disturb her," Edric said. "I can deal with them."

Carla nodded. "Kelson is dead, then?"

"He is."

"Good riddance. I don't know why you let him live in the first place." She said what the others had not dared say to their Alpha.

"I know it was stupid of me, especially since he came after Jillian. But he is gone now. Let's just hope that no one else comes after her."

Edric headed to his room and tucked Jillian into his bed. It was time she started sharing his bed. They shared everything else. He covered her up and walked out of the room and back down the stairs.

Warren met him there. "Dr. Hess is on the phone in your office. Emerson is talking to him, but he wants to speak with you."

Edric nodded and headed to his office. He walked in, closing the door. Emerson put the phone on speaker. "Doc, Edric is here. Tell him what you discovered."

"Alpha, I found out something interesting with your Luna's blood."

"Oh? What is that?"

"She has healer's blood in her."

"I kind of figured since she's not a wolf."

"Yes, but another interesting thing is that she has the capability of healing others."

"How do you know this?"

"The plane crash and the six kids that were sitting around her. They all miraculously healed. Not one of them spent over a day in the hospital."

"You are sure she healed them? How is that possible?" "There is no other explanation. By all means, all of them should be dead. You saw the plane; there wasn't much left of it."

"I wonder if it runs in her family."

"Do you think she knew she was healing her classmates?" Emerson asked.

"You'll have to ask her," Dr. Hess replied. "I have only heard of one healer, and that was the High Luna Queen."

"Do you think she could be related in any way?" Edric asked. The High Luna Queen was the greatest Luna who had ever lived and was murdered when he was but a child, along with her husband, the Great Alpha King.

"I will check into it and let you know. But I think when you marked her, it woke up her skills," the Doctor said. "You are a lucky man Alpha. Keep her close to you."

"What of her dreams that come true?" Edric asked him. He had told Dr. Hess about Jillian dreaming of the plane crash and the yacht overturning.

"Yes, that is interesting also. If you will recall, the great Queen was also a seer."

Edric frowned. "You think she could be a seer also?"

"I am pretty sure she is. A healer and a seer. You have one powerful Luna on your hands, Alpha. If I were you, I wouldn't let anyone know. Her life would be in greater danger."

"I wasn't planning on it."

"Let's hope not, or things could get ugly."

"Thanks, Doc, for informing us. Do you think that her talents will pass along to our child?"

"I do not know. Only time will tell. Take care of her, Alpha. Her life is in danger, carrying that baby. I would keep her pregnancy a secret for as long as you can."

"I will try," Edric replied.

"Good day then. Keep in touch with me. I want to see her in a few weeks to see how the baby is doing."

"Will do," Edric said and hung up.

He looked at Emerson. "Oh boy, what have I gotten myself into?"

Emerson chuckled. "A whole heap of trouble, that's what."

Chapter 17

When Jillian woke up, it was dark, she was in bed, and a warm arm was over her stomach. She turned over to see Edric sound asleep beside her. She was also in just a t-shirt and underwear. Had he changed her? She must have been really out of it, but she had been exhausted. He sighed in his sleep, and she smiled. She was a lucky girl. He was taking such good care of her. She couldn't believe it had been less than a month since she had met him, but she was glad he had walked into the school and claimed her. She had fallen deeply in love with the man.

He sensed her watching him and woke up. "My lovely Luna, how are you feeling?" he asked her softly.

"Better," she replied, "but,"

"But what?"

"I know something that would make me feel even better," she grinned cheekily.

"Are you up to it?" he asked in concern.

"When it comes to you? I will always be up to it," she teased.

He grinned, pulling her on top of him and kissing her. "I missed this," he said as he pulled her shirt off.

"Me too," she whispered.

It was dawn by the time they fell asleep in each other's arm, content and happy.

When Jillian woke up later, Edric was gone. She shouldn't have been surprised. It was almost noon. She got up, showered, and dressed, then headed to the kitchen; she was starving. She rubbed her stomach, wondering if she would start craving weird things.

Carla was in the kitchen making herself some lunch. "Hi Luna, how are you feeling?"

"Good," she shrugged. "Just hungry."

"Here, you can eat my sandwich; I will make another."

"Are you sure?"

"Positive. You are my Luna, after all. I need to take care of you before myself."

"I thought that was Edric's job," Jillian grinned.

Carla laughed. "It is, but it is also ours. Your comfort comes before our own."

"Oh, but that will make me feel weird."

"Don't let it; that is just the way things are run around here," she shrugged, pushing the sandwich to Jillian.

"Thanks," Jillian said, sitting at the table.

"What are you planning on doing the rest of the day?" Carla asked.

"I'll probably go paint, and then tomorrow head back to school."

"If the Alpha lets you."

"He told me I could."

"Do you think you will be safe?"

"I think so; why, what aren't you telling me, Carla?"

She flushed. "Ask the Alpha; he can tell you."

"Carla," Jillian warned.

Carla could tell Jillian was getting angry, and she could feel great power emanating from her; she was forced to expose her neck to her Luna and answer.

"It's just that,"

"Yes?" Jillian asked, wondering why Carla was exposing her neck; she wasn't a wolf.

"The doctor called while you were sleeping yesterday; he found out you had healing powers. You can heal others and yourself."

"Oh, I thought it would be something bad."

"Oh no, it is wonderful," Carla sighed, feeling the power lessen. "Plus, he said you had seer blood in you; that is why you can dream of the future. But you didn't hear that from me. I'm not supposed to say a word, or your life could be in danger."

"Then how do you know?"

"Emerson, but I swear to you, not a word will be said; the Alpha would have our hides if anyone else knew."

"I wonder how I inherited my abilities."

"The doctor thinks that your abilities awoke when Edric marked you."

"No, I don't think that is the reason," Jillian muttered. "Why do you say that?" Carla asked her.

"Because I have had those abilities my whole life, except for the healing others part," she shrugged, finished her sandwich, and then stood. "Is Edric in his office?"

"I think so," Carla told her, in awe of the Luna. She had just forced her to tell her the truth, and she had been born with seer and healing powers?

"Anything else?" Jillian asked her, knowing she was hiding something.

"He told us you were pregnant," she whispered, feeling the power roll off of Jillian once again.

"Why would he do that?" Jillian asked, upset. "I asked him not to tell anyone, not until I was further along."

"Only myself, Emerson, and Warren know," Carla said, "and only so we can protect you more. The Alpha doesn't want you to get hurt or have something happen to you and lose the baby."

"Oh," Jillian sighed. "I suppose that is okay then."

Carla could feel the pressure release from her again, and she sighed. She was in shock. Even the Alpha wasn't that powerful. He could put pressure on them, but he could never force them to tell the truth.

"Carla, are you okay?"

"I am, Luna," Carla nodded. "I didn't realize how powerful you were. Remind me not ever to try and lie to you."

She knew that she had forced Carla to tell her the truth. She had seen the waves of power coming from herself as she made Carla talk.

It was interesting. She didn't know she had that ability, but it was good she did. Then people would have to be honest with her. "I would hope you don't," Jillian said, then walked out of the kitchen. She headed to the office and walked in, not bothering to knock.

"Get back with me as soon as you can," Edric was saying, and then he hung up. He stood and walking around the desk; he pulled Jillian into his arms and kissed her.

"How are you feeling, love?"

"Upset at you."

"Why?"

"Because you told your men and Carla that I was pregnant."

Edric frowned. "Carla said that I told her?"

"I made her tell me."

Edric exchanged glances with Warren, who was standing by the window.

"What do you mean, you made her tell you?" Edric asked.

"Why did you tell them, Edric?" Jillian asked, "when I asked you not to?" she asked, ignoring his question.

"It is for your safety, love," he told her, "and I only told Carla, Warren, Emerson, and my two guards. Your secret is safe with them," he said.

"I'll just wait outside," Warren said, walking out. He knew they needed to discuss a few things.

"She also told me that you found out I was a seer and healer."

"How did she know?"

"Emerson."

He growled.

"I am sure she read his mind."

"And how did she tell you this?"

"I made her."

"How?"

"I asked her, and she wouldn't answer, so I used some of my Luna power to make her answer."

"Luna," Edric said.

"Don't Luna me," Jillian growled. "I don't like that everyone knows of my abilities. You know that I won't be safe if everyone knows."

He pulled her into his arms. "I swear to you, my Luna, that only Emerson and now Carla knows; not one other person does." He pulled her to sit by him on the couch. "Tell me how you forced Carla to answer you. I can't do that."

She shrugged. "I don't know, but I could tell she was hiding things from me."

"But how?"

"I just did. I could almost see the power rolling off of me when I made her answer. She exposed her neck to me, and she couldn't lie to me."

"You can see the power rolling off of yourself?"

"Yes, just like how I can see the power rolling off of you." "You can see my power?"

"I can. It's blue and comes off you in waves when you are upset or need your men to listen."

Edric kissed her. "You just keep amazing me, my Luna, but next time you want a straight answer, don't hurt my Omega's wife, okay?"

"I didn't hurt her; I just made her obey."

"Yes, even I can't do that to my men," he said, shaking his head. "I am glad you are here. I wanted to ask you something."

The door opened then, and Emerson walked in. He was smirking. "Luna, Carla told me what you did to her; I am impressed." He shut the door behind him.

"Emerson and I wanted to ask you about the students you saved on the plane," Edric told Jillian.

"What do you mean?"

"Don't play dumb, Jillian. None of them should have lived, but six did and healed faster than normal. Not one had to spend more than a night in the hospital. I want to know how you did that."

She sighed. "It was kind of an impulse thing, I guess. I was mostly trying to save Kim."

"So, what happened?"

She glanced at Emerson. "My lips and mind are sealed," he said.

"Oh yeah, because that worked out so well earlier," Jillian frowned at him.

"Sorry about that, I was thinking of you when I went to bed last night, and she saw. She won't say a word, though."

"I know she won't. I made her promise."

"Yes, she also said you forced her to tell you," he chuckled. "You are something else."

"Jillian, tell us what happened on the plane," Edric told her, turning her attention back to him.

"Just before the plane crashed, I knew I didn't want Kim to die, so I put out my hand to save her. Blue sparks came from my hand and hit her and some of the other students."

Edric's mouth dropped open, as did Emerson's.

"Incredible," Emerson whispered.

"Because of that, those six lived," Edric told her. "They were injured, but they healed like you did. Their parents are in shock that they healed so fast."

"You won't tell them?"

"Of course not. I don't want everyone on our doorstep thinking you can heal them of every ailment," he chuckled.

"Why do you think I am this way?" Jillian asked him.

"I don't know. But I have a friend I am going to call. He can help figure this out, I think," Edric told her.

"That would be nice," she sighed. "I wonder if our little one will inherit my abilities? Or if he is just going to be a handsome troublemaker like his dad."

"Troublemaker?" he asked, raising an eyebrow, "excuse me?"

"I'll leave you two lovebirds alone," Emerson chuckled and walked out.

"Now tell me again how you think I am a troublemaker?" Edric teased Jillian, grabbing her and tickling her, making her burst out with laughter.

"That's what you are," she gasped out.

"I'll show you, troublemaker," he said, then attacked her mouth with his.

Chapter 18

Jillian decided to go out to the studio and paint because the Alpha had work to do. She spent the rest of the day there, only coming in for dinner. The Alpha wasn't there, and she frowned, wondering where he was.

Carla walked in as Jillian sat at the table, picking at her food. She wasn't hungry and wasn't happy that Edric wasn't there. He hadn't told her he was going anywhere.

"Luna?" Carla asked.

Jillian looked at her. "Yes?"

"The Alpha wanted me to let you know he had to leave town for a few days. One of the packs is having problems with some rogues. He'll be back this weekend."

"Why didn't he take me with him?" Jillian asked, "and why didn't he tell me?"

"Something about you being pregnant," she whispered, "and he didn't want you upset with him because he left you behind."

Jillian frowned. "I am not a china doll Carla."

"I know Luna, but he wants you treated as one."

Jillian shook her head, rolling her eyes.

She stood up then.

"Aren't you going to eat Luna?"

"I'm not hungry," Jillian sighed and headed to her room. She showered and then headed to bed. She was tired, and she was tired of being tired. She knew that the baby would be sapping more of her energy as it grew, and she was sure that was one reason why she was tired.

Just as she was about asleep, the phone rang by the bedside. She picked it up.

"Hello?" she mumbled.

"My love, did I wake you?" Edric asked.

"I'm mad at you," was her response.

"I am sorry, love. I didn't want to tell you I was leaving because you would have insisted on coming with me, but I have to help deal with some rogues in another pack, and I don't want you hurt."

"You could have at least told me all of that before you left," she said.

"I know; I am sorry, love. It's a last-minute thing."

"Promise me you will be careful?" I don't want you hurt, either."

"Of course, my love. You be careful also. Wes and Orson are there for you if you go to school tomorrow."

"Okay, thank you."

"I love you, my Luna, sleep well, and I will call tomorrow. I am hoping that we can deal with this problem quickly so I can return home. I love you, Jillian."

"I love you."

"I am doing this to keep us safe, okay?"

"I know."

"Goodnight, my love, have good dreams, okay?"

"I will try."

"I love you," he said again and then hung up.

Jillian sighed and rolled over to Edric's side of the bed, pulling his pillow to her, breathing in his scent. Good thing he cared for her and his pack so much. He was a good Alpha; she saw that every day she spent with him.

The following day Jillian got up early, got dressed, then headed down the stairs, her backpack on. Orson was by the front door.

"School?" he asked her.

"Yes, I have work to catch up on."

He nodded. "We'll need to be there with you."

"Yes, I know, Edric told me."

"Where are Warren and Emerson?" Jillian asked.

"Alpha took them with him," Orson told her.

"But doesn't the Alpha need guards?"

"He has Warren and Emerson and Travis and Zack."

"Oh, I don't know Travis and Zack."

"They are guards; they just usually guard the palace, not the Alpha."

"Oh. So I took you from the Alpha."

"Yes, but he is more worried about your safety than his."

"That is nice of him, but he needs just as much protection."

"Glad you think we are the only ones who can guard him," Orson chuckled, "but the other men are just as capable; besides, Edric could kick anyone's ass any day."

Jillian laughed. "Yes, I am sure he could."

Orson helped Jillian into the limo, and Wes drove her to the school, Orson sitting by her. Wes parked the limo in front of the school, then opened the door so Jillian could get out. The students stopped and bared their necks to her as she headed inside, her two guards right behind her.

When she saw Jillian, Kimberly and Ruben were just headed inside with some other students. She shrieked and ran back down the stairs, hugging her friend.

"Hey," she said, eyeing Jillian's guards. "Guards at school now, huh?"

"Yes," Jillian grumbled. "It's the only way I am allowed to come to school."

"Cool," she grinned. "Come on; you have missed a lot since you have been gone."

"What?"

"Oh, well, let's see. Forty girls have found their mates here at school."

"I've only been gone a week."

"I know," she smiled, and Spring Ball is this next week."

"Spring Ball?"

"Yes, it's like Prom, you dress up all fancy, and it's decorated like Spring, it is so beautiful," she sighed.

Jillian laughed. "Okay, sounds fun."

"Yep, and you can bring the Alpha as your date."

"Oh," Jillian said, stopping at her locker. "I don't know if he would want to come to some silly high school Ball."

"I bet he would, for you," Kimberly said. "Ask him."

"I don't know," Jillian said.

"Ask him," Ruben smiled. "You know he will. I know for a fact he would do anything for you."

"Okay," Jillian sighed. "I'll ask him."

Kimberly squealed in delight. "Want to go dress shopping this afternoon?"

Jillian looked at her guards, who were shaking their heads.

"I don't know, Kim; remember last time we went shopping?" Jillian said.

"Oh, yeah, I forgot," she sighed, "but how are you going to get a dress?"

"The Alpha has a clothes designer," Orson spoke up, "he can come in and make dresses for you girls."

"A guy?" Kimberly snorted, "yeah, right." She looked at Jillian. "We'll figure something out, even if it means sneaking out to get you a dress."

"We are standing right here, you know," Wes said, but he was grinning.

"Oh, be quiet, you," Kimberly teased. She grabbed Jillian's hand, "come on, or we'll be late for class."

Jillian nodded and let Kimberly lead her down the hall, Jillian's guards on her heels.

They stood sentry outside the door as Jillian headed into her class.

When she walked in, the whole class stood along with the teacher and bared their necks to her.

Embarrassed, Jillian sat down, them sitting after she did. Great, why were they doing that now?

"Luna, welcome back," Mr. Flynn said. "I am glad you are okay."

She nodded, looking around the room, at the empty seats, guilt hitting her a hundredfold.

The teacher saw her face and smiled sadly. "There will be a memorial in the gym right before lunch for those students who lost their lives."

"That's good."

"I know that the parents would want you to say a few words."

"That is not good," she said, making the students and the teacher chuckle.

"Class, as you know, what with everything going on, I have pushed back your essay being due for another week."

All the students sighed in relief, including Jillian.

The other classes were just like the first, everyone bared their neck to Jillian out of respect, and then the teachers continued on with their lessons like Jillian hadn't even been gone.

As soon as her third class let out, all the students headed to the gym. Jillian found herself at the front of the students, her guards right behind her.

When Jillian walked into the gym, all the students filed in behind her and then stayed standing. Parents then filed in to stand by their students and the parents who lost their children. Several pictures on easels lined the front of the gym of the students who had died. Tears came to Jillian's eyes as she looked at them.

"Luna, we have a seat for you right here," the Principal told her, leading her to the front, where half a dozen chairs were set up. Sure, put her on display; she sighed and followed the principal, Wes, and Orson right behind her.

Jillian sat down, and then everyone else sat. They were waiting for her to sit? How embarrassing. Wes and Orson then took sentry positions behind her chair.

The principal walked to the microphone. "Students and parents, thank you for gathering with us today. We wanted to honor the students who lost their lives these past few weeks." He smiled sadly. "I want to let the parents know how sorry I am that such brilliant minds were lost to us. I know that the Alpha and Luna feel your pain."

Parents and students were wiping their eyes as their tears fell. Jillian started to cry also. She couldn't help it. There were just too many students gone.

"We are grateful that some survived," the principal said, nodding at a group of students and their parents who were sitting together. "Johan, Libby, Faris, Bart, Carol, and Kimberly, we are so glad you lived but most important, that our Luna survived. I would like to turn a few minutes over to her." He stepped back and looked at Jillian.

She stood up, feeling like a nervous wreck. Jillian hated public speaking, especially in front of the whole school, plus the parents and teachers.

She took a deep breath and looked back at Orson and Wes, who gave her nods of encouragement. She stepped to the microphone.

"I am not sure what to say," Jillian said, looking out to the audience, spotting Kim. She smiled at her friend. "But I do want you to know how loved all of you are and that the Alpha and I are with all of you in feeling your sorrow. I wish none of this had happened, that we could go back in time, but as much as I wish that, it isn't possible. All I can do is tell all of you how sorry I am. I care deeply for all of you. You are my pack, and I want you to know if you need anything, especially a shoulder to cry on; I am here for you." She then sat down amid thunderous applause. Then everyone stood and bore their necks to her, a great sign of respect. Tears came to Jillian's eyes, and she bowed her head back to them. Things would be okay. The students saw her in a new light and felt respect for her now.

The principal then got back up and spoke for a few minutes, then he turned the time over to a few of the parents who had lost a child, and then he turned the time over to one of the parents whose child had lived.

The woman walked to the microphone, tears in her eyes, and then she looked back at Jillian, bowed her head to her, and then turned around. "I just wanted to say how grateful I am that my son Faris is alive. I can't even describe to you how it feels. I thought he was lost to me, just like all the others." She choked back a sob, "but I know for a fact that the Luna protected him and the others who lived."

Everyone gasped, and Jillian frowned. "I know you think that impossible, but how else do you explain that those who were sitting by our Luna lived. They were the only ones," she whispered. "I know that our Luna is powerful; I can feel it; she is so good for all of us; thank you, Luna, for saving my son." She then stepped to Jillian. Jillian stood up and hugged her. "How did you do it?" the woman whispered in her ear.

"I don't know," Jillian said.

"I will forever be in your debt," she then knelt at her feet, making Jillian blush. The other parents, whose students were alive because of her, knelt also. Then all of the students, and soon everyone was kneeling.

"Please, please, stand," Jillian said to them, tears streaming down her face. "I am not worthy of your fealty." They stayed where they were. They all could feel her power. They knew she wasn't a weak human, after all.

"Yes, you are worthy," the principal told her. "You are the greatest Luna we have had since the High Luna Queen."

Jillian looked at him, a question in her eyes. He turned to the audience. "The High Luna Queen was the most powerful woman alive; she was just like you, Luna Jillian. The High Queen cared for each and every one of us, but then rogues murdered her and her husband." He sighed. "I am just glad that you are here now. You will make us wolves great again."

The students and parents all sat down then, and the principal said, "Parents and students, we have grief counselors here if you need them. I know that the Luna will also talk with those who might need comfort." He then dismissed everyone. But they waited until Jillian stood and walked out, her guards behind her.

"Okay, that was so crazy," Jillian breathed out, heading to the lunchroom.

Orson chuckled. "They are smart, Luna; they know a great and powerful woman when they see her."

"I am not all that great or powerful."

Wes scoffed. "So you say. We can feel the power in you. Don't kid yourself."

Jillian walked into the lunchroom to get her food, and soon the other students followed. She took her food to her table and sat down; Orson and Wes grabbed some food also and came to sit by her. A few minutes later, Kimberly and Ruben came to sit with her. "Permission to sit with her almighty, Luna?" Kimberly asked seriously, but she had a twinkle in her eye.

"Yes, Kim, sit your butt down and quit embarrassing me," Jillian grinned.

She laughed. "Very well." She sat down, Ruben by her side.

"You did well in there," Ruben told Jillian. "You are greatly respected now. You shouldn't have any more problems with any of the students."

"I hope not; I hate being talked about or bullied."

"What you said," Kim whispered, wiping at her eyes. "You meant it, and everyone could tell."

"I just don't know why that mom would tell everyone I saved her son."

"Because you did," Kim insisted. "You saved me, and as she said because the others were sitting by you, your Luna power saved them. I have a feeling you are going to have some worshipers on your hands now."

"Oh, dear, that is not what I wanted."

Ruben chuckled. "Enjoy it; it's about time everyone started treating you with respect."

The three boys she had saved suddenly walked up to the table, and Orson and Wes stepped in to stop them.

"It's okay, Orson, Wes, let them through," Jillian said.

Her guards nodded and stepped back, but only to stand behind Jillian.

"Luna," Faris said, exposing his neck to her. "Bart, Johan, and I would like to thank you for saving us. We owe you everything, and we were wondering, well, if," he looked at the other boys, who nodded. "Well, we were wondering if you would let us be your guards after we graduate high school."

Jillian looked back at Orson and Wes, who shrugged.

"Can I get back with you on that? I would need to ask the Alpha."

"Of course," Faris nodded. "We can go to school, whatever it takes, so that we can protect you; after all, you saved us. It is the least we can do, Luna."

Jillian felt at such a disadvantage sitting down, so she stood and walked to them. The three knelt at her feet, making her feel embarrassed all over again. The cafeteria had gone quiet. Everyone was watching them.

"Gentlemen, please, stand," she said.

They nodded and got to their feet. She then hugged them. They were pretty surprised that their Luna would embrace them, but the three hugged her back. "I would be honored if you were my guards, but the Alpha is out of town, so I will let you know in a few days, okay?"

They nodded at her, then bowing their heads to her one more time, they went back to their table.

"Man, that was embarrassing," Jillian sighed, sitting down as the students went back to eating.

"That is a great honor," Ruben told her, "for guys like that to swear their lives to protect yours. You don't see that happen, like ever."

"I do feel honored," Jillian replied.

"So, girl, how about dress shopping?" Kim asked her, trying to ease the tension.

"You are not going shopping," Orson growled out.

"Orson, what are the chances of me being attacked twice? Kelson is dead; I should be okay."

"I don't know, Luna," he frowned.

"Orson, you can't keep babying me. I will be fine. The Alpha doesn't need to know."

"Luna, we just got you back from the hospital again," he frowned.

She sighed. "Okay, I won't go shopping today, but I need a dress."

"Wait until the Alpha gets back, and then he can take you," Orson said.

"Yippee, I am sure he would be thrilled to have me drag him around looking for a dress."

The two men chuckled, but they were relieved.

Wes growled then, his wolf wanting to come out, as Jarem approached them. He had skipped out on the memorial. He hated that stuff, and he didn't care how great the Luna was; she was still human.

He smirked at Jillian but bowed his head at her, mocking her.

"Luna."

"What do you want?" she said, getting angry. He could feel her power and backed away.

"I wanted to thank you for making me work with horse crap," he smirked. "It has really opened my eyes to see something."

"Oh?"

"Yes, on how to get revenge," he chuckled. "By the way, Kelson may be dead, but he had many followers," he replied and walked away.

Wes growled, ready to head after him.

"Wes, stop," Jillian demanded.

He stopped and looked at her. He could feel her power, and he couldn't deny her.

"Luna, he threatened you," he growled.

"I know, but he wants you to follow him and leave me vulnerable."

Wes nodded, frowning. "I am sorry, Luna, I didn't think about that."

"I know," she frowned. She looked at Orson. "Don't tell the Alpha about this."

"He has to know."

"No, because then he will lock me away, and I don't want that; promise me, both of you."

"But," Orson said.

"No, Orson. I will not be a prisoner."

He sighed. "Yes, Luna."

"Good," she said and stood. "I need to head to class." She hugged Kimberly. "I'll see you there?"

"Of course," she nodded, watching her friend walk out, her guards following.

She looked at Ruben. He looked worried.

"Ruben, Jillian did not tell us not to say anything," she said.

He nodded. "I will let the Alpha know. Her life is in danger."

Kimberly nodded. "I wonder who Kelson had following him? It worries me if he has a group of wolves that were under him."

"I know. I just hope we can stop Jarem before he does something stupid."

"I hope so too," Kimberly whispered, worried about her Luna.

Chapter 19

The rest of the day was uneventful except for the fact that now everyone exposed their necks to Jillian and then didn't sit until she did. She was glad to head to her last class, one of her favorite, her dutch oven cooking class.

The class cooked some potatoes and bread and sat around eating it when Jillian suddenly stood up, holding her mouth. They were outside, and the class watched as she sprinted away, Orson and Wes on her heels.

She found some bushes nearby and threw up.

Orson frowned and looked at Wes, who shrugged.

The teacher walked over a moment later and handed her a water bottle.

"I am sorry, sir," Jillian said, "I guess the food didn't sit right."

He nodded. "It's okay, Luna; I am sure your body is still healing from your trauma. Why don't you go home early, so you can rest? I will excuse you."

"Thanks," she whispered as she dry heaved.

Orson put an arm around her as Wes grabbed her backpack, and they headed to the car.

"Don't throw up in the car," Wes teased as he got up front. "I don't think the Alpha would appreciate it."

"I'll try not to," Jillian whispered, her face pale.

Wes hurried them back to the palace. Carla was waiting for them, and took Jillian to her room, made her lay down, and then ran to get a wet rag and some crackers. She brought them back, put the cloth on Jillian's forehead, and handed her the crackers. "The first few months of pregnancy are the worst," Carla said.

"Oh, yes, I guess it would be morning sickness," Jillian muttered. "This is going to suck."

Carla chuckled. "Just make sure you have crackers with you all the time, and you should be okay."

"When will it go away," Jillian asked as she nibbled on a cracker.

"Usually after the second month, sometimes the third."

"Oh, great," Jillian moaned.

"I'm sorry, Luna," Carla said.

Jillian nodded and hopped off the bed, running to the bathroom again.

Carla followed her, holding Jillian's hair back for her as she threw up again. Carla handed her some water to wash her mouth out.

"I am so screwed," Jillian whispered as Carla helped her back to bed.

"Just rest, Luna," Carla told her.

"What am I going to do about school? If I keep throwing up, I won't be able to be there; I'll always be running to the bathroom."

"You can either stay home and finish school online, or you can just make sure you carry crackers with you and let the teachers know," Carla shrugged.

"I don't want anyone to know yet," Jillian whispered, "especially my parents."

"Speaking of your parents," Carla said. "They want to come to dinner tomorrow."

"That's fine," Jillian said. "Hopefully, I'll be able to hold something down."

"I can call them back," Carla said.

"No, let them come. I want to see them."

"I heard about what happened at school today," Carla smiled at her Luna. "You were wonderful. Orson and Wes are singing your praises. They said that the whole student body knelt for you? And that three young men want to be your guards? Luna, that has never happened in the history of Luna's except for the Great Queen."

"Did she go to school too?" Jillian asked her.

"You had better believe it, and she started showing her powers when she was your age. The students loved her, and she loved them."

"Tell me about her."

"I was just a child when she died, but the stories told about her are wonderful."

"The principal said rogues murdered her."

Carla nodded. "Yes, her and her husband, and their newborn child."

Jillian gasped. "They had a child?"

"Yes. She wasn't even a day old when rogues attacked the nursery and killed her and her parents while they slept."

Tears fell down Jillian's face. "That is horrible."

"I know, it makes all of us sad when we think of how great a Luna that little girl would have been, just like you are turning out to be," Carla smiled at her, but that became a frown as Jillian headed to the bathroom again.

After she was cleaned up again, Carla helped her back into bed. "I'll go find a bucket," Carla told her, "and then you won't have to keep getting out of bed."

She was back a few moments later, Orson and Wes with her.

Jillian raised an eyebrow at them.

"Carla said you couldn't stop throwing up. Maybe we should take you to the hospital," Orson said. "You are probably getting dehydrated."

"No, I'll be okay," Jillian said, as once again, she got up and ran to the bathroom.

"Luna," Orson said, "you need to be taken care of. This is not normal."

"I thought morning sickness was normal," Jillian panted, sitting on the floor of the bathroom.

"Not like this. My sister was never this sick with her pup," he said.

"Okay, maybe I will go," Jillian panted as she once again threw up.

Orson nodded at Wes as Orson picked up Jillian into his arms. Carla followed them out of the room and down the hall to the door. She watched Orson get into the limo with Jillian.

"I'll stay here in case the Alpha calls."

Wes nodded, and he got in and headed out of the drive.

Carla went back inside. She hadn't been able to mind-link with the Alpha. She was sure it was because he was busy in meetings, but she hadn't been able to get hold of Emerson or Warren either. What was so important that they would shut her out?

Carla sighed as she headed back inside. She headed into the office and dialed the Alpha's number. It went right to voicemail.

"Alpha, give me a call when you can; it's important," Carla said, leaving a message, hoping that the Alpha would get it soon.

Carla didn't want to let the Alpha know that his Luna was having problems, or he would stress out and possibly wreck when he came racing home. She didn't want that, so she tried to sound calm on the phone.

Jillian felt cold to Orson as he held her on the way to the hospital. She didn't look good at all.

"Step on it, Wes; she looks awful."

"I don't want to drive too fast," Wes ground out, "I don't want to get in an accident."

Orson nodded and then swore as they headed into the intersection. Their light was green, but he watched in horror as a car came speeding through the red light and slammed right into the limo, sending it skidding across the lane and into a building.

Jillian screamed as she was thrown across the limo, and everything went black.

Chapter 20

Edric was sitting in an important meeting with other Alpha's. He had informed them about Kelson and that he was probably leading the band of rogues when he suddenly dropped to his knees, a severe pain ripping through his gut. He gasped and swore. Something had happened to Jillian again.

Emerson and Warren were by his side. "Alpha," Emerson said, "what's wrong?"

"Jillian," he moaned.

"Crap," Emerson said, "not again." He helped haul the Alpha to his feet. Edric's face was ashen, and his nose was bleeding.

"We need to leave now," Edric said.

The men nodded. The others in the room knew how it was when their mate was hurt. They watched in concern as his men helped him out.

Jillian groaned in agony as she came to. She looked around her, realizing that she was still inside the limo. The side of the limo she was on was crushed into a building. Jillian then saw several people running to them, and she looked over at Orson. He was out cold, his face cut and bleeding, and she couldn't get up to see how Wes was because a great pain ripped through her, making her gasp, and suddenly she was bleeding all over. She moaned in pain as a door was ripped off its hinges. "Hold on, Luna, help is on the way," she heard, and then she gave in to the blackness calling her name again.

When Jillian woke up, she found herself hooked up to several machines, a saline drip, and blood. She groaned in pain, but then it started to ease up. She sighed, wondering what had happened.

The door opened, and Dr. Hess walked in, looking upset.

"Luna," he said.

"Orson and Wes?" she asked, "how are they?"

"They will be okay, just some cuts that are healing, but you, on the other hand."

"What?" she whispered.

He smiled sadly at her. "You lost the baby. When the car hit the limo, you were thrown, and the impact killed your baby," he whispered.

Jillian began to cry. "Where is Edric?"

"Flying back as we speak. He will be here as soon as he can. He knew you were injured, so left as soon as he could. He should be here soon."

She nodded, tears streaming down her face.

"I am sorry, Luna," he said. "I am keeping you here for a few days. You lost a lot of blood, and I have a counselor who is here if you need to talk to her." He again smiled sadly at her and walked out.

Carla walked in then, her face pale, tears in her eyes. She walked over to Jillian and hugged her softly.

"The baby," Jillian sobbed.

"I know," Carla whispered sadly. "The doc told me. I am so sorry, Jillian."

"What is Edric going to say?" Jillian cried. "He so wanted a baby."

"You will have more," Carla assured her.

"Oh, Carla, I feel devastated."

"I am sure you do," Carla said. "I feel devastated for you."

"Did they catch who hit us?"

Carla nodded. "It was Jarem. He admitted to hitting the limo on purpose."

Jillian gasped. "He threatened me at school today."

"I heard," she frowned.

"Where are Wes and Orson?"

"Outside your door, guarding you."

"Where is Jarem?"

"In a jail cell. He won't tell the officers why he hit the limo. He is going to be charged with attempted murder, and murder, for killing your baby," she said.

Jillian swallowed. "And my parents, do they know?"

Carla shook her head. "We were going to let you decide if you wanted them to know about the accident and the baby."

"They are going to find out about the accident anyway, but I don't want them to know about the baby."

"Of course," Carla said. "I will have Orson call them."

"Will you have him and Wes come in here?"

Carla nodded, and, walking to the door, she opened it, motioning them in.

They walked in, their faces solemn and grim.

"Luna," Orson whispered. "We are so sorry."

Jillian smiled sadly at them. "I know Orson. Are you two okay?"

"We are okay. We only had a few cuts."

"Then why was I so injured?"

"The baby," Wes said. "You were weak already from throwing up, and when the limo got hit, you were thrown into the window. If you weren't a Luna, you would have died."

"Does Edric know about the baby?" Jillian asked.

"Yes," Orson whispered. "We have been keeping him informed about you."

"Oh."

"He will be here soon," Wes said softly. "He is worried about you."

"I am worried about me," Jillian sighed. "Will you call my parents?"

"Already did," Orson said. "They are on their way."

"Please, no one mention the baby," Jillian whispered.

Everyone nodded.

"I am sorry I couldn't help keep you safe," Orson said.

"There was nothing you could do about it, Orson."

"I could have buckled you in."

"I know, but you didn't know that we were going to be hit, either."

He nodded. "I just don't know if the Alpha will forgive us for letting you get injured and for the baby dying," he said, swallowing back tears.

"It was not your fault," Jillian said again as the door opened and her parents walked in. Her mother was crying. When she saw Jillian was awake, she threw herself onto Jillian, sobbing.

"Oh, Jillian, I am sorry," she sniffled. "Orson called and said your limo got hit as he was taking you here because he said you had the flu."

"Did the person get caught that hit the limo?" Jillian's dad asked.

"Yes, sir, he is in a jail cell," Wes said.

"Good." He sighed. "Jillian, what are we going to do with you? This is the third time in just a few weeks that you have been in here." He then glared at Jillian's guards. "She never got into accidents or had trouble before she met Edric. Why is her life suddenly in danger?" he demanded to know.

Wes shook his head. "I don't know, sir."

"It's because of who she is living with," Jillian's mom said. "He is a King. Maybe someone wants him dead, so they are coming after Jillian to get to him."

"Mom, no," Jillian said. "The airplane crash was an accident."

"And what about the almost kidnapping?" her mom glared at Orson.

"Okay, they did want revenge on Edric," Jillian muttered.

"And now? Did the person hit the limo on purpose?" Jillian's dad asked angrily.

"Yes," she muttered again.

Her father glared at the guards. "See? How dare you let her be injured? How dare you let her life be in danger. Where is Edric? I am taking Jillian home; she has been hurt enough," he growled.

"He was in some meetings in New York; he is flying back now," Orson said.

"Well, you can tell him when he gets back that we are taking our daughter home. I don't care if he threatens us with jail. I don't want my daughter dead because of him," he growled.

"Mr. Everett," Orson said.

"Don't," he snarled. "I don't want to hear about it; her life is too precious to let her keep getting hurt; enough is enough."

"I'm 18, dad; you can't make me come home," Jillian whispered.

"Watch me," he said. "If I have to get a restraining order against the King, I will. I have had enough of my baby girl getting hurt."

"Dad," she pleaded.

"No. You are coming home with us."

The door opened then, Dr. Hess walked in, and he was unhappy.

"Jillian's heart monitor is jumping off the charts, and I heard yelling in here; what is going on?" he said angrily. "Jillian is severely injured. If all of you can't keep your voices down, you are going to have to leave."

Jillian's dad sighed, running a hand through his hair. "I'm sorry, Doctor. I just don't want her around Edric anymore. She keeps getting hurt."

"I understand, Mr. Everett, but you can't take her home right now. She is seriously injured, if you haven't noticed," he said, pointing at the machines hooked up to Jillian.

"Oh," he whispered, "I am sorry; it's just that she is my daughter, and.."

"I know, sir, but she needs to stay for a few days. She was more injured this time than in that plane crash," he frowned.

"When she heals, I want her home," her father said.

"No, I am sorry, Mr. Everett, but as your daughter said, she is 18; she gets that choice."

"She does not," he ground out.

"Dad, please," Jillian said.

"No, Jillian. Enough is enough."

The door flung open then, and Edric walked in, his face pale but angry. He had heard everything, and he was ticked.

"Everyone leave, but Orson, Wes, and Emerson. Now," he demanded. His voice was calm but deadly sounding.

Everyone hurried out of the room, including the doctor and Jillian's parents. They could feel the power flowing from him.

Carla closed the door behind her.

Edric's face suddenly softened, and he hurried to Jillian's side, kissing her softly. She began to cry again.

"Shh, love, it will be okay," he whispered.

"No, it won't, Edric, the baby," she sobbed.

"I know, love, I know," he said, tears in his eyes. He climbed onto the bed with her and gingerly picked her up, setting her onto his lap. She buried her head into his shoulder and wept.

He kissed the top of her head. "Shh, love, I am here. I am so sorry I wasn't here to protect you. I am here now, and I won't ever leave you again," he promised.

He then looked at his men. "Orson, what happened?"

"Your Luna was extremely ill. She had bad morning sickness and couldn't stop throwing up. She ended up coming home from school early because of it. We took her home, but she just kept throwing up, so we decided to take her to the hospital. We were going through the intersection when we were broadsided. The impact sent us into a building. I was thrown into the door; your Luna hit the window; she got the worst of it."

"Why was she not buckled?" he growled.

"I am sorry, Alpha, we were worried sick about her, and we wanted to get her here as quickly as possible. It was easier holding her."

"My baby is dead because she was not buckled in," he ground out.

Orson nodded, his face grim. "I am sorry, Alpha."

"My baby is dead!" he roared in anger, making Jillian jump. She touched his face, calming him. "Alpha," she whispered.

His face softened as he looked at his Luna. "I am sorry, Luna," he said, kissing her forehead. "I am just so angry."

The door opened, and Dr. Hess walked in again, shutting it behind him. "Alpha, I heard what you said, and the baby would not have survived, even if the Luna was buckled up."

"Why?" Edric growled.

"The limo crumpled on impact. If your Luna had been buckled in, she would have been instantly killed. She is lucky," he said.

Edric swallowed, tightening his hold on Jillian. "So, her being unbuckled saved her life."

"Yes, it did. Yes, she got severely hurt, but she will heal. Give your guards some slack, Alpha; they saved her life."

Edric nodded, taking a deep breath. "I am just incredibly ticked off."

"Understandable. She will need to stay a few days. She bled pretty heavily after miscarrying. She will need a few blood transfusions, and she needs time to heal."

He then walked out again.

Edric wrapped his arms tighter around Jillian, not wanting to let her go. He had almost lost her again because he hadn't been there for her.

He then looked at his men. "Jarem did this?"

"Yes, Alpha," Wes said. "He said he was getting revenge."

"For me punishing him?"

"Yes, but he said something about revenge for Kelson."

Edric went pale. "He was in league with Kelson?"

"That's what he said to the Luna when he confronted her in the lunchroom today."

"What did he say?" Edric growled in anger.

"He wanted to thank me for making him clean out stalls," Jillian whispered, "that it helped him plan his revenge on me. He is blaming me for Kelson dying."

"I was going to go after him, but Jillian stopped me," Wes said. "She told me that if I did, she would be left vulnerable for him to attack her."

Edric nodded, frowning. He kissed the top of Jillian's head. "I heard what you did today at school. I am proud of you. Orson said he was in awe that you had the whole school kneeling for you and that three young men want to be your guards? Even I am impressed. You are incredible, my sweet Luna."

She looked up at him. "I don't feel so incredible. All I did was tell them that I was sorry for their losses, and then one of the moms had to get up there and tell everyone that she knew I saved her son."

Edric frowned. "She did?"

"Yes," Orson confirmed. "She believes that because those students that were sitting around the Luna, they were saved."

"Jillian's life is going to be in greater danger then."

"We know," Orson nodded.

"We'll have to have more guards for her, and I'm sorry Jillian, but it would probably be best if you stayed home for a bit until all this died down."

She sighed. "I understand."

"What, no arguing?" he teased her.

"I'm not exactly feeling up to that right now."

He kissed her softly. "I can tell. Orson, Wes, let Jillian's parents and Carla come back in and stand guard outside. I want guards around the clock for her. I am going to go and have a little visit with Jarem at the jail."

Edric carefully set Jillian on the bed, kissed her again, and then turned to his men. "I want to go see him now."

Orson nodded. "Yes, Alpha, but your Luna needs someone to watch her."

"I will take my other guards. I am going to go kill that fool," he growled.

His phone rang then. "Yeah," he growled into it. His frown got deeper. "You are kidding me."

He threw his phone into the wall, shattering it, making everyone flinch.

"Alpha?" Orson said.

"He hung himself. That idiot hung himself. Now we won't know if anyone else is after Jillian." He punched his fist into the brick wall, leaving a huge hole, but he didn't even notice that his knuckles were bleeding. His wolf wanted out; he was so mad.

Jillian watched Edric as he punched the wall. She had never seen anyone so angry before; it made her a bit scared. She whimpered without meaning to.

Edric whipped to her, and his face changed from anger to worry as he saw Jillian cowering in her bed, her eyes frightened.

"I want everyone out," he whispered.

His men hurried out the door as Edric headed to the bed. Jillian flinched as he sat down by her.

"Love," he said, as he tried to pull her to him, but she moved away.

"Jillian, love, my Luna," he whispered, "please listen to me," he said softly.

He turned her face to him, and he cussed, seeing her tears. "I am so sorry," he said. "Sometimes, my anger gets the best of me. My wolf was begging to come out. He wanted to tear everything apart. I had to control him, so I punched the wall to relieve stress. I am so sorry; I scared you."

She still didn't say anything. He picked her up, setting her onto his lap again. She was shivering.

"Oh, Luna," he said, tears in his eyes. "I am so, so sorry. Sorry for getting angry, and sorry for the baby."

He kissed her temple and then turned her face up to him. He wiped the tears away and kissed her softly. "I promise you, love, that I will find out if any more wolves are after us, and I promise never to leave you home alone again. If I have meetings, I will bring you with me."

She nodded against him. He rubbed her back softly. "I love you, Jillian. It almost killed me when I felt your pain. I flew back as soon as I could. I wish I had been here, then maybe this wouldn't have happened."

"Then you would have been hurt," she whispered.

"I would have been okay, and I probably would have been able to protect you."

She looked up at him. "I am glad you weren't. If you had been sitting where the car hit the limo," she cried.

"Shh, love, it will be okay." He held her against him, soothing her.

"We will try again for a baby," he promised her, "as soon as you are up to it." He sighed. "I can't believe Jarem hung himself."

"He probably knew you would come after him; that is why."

"He is a coward. I hope he rots in Hell."

Jillian giggled. He frowned down at her. "Did you think that was funny?"

"Yes," she giggled again. "Sorry, but it was."

He kissed her, chuckling. "You laugh at the strangest things, my Luna." He sighed then, tucking her against him. "I love you more than you will ever know."

But she didn't hear him because she was asleep, feeling safe in her Alpha's arms.

Edric set Jillian gently on the bed and covered her up.

He walked to the door and opened it. He had his own waiting room next to his hospital room and as he opened the door, everyone hopped to their feet.

"She is asleep. I am sorry everyone for losing my temper," he said, closing the door behind him. He raked a hand through his hair, frustrated.

Jillian's mom walked over to him and hugged him. "We know you love her; understandably, you are upset."

"I want her to come home," Henry said, walking up to Edric. "I am tired of her getting hurt."

"She is not safe at your home," Edric said.

"Why not?"

"Because, if whoever is after me comes after Jillian again, and she is home without guards, she would be in danger. Do you want that?"

Henry shook his head. "No, of course not."

"Then, she stays at the palace."

Edric then looked at his men. "I am staying the night. Orson and Wes, go to the police station, find out what you can do there. Travis and Zack, stay here to guard the room."

The men nodded. "Emerson and Warren, go home and get some rest, you also, Carla. I will need you three tomorrow."

They also nodded. He then looked at Jillian's parents. "She will be safe from now on. I will personally see to it. I will not let her leave my side."

"What about school?" her mom asked.

"As of now, she will be homeschooled. I don't want the chance of her getting hurt again."

"That's good. Can we come and see her tomorrow?"

"Of course, I know Jillian would enjoy the company."

Jillian's mom wiped a tear away. "Take care of her, Edric; she is all we have."

"I know," he said, "and when she is up to it, I want us to get married."

"I thought you were going to wait," Jillian's father said.

"I think she would be safer if we were married," Edric replied. "I want to have it in a month." He looked to Jillian's mom. "I want you to help her plan her wedding, and Carla also."

"Okay," they both said.

"Where is her ring?" Jillian's father asked him.

"I haven't gotten her one yet, but I will, don't worry."

"I want my girl to be proposed to properly and you to be married before you have your way with her," Jillian's father ground out.

Warren and Emerson hid smirks.

"Yes, sir," Edric said, "now, if you will excuse me, I am going to go make sure Jillian is okay."

He left the waiting room to head back into the hospital room, and everyone dispersed, leaving Zack and Travis to watch the door.

Edric slid into bed beside Jillian, pulling her to him.

"Until my dying day, I will protect you, my Luna," he whispered. He sighed, mind linking with his men. *"Men, be vigilant; I have a feeling that this is only the beginning."*

"Yes, Alpha," came the response.

"I wish we could have killed him," Raul said. *"It would have been gratifying."*

"I know, for both of us. One thing is for sure, Jillian will not go unprotected from now on, especially after that woman spoke about Jillian saving those kids. I hope they don't think that she can heal people, or we are going to have a problem."

"You need to call your friend."

"I will when I get a chance. Right now, the only thing on my mind is keeping my Luna safe."

"You and me both," his wolf replied. *"Let's hope that we can."*

Chapter 21

When Jillian woke up again, she was alone. She wasn't sure where Edric was, hoping he was just outside. She stretched and frowned as pain shot through her stomach. She gasped, and her heart rate suddenly skyrocketed.

The door opened, and Edric and the doctor walked in. Edric looked worried.

"Luna," the doctor said, "let me get you some pain meds into your I.V. With you losing the baby, your body is trying to right itself again to where it was before you got pregnant. It will take a few days."

"It hurts," she whispered.

"I am sure it does," he sympathized. "I'll be right back."

Edric came to sit by Jillian on the bed as she cringed in pain again.

"Why am I not healing like before?" she asked him.

"I'm not sure, love," he said, kissing her softly. "I am sorry you are in pain."

"Can you feel it when I hurt?" she asked him.

"Yes, but not as half as bad as you can," he said. "It feels like mild cramps to me."

"I'm sorry you have to feel my pain," she gasped out.

"I'm not. I will take your pain any day. It assures me you are alive and healing."

The doctor walked in, then with a syringe. "This should help your pain," he said and inserted it into Jillian's I.V.

Moments later, she sighed. "That's much better."

"I am sure it is. You are healing quickly, Luna, but I am amazed that you only lost the baby. I figured you would have broken bones among internal injuries. But everything checked out okay. You are one lucky Luna," he said.

The door opened again, and Kimberly walked in with some flowers. She smiled at her friend and set the flowers down. "How is my best friend?" she asked.

"I've been better," Jillian sighed.

"I'm sorry about your accident," she said.

"How did you find out?"

"The Alpha mind linked Ruben to let him know. He then told me."

"I hope no one else knows," Jillian said.

"Nope, my lips are sealed."

"Good. So did you bring me some food?" Jillian grinned at her friend.

Edric chuckled. "Someone is feeling better."

"Sorry, friend, I didn't know if I was allowed to," Kimberly shrugged.

"Dang," Jillian said.

Edric kissed Jillian's cheek. "How about I go get you something. You name it."

"I would love some fish and chips," Jillian said.

"Okay, my love, I'll be back soon," he said, and kissing her again, he left.

Kimberly pulled up a chair. "So, will you tell me what happened?"

"I'll just leave you two," the doctor said and walked out.

Jillian sighed. "Promise not to say a word if I tell you?"

"Yep, my lips are still sealed."

"I was pregnant," Jillian whispered.

Kimberly's face lit up, then fell. "Wait, you said you *were* pregnant."

"Yes. I was really sick with morning sickness, and Orson and Wes were bringing me to the hospital because I was so sick. Someone ran the red light and hit us. I hit the passenger window when we crashed, and the impact killed the baby," Jillian whispered, the tears falling once again.

"Oh, my friend," Kimberly said, standing to hug her friend. "I am so sorry."

"Me too," Jillian said. "I know I am still young, but I was kind of looking forward to being a mom since I found out."

"Yeah, I know the feeling. Ruben and I are trying now since we graduate in a few months," she shrugged.

"I didn't know I would get pregnant so easily," Jillian said.

"So, you gave in to the Alpha? Must have been because he was always shifting in front of you?" Kimberly teased.

Jillian blushed. "No, that wasn't it. After he marked me, I just felt an intense love for him, and well, I wanted to complete the mating."

"Hmm, yep, you have it bad," she teased.

"What?"

"You love him a lot, don't you."

"I do," Jillian said. "He has been incredible, patient with me, and concerned when I get hurt."

"Which has been way too much lately, Missy," Kimberly said.

"I know. My dad said I had never been hurt until I met Edric, which is true," she sighed.

"I bet your dad is ticked."

"Very. Especially when he realized I keep getting hurt because someone is after Edric."

"But Kelson is dead."

"Yes, but it kind of sounds like he recruited some others to come after us."

"Oh, that is bad."

"Yeah."

"So, what happened in your accident? I heard it was Jarem."

"It wasn't an accident. It *was* Jarem; he hit our limo on purpose."

"How did he know it was you?"

"I don't know," Jillian said. "He must have been following us."

"But how would he know you were going to the hospital?" Kimberly asked.

Jillian frowned. "He would if the car had a tracking device on it, or if someone's phone is bugged."

"Dang girl, you should be a cop," Kimberly smiled.

"Orson, Wes, get in here," Jillian said. She knew they could hear her.

"We heard," Orson frowned as the two men walked into the room. "So you think the car has a tracking device and possibly someone's phone?" Orson asked.

"It's the only explanation as to why Jarem would know where we were," Jillian pointed out.

"Crap," Orson said. He frowned for a moment, then said, "I just let the Alpha know. He's on his way back, and he will let the police know. They will probably search the palace and the cars."

"Good thinking on your part Luna," Wes smiled at her. "We wouldn't have thought of something like that."

Edric walked in with a bag of food moments later and handed it to her, kissing her as he did so. "I didn't think about the palace or limo being bugged either; good thinking, Jillian."

Edric looked at Orson. "Have the police search the wrecked limo and this limo to see if there is any tracking device on either one."

Orson nodded and left the room.

"Sorry I am so much trouble," Jillian said, pulling the food out to eat.

"You are no trouble at all," Edric said. "I am. They are after me, and to get to me, they are coming after you first."

"If the palace is bugged, who do you think did it?" Jillian asked.

"I don't know. I trust every single person that lives or works there. It worries me that someone is following in Kelson's footsteps."

Orson walked back into the room with a frown on his face.

"We have a problem Alpha."

"What is it?"

"Someone torched the wrecked limo. The fire department is putting it out as we speak."

Edric swore. "So, someone didn't want evidence found. Get several of the pack and head over to the palace. I don't want it burned to the ground, and make sure the officers are thorough in searching the place."

"Yes, sir," he said and headed out again.

Edric sighed. "This is not good. I had no idea that Kelson had such a grudge."

"You should have just killed him in the first place," Wes said.

"I know, but I was too nice. He promised to leave and that I would never see his face again."

"Next time Alpha, just kill the wolf."

"I will, believe me," he said.

"Are my parents safe?" Jillian then asked.

"I don't know, love; I can have officers watch their place also if it would make you feel better."

"It would," she assured him.

He nodded at Wes. "Let Orson know to have the cops patrol in front of Jillian's parents."

"Yes, Alpha," he said and walked out the door.

"Now what?" Jillian asked, handing over her empty food wrappers to Edric.

"You are going to heal, and I am going to figure out how many followers Kelson has."

"If you find more, what are you going to do with them?"
"Send them to prison, or kill them if they put up a fight."

Jillian flinched.

"I'm sorry, love, but that is the werewolf world. If I don't defend my territory and my pack, we could die. Which would you rather have; them dead, or me?" he asked.

"Them, of course," she whispered.

"Then let me handle it, okay?"

She nodded, hoping that it wouldn't have to come down to fighting other wolves.

"Rest love, I am right here," he told her.

He then looked at Kimberly. "You are welcome to stay."

"I think I will head home," she said. She hugged Jillian. "I'll drop by tomorrow, okay? You look like you need some rest."

"Okay, thanks for visiting and for the flowers."

"No problem, friend, see you later." She then headed out the door.

Edric started pacing the floor, a frown on his face. He kept shaking his head, getting angrier by the moment.

"What is it, Edric?" Jillian asked.

He held up a finger to tell her to wait a moment. A minute later, he looked at her, great worry on his face.

"The officers found bugs in every single room, including ours."

"Oh," Jillian gasped out. "So, there is a rat in the palace."

"Yes, a huge one," he growled, "and I am going to find out who it is. This sickens me that I am not safe in my own home," he growled.

"*We can always interrogate everyone the hard way*," his wolf chuckled.

"*If no one confesses, it might resort to that*," Edric responded.

He turned back to Jillian, who looked worried. "Are we going to be okay?"

"We will be, I promise. Now the palace is free of bugs; we should be fine. I will just make sure it doesn't happen again."

He walked to the bed and laid down by her, kicking off his shoes. "Get some rest, love," he said.

"And how am I supposed to do that when a sexy man is in my bed?" she asked, making him chuckle.

"Now, love, I have a ridiculously sexy woman in my bed, and I am going to get some sleep because she needs some, and so do I. It's been a long day." He tucked her against him. She sighed against him, making his wolf smile. He would make sure she was safe, even if it meant torturing his wolves to find out who was behind everything. He hated to do it, but he would. He loved his Luna that much. He would do anything for her, and he would kill them personally when he found out who was behind all that was going on.

Chapter 22

Edric got up early the following day, and after showering, he walked back into the room. Jillian was still asleep. Edric smiled as he watched her; she was so beautiful.

Edric walked out of the room then to talk to his guards, and he wanted to check in with his Beta and Omega to see if they had found anything else in the palace. He was chuckling, though, at the thought of the bug being in their bedroom. Good thing Jillian wasn't a screamer, or someone would have gotten an earful. "*Alpha, the house is clean,*" Emerson responded.

"*Good, I'll be home with Jillian in a while.*"

"*Yes, Alpha.*"

Jillian was dressed and waiting on the bed when he walked back into the room, but she looked sad. She had her head down but looked up when he walked in. He could see that she had been crying.

"What is it, love?" he asked, pulling her to her feet and holding her close.

"I was just thinking about what might have been," she said sadly.

"I know, my love, and I am truly sorry, but I promise you, we will try again, as many times as you want," he grinned.

She blushed, and he held her closer. "I love you, Luna. I know this is hard, and I am sorry Jarem took the easy way out because I wanted to find out who is behind this. Now we don't know, plus I kind of wanted to kill him myself."

She looked up at him and kissed him softly. "I am glad you didn't have to."

"Are you ready to go home?" he asked her, feeling overprotective of her. He picked her up into his arms.

"I can walk, you know," she protested.

"I know, but you are still weak, and I don't mind carrying my Luna," he replied.

Warren, Emerson, Wes, and Orson were waiting outside the room as Edric walked out the door with Jillian.

"Luna," Emerson said, "How are you feeling?"

"Okay, I guess," she sighed.

He nodded. "The palace is clean, and the alarm system up and going," he said.

"You installed an alarm system?" Jillian frowned.

"Yes," Edric said, "we need to keep you safe."

"And you," she replied.

"I can take care of myself, Luna, but you are still human," he pointed out.

"Partly," she reminded him.

He shook his head. "You are still frail. You can get hurt."

"Like you can't?"

"Yes, but I heal quickly."

"And I don't?"

Warren chuckled, earning a glare from Edric.

"Just saying," she said cheekily.

"What am I going to do with you, Luna?" Edric chuckled as Warren opened the limo door for them.

"Make me your wife?" she smiled.

"I will, and soon, but I would like to catch whoever is after me so we can get married without having to worry about if someone is going to interrupt our wedding. I want you to have a dream wedding."

"In Hawaii?"

He chuckled. "Sure, why not."

Emerson pulled up to the palace a few minutes later. More guards were walking the grounds, and when they went inside, more guards wandered the castle.

"A little overprotective?" Jillian teased Edric.

"I want us safe, love, and need to figure out who planted those bugs."

"Did you leave any of them?"

"I don't think so. Why?"

"I was just wondering if we left some, we could draw out the person who planted them."

Edric frowned. "What do you mean?"

"Well, if we had a few conversations that talked about us getting closer to catching the culprit, making sure we were standing by said listening device, maybe that person would make a mistake and come and try something."

"She's a smart one," Warren teased Jillian.

"I know," Edric frowned. "I guess we should have, but it is too late. I am sure whoever planted them knows we found them."

"Are you sure? But then, you are probably right; they would have found out when the bugs suddenly went quiet. So now what?"

"Well, we have extra security, if you didn't notice," he said, nodding at four men wandering the front hall, "and a security system in the whole place."

"Who installed it?"

"What do you mean?"

"Just wondering who installed it. Do you trust them?"

"I do."

"Good," she nodded.

"She makes a good Luna, sir," Emerson smiled. "She's brilliant for a girl."

"Ouch," Jillian said, punching his arm.

"You hit like a girl, too," he laughed.

"Just don't make me mad," she warned him.

"She's right, don't do that," Edric smiled, rubbing his jaw, remembering how hard she could hit.

"Whatever," Emerson chuckled.

"You are in for it, Emerson; just you wait. I am going to tell Carla that you are a sucker for girls' underwear."

Emerson stared at her. "But, I'm not."

"She doesn't know that."

Edric chuckled. "All right, you two," hugging Jillian to him. "Let's go eat breakfast, and then we can decide what to do for the weekend."

"A boat ride or plane ride, perhaps?" Warren asked.

Jillian went absolutely pale. Edric growled at him. "Warren, that was the stupidest thing I have ever heard coming out of your mouth."

"I am sorry, Alpha and Luna, I didn't mean it; I was just trying to lighten the mood," he said.

"Don't ever talk about the accidents, again, or you are being demoted back to a regular wolf."

Warren bore his neck to his Alpha and the Luna. "I am sorry," he murmured.

"I know he didn't mean harm Edric," Jillian said. She then looked at him. "Are we going to go have breakfast or what?"

He chuckled and followed his Luna; the others headed away to give them some private time.

Jillian sat at the table while Edric cooked up some food. He then set it down in front of her.

She smiled up at him, then kissed him as he sat by her. "Thank you."

"Anything for you, love," he said, beginning to eat.

They sat in comfortable silence until they were done, then Edric pulled Jillian onto his lap and nuzzled her neck with his lips. She sighed against him.

"I know we can't do anything for a few weeks, doctors orders," Edric said, kissing Jillian thoroughly, "but that doesn't mean I can't drive you crazy until then."

Jillian smiled and pulled away. "You know, two can play at that," she teased.

Edric's phone had to ring right then, of course. He chuckled as she kissed his ear and his neck.

"Hello," he said, trying hard not to sound distracted as Jillian kissed down his neck and to his shirt collar.

"Yes, okay, that's fine. See you tonight."

He then hung up and pulled Jillian back, kissing her soundly. "Your parents are coming for dinner."

"Okay."

"I need to go get some business done in my office. Why don't you go into the studio and paint for a while? I noticed you had some more scenes you were working on."

"Yes, of the view from our room."

"They are incredible. How about next weekend we go set up the gallery with your paintings and have a show."

"Can we?" she smiled.

"Of course, love," he said, kissing her soundly and setting her onto her feet. He then headed out, but not before winking at her.

Jillian put the dishes in the sink and headed to the studio. She wondered if it had been checked for bugs. She assumed it had been since Edric had seen her newest paintings.

She was just pulling out some paintings when she felt lightheaded.

She sat on the couch, putting her head down. Why was she so lightheaded? But then she knew as a vision flashed across her sight. She wasn't used to having a waking nightmare, but there it was. She gasped when she saw what it was and hurried to her feet, running inside.

She headed to the office and opened the door. Edric was going over paperwork and looked up. "Miss me already?" he teased but then frowned when he saw her face. He jumped up and walked to her. "Jillian, what's wrong?"

"Did you just send Warren and Emerson out?"

"Yes, why? There is some pack business back West, and I don't want to leave you here alone, so they are going in my place."

"The plane," she whispered. "It's been sabotaged. It's going to explode in the air."

He cussed and mind linked with Warren.

"*Warren, where are you?*"

"*Just getting on the plane, why?*"

"*Get out of there now. Jillian said it was set to explode in the air. Get off, and get the police there; I will be there as soon as I can.*"

"*Yes, sir,*" he replied.

"We got to them in time?" Jillian whispered.

"Yes, they were just boarding. I need to go see why the plane was going to explode."

"A bomb, set for two hours from now," Jillian whispered.

He nodded and dialed a number on his phone. "Hey, it's Edric. I need the bomb squad out to the private airport. There's a bomb on one of my planes."

He then hung up and pulled Jillian into his arms; she was still pale.

"It will be all right, love. I am just glad you saw it in time; you just saved the lives of my two best men." He then took her hand. "Come on; I want you with me. I don't want you out of my sight."

She didn't even argue as they headed out the door. Orson and Wes were waiting by the limo, and they got in, headed to the airport.

When they arrived, the police were there already, along with the bomb squad.

Warren and Emerson were behind the fence, staying out of their way. They saw the limo pull in and hurried to it. Emerson pulled open the door and pulled Jillian out, giving her a huge hug. Edric frowned but knew Emerson was doing it because he was grateful.

"Luna," he said. "You saved our lives. A bomb in the wheel well was set to go off when we were in the air. You are my hero."

He then stepped back. Warren nodded at her. "Thank you, Luna, for saving our lives," he added.

She blushed. "You are both welcome," she said.

One of the officers hurried to the fence then. "Alpha, we diffused the bomb, taking it in for analysis. We will let you know what we find."

"Thanks, Detective."

"How did you know?" he then asked.

Edric frowned. He didn't want anyone knowing of Jillian's gift, so he said, "With what has been going on lately? I wanted to make sure that my plane was safe. I am glad I did."

He nodded. "We'll get back to you soon." He then walked away.

"Why didn't you tell them how you knew?" Emerson asked Edric.

"Because I don't want anyone knowing about Jillian's gifts, except us," Edric said, "I don't want everyone thinking that they can use her for their fortune teller."

Emerson nodded. "Understandable."

"Good. Her gifts stay within our circle, got it?" Edric said.

"Yes, sir," the men nodded.

Edric then tucked an arm about Jillian. "Come on, let's head back. Let the men do their jobs, and I will call the Western Pack; let them know you two aren't coming today."

"Will it be safe to go at all?" Warren asked.

"I don't know Warren, that is an excellent question. Someone is greatly determined to stop me."

"Did you debug the phones?" Jillian asked, "maybe that was how the person knew you were sending out Warren and Emerson."

Edric frowned. "I thought it was debugged. I will recheck it," he said as he helped Jillian in. He then looked at Warren and Emerson. "When you get back to the palace, meet me in the office. We obviously need more security measures."

"Yes, sir," they replied and headed away to a different car.

They headed right to the office when they got back to the palace. Edric took apart his desk phone and didn't find anything. He sighed as he sat down, pulling Jillian onto his lap. "You are incredible, you know that?" he said, kissing her cheek.

Warren and Emerson walked in then. "Wes, Orson, stand outside the door," Edric told them.

The men nodded and did as told, closing the door behind them.

"No bug in the phone," Edric said. "I don't know how someone knew you two were going on that flight."

"Maybe they planted the bomb, thinking you would be on the plane," Emerson said, "but instead, we were."

Edric nodded. "I guess that is a possibility, which would mean that I would have ended up dead, instead."

He kissed Jillian's temple. "But thanks to my lovely Luna, we are all okay. Emerson, I want you to post four men out at the airport from now on. I don't want my planes compromised again. I also want the mechanic checked out."

Emerson nodded. "I will get on it right now, sir," he said and left the room.

Edric then turned to Warren. "I am worried, Beta. I trust all of you, but someone is still getting through."

"Maybe not, sir, now that we debugged the place, and if that bomb was on there earlier before the palace was debugged," he pointed out.

"Let's give it a few days," Edric said. "I will send you to the Western pack then. But I don't want anyone knowing you are going, except Jillian, I, and Carla."

Warren nodded. "Yes, sir."

"If there ends up being a bomb on board again, I won't know what to do," Edric said.

"I certainly hope not, sir, but with our good luck charm here," he winked at Jillian, "we should be okay, right?"

Edric nodded. "I hope so. It still worries me, though."

He held Jillian to him as Warren headed to the door. "I'll let you two get back to business," he chuckled and headed out of the door, closing it behind him.

Jillian kissed Edric. "You really care about your pack."

"I do, love. They are good people."

She nodded and cuddled up to him, making him sigh with happiness.

"Now I have a few minutes; want to go watch a movie in my theater?"

"You have a theater?" she grinned.

"I do, it's just down the hall from my office, but no chick flicks," he teased her, helping her stand.

"Fine, but no fighting movies either."

"Well, then what are we going to watch?" he asked her.

She took his hand, leading him to the door, "I am sure we can figure something out," she winked.

He chuckled as he followed her. "Now, you heard the doctor," he teased.

"I know," she laughed, "you have one dirty mind, Alpha," she teased him.

"I can't help it; you are just so sexy," he teased as he took her to the theater.

Chapter 23

Jillian fell asleep halfway through the movie, so Edric carried her upstairs and to bed, planning to wake her in time for dinner with her parents. He then walked into the kitchen and let Den know about their dinner plans. "Let's make it a BBQ out on the back porch; I think the Luna would like that," he said to him.

Den nodded. "Okay, Alpha, I can do that."

"Do you need some help? I can send Carla in here."

"Sure, why not," he said.

Moments later, she walked in. "Okay, Den, tell me what I need to do. We need to keep our Alpha and Luna happy," she teased.

"Our Luna needs to be the pampered one, not me," Edric pointed out and walked out, smiling.

He found Emerson and Warren in the hall, nodding at each other, frowns on their faces.

"What's going on?" he asked the men.

"Just going over more security plans at the airport," Warren said. "I've got six of the pack out there, and I asked for the background check of the maintenance man from the police. They'll get it as soon as they can."

"But?" Edric said, knowing he was holding back something.

"Well, Alpha," Warren frowned, "I got a call from the police. They found the mechanic tied up and beaten to death out behind the plane hangar."

Edric growled, making his men jump. "Find out who did it; I will personally have their head."

"I'll get on it right now," Warren replied, walking away.

Edric looked at Emerson. "I don't like that someone is trying to sabotage my planes." He then frowned deeply. "I wonder," he said and pulled out his phone, dialing the police department. "I want to speak with Detective Campbell; it's Edric."

"Alpha," the detective said when he came on the phone.

"Campbell, I want the plane that my Luna was on searched more thoroughly."

"Alpha, are you thinking that there might be another reason it crashed?"

"I do. I think there was a bomb on board."

"Why do you say that?"

"Because of the bomb found on my plane, and my mechanic was just found beaten to death."

"I'll get right on it, Alpha," he said and hung up.

Emerson was frowning. "Do you really think there was a bomb on board?"

"I do. Why else would it have exploded like it did."

"Why would someone plant a bomb?"

"To get to Jillian."

"Damn," Emerson swore.

"But we will not say a word. She already feels guilty enough, got it?"

"Yes, Alpha."

"I'm going to go and check on her," Edric said and headed up the stairs. He opened the door to the bedroom, but the bed was empty. He went into her room, but it was also abandoned, so was the bathroom.

Growing concerned, he ran down the stairs and out front, looking around. No Jillian. How had she gotten past him without him seeing her? Did she sneak by when he was visiting with Warren and Emerson? He didn't think she could have; he would have smelled her and heard her. He then headed out back. Den had the grill lit and warming up.

"She headed to her studio," Den said, knowing that Edric was looking for Jillian.

"Thanks," Edric sighed, relieved, and hurried that way.

When he opened the door, he smiled. Jillian was standing in front of a picture, doing some touch-ups. It was of her and her parents standing on a beach. It was an excellent painting.

"That is incredible, Luna," Edric said, walking up to her and kissing her cheek.

She smiled. "Thanks, I was going to give it to my parents tonight. Do you think they will like it?"

"They will love it. I know I promised you that we would have an art show this weekend, but with everything going on," he sighed.

She turned and kissed him. "It's okay. I'm not in any hurry. Besides, I need to have more paintings done."

"I promise I will make it up to you as soon as we catch whoever is trying to harm us, okay?" he said.

She nodded, and he kissed her softly. "If you are ready, your parents should be here any minute."

Jillian picked up the painting, dried it with a hairdryer to set the paint, and then taking Edric's hand, she walked out of the studio with him.

Jillian's parents were just walking outside with Warren when Edric entered the backyard.

Her mom hugged her.

"What's that?" she asked Jillian of her painting.

"It's for you and Dad; I painted it," Jillian said, showing it to her mother and father.

Jillian's mom teared up. "Oh honey, that is incredible; you have such talent," she said. "I remember that trip. That was one of our favorites on the beaches of Puerto Rico."

"I figured you would like it," Jillian said as her mother took the painting reverently.

"So, that is what you have been doing instead of going to school?" her dad asked, frowning.

"Dad," Jillian protested.

"She has been painting because I am not letting her go back to school," Edric said. "She is homeschooling from now on. Plus, you have to remember she is recovering from her car accident," Edric pointed out.

"There is no reason that she can't go back to school next week, though," Henry frowned. "You shouldn't have any say whether or not my daughter goes or not."

"Excuse me, dad, but you wanted me to come home with you, and you think that was fair?" Jillian pointed out. "You are saying that Edric doesn't have the right to control me, but what are you trying to do?"

Both men flushed.

"Let me do my own thing, okay? I am 18; let me live my life. I am not a child anymore," she glared at both of them. "You both should know better than trying to control me."

Edric nodded, feeling power come off of her. Carla and Emerson were standing close by and whimpered, baring their necks to her.

Edric even felt the pull. "Lay off of it, Jillian," he said, nodding at Emerson and Carla.

She sighed, and they also did. "Sorry." She then looked at her dad, who was watching her curiously.

"I don't know what you see in him," Henry said to Jillian.

"Dad," she growled.

"Okay, you two," Nadine stepped in, "Let's not fight. Henry, our daughter, is a grown woman, you can see that. She's not a helpless girl."

"But her life is still in danger," Henry frowned.

"How you know that dad, I won't even ask," Jillian frowned. "But I am safe here. You have seen how many guards Edric has."

"I hate that you are staying here, and you aren't married," he muttered.

"Dad, we are getting married in Hawaii in a month."

"That's going to be extremely expensive and over the top." "Dad, it will just be a few of us. Besides, we will be flying over on Edric's plane."

"Is that safe after today?" Carla asked, then covered her mouth. "Sorry, you didn't hear that."

"What happened?" Henry glared at Edric.

"Nothing, dad, it was just a plane malfunction, but it is being fixed," Jillian assured him.

Edric nodded at her, grateful she had sugar-coated it.

"Who's up for a burger?" Den interrupted.

"Burgers?" Jillian grinned. "Thank you, Den; I have wanted a good burger; those fast-food ones just don't cut a homemade one."

"You can thank Edric, he thought it would be a good idea," Den said.

Jillian kissed Edric, making her dad frown. "Thank you, Edric."

"You are welcome," he grinned, kissing her back.

"Now, enough of that," Henry growled out. "My daughter is only 18. I don't want you taking advantage of her, especially in front of us," he ground out.

Jillian flushed. "Dad quit being such a fuddy-duddy. You and mom kiss in front of me all the time."

"Of course we do; we are married and much older. You are still a teen, Jillian."

She sighed. "Dad, let's just eat, okay?"

Henry glared at Edric again. If Henry only knew what Edric had done to Jillian. He would probably kill him.

The seven of them sat down to eat at a large round table on the patio while Orson and Wes stood guard by the back door.

Jillian's mom noticed and took them each a plate of food. "Here you are, young men," she smiled. "You can't stay alert if you haven't eaten."

"Thank you, Mrs. Everett," Orson smiled at her.

She blushed. "You are welcome," she said and headed back to sit by Jillian.

"He is handsome, too bad I am married," she whispered to Jillian.

Jillian gasped. "Mom, I can't believe you said that," she hissed back.

Edric covered a laugh with a cough. He had heard every word.

Henry looked at his wife, seated on the other side of him.

"What's going on?" he asked.

"Nothing," Nadine grinned, making Jillian laugh.

"Nothing at all, dad. Mom was just telling me something funny is all," Jillian said innocently.

"Hmm, why do I not believe that?" Henry frowned. He had ways of making his wife talk. He would have to find out later.

"So, what's for dessert?" Nadine asked Carla.

Edric waggled his eyebrows at Jillian, who blushed, making Edric chuckle.

"How about strawberry shortcake?" Carla said.

"We love that, don't we, Henry?" Nadine asked him.

"Of course. That was one of our favorite summer desserts when Jillian was growing up. She used to ask for it all the time," he smiled at his daughter.

"I can think of some things we could do with strawberries and whip cream," Edric whispered into Jillian's ear.

She blushed bright red again, making him grin.

"Are you making crude remarks, Edric?" Henry frowned. He had seen Jillian blush when Edric whispered in her ear.

"No, sir," Edric smiled. "I am innocent."

Jillian began to choke on her lemonade that she had just taken a swallow of.

Edric patted her on the back, hiding a smirk.

"Are you okay, love?" he asked her.

"Sure," she choked out. The wolves were trying not to laugh. They had heard Edric's remarks.

"Are you sure?" he asked her, winking at her.

"You just wait," Jillian replied, "you are in so much trouble later."

"I can't wait," he grinned.

Emerson, Warren, and Carla were hiding smiles as the two joked around, but Henry was fuming. He stood up. "Might I have a word with you, Edric?" he snarled.

"Yes, sir," Edric said, following Henry into the house.

The others heard Henry yelling through the door at Edric moments later.

"How dare you treat my daughter like she is some, some hooker!" he yelled.

"Sir, she is not and never will be treated like that. I love your daughter."

"If I find out you have had your way with her," he ground out, especially since you aren't even married yet, you are a dead man."

"Haven't we had this discussion already?" Edric asked Henry.

"I am going to keep having this discussion if you don't behave! That is my daughter, my only child! Her life is in danger, and all you want to do is make crude jokes!"

"I assure you, sir, it was all meant in jest."

"Jest my ass!" Henry yelled.

Nadine walked into the house then and glared at Henry. "You calm down right this minute. Edric is innocent; Jillian told me so. If you can't behave, then we are leaving, and I won't let you visit your daughter next time. I will just leave you home."

"I can't help it," Henry muttered. "He brings out the worst in me."

Edric hid a laugh. He wanted to say the same thing to Henry.

Jillian walked in then, her face worried.

"Dad, please calm down. We could hear you outside; I think the neighbors could hear you; you were yelling so loud."

Henry flushed. "Okay, I will calm down, but you must promise me something, Jillian."

"What is that, father?"

"That you will save yourself for your wedding night. Do not let this scoundrel try to talk you into something you shouldn't be doing."

Jillian frowned at her dad while Edric hid a smirk.

"Dad, that *scoundrel* is paying for your dig, if I remember correctly, and without him, you wouldn't have work. He is also a King, and you just insulted him." Jillian was trying to control her anger, she really was, but the power started to ooze from her again. Edric put an arm about her waist to calm her. She smiled at him gratefully.

"Well," her dad stuttered.

"Now, if you are done throwing a five-year-old tantrum, can we go have dessert? "

"Fine," he sighed. "I am sorry, Jillian, I am just worried about you."

"I know, father, but I am okay, I really am. Come on; I heard Carla makes a killer cake for her strawberry shortcake," Jillian said and dragged her dad by the hand and outside again.

Nadine put her hand on Edric's arm as they walked outside. "I am sorry about Henry. He is just so overprotective."

"It's all right, Mrs. Everett; I would feel the same way if it was my daughter."

"You know one day, you two are going to have the most beautiful babies," Nadine smiled.

Edric nodded, watching Jillian, who had turned pale.

Edric hurried to her side. "Are you okay, Jillian?" he asked in concern.

Jillian had heard her mom's remark, and it had made her suddenly sad.

"I'm okay," Jillian whispered. "Maybe I just need to go lay down for a bit."

"Of course, love," he said, and picking her up, he carried her inside and up to his room.

He gently laid her on the bed as she wiped at her tears.

"Jillian, love, I know it still hurts," Edric said, sitting by her and pulling her into his arms, "but as I said, we have many more years to practice making babies, right?" he asked, kissing her softly.

"I know," she whispered, "it just still breaks my heart, even though I wasn't very far along."

"I know, love, I know," he said. He made her lie down and took her shoes off.

"Don't leave me," she whispered.

"Never," he assured her, laying down by her and pulling her close to him as she cried herself to sleep.

It broke Edric's heart to see Jillian so broken. He didn't know what it was like to lose a child, but he knew that he would do everything to help Jillian recover; it was the least he could do for his Luna.

He went back outside to tell everyone that Jillian was weary.

"I am sure she is; she has been through so much lately," Nadine sighed. "But, I am glad you are all here for her, especially you, Your Highness."

"I love your daughter Nadine; she is my life now."

"Good, she has needed someone like you in her life. I can see how good you are for her. I can tell she adores you also."

She then looked at her husband. "As much as you don't approve of his Highness, you have to admit that they are good together."

He sighed. "Yes, I suppose they are."

Carla handed out the plates with the strawberry shortcake. "I will save some for Jillian. I am sure she will want some."

She knew that Jillian had been crying over losing the baby. She didn't blame her. She had miscarried several times; that was why they didn't have any pups. She wasn't able to carry them full term.

They sat around visiting, but Emerson kept glancing up at Jillian's window and shaking his head.

"*Emerson, what's going on?*" Edric mind-linked.

"*Your Luna, I have never felt such power. To make us bare our necks to her, and it hurt.*"

Edric chuckled. "*I know, even I wanted to bare my neck to her. She is something else, isn't she.*"

"*Have you called your friend yet?*"

"*No, I will tomorrow. He is always busy.*"

"*Knowing him, no surprise. Good thing her parents aren't wolves,*" Emerson chuckled.

"*They wouldn't believe it if we told them what she can do,*" Edric responded.

"*I wonder if they know about her powers?*"

"*I don't know, but I'm not going to ask.*"

"*You're right, don't want to open that can of worms,*" Emerson chuckled.

Chapter 24

Jillian woke later, restless, and noticing it was only 9:00, she got up and went in search of Edric. Not seeing him in his office, she decided to head out back. Emerson and Carla were sitting on a porch swing, visiting.

"Are you okay, Luna?" Emerson asked her.

"I am; I was just a bit sad over my mom mentioning having kids."

"You will have more. I am sure of it," Carla smiled softly.

"About earlier," Jillian said. "I am sorry."

"Don't be," Emerson chuckled. "I didn't realize how incredibly powerful you are."

"When I get mad, I can do that," she sighed.

"You can also make people talk," Carla pointed out.

"Plus, you can heal, and you can see the future. What can't you do, Luna?" Emerson teased her.

"This," she said, pointing to her head. "It drives me crazy that I can't mind link with Edric to see where he is."

"He went to the airport to make sure that his men were guarding the planes and to make sure nothing happens to them."

"Planes?" Jillian asked.

"He owns a whole fleet of them," Emerson said.

"Of course he does," Jillian replied, sitting on an outdoor wicker chair that was next to the swing. She just kept being surprised over how much Edric owned and how wealthy he was.

"Want to go swimming?" Carla asked Jillian. "The pool is lit up so we can see."

"I'm not much of a swimmer," Jillian admitted.

"That's okay, you can sit in the shallow end," Carla assured her.

"It does sound nice," Jillian admitted, "I'll go get my swimsuit on."

She stood and headed inside, but as she headed inside, a vision flashed in front of her eyes. Carla wasn't a strong swimmer either;

Emerson knew it, but teasing her, he threw her into the deep end of the pool, and Carla didn't resurface.

Jillian gasped, and, turning around, she ran back outside. The two of them were headed to the end of the pool, Carla screaming for Emerson to put her down, but she was laughing.

"Emerson, put her down now!" Jillian screamed, but it was too late, and he threw her into the deep end.

Carla screamed as she hit and went under.

"Get her out now, before she drowns!" Jillian screamed at Emerson, running to the end of the pool where he had thrown Carla.

"She can swim, Jillian, don't worry," Emerson grinned, but then his face turned to a frown as Carla didn't surface.

"She's drowning; get her out, now!" Jillian yelled at him.

"What's going on here?" Edric said as he headed to the backyard.

He watched as Emerson dove into the deep end and moments later pulled Carla out of the water.

He laid her onto the cement and knelt by her. She wasn't breathing, so he started mouth to mouth.

"Edric, get an ambulance, now!" Jillian shouted at him. He nodded and pulled out his phone to call for one.

"Breathe damn it," Emerson said, tears leaking down his face.

Carla suddenly took a deep breath, then spit out water.

"Thank goodness," Emerson wept, holding Carla to him. "I am so sorry, my love, so very sorry. If Jillian hadn't warned me, I wouldn't have jumped in after you."

He then looked at Jillian. "You helped save her, Luna, thank you."

"Yes, thank you," Carla said weakly. She then glared at Emerson. "You are in so much trouble."

"Forgive me, love," he whispered to her.

Two men walked into the backyard then with a stretcher and began to check out Carla.

Jillian frowned. The men didn't look right. They seemed too shabby to be paramedics, their outfits too small for them, and why were they there already?

"Edric, those men are not real paramedics," Jillian warned him.

Edric frowned and hurried to the men, who were strapping Carla down. One of them had a needle he was about to insert into her arm.

"Stop right now!" Edric yelled, his Alpha power emanating from him.

The men whimpered, unable to disobey him. The one with the needle dropped it and fell to his knees.

"Forgive us, Alpha," he moaned. "We were sent to kidnap her when we heard the call you made for the ambulance."

"How did you know?" Alpha growled.

"Your phone has to be bugged," Jillian said.

"There is no way my phone could be bugged; I keep it on me at all times, except at night."

"Check it, Edric," Jillian insisted. He nodded, wondering how such a thing could have happened.

She then looked at Orson, who was ready to step in. "Call the cops, tell them to come and pick these two up, and let's hope that the real paramedics show up."

Orson pulled out his phone to call for help as Warren walked to the backyard, the real paramedics in tow.

"Edric, here's the real paramedics."

"Good," Edric said as he tied up the other two men with the straps they were using on Carla.

The two real paramedics headed to Carla and transferred her to their stretcher, checking her vitals and putting oxygen on her.

"Luna, thank you," Emerson hugged Jillian. "You saved Carla twice tonight. I will never be able to repay you."

"It's the least I can do for my friends," she said as two officers walked to the backyard. They sure had shown up quickly, but then again, when the Alpha calls you, you had better drop everything and come running.

"Alpha, more trouble?" one of the officers asked him.

"Yes, those two men were trying to kidnap one of my wolves, and I found my cell phone had been bugged. I don't know how, but it has been," Edric said angrily. "I keep my phone on me at all times except at night, when I am asleep. Someone must have come into my room and bugged it."

"Who let the fake paramedics through the gate?" Jillian asked then.

Warren frowned. "Sorry, it was me. I thought they were the real ones."

"Really, Warren? I didn't know you were that stupid," Jillian growled. Jillian was mad, mad that he hadn't been able to tell, furious that her friend had almost died.

"Jillian," Edric said.

"No, Edric, it is ridiculous. Those men were in stolen uniforms. They didn't even fit, and didn't it cross your mind that they were a little too unkempt for paramedics?"

Warren bared his neck to her. "Luna, I am sorry," he gasped out.

Edric put his arms about her. "Luna, ease up."

She took a deep breath and then released it, releasing Warren from her power hold over him.

"Sorry, I'm just extremely ticked."

"Understandable love, but please don't take your anger out on my men."

"I really am sorry, Warren."

Warren nodded at her. "Forgive me also for not realizing those men weren't the real paramedics."

Edric was proud of her, though. He had never made Warren bare his neck to him like that.

"Why would those men kidnap my mate?" Emerson asked as the real paramedics headed to the front of the house with Carla.

"That is a good question, and I will find out," Edric promised.

"And how the hell did someone bug your phone?" Orson frowned at the Alpha. "You have that thing on you 24/7. This is not good, Alpha."

"You are telling me. It really ticks me off. I might have to install cameras in the halls to see who is getting into my room."

Warren frowned. "I don't think we need to go that far, Alpha."

"Then tell me, Warren, how am I going to protect my Luna and all of you?"

"I am sure we can figure something out, but spying on everyone might not be the answer."

"Well, if you can think of something better, let me know, but for now, I want someone to install cameras around the perimeter. Warren, get on that for me."

"Yes, Alpha," he said, heading to the house but letting the officers through the house first, their prisoners in tow.

Wes frowned at the Alpha, watching him.

Jillian noticed his frown. "Wes, what's wrong?"

"Just worried about this whole mess, wondering what the purpose of trying to kidnap Carla is."

"I don't know, but we need to get it figured out."

"I hope it wasn't that they thought you were her," Orson said to Jillian. "Those fake men might have thought Carla was you."

Edric growled. "That would make sense. Orson, I want a camera on the gate also. This is getting ridiculous."

"Yes, Alpha."

Jillian yawned then; she was suddenly drained. Even though she hadn't physically saved Carla, she almost felt like she had.

Edric saw her yawn.

"Head to bed Jillian, I will be up in a bit."

"Orson, Wes, watch her room. I trust no one but those here," Edric said.

"Yes, Alpha," they responded, following their Luna.

Edric sighed as he stood alone in the backyard. He looked at the moon. "Why her?" he whispered as if the moon would answer back.

Chapter 25

Jillian walked down the stairs the following day, her backpack on. She had slept soundly, but it helped that she had a handsome man in her bed.

"Warren, do you think the Alpha would kill me if I snuck out to school?" she asked him when she saw him standing in the entryway.

He chuckled. "Probably, but you do need to graduate. I say go for it, just take Wes and Orson with you."

"Thanks, Warren, just let the Alpha know where I am; he's still sleeping."

"Of course, Luna," he nodded. Wes and Orson were waiting outside for her as she climbed into the limo, Emerson winking at her.

"Sure about this, Luna? Don't want you to get into trouble." "What's he going to do, ground me?" she chuckled.

He grinned and climbed in to drive, Wes and Orson scooting in with her.

Edric woke up a bit later, but Jillian wasn't in bed. He figured she was in her studio, and he had some business to attend to, so he headed to his office after he dressed for the day. Warren was headed into the house as Edric walked down the hall. Warren stepped up to him. "Good morning, Alpha."

"Morning Warren, are the men coming today to put in cameras?"

"They are."

"Good. I know Jillian won't like it, but I want some installed in her studio. I don't want her out there if something happens to her, and I don't know about it."

"Yes, Alpha," he nodded.

"I suppose I should go talk to her about it," Edric said.

"She's not in her studio," Warren told him.

"Oh? Where is she?"

"School."

"What?" Edric roared in anger. "Who took her?"

"Emerson. Don't worry; she took Orson and Wes with her."

"I specifically told her not to go back," Edric growled.

"You can't keep her a prisoner Edric," Warren pointed out.

Edric sighed. "Fine, at least she took Orson and Wes, but I don't like it."

"I understand, Alpha, but she is getting restless here."

Edric nodded and headed into his office. "Let me know when the guys with the security cameras show up."

"Yes, Alpha," he said and walked away, glad the Alpha hadn't been too upset over Jillian going back to school.

Edric knew he couldn't hold Jillian back, but it ticked him off that she would go to school and not tell him. He hated not being able to mind link with her. She did have a phone, though, didn't she? He would have to ask her about it later.

"*We can always go check on her*," his wolf said.

"*No, I know she needs to trust me, and that won't help. I don't need to be a babysitter*," Edric pointed out.

"*But she is always getting into trouble*," his wolf said.

"*Not by her doing*," Edric replied.

"*I still think you should go check on her*," his wolf said again.

Jillian was sitting in class at school, her guards in the back of the room. The teachers didn't mind having the men there; their presence kept the students in line. Jillian tried her best to ignore them; she did a better job at it than the girls in class who kept turning around and winking and giggling. Orson and Wes tried their best to ignore the girls, but it was hard to do so. There were some beautiful female wolves that the Luna went to school with.

When the bell rang for lunch, Jillian headed to the lunchroom. Kimberly and Ruben were in line getting their lunch.

"Hey, you two," Jillian said from behind them.

Kimberly squealed with delight and hugged her friend.

"How did you escape the Warden?" she asked, looking around.

"I had to bring those two," Jillian nodded at her guards.

"Of course you did," Kimberly shook her head. "I am glad you are here. You would not believe who is coming to a concert here, at our school, in a few weeks, and we have to come!"

Jillian laughed. "Okay, who?"

"Maroon 5, of course," she squealed.

"You are kidding me."

"Nope. Our school is the biggest place to have it, and their group wanted to come and perform a charity concert to benefit homeless pups."

"Wait; what?"

"They are werewolf children, Jillian," Ruben laughed.

Jillian smiled. "I know what they are, Ruben; I just didn't realize we had homeless ones. Does the Alpha know?"

"We don't have any homeless pups here, but there are some around the territories, and Maroon 5 wants to help out."

"Maroon 5, huh? I have had a crush on Adam forever," Jillian admitted.

"I know," Kimberly sighed. "He is such a hunk."

"Hey," Ruben complained.

"I will always love you," Kimberly said, kissing him, "but Adam is truly drool-worthy."

"Whatever," Ruben said, growling at her.

Jillian laughed. "So, in a few weeks, then?"

"Yeah, not sure the exact date, but soon."

"Hmm, okay."

"Why?" Kimberly asked.

"Edric wants to get married soon, but I can move it up to see Maroon 5 in concert."

Ruben laughed as he put food on his tray. "You would move your wedding so you could see them perform?"

"Of course," Jillian grinned.

"Don't let the Alpha hear that," Ruben shook his head. "Moving your wedding for a rock band."

"You know, Luna," Kimberly grinned, "I bet if you asked, he would perform at your wedding."

"That would be awesome, but he is probably too busy."

"No one is ever too busy for a Luna," Ruben pointed out.

"I don't want to inconvenience him if he has a concert somewhere," Jillian said.

Her two friends laughed. "You are something else, Luna," Kimberly shook her head.

Jillian grabbed some food and headed with her friends to her table. The other students stood until she sat down, but Jillian didn't really notice. She had her back turned to them until Orson pulled out a chair for her so she could sit.

"So, any troubles lately?" Kimberly asked Jillian as they began to eat.

"No, not really. I mean, other than the Alpha's plane almost getting blown up and Carla almost drowning," Jillian shrugged.

Ruben paled. "How could you say that wasn't trouble?"

Jillian sighed. "I guess so much crap has happened that I am getting used to it? I don't know. There is always something happening. It is getting kind of old, you know?"

"Well, spring break is next week," Kimberly said, "and I have always wanted to go to Florida; we could go, get our minds off things, party, get drunk, hit on men," Kimberly teased.

Ruben growled at her.

Jillian grinned. "Okay, let's do it without hitting on men or getting drunk. But going to relax on a beach, just to get away, that would be nice," Jillian admitted.

"But no flying," Ruben said.

"And no boats," Kimberly added.

"Driving it is," Jillian said, "but to convince the Alpha."

"Just let him know you need to get away from the stress of things," Kimberly told her, "he has to understand."

"I suppose so, okay, I will do it."

"And don't forget the Prom is this weekend."

"Oh, crap. Of course, it is."

Kimberly laughed. "You don't have to go, you know."

"I know, but it would be kind of fun, but then again, I don't have a dress, and I haven't asked Edric."

"Just ask him when you get home."

"Yeah, that will work. Edric, I know I escaped this morning to go to school, but can we go to the dance on Saturday, and will you buy me a dress?"

Ruben snickered. Kimberly hugged her friend. "You are so funny. I'm sure he would love to take you. Just think, the Alpha and Luna at the dance. That hasn't happened in like 20 or more years."

"Really?"

"Yes, when the Great Luna Queen and Alpha King were in high school. Of course, they were just a normal Luna and Alpha; they hadn't been made the High King and Queen yet."

"How were they made the High King and Queen?"

"Not sure, the story is the Moon Goddess bestowed it on them, but no one really knows."

"So, did they meet in high school then?" Jillian asked Kimberly.

"Yes, and I guess that they were the most incredible couple you have ever laid eyes on. Everyone was in awe of them, kind of like we are with you and Edric."

"You are in awe of us?" Jillian asked, surprised.

"Well, yeah. I mean, come on. I have never seen the students act as they do around you."

"What do you mean?"

"The reverence they hold for you, like when you walk down the hall, and the hall goes quiet, and they all bare their necks to you."

"Oh," Jillian blushed. "I figured that was what they did for all Luna's."

"They do, but more so you. You are special, Jillian, and everyone can feel it."

"Guess I won't be bullied anymore, then?" Jillian grinned.

"Nope, and if you are, you or your guards can take them down; you have permission to do so."

Orson and Wes were standing behind Jillian as she ate, nodding. "We can Luna, it is our job," Orson told her.

"Well, I feel better then," Jillian grinned. "And at least Jarem is gone."

"He is?" Kimberly asked her.

"Yeah, he went to jail, but then he hung himself because he wanted to take the chicken way out."

"That's crazy," Ruben whistled.

"It's cowardly," Jillian frowned. "All because the Alpha wanted to go and question him. But at least we don't have to deal with him anymore."

The two of them nodded; both of them held great respect for their Luna. She would lead the wolves and make everyone whole again; they could tell.

Ruben and Kimberly exchanged glances and smiled.

Jillian stood then, ready to head to class. She knew she needed to graduate, but school seemed so dull now with what had been going on. The students still in the lunchroom stood with her, even Ruben and Kimberly.

"I will never get used to this," Jillian smiled.

"Let me take your lunch tray, Luna," Kimberly told her. "You shouldn't have to do that."

"Thanks, Kim, you are sweet."

The students waited until Jillian left the cafeteria before they sat back down.

When the bell finally rang to signal the end of the day, Jillian headed to her locker and suddenly felt an arm about her waist. She looked up to see Edric.

"Hi," he said.

"Hi," she replied, opening her locker and putting her books inside.

"Are you mad at me?" she asked him as he took her hand and walked with her, the students parting down the middle of the hall to let them through, all of them bowing their heads as they walked by.

"No," Edric said, walking with her outside, ignoring the students, Orson and Wes following. "I was kind of angry this morning, but I know life has been stressful lately, and for that, I apologize," Edric said.

"It is not your fault Edric," she shook her head.

"It is my fault. You had a normal life, with normal friends, until I crashed into it, and since then, you have had nothing but trials."

"What are you saying?" she asked him, stopping at the limo.

"I am just apologizing. I am sorry for all of this."

"Oh, I was thinking you were going to say something bad."

"Like what?" he asked her.

"Like calling off our wedding."

He smiled softly at her. "You think that would be bad?"

She nodded. "I love you, Edric; I want to spend my life with you."

He pulled her to him and kissed her softly. "And I love you, my Luna, more than life itself. I would never cancel our wedding, although I did hear you wanted to move it up so you could attend a certain concert?"

Jillian flushed. "How?"

He pointed to his head. "I know, remember?"

"I am going to kill my friends," Jillian growled.

Edric laughed and kissed Jillian again before tucking her into the limo. He climbed in after her, along with Orson and Wes.

"We can move the wedding, and I know Adam would be honored to perform for us," Edric said as Emerson pulled out to the street.

"He would?"

"Of course. He and I are good friends. He suggested this concert, so I invited him here; I was hoping to keep it a surprise, though," he chuckled, "but your friends talk too much."

Jillian grinned. "I am glad Kimberly told me, so then I wouldn't miss the concert, and I can have him at our wedding."

"As long as you don't run off with him," Edric teased.

"Why would I? You are much better looking, although I don't think you can sing as well," Jillian teased, making the guards chuckle.

Edric began to tickle Jillian. "Take that back," he said as she laughed.

"No, never," she gasped out as he tickled her.

"I will make you sing later," he then whispered in her ear. She blushed bright red, making him chuckle. "So, what is this about Prom?" he asked after kissing her cheek.

"Oh, you heard about that also."

"Yes, Kim wants you and I to go?"

"Yes, she thinks it would be good to have the Alpha King and his Luna at the dance since that hasn't happened in a long time."

"I think we could do that, but I will get your dress. I don't want you go shopping and for something to happen to you."

"Okay."

"You are giving in?" he chuckled.

"You are letting me go to the Prom; I don't want to bite the hand that feeds me."

He leaned in and whispered. "You can if you want."

She laughed and punched his arm, making him chuckle. "Emerson is right; you hit like a girl. Maybe we need to get you training with my men," Edric teased.

Jillian frowned. "You want me to train?"

"Why not? Then you can defend yourself if someone tries to hurt you again."

"Who would train me?"

"I would, of course. I don't want anyone touching your body but me."

"Okay, when?"

"We can start this afternoon if you are up to it."

"Bring it on."

He chuckled. "You asked for it."

They pulled into the driveway, and he sent her to change her clothes. She put on some leggings and a sports bra with a t-shirt over it, then her shoes, and headed down to the front door. Edric was waiting for Jillian, dressed in a t-shirt and workout pants. Jillian took a deep breath and let it out, feeling faint. Edric's shirt outlined all his muscles, and the pants outlined everything from the waist down. She fanned herself. "Wow, if I had known you would look so hot in those clothes, I would have you dress like that every day."

Edric chuckled and pulled her to him, kissing her. "I can if you would like," he whispered, "but I like it better when we aren't wearing a thing."

She blushed and pushed him away. "What are we going to learn today?"

"I want to start easy. We'll warm up; then I want to show you a few hand-to-hand combat moves."

"Very well," she said, following him outside and to the training facility. He opened the door, and she stepped in, looking around in awe. The place was huge. Weapons of every kind lined the walls, and mats were on the floor to cushion everyone's falls.

The men in the building practicing bowed their heads to their Alpha and Luna.

"Keep working, men," Edric told them. He then turned to face Jillian. "Okay, let's warm up."

He showed her how to warm up properly, and he watched her graceful moves. She caught him staring and winked at him. He cleared his throat. "Okay, let's start with a few basic moves. First, I want to work with our hands, and then with a knife. I want you to learn to disarm me."

She nodded as he stepped forward and showed her how to work with her hands. She began to block Edric with ease, and he smiled at how fast she was learning.

"Okay, I'm going to get a knife, and we will see how well you can disarm me," he said. He headed to the wall, grabbed a knife, and then headed back to Jillian. She had her shirt off and was wiping the sweat off her brow with it. All the men had stopped their training to watch her since she was only in a sports bra. Edric growled at them, and they got back to work.

"Luna, you are driving my men crazy," he said, and taking her shirt, he put it back on her.

She laughed. "Sorry I was warm."

"We have towels and water," he said, nodding to an area by the weapons.

"Fine, I want a break then."

"Very well," he said, "Five minutes."

She nodded and headed to get a towel and a drink. Edric did the same, and a few minutes later, she was back with him, and in moments had him disarmed. He was impressed and told her so. "You learn fast."

"Thank you. I did take some self-defense growing up; my parents insisted on it."

"Oh, what did you learn?"

"Some Judo and a bit of karate."

"No wonder you are so good with your hands."

"Thanks, glad you think so," she winked at him, making him chuckle.

"Later, love," he promised her. "Now, show me what you know."

She nodded. The men who had been working out stopped to watch. They wanted to see what she was going to do.

"Grab me around the neck," she told him.

He nodded and stepped behind her, putting his hands gently around her neck. She crouched down, grabbed his arms, and he suddenly found himself on his back.

The men cheered. Edric laid on the mat, stunned. His Luna had just tossed him flat on his back.

She smiled cheekily down at him.

"How did you do that?" he asked her.

"Practice," she winked.

He stood up and pulled her to him. "Why didn't you do that when you had a gun to your head?"

"I was scared. It's harder to think straight when you have a gun pointed at you."

"Then we need to practice that, so if there is a next time, you can do what you did to me."

She nodded, and they got to work.

They were both exhausted and sweaty when they headed into the house for dinner a few hours later.

"Dinner in our room?" Edric asked her.

"Yes, shower first."

"I like that idea," he growled hungrily at her.

She laughed and ran up the stairs, him on her heels.

Chapter 26

The next day at school, Kimberly walked up to Jillian as she was headed to class.

"Hey, Ruben and I were thinking of going to the park just down the street for lunch; want to join us?"

"Sure, what are we going to take for lunch, and whose car? Emerson drops me off and picks me up."

"I have a car, and we already packed a lunch."

"So, what's the occasion?"

Kimberly grinned, "Nothing, it's just a nice change from school."

"Sounds good to me," Jillian said, and after hugging each other, the girls headed to class.

Jillian was sitting in her class, daydreaming. Last night had been incredible. Edric knew she was still healing, so he had been gentle with her, but he was very talented in the lovemaking department. She tried not to be jealous as she thought of the other girls he had had in his palace before he had met her. She was glad that they weren't around anymore. She wondered then where the hussy Jessy was. She had been so determined to get her claws into Edric. Jillian hoped that she had found her mate so she wouldn't have to worry about her anymore. She trusted Edric now and didn't want someone like Jessy barging into their lives now.

Class ended, and she headed to her next class, nodding at the students who bowed their heads at her. Classes were boring as usual. Her teachers treated her just like the other students, which was good. She didn't need to be treated differently because of who she was.

Soon, lunch rolled around, and Jillian headed outside to see Kimberly and Ruben already waiting for her. Kimberly led her to a Dodge Charger, and Jillian was about to climb in when Orson and Wes walked up to her.

"And where are we going to sit?" Orson asked her. "You know you can't go anywhere without us, Luna."

"Tight fit in the back seat, then?" Jillian said, a grin on her face.

The men chuckled. Orson climbed into the front by Ruben, Wes climbed into the back, Jillian in the middle, and Kim on the other side.

"Well, this is cozy," Wes chuckled as Ruben drove to the park.

"At least you *and* Orson aren't back here," Jillian laughed. "I would be a pancake."

Wes nodded. "Yes, and I am sure the Alpha would love that when you went home to see you flat."

"Wes," Jillian gasped, smacking his arm and making everyone laugh.

"What? I wasn't being a pervert, I promise," he laughed.

"Sure you weren't," Jillian laughed with him.

Jillian smiled as they got out of the car a few minutes later. It was a large park. There were several large trees for shade, a pond in the middle for fishing and feeding the ducks, and even a large playground and picnic tables under a large roof. That is where Ruben headed to take their picnic.

Jillian started to follow them when she felt lightheaded again. She cussed as a vision flashed across her sight. A dark car came barreling through the park, across the grass, aimed for them. It was going to hit Ruben head-on, and he would not survive. What the hell would a car be doing in the middle of the park unless it wanted to kill Ruben on purpose?

"Ruben!" Jillian screamed, running to catch up to him and Kimberly, who were both several steps ahead of her.

Ruben turned to see what Jillian was yelling about, just as a dark car came barreling through the park. People jumped out of the way, yelling at the driver, some pulling out their phones to call the cops.

Things moved in slow motion; it seemed as Jillian leaped at Ruben, pushing him out of the way as the car barreled past, catching Jillian with the front bumper of the vehicle.

She went down, feeling her leg bust in two, as the car took off and pulled out to the street, roaring away.

Jillian cried out in pain as she hit the ground, Ruben and Kimberly instantly by her side.

"You saved my life," Ruben said, his face ghostly pale.

"They were trying to kill you," Jillian gasped out, feeling her leg heal. She grimaced as the bones snapped back into place.

"You broke your leg," Kimberly whispered but then watched in fascination as Jillian's leg straightened out.

"That was fast," Ruben commented, shaking his head in disbelief as he sat down by Jillian, feeling extremely shaky.

"That was insane," Orson said, kneeling by Jillian. "I called the cops and got a license plate. The Alpha's not going to be happy."

"You let him know?"

"Of course. I am sure he felt your pain again."

"Yes, I suppose he would have," Jillian frowned.

"Thank you for saving my mate," Kimberly told Jillian, hugging her tightly. "Thank you so much," she began to cry.

"It's okay, Kim; I am just glad I could."

Wes was shaking his head. "Unbelievable. You are something special, Luna, saving so many people like you have."

Cop cars pulled in then, along with a limo.

Edric leaped from the limo and raced to Jillian's side, Emerson, Warren, Zack, and Travis on his heels.

"Jillian," Edric said, kneeling by her.

"I'm okay," she whispered. "The car hit me and broke my leg, but I am okay now."

Edric shook his head. "What happened? I heard your scream and felt your pain again."

"Someone was trying to hit and kill Ruben; I pushed him out of the way," Jillian said.

"Did you get a plate?" Edric asked the three of them just as four officers approached them.

"What happened, Alpha?" one of the officers asked him.

"Someone just tried to hit and kill the Luna's friend," Edric frowned.

"I called in the plate," Orson said.

"I did also," a guy said, approaching them. "My wife and I were taking a walk through the park when that guy came barreling through. We barely jumped out of the way in time."

The man knelt by Jillian. He was a handsome man and human, Jillian could tell.

"I saw your heroics, young lady. You move pretty fast; how did you know to push him out of the way?"

"I saw that the car wasn't going to swerve; it seemed he was headed right for us," Jillian told him.

"I'm a paramedic. I saw that car hit you. Can I see if you are okay?"

"Just a few bruises," Jillian assured him.

"I think you should be checked out anyway," his wife said. "That car hit you pretty hard."

"I'll be okay," Jillian insisted.

"I'll take her to the hospital," Edric told them.

"Are you related to her?" the man asked, eyeing Edric up and down with distrust.

"She is my fiancée," Edric stated.

"Don't you know who that is, honey?" his wife hissed. "That's Edric Ventin; he owns over half the town, you know the one who owns the huge mansion on the hill?"

The man flushed. "Sorry, sir, I didn't recognize you. You said this young lady is your fiancée? She looks a bit young."

Warren chuckled, earning a look from Edric to be quiet.

"He is my fiancé," Jillian said, trying to stand, but her leg gave out; it was still weak from healing.

Edric caught her before she fell and tucked her into his arms. "I'm okay," she whispered.

"No, you are not; let's get you back home."

"I have school," she said.

"I knew she was too young for you," the man frowned. "You are engaged to a high school student? That's just not right, sir."

Kimberly and Ruben chuckled. This was going to get interesting.

"I am 18, sir," Jillian said from Edric's arms. She felt at a disadvantage being held.

"Still too young," the man shook his head.

"Now Frank, we were 18 when we got engaged," the woman said, putting a hand on the man's arm.

"I know, but we are the same age; he looks to be at least ten years older," he was frowning at Edric.

"I assure you, sir, I am not that much older, and it is a consensual relationship."

Jillian coughed with laughter at his use of consensual. He squeezed her sides, trying to hush her.

"Edric, can you put me down now?" Jillian asked him. "I never did get to finish my picnic."

"You want to finish your picnic after what happened?" Edric looked at her incredulously.

"Maybe she hit her head too," the man muttered.

"Alpha, the plate came back stolen," one of the officers said, approaching him.

"No surprise," Edric frowned.

"Alpha?" the man had gone pale. "I have heard of you—King of the Werewolves. I have heard of your weird cult or whatever it is. You have mates, as you call them. Well, listen here, bud, I don't believe in all that wolf business. They don't exist."

"*Prove to him we do exist,*" Raul growled at Edric.

"No, we don't need to make a scene in front of the humans," Edric replied.

More people had gathered around them, curious about what was going on. Some had witnessed the car racing through; others wondered why there were so many cops in the park.

Jillian pushed Edric's arms away and hopped down, her leg now totally healed.

"I assure you, sir, whatever you have heard is false. Edric is a good man."

"Is that so? Then why is he engaged to such a young girl like you? He might have a sex trade going on in that big mansion of his."

"That is enough!" Jillian shouted, her anger and power spilling out again. The few wolves in the park all whimpered in pain and fell to their knees.

"You need to apologize, now," Jillian said, glaring at the man.

The man could tell there was something different about this girl. He nodded. "I apologize to both of you. I am sorry I jumped to conclusions."

"Very well then," Jillian said, her power withdrawing. Edric hid a smile. His Luna was really something.

"Now, if you would like to discuss with the police what you witnessed, then by all means, but leave our relationship alone," Jillian said.

She then looked at Ruben and Kimberly. "I'm hungry; let's go eat."

Ruben chuckled, getting off the ground where he, Kimberly, Orson, Wes, Warren, Zack, and Travis had ended up.

"Sorry," Jillian apologized. "I did it again."

Edric chuckled. "Maybe you need an anger management class, love."

Jillian frowned at him. "Edric."

"Okay, okay, no anger management classes." He leaned down and whispered, "maybe just more lovemaking, that will tame you."

The wolves snickered. Jillian just shook her head at him. "Want to join us for lunch?"

"No, but I am not leaving your side either. I cannot keep you out of trouble."

"It wasn't me they wanted this time," Jillian said as she walked to the picnic tables, Ruben, Kimberly, Edric, Warren, Emerson, and the guards right behind her.

The cops stayed where they were to get witness statements.

Ruben pulled out a sandwich and handed it to Jillian. She smiled and sitting down; she bit into it.

"I can't believe you are hungry after that," Ruben shook his head. "I am still scared spitless."

"I'm getting used to it; I guess," Jillian shrugged. "Besides, when I am stressed I get hungry."

Kimberly sat down by her friend and grabbed a sandwich.

"So, you are sure the car was headed for Ruben?" Edric asked Jillian sitting down by her and putting his hand on her leg.

"No, not positive, but when I had a vision a few minutes ago, the car was aimed for him, so I pushed him out of the way."

"You are a seer too?" Kimberly squeaked.

"Wow," Ruben said. "You are one special Luna. A healer and a seer. No wonder someone wants to get to you."

"No one knows but those of you right here," Jillian pointed out. "I don't think the people are after me for my gifts; they don't know I have them. They are after me because I am a Luna and to get revenge on the Alpha."

"Do you think that was a rogue?" Orson asked Edric.

"I would not be surprised. What I want to know, though, is how the person who was in that car knew where my Luna was today."

"But how? We checked everything for bugs," Orson said.

Edric shook his head. "This is getting to be ridiculous."

"Are you sure the car was after the Luna or Ruben, for that matter?" Wes asked all of them. "It could have been just some crazy drunk barreling through the park."

Emerson nodded. "He does have a point; it could have just been a drunk."

"But why aim directly at Ruben?" Edric frowned.

"He could have just been in the wrong place," Kimberly said. "We were visiting and not paying attention to anything. Everyone else jumped out of the way when the car came barreling through; Jillian is the only one who noticed it heading for us."

Edric turned to Jillian, "Love, do you think that is what it was? A drunk?"

Jillian shrugged. "I don't know Edric, it seemed to me that the person aimed directly for Ruben, but he didn't care who he hit on his way to get to him."

Edric frowned. "If that is true, then none of your friends are safe either."

Kimberly shuddered. "Why would someone come after us?"

"Because you are associated with me," Jillian said sadly. "Maybe it would be a good idea just to stay home and not go to school."

She then walked away, feeling defeated.

Edric took off after Jillian, and stopping her, he pulled her into his arms.

"Love, none of this is your fault," he said, wiping at her tears. "But I think it *is* a good idea for you to stay home from now on; it would be safer."

"Do you believe me that the car was headed for Ruben?" Jillian asked him. "I could see the doubt in the others' eyes like they didn't believe me."

"I will always believe you," he said, kissing her forehead. "Come on, let's get you home before something else happens."

Jillian sighed. "Maybe I should just go into hiding until whoever is after us gives up."

Edric looked down at Jillian. "I think that is a brilliant plan. I heard you wanted to go to Florida. I suggest you go now before something else happens."

He took her over to where the others were standing around visiting.

"Kimberly, you wanted to go on vacation next week?" Edric asked her.

"Yes, Alpha. Jillian and I wanted to go to Florida."

"Leave tomorrow, both of you. I will inform the school you will be gone for a while. I want you to go and be with Jillian for a few weeks until this whole thing calms down."

Kimberly looked at Ruben. "Is that okay?"

"I don't know," he said, "after what happened today, I am afraid that something might happen to them in Florida."

"I will make sure she is safe," Edric said, then looked around at everyone. "I trust all of you, but if I find out that one of you is leaking our whereabouts to whoever is after us, I will personally kill you, do you understand?" Everyone nodded, baring their necks to him, but Jillian.

"Good. Jillian, you are going, Kimberly or no Kimberly. I want you safe. I will tell your parents that you are taking a much-needed vacation. I need to stay here to see if I can figure out things from my end."

The officer who had talked to them a few minutes before about the stolen car came back to them.

"Alpha, can I have a word?" he said.

Edric nodded and headed away with the man.

Jillian looked at Edric, he was frowning deeply, and she noticed her friends were also frowning. She knew they could hear what the officer was saying.

"What's going on?" Jillian whispered to Emerson.

"The car that almost killed Ruben? They found it; the driver was dead, shot in the heart."

Jillian gasped. "He had to have been shot after he went through the park."

"Why do you say that?"

"Because as soon as he hit me, the car went roaring away. The guy didn't crash like he would have if he had been shot beforehand."

Edric headed back to Jillian and took her by the arm. "You are leaving tonight."

"But," she protested.

"That man, *if* he was alive before he tried to run over Ruben and was shot afterward, or if he was shot before and that is why he came sailing through the park like that, doesn't matter, you are going." He frowned then. "Detective Campbell just informed me that the man was shot after he tried to hit Ruben. The gunshot is fresh."

"See, I knew he hadn't been shot before," Jillian told him.

"Dang," Kimberly went pale.

"Am I even going to be safe if I leave?" Jillian asked.

"I will make sure you are. I will send Wes with you; he will keep you safe."

Jillian nodded. "Okay."

"Good, let's go home and pack your stuff. Kimberly let us know within the hour if you are going with her," Edric told her.

"Yes, Alpha," Kimberly nodded.

Edric put his arm about Jillian and helped her into the limo.

He climbed in beside her, the guards and Warren following Emerson up front to drive.

Jillian wiped at her tears as she looked out the window on the way back to the palace.

"This is for the best, love," Edric told her softly. "I want you safe until we can catch these wolves or whoever it is after us."

"I will miss you," she whispered.

"I will miss you also, love," he replied, kissing her cheek, "but I want you alive and well. We are to get married in a few weeks. I want to be able to marry you, and for that to happen, you need to go into hiding."

She finally looked at him. "I understand."

"I love you, Jillian, my Luna; I would die if I lost you, you know that."

She nodded. "I know, and I would feel the same if something were to happen to you."

"Then go, be safe, let me handle this, then send for you when they have been apprehended, okay?"

"And if they follow me?"

"Then, there will be hell to pay," he growled.

Chapter 27

Jillian headed to her studio as soon as they got home. She wanted to be alone. She was feeling guilty about everything. She couldn't believe that her friend had been almost hit and killed.

Edric sighed as he watched Jillian walk outside. He turned to Warren. "I am sick of what is going on. I can't believe that someone is still after us; how the hell are they finding Jillian? Everywhere she goes, someone is after her."

"It might be the mind connection within the pack, Alpha. There is always someone with Jillian, and everyone has a mind link but her. So if someone is thinking about her, then whoever is doing this knows exactly where she is."

Edric's wolf growled in anger. "*She will never be safe then*," Raul said.

"Warren, I trust you with my life. Do you think someone in my pack is the one who is trying to kill us?"

Warren shrugged. "I can't be positive, Alpha, but I think it is a great possibility."

"Then how do I get Jillian to safety without anyone knowing? If anyone knows where she is because of a mind link, we are all screwed."

"I have a suggestion, Alpha."

"Go ahead."

"Send Jillian away with her parents, somewhere where no one will know. They are all human, so no one could try and mind link with them. Leave her friend here, since she is a wolf, and don't send her to Florida; everyone knows they are going there, and don't tell me or anyone else. Give her a phone to keep in touch, but make sure it is encrypted so no one can find out where she is."

"I like your thinking Warren. I will call Jillian's parents now."

Warren left Edric to call Jillian's parents as he headed to the kitchen to eat lunch.

Out in her studio, Jillian sighed heavily. She was working on another painting, but it was dark. It represented her pain and loss. The colors were dark and swirling like an angry storm, but right in the middle was a little speck of silver, the light in the storm. Jillian hoped that the light would grow and that things could get back to normal, but she knew the only way for that to happen would be to leave and to let Edric find out who was behind everything going on.

A little while later, Edric found Jillian on the couch in the studio. She had been crying.

He sat down by her and pulled her onto his lap.

"My sweet Luna, I am so sorry that all of this is happening," he murmured. "I have a solution, though," he said, wiping at her tears.

"Oh?" she asked, hope in her eyes.

He smiled softly.

"I called your parents. I told them to pack clothes for a few weeks. I am sending the three of you away while we deal with us."

"Where to?"

"I won't say. I don't know who is listening," he replied. "I don't want to take chances of anyone finding you. Detective Campbell is encrypting a new cell phone for you so you can stay in touch with me without giving out your location."

"You are sending my parents with me because we are all human and letting Kimberly stay home because she is a wolf."

"Yes. No one can read your minds or mind link; I think you will be safer that way."

"I take it you won't be sending any guards with me then."

"I want to, believe me, I do, but I won't. I don't know who I can trust right now, and with everyone mind linking but you, I trust no one."

"How long do you think I will need to be gone?"

"I am not sure, but hopefully not too long."

He then looked around the room. "Did you notice that you had a camera out here?"

She nodded. "Yes, I was assuming it was for my safety."
"Yes. I have the monitors in my office so someone can watch the palace and grounds. That way, we will know if anyone tries to come onto the property. I hope you are okay with that."

"As long as there isn't one in the bedroom."

He laughed. "Do you want there to be one?"

"No," she blushed. "We don't need your guards getting an eyeful."

He kissed her. "No, but I am sure whoever planted the bugs in our room got an earful."

She blushed again. "I didn't think of that; how embarrassing."

He smiled. "My sweet innocent Luna, how I love you."

"Innocent, huh?"

"Well, maybe not so much now," he teased.

"Good thing my dad doesn't know."

"I am sure he suspects, though. But it's kind of hard not getting it on when I have such an incredible-looking Luna," he said, kissing her. He laid her on the couch and laid on top of her.

"You know, Alpha, if any of your guards are in the office, they *are* going to get an eyeful," she grinned at him.

He laughed and kissed her. "You are right, my love; we don't need them to see that." He pulled her up and into his arms.

"So, do you have an idea of who might be after us?" Jillian asked him.

"No, but we think it is rogues, probably that were under Kelson. That is why I want you to leave so that you will be safe. I want to get married soon, and I don't want to have to worry about watching our backs every day."

"What about a ring?" she asked him. "You want to marry me, but you haven't even properly proposed."

He chuckled. "I need to do that, don't I. It's just in the werewolf world; technically, we are married since you are marked, and we have mated."

"But in the human world, this girl would like a ring on her finger," she teased.

"Of course, my love, and I will do that soon."

Jillian nodded and held onto Edric. "What will happen when we are separated? I heard it is painful."

Edric nodded. "It will be more painful for me than you. Since you are not a wolf, it won't affect you as much."

"Then I can't go. I don't want you to hurt," she whispered, looking at him.

"My love, I will suffer great pain to keep you safe. You mean more to me than my health. I will be okay."

"Are you sure?" she asked, totally unconvinced.

"I promise," he said, kissing her softly. "Now go pack. I want to send you out of here tonight."

She sighed. "Okay."

"I love you, my Luna, always."

"I love you, Edric."

He kissed her soundly, and then tucking an arm about her waist, they headed out the door. "While you pack, I will make sure the plane is fueled and ready to go."

Edric glanced at Jillian's painting as he shut the door behind him, feeling just like the storm she was painting. He would be that storm and destroy everything in his path if anyone hurt his Luna again.

Chapter 28

Jillian went to the phone in the room before she started to pack. She dialed Kim.

"Hey, friend," Kim answered.

"Hey, look, Edric wants to send me alone with my parents on a trip."

"So, does he think I will cause too much trouble?" Kim laughed.

"No, but he knows where you are a wolf, that someone might read your mind and put us in danger."

"Yes, that makes sense. So off on your own, then, huh?"

"Just my parents and I, just like old times."

"Boring," Kim laughed.

"I agree," Jillian laughed with her, "but if it keeps us safe."

"I know, friend, and you had better stay safe."

"I will most certainly try."

"Good, so I will see you when you get back, whenever that is?"

"Yes, whenever that is, which means probably no prom this weekend."

"That's too bad; I think that everyone was looking forward to having you there."

"I know, and I am sorry. Is there another dance before the year ends?"

"Yes, graduation dance."

"Good, I will plan on that one then."

"Very well, my friend, take care of yourself, okay?"

"I will, and you too." Jillian then hung up and began to pack, wondering what she should pack. Was she going somewhere cold or warm? She was hoping warm. She liked the heat; a tropical place would be lovely. Maybe somewhere she hadn't been before.

A little later, Edric walked into Jillian's room to see that she had two full suitcases open on the bed. One with summer clothes, one with winter clothes.

She turned when he walked in. "I didn't know where you were sending me, so I packed both."

"Good idea," he nodded, pulling her into his arms and kissing her. "The plane is fueled and ready to go."

"Is that safe?" she asked. "Do you trust your pilot? Wouldn't I be safer on a commercial flight?"

He winced. "Jillian, after what happened last time, I don't want you on a commercial flight."

"Edric, what are you not telling me?" she asked him. She could tell he was hiding something from her.

He sighed. "I called Detective Campbell earlier and asked him to look into the plane you were on. I had a feeling there was something on that plane that made it explode."

"And?"

"A bomb was in the cargo area. It exploded on takeoff, and that's why the plane crashed."

"No wonder I heard a boom when we took off."

"You heard a boom?" he frowned.

"Yes, right after takeoff, and then the plane hit the ground. If there was a bomb, that means they were after me," she whispered.

"I'm afraid so, love."

"Oh, Edric, now I feel even more terrible," she began to cry. Jillian sure did that a lot, but considering what she was going through, she figured she had every right to do so. "Why? Why would someone be so sick that they would kill several people just to get to me?"

"I do not know love. I am trying to figure that out." He rubbed her back, trying to soothe her. "Whoever it is will die when we find them."

"You will have your wolf kill them?" she whispered.

"Yes. My wolf is restless and is not happy that you keep getting hurt," he frowned.

"*You've got that right*," Raul harrumphed.

"You would kill for me?" she asked.

"I would," he nodded.

She wasn't sure if she should be mortified or not, but she was tired of being chased after. She wanted it to end. "I am glad you are here to protect me."

He kissed her. "I trust my pilot, he will not harm you, and right now, he does not know where you are headed either. I will tell him when you are in the air. The plane has been checked thoroughly for anything suspicious, and I have six of the pack there to make sure no one touches it."

"Thank you."

"I love you, Luna; I would give my life to keep you safe," he told her, "I hope you know that."

"I do," she said, looking up at him. "And I would do the same."

He smiled softly and kissed her again. "Finish packing; your parents should be here soon. I'll have Carla cook some dinner for all of us, and then I will send you to the airport, okay?"

"That's fine," she replied, and after kissing Edric once more, she watched him walk out of the door.

She sighed; he was so good to her.

She had just finished packing when her vision went blurry again.

Her parents were driving to the mansion when a dark SUV came up from a side street, going fast. It breezed through the stop sign and t-boned her parents' small car, sending it flying through the air to crash upside down in a field.

Jillian screamed.

Edric heard her and rushed back into the bedroom.

"Jillian," he said.

"My parents," she sobbed. "Someone is going to hit them on purpose."

Warren appeared then, along with Orson and Wes.

"Try and get to her parents before they get hit," Edric said.

The men nodded.

"Please, stop them," Jillian whispered.

"Where love, where are they?" Edric asked.

"Just a few blocks from here, they are headed this way."

"You heard her; get going," Edric replied.

The men nodded, and all of them shifted to their wolves. Jillian had never seen them shift. They were huge and beautiful. Warren was dark brown with a white spot on his forehead, Orson was pale brown mixed with white, and Wes was brown, white, and gray.

All of them headed out the door as fast as they could.

"Jillian, love, they will be okay," Edric soothed. "The men will get there in time to stop them, I promise." He kissed her softly then. "I hope they won't be too late," she whispered against his chest.

"I hope so, too," he replied.

"Do you know who it is?" he then asked her.

"No, all I saw was a dark SUV."

"Maybe I should go see if I can help," he said; he then looked at Jillian. "Will you be okay? I want to find out who is trying to kill your family."

"I am okay, go," she whispered.

He nodded and shifted. He nudged her with his nose and took off out the door.

Jillian shuddered. She just hoped that they would get to her parents in time.

"Very good," she heard then, "It's about time they all left."

Jillian turned to the balcony doors. Jessy stood there, a gun in her hand, aimed at Jillian.

She sauntered in, dressed in tight jeans and a low-cut shirt. "I was hoping he would leave."

"What are you doing here?" Jillian ground out angrily.

"I am here to get rid of you, of course," she chuckled.

"Edric will know."

"I am planning on it," Jessy said and pulled the trigger.

Chapter 29

Jillian felt the bullet hit her shoulder, and she fell to the ground, knocking her out.

When Jillian came to, she was bound and gagged in the back seat of a car. Her shoulder hurt like crazy, and she wondered if Jessy was just a horrible shot, or had she shot Jillian in the shoulder on purpose? Jessy was driving and talking on the phone to someone. "Yes, I have her, no, the Alpha has not noticed her being gone, or he would be after her. It makes me wonder if they really are mates," she snickered. "Yeah, yeah, I'll be there in a few."

She then hung up. Who was Jessy talking to? Jillian didn't want to move, even though her shoulder was healing already. Did Jessy know she healed fast? She hoped not, but Jillian didn't really want to stick around to see who had ordered Jessy to come after her and her parents. She was sure it was the same person, but who? She pondered on escaping, or should she wait and see where Jessy was taking her to see who she was talking to? What to do, what to do. She decided on the first choice. She sat up after tearing her restraints off easily. Jillian was either becoming stronger, or Jessy didn't know how to tie someone up properly.

"So, witch, what are you planning on doing with me?" Jillian hissed into Jessy's ear.

Jessy screamed and jerked the wheel hard, sending it sailing across the lane and into a field, right into a tree. Right before impact, Jillian saw the accident happening, so she ducked back down and braced for impact. Maybe she shouldn't have done that to Jessy, scaring her that bad, but too late for regrets now.

The car hit the tree hard. Jillian hit the back of the driver's seat with a hard oomph, making her let out a scream, while Jessy hit the steering wheel, making the airbag deploy.

"Ouch," Jillian moaned. She sat back up and shook her head. It hurt a lot. She touched it and noticed it was bleeding, no surprise.

"Stupid idiot," she muttered, cursing both her and Jessy out, then leaned over the seat to make sure that Jessy wasn't dead, not that she really cared; she did kidnap her after all. Jessy was unconscious, no surprise. She *had* hit a tree head-on. She sat back on the seat, knowing Edric would soon be there, wouldn't he? She was sure he had felt her pain, but then, did he even know she had been kidnapped? It's not like she had a phone on her to call anyone.

Suddenly her door was ripped off the hinges, and Edric was there. He tossed the door into the grass and looked at her. "Are you okay?" he asked softly, great worry on his face.

"I'm better off than Jessy," Jillian told him.

Edric leaned in and pulled Jillian out and into his arms, bridal style.

"Your head is bleeding."

"It will heal. How did you know where I was?"

"Well, I was kicking myself for leaving you alone, and I headed back to the house just as Jessy was pulling out of the gates. I wondered what she was doing there, and so I followed. I knew you were injured somewhere; I could feel your pain. Did she hurt you?"

"She shot me, then tied me up and dumped me into the car," Jillian admitted. "But that doesn't explain how you knew I was in the car."

"I didn't know until I heard you scream."

"I screamed?"

"Yes, when the car hit the tree. I wanted to kill Jessy for crashing. Why did she crash anyway?"

Just then, Emerson showed up. He tore off the front door and looked in on Jessy. "Sorry it took me so long; I had to make sure Jillian's parents were okay." He looked down at Jessy, then felt for a pulse. "She's alive, but she looks to be hurt badly. I called for an ambulance." He then turned back to Edric and Jillian.

"I'll be fine," Jillian said to his unanswered question.

"I know, love," Edric said, holding Jillian tighter, "but we aren't taking any chances. You have been hurt too many times lately."

"I know, and I'm sick of it," she sighed.

An ambulance pulled in moments later, followed by the three other wolves. They changed into their human forms behind the trees and walked out clothed. It was Warren, Orson, and Wes.

"Is she okay?" Orson asked, walking up to them.

"Jillian should be okay," Edric nodded, "we'll see about Jessy."

"What did she want with Jillian?" Orson frowned as he watched the paramedics pull Jessy from the car, still unconscious.

"She wanted to take me to someone; I am not sure who," Jillian replied.

"Who, I wonder?" Emerson frowned.

"Jillian, can you tell us what happened?" Warren asked as a paramedic walked over to them.

"Alpha, can we look at the Luna? It looks like her head is bleeding," the paramedic asked, interrupting Warren.

Edric nodded and set Jillian onto a stretcher that the paramedic had wheeled over to them.

"This conversation can wait until we make sure Jillian is okay," Edric told his men. He didn't give a rat's ass about Jessy. He then turned to Wes and Orson. "I want a guard on Jessy. I don't trust her. If she tried to kidnap Jillian, someone is going to come looking to see why she didn't show up."

"Yes, Alpha," both men nodded.

"But I don't want you two watching Jessy. I want Zack and Travis. I would rather have you two watching my Luna; I trust you more."

"Yes, Alpha," they said again.

Jillian listened in to the conversation as the paramedic checked her over. He wiped her head clean with a soft cloth and checked her for bruises.

"How are you feeling, Luna?" he asked her.

"I feel okay."

"Your head is healed already. But I am worried about internal injuries. It looks like you were also shot," he pointed to her shoulder, "and did you hit the back of the seat with just your head?"

"I don't remember. It happened so fast," Jillian admitted, "and yes, Jessy shot me," she sighed.

"Maybe we should take you in to get you checked out for internal injuries then."

"I think I agree," Edric replied. "The car was totaled, and if you hit the back of the seat as hard as Jessy hit the steering wheel, you are probably really bruised up."

"I'm fine," Jillian insisted, "and I am so sick of hospitals."

"I know Jillian, and I am sorry, but for me, please?" Edric asked.

"Okay, for you, but I want to know if the men find out anything. Like who Jessy was talking to when she kidnapped me?"

"Warren just checked; it came up as a private number. We are going to see if it can be traced."

He then looked at the paramedic. "We will meet all of you at the hospital."

The man nodded, and with the help of another paramedic, they loaded Jillian into the ambulance, right next to Jessy. The ambulance was wide enough for two stretchers. Jessy was still unconscious, her bruises not healing, or the bleeding on her head not stopping.

Jillian frowned as the paramedics worked on Jessy. "Is she going to be okay?"

"We're not sure," one of them said. "She hit that tree at a very high rate of speed. I am sure she has some serious injuries."

"But why isn't she healing? Most wolves start healing by now."

"I don't know," the paramedic shrugged. "That is also something we need to look into."

The paramedic who was driving turned on the lights and sirens, and they sped through the night; it was only as Jillian lay on the gurney, her eyes closed against the headache pounding away, that she wondered where her parents were and how they were. Were they okay? But the biggest question of all, who had sent Jessy to kidnap her? And did they want Jillian dead or just injured? Jessy had only shot her in the shoulder, so either she was a bad shot, or the person who wanted her, wanted her alive.

Chapter 30

Jillian wondered if the whole thing with her parents was a setup to get everyone out of the palace and leave Jillian alone. It had to be, but why? She sighed then, the headache finally easing up.

"She's crashing!" one of the paramedics yelled. "Hit the gas, Fred!"

The driver gunned the engine, racing down the street to the hospital, as two paramedics worked feverishly on Jessy.

Jillian opened her eyes and looked over at the frantic movements. She sighed. She knew she should be more concerned, but Jessy had belittled her, tried to steal her mate, and kidnapped her; why would she care? She supposed she should care; it was, after all, another human, well, wolf. That was the most curious thing. Why was Jessy not healing? She seemed to be bleeding a lot.

Jillian sat up. She didn't want the girl to die, even though she hated her guts.

"Move over," Jillian told one of the paramedics.

"Luna, she is dying; I need to save her."

"As do I. Just let me take her hand."

The paramedic nodded and let Jillian grasp Jessy's hand, which was ice cold. Her lips were turning blue. Jessy was not going to make it if Jillian didn't do something.

She had saved her classmates on the plane so she could save this rotten girl now, right? Jillian cleared her mind and sent healing vibes into Jessy.

The paramedics watched in awe as Jillian's hand began to glow a light blue, and then they watched as the light traveled across Jessy's body, healing wherever it went.

Jessy finally took a deep breath and settled into a peaceful sleep. The bleeding had stopped, and her color was returning.

Jillian lay back down; the healing had exhausted her.

"Good job Luna," one of the paramedics said in reverence. "You saved her."

"Yay, me," Jillian muttered.

Jillian heard a snicker from one of the men at her sass, but she didn't care. She was tired. "Don't you dare say a word to anyone," she warned the men.

"Of course not, Luna," they replied.

The ambulance stopped then, and the doors were flung open. The men hopped out and pulled the stretchers out. Edric was right there, as were Warren, Orson, and Wes.

"How are they?" Edric asked, walking alongside Jillian's stretcher.

"They will both be okay," one of the paramedics replied. "Your Luna is exhausted, and Jessy had a rough time of it, but I think she will pull through."

"Good, then I can kill her myself," he growled.

Jillian frowned and looked up at Edric. He was watching her in concern.

"She will pay for what she did to you," Edric promised.

"I am sure she will, but I don't want her dead," Jillian responded.

"Why not? You have every right to pronounce a death sentence on her."

"I want to find out why she wanted me and who made her kidnap me."

"Oh, we will," Edric growled angrily, "and then I am going to do away with her. She has caused enough problems unless you can convince me why she should live?" he asked Jillian.

"Alpha, I assume you want to be in the room when we examine the Luna?" the doctor asked, walking over to them, cutting off Jillian's answer.

"Of course. I also want to know the condition of the girl who kidnapped my Luna."

"Of course, Alpha." He nodded at two nurses who wheeled Jessy into one of the rooms while he and another nurse wheeled Jillian into another room.

"I'm fine," Jillian protested, sitting up.

"Let the doctor be the one to tell you if you are okay," Edric replied, the concern seemed to be etched on his face.

Jillian sighed; no use in arguing.

The doctor rolled over a portable x-ray machine and, using the wand, ran it over Jillian's body.

He nodded his head when he got done. "She is fine, Alpha, but I suggest rest and a lot of it. She looks exhausted."

One of the nurses stepped into the room then. "Dr. Benson, can I have a word?"

He nodded and stepped out of the curtained-off area.

Edric frowned when he heard the nurse's whispered conversation.

"Sir, the other girl will be okay, but not because she was able to heal herself."

"What do you mean?"

"Her wounds were healed from the outside in. It was not her own body's doing."

"Interesting. I will be in, in a few minutes. Make sure our patient is comfortable but doesn't escape. She is a danger to the Luna."

"Yes, sir," the nurse said.

Edric turned back to Jillian, who had her eyes closed. Her face was pale, and she didn't look good. He was going to have a word with her later. He knew that it had been her that had saved Jessy, but why?

The doctor hurried back into the room. "I am sure you heard what my nurse said?" Dr. Benson asked, looking at Jillian, who was asleep.

"Yes," Edric nodded.

"Do you think our Luna healed her?"

"I have no doubt," Edric frowned.

"But why?"

"That is the question of the day, doctor."

"Not to be a heartless person, but I would have let her die," Orson said, walking in with Wes, Emerson, and Warren. Zack and Travis walked in, right behind them. Edric wanted them there; he didn't trust Jessy. His Luna might have healed her, but he wouldn't put it past Jessy to try something again.

"Zack, Travis, I want you to make sure Jessy does not escape. I want to question her tomorrow."

"Yes, sir," the men nodded.

Edric then leaned over and picked up Jillian into his arms. "I am taking her home. Emerson, bring the car to the front door."

Emerson nodded and hurried away.

"What of Jillian's parents?" Warren asked Edric.

"Are they at the palace?"

"Yes. Carla put them in a guest room."

"Good. Do not let them know what has happened today. They do not need to know. I'll make up some story as to why I am bringing her home like this." He looked down at his sleeping Luna. Her hair was matted with blood, and her shirt also, where Jessy had shot her.

"Good luck in trying to convince Jillian's parents that nothing happened to her," Orson chuckled.

"I know; I'm hoping I can sneak her in. I hope they went to bed."

"I doubt it," Wes replied. "Did anyone tell her parents where she was?"

"No, we were all too worried about getting to Jillian," Edric frowned.

"So, they are probably pacing the floor right now," Orson replied.

"More than likely."

Emerson walked back into the room. "Ready whenever you are Alpha."

Edric nodded and carried Jillian out the door, Warren, on his heels.

Edric slid into the car with Emerson driving; Orson and Wes sat across from Edric, Warren next to his Alpha and his Luna.

"Warren, when we get back, I need you to distract Jillian's parents so I can get her into the house," Edric told his Beta.

"What do you want me to do?"

"I don't know. Tell them that I found Jillian at her friend's house, that they were going to run away on their own, and that I am bringing her home."

"Will they believe it? Especially when all her luggage is still on her bed?" Warren asked.

Edric sighed. "Well, we have to think of something."

"I am sure we will," Warren replied. "Are Jillian's parents going to stay for a while?"

"Yes, until we get things figured out. I still want Jillian to go with her parents, but this whole mess today has made me wonder if she will be okay with just her parents. I am tempted to go with them."

"I'm not sure that will be any safer, Alpha, especially since they are after both of you," Warren reminded him.

"Yes, and we are no closer to finding out who is after us. Kelson is dead, and until Jessy wakes up, we will have no clue who else is after us. I just hope she doesn't end up killing herself or that no one else kills her until after we find out who sent her to kidnap Jillian."

"Do you think she will end up dead like the others?" Emerson asked. "There sure have been a lot of bodies and no witnesses."

"I know; that is why I have Zack and Travis at the hospital. Hopefully, they can keep Jessy alive until I get there to question her in the morning."

"I just hope she will give us answers," Warren pointed out.

"She had better, or she will be tortured until she does," Edric growled.

"Better not tell Jillian that; she has a soft spot for pitiful people, even her enemies," Warren chuckled.

"I know, that is a weakness for her, and I admire it, to a point, but not when it comes to someone trying to harm her or me. If she does not answer my questions, she dies."

"Yes, Alpha," came the response from the men.

Jillian had heard the whole conversation. She was awake but wanted to listen in, so she was faking sleep. Should she care that Edric was willing to torture Jessy for information? Unfortunately, she did. Like Warren had said, she had a soft spot for pitiful people. She just hoped that didn't end up being her downfall.

Chapter 31

Warren headed into the palace first to see if Jillian's parents were still up. They were waiting in the sitting room off the entryway when he walked in.

They hopped up. "Where is Jillian?" her dad asked.

"Edric is bringing her home."

"Where was she?"

"At her friend's house. They wanted one last night together before the three of you left."

"Did anyone know she was there?" her mom asked.

"Not until just a bit ago. We've been out looking for her, but she finally called."

"She needs to be grounded for a month," Henry growled, "and does she even know we were almost in a car accident?"

"She does," Warren replied. "I am sure you are both exhausted; why don't you head to bed. I know Jillian will be headed straight to bed when she gets home."

"Hopefully, not to the King's bed," Henry muttered. He took his wife's hand. "Come on, let's head upstairs. We can have a word with our daughter tomorrow."

Jillian's mom nodded, and the two of them headed up to bed.

"*Okay, the coast is clear,*" Warren thought to Edric.

"*Thanks, Warren,*" came the reply.

Edric came in the front door, carried Jillian upstairs, and laid her onto his bed. He then took off her bloodied shirt and pants, and after wiping the blood from her hair, he climbed into bed by her. "Goodnight, my Luna," he whispered, pulling her close to him. Her only response was a sigh.

The following day, Jillian woke up with a start. The bed was cold next to her. She knew that Edric had tucked her in last night, so where was he? Then she remembered. He was probably at the hospital interrogating Jessy. She wanted to be there too, but how would she escape and go see her? Jillian got up and went into the bathroom, sighing at her reflection. She looked like a mess. She got into the shower and cleaned up, and then after dressing, she headed down the stairs. The house was quiet. Where were her guards? Where were Carla and Emerson? Did they all go to the hospital? Jillian headed into the kitchen. No one was there either. It was kind of eerie. She found some food, and after preparing it, she sat to eat. As she ate, she heard a door open and close, and then a few moments later, Carla walked into the kitchen. "Good morning Luna," Carla said.

"Where is everyone?" Jillian asked her.

"At the hospital. The Alpha is there talking to Jessy."

"And my guards?"

"Everyone is there but the ones outside guarding the palace."

"Why would he leave me here alone? Especially after what happened last night?"

"He said to tell you that you were in good hands with me and that there were twenty men outside to guard the palace and you."

"Okay, then. What I wouldn't do to go and talk with Jessy."

"You and me both. That woman has been a thorn in our sides since she got here."

"Then why can't we go and see her also?" Jillian asked her. "No way, the Alpha would have my head if he knew that I took you to the hospital."

"You could always tell him I didn't feel well; that would be an excuse."

"You are evil, woman, but that would work," she grinned. "I am quite curious myself as to what is going on. They are shutting me out."

Jillian hopped up. "Then what's stopping us? Let's go."

"Look sick," Carla whispered to her.

Jillian nodded and suddenly fell to the floor.

"Luna!" She cried out. The back door opened, and in ran two men.

"What happened, Carla?" one of them asked.

"I don't know, but the Luna just passed out. I need to get her to the hospital."

"Okay," the man said, and leaning down, he scooped up Jillian into his arms.

"Gerald, go get a car and meet us out front," the man said.

Gerald nodded and ran out of the door.

Jillian opened her eyes and winked at Carla, who smiled with relief because she hadn't known if Jillian was acting or not.

"What happened?" Jillian whispered.

"You passed out, Luna," the man said. "Gerald went to get a car. We'll get you to the hospital."

He headed out the door with her and loaded her into the back of a car, climbing in by her. Carla sat in the front with Gerald, and the four of them headed out through the gates.

Jillian closed her eyes. That was one way to get to see Jessy, fake being sick.

A few minutes later, the car stopped, and the door opened. Jillian felt herself being lifted into someone's arms, and she opened her eyes. It was Edric. Crap.

"Love, what happened?" he asked in concern, walking into the hospital with her.

"I passed out," she sighed.

"You probably overdid it yesterday," he told her, taking her into the emergency room.

A nurse was waiting for Jillian and put her into a wheelchair, and then took her into the Alpha's room. Edric lifted her into the bed.

"The doctor will be in as soon as he can," the nurse assured and hurried out.

Edric frowned and looked down at Jillian. "Love, I need to go back to Jessy's room. Emerson and Warren are interrogating her, and I need to be there."

Jillian sighed in relief. She didn't want him sticking around anyway, especially since she had faked the whole thing.

"Okay. I'll probably be here for a bit anyway."

He kissed her then left the room, nodding at the two men who had brought her in and Carla. "Thanks for bringing her in," he told them.

"Anytime, Alpha," Carla told him.

The two guards stood outside the door as Carla stepped in. "Come on; we can get past Gerald and Tom."

"How?"

"I'm going to tell them you need to walk until the doctor comes in; it will help you feel better."

Jillian nodded, and the two of them headed out the door. "She needs to walk before the doctor comes in; it will help her feel better," Carla told the men.

They nodded, and they headed down the hall, Carla in the lead.

Carla opened the door quietly to Jessy's room, but the men inside ignored her. They were too busy glaring at Jessy, who was lying in bed, looking terrified.

"Jessy, answer us now," Edric growled at her. "Who sent you to kidnap my Luna?"

"I can't say," she whispered.

"Why not?"

"Or they will kill me."

"I will kill you if you don't answer."

"No, please, Alpha, I love you, please don't kill me."

Jillian gasped, and the men turned. Edric frowned at her and pulled her into the hall.

"You are supposed to be waiting for the doctor."

"We are," Jillian said, "but I wanted to see how Jessy was doing. She said she still loves you."

"Yes, and that is a problem."

"Why?"

"Because I was going to kill her."

"You won't kill her."

"Yes, I am. She won't give us an answer, she is worthless, and she brought harm to you. Now leave."

Jillian frowned. She knew better than to argue, but she did feel bad for Jessy. "You are going to kill her after I healed her?"

Edric frowned. "So you did heal her. Why?"

"Because I couldn't just let her die."

"Why not? She hates you; she tried to kill you, Jillian, you should have let her die, but since you didn't, I will have to kill her."

"You are going to kill someone who loves you still?"

Edric growled, his eyes turning black, his wolf fighting for dominance. His wolf was ticked. Not at Jillian, but at the whole situation with Jessy.

"Jillian, get out of here now," Edric growled as he tried to hold his wolf back.

Jillian stepped back. She was suddenly scared. She had never seen Edric so angry.

"Leave," he growled, "before something happens," and then he shifted.

Jillian turned and ran.

"Luna!" Carla yelled, but Jillian didn't stop. She had to get away. She knew it was childish to run, but it seemed to be the logical answer right now. She only wanted to save Jessy. True, she wasn't innocent by any means, but she didn't deserve to die, did she? Besides, if Edric killed Jessy, how would they find out who was after her?

Jillian ran outside to the car, trying to catch her breath. Maybe she had been stupid to try and see what Edric was going to do to Jessy, but she wanted to know. She hated to see anyone die, enemy or not.

Jillian sat in the car, closing her eyes. Ever since she had met Edric, her life had been in danger. Maybe she needed to leave for a day or so. If she did, then no one could find her, especially whoever was after her. She would get hold of Edric later to let him know she was gone. He wanted her to leave town anyway. She knew he would be mad with her, but she needed to be safe, right? Besides, if she were gone, maybe whoever was after them would give up trying to harm Edric and her.

Jillian started the car and peeled out of the parking lot. Carla, Gerald, and Tom ran outside to see her driving away as fast as she could.

"We had better go after her," Gerald said.

"Give her a few minutes to calm down," Carla told him. "You don't want to be by her when she is that angry."

"But if the Alpha finds out."

"He won't. Let her be for a few; then we can go after her."

The men nodded and headed back inside to wait. They would give her a ten-minute head start, and then they were going after her.

Dr. Hess walked into the Alpha's hospital room a few minutes later to check on Jillian, but no one was there. Had the nurse been mistaken that the Luna had been brought in? Perhaps so. He knew that the Alpha was there questioning the girl who had kidnapped the Luna the night before. He suddenly heard a terrified scream and then silence. The girl was dead. She deserved it, though. The Luna was important, more important than any Luna before her. He would have to tell the Alpha that he had found out some very interesting things about the Luna.

Jillian drove for a few miles and then stopped and looked at where she was. She was outside the mall. She wasn't sure it was wise to go to the mall, but no one there would know who she was, would they? She got out of the car and walked inside the mall. She might as well get her mind off of her worries. People looked at her in concern as she walked the mall. Why were they looking at her funny? She had been crying a bit, but she didn't think she looked that bad.

Moments later, two security men hurried up to her. "Miss, are you okay?" one of them asked her.

"Yes, I think so," Jillian said.

"Maybe you had better come with us," the man said as the other man followed her down a long hall.

"Did I do something wrong?" Jillian asked the man.

The two men led Jillian back to an office, where a woman stood by a desk. She pointed at a cot in the corner of the room and then looked at Jillian.

"Did I do something wrong?" Jillian asked again, sitting on the cot.

"No, Miss, some people just noticed that you had been crying and wanted us to make sure you were okay," the woman said. "I'm Julie, by the way."

"Nice to meet you, Julie," Jillian said.

"Are you okay? You look like you had a rough day."

Jillian chuckled dryly. "You could say that."

"Is there someone we should call?" Julie asked her.

"No, I am sure someone is already on their way to find me," Jillian sighed.

"Oh?" one of the men asked, "how do you know?"

"My fiancé likes to have bodyguards watch me; I am sure one of them followed me."

"You must be important," Julie said.

"Not so much," Jillian sighed, "more so my fiancé."

"Who is your fiancé?"

"It's not important," Jillian sighed. "Besides, knowing my guards, I am sure that they will find me soon enough. Can I go now? I'm okay, I really am."

Julie frowned. "Okay, but don't leave the mall. We don't want your fiancé to wonder where you are."

"Okay," Jillian said and headed out the door. She was surprised that Edric wasn't there, that Gerald and Tom hadn't informed him that she was gone, but then again, he was probably dealing with Jessy still. Jillian shuddered. Did Edric kill Jessy? Did she deserve to die? Jillian supposed she did, but she still hated it.

Jillian sighed as she wandered the mall. She wished she could go back to before she met Edric. What if she hadn't met Edric? She supposed her life would be extremely dull. She loved Edric, but right now, she needed to clear her head. Edric had been incredibly ticked, and Jillian didn't want to see him until he had calmed down. Jillian took a deep breath and headed back outside. She just hoped that the mall security wasn't watching her escape, but it's not like they knew who she was to tell Edric. She climbed into the car and left the mall. She wished she had Kim to talk to; oh wait, she did. But if she went to Kim's house, then Edric would find out where she was because he would see it in Kim's head. Jillian was glad that Edric couldn't read her mind right now. He didn't need to know where she was at the moment. She would go home later after she had time to think.

Jillian drove for a while before the car started to sputter. She cursed as she looked at the car's gas gauge. It was on empty; of course, it was. She sighed and pulled off the road under some trees, next to a huge pond.

She sat in the car for a few moments, looking at her bare fingers. Edric had promised her a ring. Would he ever get around to getting her a ring? Did it really matter?

Jillian got out of the car and started walking. She heard a creak behind her moments later, and if by fate, the car started rolling backward and turned right into the pond. Jillian just shook her head as she watched the car sink under the water, only the roof showing. She must not have put the car into neutral since it was a standard. "Oh well," Jillian sighed and started walking again. She knew she was acting careless, she knew she was being selfish, not letting anyone know where she was, but she was so done with everything at the moment. She had almost died how many times, her life threatened how many times, all because she had to go and meet Edric and be his mate. Did she love him? More than anything, but at the moment, she was scared. Her life was in danger, and she couldn't do a thing about it.

Tears fell silently down Jillian's face as she headed into the woods. She didn't want to stay on the road; she didn't want to be found, not yet, although if the wolves came this far, she was sure they would sniff her out.

"Okay, it's been ten minutes," Gerald told Carla. She nodded, and the three of them headed outside, shifted, and took off down the road, following her scent. It ended at the mall. The three sniffed around the mall, knowing they couldn't go inside as wolves, and they didn't have extra clothes to change into.

"*I think she's still in there*," Gerald thought to Carla.

"*She has to be. But we can't go in like this and scare the humans; we will wait until she comes back out.*"

Gerald nodded, and the three sat down to wait. If only they had known that Jillian was on the other side of the mall, and that was where she escaped from.

Darkness was settling in when Jillian happened upon a small house in the middle of some fields. She wondered if they would take her in for the night, but then again, would they find out who she was and call Edric? Perhaps she would just turn around and find somewhere else for the night, but where?

Jillian's mind was made up for her when she heard a dog bark, and suddenly a dog was in front of her, barking but wagging its tail at her.

"Shh," Jillian said to the dog, but it only barked in response.

"Joe, who's out here, old boy?" came a man's voice as the front door to the home opened.

The dog barked in response. "Shh," Jillian said again, but the dog barked again and licked Jillian's hand.

An older man approached Jillian. "Well, I'll be, a young lady. What are you doing out here in the middle of nowhere?"

"I think I am lost," Jillian told him. "My car ran out of gas, and I didn't have a phone to call anyone."

"Well, young lady, you're practically out in the middle of nowhere. Come on in; we have a phone. You can call someone if you need to."

"I don't know anyone's numbers," Jillian confessed.

"Well, come in anyway; let's get you out of the chilly night. We can figure things out later. My wife Helen just cooked a lovely meal; perhaps you can join us?"

"I would be forever grateful," Jillian smiled and followed the man through the field onto a paved walk and into a small but cozy home. Jillian sighed as the warmth of the house hit her. She hadn't realized she was cold.

"Helen, I brought home a stray," the man chuckled.

"Albert, what mangy creature did you find this time?" Helen asked, walking into the small living room. She stopped short and chuckled. "Well, I suppose you definitely are not a mangy creature."

"No, ma'am," Jillian grinned. "I just seem to have lost my way."

"I invited her for dinner, and we can figure out where she needs to go later," Albert told his wife.

"Very well then, I will set an extra plate, come into the kitchen," Helen said and led the way. Jillian followed and smiled as she walked into the modest kitchen. It reminded her of home, not Edric's massive castle, but her parents' home, warm, cozy, and comfortable. A small dining table sat by a window, where there were two place settings and soon to be three. The kitchen was bright, the cupboards white, with bright yellow walls. Jillian looked around as she sat at the table.

"I apologize for my humble home," Helen said, watching Jillian.

"Oh, please don't, it is so lovely," Jillian sighed. "It reminds me of home."

"Do you live far from here?" Helen asked her.

"I'm not sure. I was driving to get away and clear my head, and the next thing I know, I ran out of gas and ended up here."

"Well, we can have Albert fill your car up if you aren't too far down the road," Helen said, setting a roast with potatoes and carrots onto the table.

"Well, the thing is, the car kind of ended up in the pond," Jillian blushed.

Albert chuckled as he sat down after his wife did. "How did that happen?"

"I'm not sure exactly," Jillian replied. "I thought I put it into neutral, and I got out, and the next thing I know, it is turning into the pond; it was the craziest thing," Jillian shook her head.

"There is a bit of an incline there," Albert nodded, helping himself to some food, "the car could have slipped gears."

"It probably did," Jillian nodded, not caring at all. Edric had plenty of cars.

"Well, I have a friend in the next town over who can come and tow it out," Albert said as Jillian put food onto her plate.

"No, that's okay. I am sure my boyfriend will find it eventually."

"Is that why you were running? Boyfriend troubles?" Helen asked her.

"Not really. I just needed some time to myself."

"He's not abusing you, is he?" she asked in concern.

"No, but he gets angry sometimes," Jillian said.

"Oh, dear, one of those types. One of these days, he will probably get angry and take it out on you, my dear; it is probably good that you are leaving that life behind, and you can stay here with us," Helen told Jillian, "for as long as you need. You are a bit smaller than me, but you can borrow some of my clothes if that is okay with Albert."

Albert chuckled. "Why not? We never had children of our own; it would be kind of nice to have someone here for Helen to visit with while I work in the fields."

"How big are your fields? I didn't see since it was getting dark out."

"Over two hundred acres."

"Do you hay?"

"Yes, and barely squeak by. The taxes are so high; I can barely manage my house payment and food on the table. I have talked to the Alpha King, but he is so busy with everything else, I think he has forgotten about us little folks."

"You know the Alpha King?"

"Yes, I take it you do also?" Helen asked her.

"Yes," Jillian nodded but didn't elaborate.

"Oh dear, you sound unhappy, don't tell me you were one of his concubines."

"You knew about that?" Jillian gasped.

"Every wolf knew about that," Helen shook her head, "but then we heard he found his mate and got rid of them."

"Yes, that is what I heard, and no, I wasn't one of his concubines," Jillian shook her head.

"Oh, that is a relief. So how do you know him?"

"My parents have worked for him," Jillian said.

"But you are human, you smell human, but a very nice smell," Albert smiled at her.

"You are a wolf, then?" Jillian asked him.

"Yes," Albert nodded.

"What do you know of the King?" Jillian asked them.

"He is a nice and fair king, but he seems to forget about his people sometimes."

"More than likely because he found his mate," Helen chuckled. "That woman would have to have balls of steel to put up with him."

Jillian choked on her potatoes, and Albert patted her on the back.

"Helen, we are eating," Albert chuckled.

"So, honey, what is your name?" Helen asked her, smiling. What she had said was true. Any woman would have to be strong to be a Luna.

"Carly," Jillian said; that was her middle name.

"Do you go to high school?"

"I do. It was weird finding out the whole school consisted of wolves."

Albert chuckled. "I bet. But hopefully, you have made some friends?"

"I have," Jillian smiled. "I am just glad that the King found his mate and quit coming to the school to find girls for his harem," Jillian said.

"Yes, we heard about that," Helen frowned. "Imagine being in a harem; that is so wrong. If I were his mate, I would be getting rid of those girls so fast."

"He did, from what I heard," Jillian shrugged.

"Good, that is just so wrong."

"What's wrong is that the school secretary dressed as bad as the other girls, hoping to be chosen for the harem," Jillian snickered. "She was as old as my mom."

The two laughed. "Oh, dear, that is awful. Speaking of parents, where are yours?"

"Home," Jillian shrugged.

"Don't you think they will be worried about you?"

"Eventually," Jillian shrugged. "But knowing my boyfriend, he is out looking for me. I wouldn't be surprised if he showed up later tonight."

"Did he hurt you?" Albert asked, getting angry.

"No. He became angry over something, so I left so he could cool down."

"Smart girl. You can stay as long as you like," Helen told her.

"Thank you," Jillian sighed, then yawned. "I'm sorry, it was a long day."

Helen scooted back her seat. "Come on, we have a spare room, and you can borrow a nightgown of mine."

"Thank you, Helen and Albert, a lot." Jillian hugged them and followed Helen out of the kitchen and down the hall into a modest bedroom.

A twin bed with a blue and white comforter was in the small room, a nightstand next to it, and a few nature pictures on the wall.

"It's humble, but it's home," Helen said.

"It's lovely," Jillian replied.

"The bathroom is across the hall; we share," she said.

"That is fine, and thank you once again."

"No problem," Helen smiled, then left the room for a moment and then returned with a nightgown.

"Thanks," Jillian said, and once Helen left, Jillian stripped down, put on the gown, and climbed into bed, sighing. The bed felt like heaven. As she drifted off, she wondered if Edric was worried about her or if he was still dealing with Jessy. She didn't really care at the moment, she was tired, and the bed felt too good.

Chapter 32

Carla was done waiting; Jillian couldn't still be in the mall, could she? She padded around the mall parking lot, hoping no one would see her and call the cops. She didn't need to terrify anyone. But she couldn't find the car.

"*Did you two find the car?*" Carla mind linked the men.

"*No, it's not here,*" Gerald replied.

"*We had better see if we can pick up her trail then,*" Carla said and headed out of the parking lot, the two other wolves right behind her.

Edric was ticked that Jessy wouldn't confess and tell him who had sent her to kidnap Jillian. She was too terrified, and so he had killed her. He didn't want Jessy hurting his Luna again, and then he felt guilty for getting so angry because he was sure Jillian thought it was directed at her. He had seen the look of terror in her eyes as she had turned and ran. He hoped she had gone back to the hospital room, but something told him she hadn't. Good thing she had Carla and two guards with her.

Edric walked into the hospital room, and sure enough, Jillian was gone. "You did terrify her," Orson pointed out to him.

"I know, but I was ticked off, and I'm sure Jillian thought it was directed at her," Edric said.

"*Carla, where is the Luna?*" he mind linked her.

"*At the mall, Alpha.*"

"*Very good; keep an eye on her and bring her home when she calms down.*"

"*Yes, Alpha.*"

Carla wasn't about to tell him that they had lost her scent. They would just have to find her and fast.

The three of them ran down the road, but Jillian's scent was gone. All they could smell was exhaust fumes from cars.

"*We had better keep looking; she can't have gotten far,*" Carla thought to the other two.

But five hours later, there was still no sign of Jillian. They had searched the city, and Carla was getting worried. She would have to admit to the Alpha that Jillian was gone.

"*Come on, we had better head home,*" Carla told the other two.

"*He is going to kill us,*" Gerald said.

"*I know,*" she sighed.

They went back to the palace, shifted, and then hurried into their rooms to change. They walked back out to see the Alpha, Warren, Emerson, Orson, and Wes waiting for them.

"Where is she, Carla? And where is the car?" the Alpha growled.

Carla hung her head. "I am sorry, Alpha, she left the mall without us knowing, and we lost her scent."

"You what?" he roared in anger, making everyone drop to their knees.

"We are sorry, Alpha," Gerald whimpered. "We didn't know she would leave the mall without us."

Edric growled again. "We have to find her."

"Yes, Alpha," everyone said.

Jillian's parents walked into the hall then, as the men and Carla were getting off of the floor.

"What's going on?" Henry frowned. "I heard you yelling, and where is Jillian?"

"She's missing," Edric growled in anger. He was more upset at himself than with Carla and the two guards.

"What?" Henry yelled. "Are you kidding me? You need to reign her in better, your Highness, or I am taking her home, and you can forget about marrying her."

"We are going to go out and try to find her."

"You had better," Henry replied, glaring at Edric.

Edric looked to his men. "Warren, come with me, Orson and Wes, head south. We'll head north. Look for the BMW. Carla, you take Gerald and Tom with you."

Edric's phone rang then.

"Alpha, it's Detective Campbell."

"Detective, what can I help you with?"

"I found one of your cars."

"What was it?"

"A BMW, black."

"Where?"

"At the bottom of a pond, about 50 miles down the road."

Edric went absolutely pale. "Was there a body?" he whispered.

"No, sir, there was nothing in the car. But we picked up the Luna's scent inside."

"You said 50 miles south?"

"Yes, sir."

"I'll be there in less than a half-hour."

"Yes, sir. We'll be waiting for you."

Edric hung up. "You heard him. He found the car. We need to meet with him."

"What's going on?" Henry asked. He hadn't heard the conversation.

"Sorry, Henry, they found the car Jillian was in."

"Oh? Where is it?"

"At the bottom of a pond."

"No," Nadine gasped out. "Is she dead?"

"There wasn't a body. We are going to go and see if we can find her."

"Can I come?" Nadine whispered, tears running down her face.

"I also, that is our daughter," Henry said.

"Yes, of course," Edric replied.

All of them headed out the front door and into the limo. Emerson hopped in to drive. Edric gritted his teeth as Emerson headed to the site. He wished he hadn't gotten so angry. He wished he had told Jillian that he was upset over the situation with Jessy, not with her.

She would probably never forgive him. "*I'm sorry, also,*" Raul whispered. "*But, I was so ticked off at Jessy.*"

"*I was also, and Jillian thought we were taking our anger out on her.*"

"*I hope we can find her,*" Raul whimpered.

"*I hope so, too; I will die without her.*"

A tear slipped down his cheek, and Jillian's mom saw it and patted his hand. "We will find her, no matter how long it takes."

Chapter 33

As the wolves headed to see if they could find Jillian, she was sound asleep in the spare bedroom, well, she was, until her stomach started protesting dinner. She got up and headed to the bathroom, and just in time, for dinner came up. She shuddered as her body expelled all of the day's food. Had she gotten food poisoning or something? She sighed and sat on the floor, but she was back at the toilet moments later. She couldn't be pregnant again already, could she?

The door opened moments later, and Helen walked in with a warm washcloth.

She knelt by Jillian and helped her clean up. "I'm sorry you are sick. I don't think it is food poisoning, or Albert and I would be sick. You're not pregnant, are you?" she then asked.

"I don't know," Jillian whispered as she threw up again.

"Maybe we had better go and get you checked out. What is your boyfriend's name? Maybe we should call him."

"No," Jillian shook her head. "I don't want him to know," She shuddered again, as if she were cold, and threw up once more.

"Albert!" Helen yelled.

Albert walked in, dressed and ready to go.

"Come on, young lady, let's get you to the hospital where they can check you out."

"Thank you," Jillian replied, and with the help of Helen, she stood up, and they helped her out to the car.

Helen made sure Jillian was buckled into the backseat and then climbed in beside her with a bucket.

"Just in case you need to throw up again," Helen told her, "and it will save me from cleaning up in here later."

"Thanks, Helen," Jillian said weakly.

Emerson pulled up to the pond where Jillian's car had supposedly gone in. Detective Campbell and two other officers were standing by the pond; a tow truck backed up to the pond to pull the car out. Edric got out of the limo with his men. Detective Campbell nodded at Edric. "No evidence here, Alpha, but her scent goes down the road," he pointed. "I figured I would wait for you before we followed it." "Thanks," Edric replied. He could also smell his Luna, but the scent was getting weak. He watched Nadine start to sob as the tow truck hooked onto the car and started to pull it from the pond. Edric knew how Nadine felt, but he wasn't giving up hope. He knew Jillian was alive, but where?

"Detective, we need to follow the Luna's scent before it is lost. Will you occupy the Luna's parents so we can track her?" Edric asked him.

He nodded. "Sure thing Alpha, and good luck."

Edric nodded at his wolves, and they all shifted, taking off into the night. Edric led his wolves as they ran down the road, following Jillian's scent. Minutes later, they stopped at the little house. That was where Jillian's scent ended. They shifted back and headed to the door to knock. The place was dark, but Edric could tell Jillian had been there or still was. No one answered, and he knocked again. All they heard in response was a dog.

"Where is she?" Edric frowned as he headed around to the windows, peeking in each one to see if Jillian was there, but no one was in the house.

The dog barked a few times but then went silent as Warren barked back, making Emerson chuckle.

"You sure told him," he laughed as the men headed to the front of the house.

Warren shrugged. "I just told it to shut up."

Edric looked at his men. "Let's search a bit further. She might have stopped here and then moved on."

"She has been under immense pressure," Warren told him, "look at what has happened to her just within the last little bit. How many times has she almost died, or had her life threatened? She is only 18 Edric, do you blame her for running?"

Edric frowned. "I don't, but she could have let me know she was leaving, or even Carla. I hate not being able to communicate with her; it drives me nuts."

"She is human. She doesn't feel emotions like we do. For her to walk away is normal; for us, it kills us," Warren pointed out.

"What will I do if she is found dead? I can't live without her, Warren."

"She's not dead, Edric, or you would have felt that. She probably just needed a break from this whole mess."

"I hate having her out here, alone. If another wolf picks up her scent," Edric frowned, "especially the rogues, that could be bad. Let's split up. Meet back here within the hour if you can't pick up her scent."

The men nodded, shifted, and all of them took off into the night, howling in frustration.

At the hospital, there was a new nurse at the desk. She didn't know Jillian, and she was human.

She stood from her desk as Jillian walked in with Helen and Albert.

"We need to be seen," Helen told the nurse. "This young lady has been throwing up all night."

"Stomach flu?" the woman asked.

"That or pregnancy," Helen told her.

"Follow me; we'll put you in the last area we have. It's been busy tonight," the nurse informed them.

They started following the nurse, but Jillian had to hurry to the bathroom and dry heave. She was beginning to feel pretty weak and wondered if she was pregnant again. That was the only thing that made her so sick the last time.

The nurse grabbed a wheelchair and then had Jillian sit in it. Her desk phone rang then, and she answered it. "Yes? Okay," she replied, then hung up. "I'm sorry, but now all the rooms are full," the nurse said, pushing her through the doors. "I'm going to have to put you in the hall for a few minutes until we get a room cleaned out. I'll have a doctor come look at you soon," the nurse assured her, and then leaving Jillian in a hallway in the E.R., she walked away.

If that woman only knew who she was, she would be in serious trouble. Edric would be fuming if he knew his Luna was stuck out in a hallway. But Jillian wasn't about to tell her. She didn't want the nurse or Albert and Helen to know who she was.

"I'm sorry," Helen said, kneeling by Jillian.

"It's okay, Helen, it's apparently busy tonight," Jillian replied, and then hopping up, once again, went into the bathroom.

She was shaking when she came back out, her face pale and sweaty.

"Oh, you poor dear. If the Alpha were here, he would probably put you in his room; he is nice like that. Maybe we should call him and ask."

"No, I don't want to disturb him this time of night," Jillian whispered, even though Edric would have come running if he had known she was there. But she didn't want him to know quite yet. She could handle this on her own.

It seemed the nurse had forgotten Jillian because she didn't come back. Jillian kept getting up to go and throw up, but no nurse. It was over two hours later when Helen finally got fed up and stormed up to one of the other nurses.

"That young lady over there has been in that wheelchair for over two hours, and not one nurse has checked on her. She is extremely ill; when is someone going to look at her?"

The nurse looked over at Jillian, then back at Helen. "I'm sorry, Ma'am, but we are swamped right now. I promise we will get with her soon."

"No, you will come and look at her now. If you do not, I will call Alpha Edric to come and talk to you about your job." She knew the woman was a wolf.

The woman paled. She knew the Alpha, she knew he owned the hospital, but her hands were tied. The hospital was at full capacity.

"Ma'am, I truly am sorry, but I will try and get her into a room as soon as possible."

Helen glared at her, her wolf wanting to come out and play. The nurse saw it and hurried away. Albert touched her arm. "Come on, love; maybe we can call Alpha Edric and see if the young lady can be put in his room for now."

"I think we must," Helen replied, "these nurses are incompetent. If the Alpha knew that the patients weren't being taken care of properly," she sighed.

"I'll call him," Albert assured and dialed the number to the mansion.

Carla answered. She had stayed home in case Jillian called. Her parents had ended up coming home also. They were of no use in searching for Jillian.

"Yes, who is this?" Helen asked when Carla answered.

"This is Carla; I help run the household. May I help you?"

"I was wondering if the Alpha was there?"

"I'm sorry, but he isn't; perhaps I can help you?"

"I hope so. You see, we have a young lady who came to us tonight, and she became quite ill while in our care, but there are no beds available at the hospital; I was wondering if the Alpha would care if she was put in his room until another bed becomes available."

"I am sure the Alpha would be okay with it," Carla assured him.

"Can I have you talk to the nurse and tell her?" Albert asked.

"Sure, what is the girl's name that is sick?"

"Her name is Carly; she didn't give us a last name."

"Go ahead and put her in the room; I'll inform the Alpha when he returns."

"Thank you," Albert said in relief. He then headed to the same nurse and handed her the phone. "It's for you."

The woman looked confused but took the phone and listened. She nodded a few times. "Very well, okay, thank you."

She then hung up. "You must have good connections. Okay, give me a few minutes, and we will get her set up in that room. The doctor should be in soon; I'll let him know there is a patient in there."

Albert nodded and headed back to Jillian to tell her the good news.

She had her eyes closed. She was weak and flushed.

"Oh, you poor thing," he said, kneeling by her. She opened her eyes and smiled weakly at him.

"Good news, one of the staff at the Alpha's mansion gave you permission to stay in the Alpha's room for now," Albert told Jillian.

Jillian nodded, too weak to talk.

It wasn't but a couple of minutes later that two doctors showed up. Dr. Hess and Dr. Benson. She ducked her head. She wasn't sure she wanted to be recognized because then they would contact Edric, and then he would be mad at her for not letting him know where she was.

But it wasn't to be. "Jillian, what are you doing here, stuck in the hall?" Dr. Hess asked her, walking up to her.

"Dr. Hess, nice to see you again," Helen smiled at him.

"Nice to see you also Helen, do you know Jillian?"

"Jillian? I'm sorry, you must have her confused with someone else. Her name is Carly."

Dr. Hess shook his head. "I'm pretty sure that is Jillian."

He knelt by her and lifted her chin. He frowned. "You look like crap, Luna."

Albert and Helen both gasped. "That is the Luna?" Helen squeaked.

The doctor stood. "It sure is. What is wrong, do you know?"

"She's been throwing up all night," Helen replied.

"Oh, dear. I'd better get her into her room. How long has she been out here in the hall?"

"Ever since we brought her in three hours ago," Albert supplied.

"What?" Dr. Hess roared, causing heads to turn towards him.

"Sylvia, get your ass over here now!"

The nurse in question came hurrying up to him.

"Do you know who this is?" he roared.

"No, sir," Sylvia replied. "Just another patient brought in. I was going to get her a room ready soon."

Dr. Hess glared at her.

"This is our Luna, Sylvia," he growled.

She paled significantly.

"Sir, I had no idea," she whimpered.

"You should have. How dare you keep her out here when she should have had top priority when she came in. Get her into her room now. I am going to go and grab some medicine to help her."

"But sir, my other patients,"

"I don't care about them right now. If the Alpha finds out about this, all of us will lose our jobs, understood?" he yelled.

"Yes, sir," she whimpered, and getting behind Jillian's wheelchair, she quickly wheeled her down the hall to the Alpha's room.

"I apologize, Albert and Helen; where did you say you found the Luna?" Dr. Hess asked.

Albert was pale; he had no idea it was their Luna.

"She ended up at our house. She said she got lost."

Dr. Hess shook his head, "I'll call the Alpha later; for now, we need to get her stabilized; are you two staying?"

"If we can," Helen replied.

"Of course, just go wait in the Luna's room. I am going to grab some medicine to make her more comfortable."

Dr. Hess then walked away, angry. Some nurses were going to pay with their jobs, and hopefully, he wouldn't lose his job too.

"We are in so much trouble," Helen whispered to her husband.

"I don't know why," Albert said as they headed down the hall. "We brought her in; I am sure the Alpha will understand."

"I wonder why she would lie to us?" Helen mused.

"She probably didn't want anyone to know who she was," Albert shrugged, opening the door to Jillian's room.

The nurse hooked Jillian up to an I.V. Jillian looked worse than before and was dry heaving into a bucket.

"You poor thing," Helen consoled her.

"I'm sorry to get you into this mess," Jillian whispered.

"Oh honey, we're not worried," Helen smiled at her, "but if we had known you were our Luna, we would have insisted on getting you in here sooner."

"I just didn't want anyone to know," Jillian sighed, closing her eyes.

"Luna, you are something else," Dr. Hess chuckled as he walked in with some drugs to combat the nausea.

Jillian opened her eyes.

"Luna, why did you not tell anyone who you were?" he chided as he put medicine into her I.V.

"I didn't want them to know."

"Why not?"

"Long story," she sighed.

He turned to the nurse. "You may leave and tell no one who this is, understood?"

"Yes, sir," the nurse mumbled and hurried out.

"I bet the Alpha is in a panic," Helen said. "He must be looking for her. She told us her car slipped into a pond a little ways from our house."

Dr. Hess paled. "Yes, the Alpha probably is greatly worried. Perhaps I should contact him and let him know where his Luna is. If you will excuse me."

He then left the room. He went to his office and picked up the phone, bracing for a chewing out from the Alpha.

"Hello?" Carla responded.

Dr. Hess sighed. "Carla, is the Alpha there? This is Dr. Hess."

"Sorry, sir, but he's out looking for his Luna right now."

"Yes, about that. Will you inform him that she is here at the hospital in his room?"

Carla gasped. "Is she okay?"

"I'm not sure. She came in here deathly ill; I was about to run some tests. Will you let him know?"

"Of course, sir. Hopefully, the Alpha's room is now available? I permitted a couple to put a sick girl in there until a room became available for her."

Dr. Hess chuckled. "That was Jillian. She changed her name; she didn't want anyone to know who she was."

"Of course she did. I will contact the Alpha right now."

"If you would," Dr. Hess said and hung up. He sighed again. At least it would be a while before he had to face the Alpha's wrath.

"*Alpha,*" Carla mind linked him.

"*Carla, I am a bit busy now,*" came the response.

"*I know, but you might want to know that the Luna has been found.*"

"*What? Where?*" he roared.

"*She's at the hospital. Dr. Hess just called to inform me.*"

"*What happened?*"

"*He said she came into the hospital deathly ill. I suggest you head over there.*"

"Thanks, Carla."

"You're welcome, Alpha."

Edric shifted back to his human form and threw on some clothes that Emerson handed over. "Jillian's at the hospital. Warren, Orson, come with me. Wes, Emerson, head home and get some sleep."

"Yes, Alpha," they replied.

After taking Jillian's parents home, the men headed to the limo that Emerson had brought back to them. Alpha got in with Warren driving, Orson in the back by Edric. The other two men took off into the night, howling at the pain that their Alpha was feeling.

"Why did I not know?" Edric growled as Warren drove. "I hate not being able to mind link with Jillian."

"You didn't feel pain?" Orson asked him.

"No, just weakness. I don't know what's going on," he said, frustrated.

Dr. Hess walked back into Jillian's room with a vial. He was pretty sure she was pregnant again, but he wanted to make sure. "Luna, I need to draw some blood, okay?" he asked her.

She nodded, keeping her eyes closed; she was too weak to open them. She felt a prick in her arm. Then moments later, she heard, "Okay, Luna, try and rest; the Alpha will be here soon." She heard the door open then close.

"I hope the Alpha will be here soon," Helen said, "and that things will be okay. I feel so bad for our Luna."

"I know, my love," Albert replied, "but the doctors will take good care of her now."

Emerson pulled into the Alpha's parking spot right next to the hospital entrance a few minutes later. Edric jumped out and ran inside. The werewolves in the room bowed their heads at him, feeling the raw power emanating from him.

He marched to the front desk. "Where is my Luna," he growled.

It was the same nurse that had checked in Jillian.

"I'm sorry, sir, your Luna?"

"Jillian Everett, where is she?"

"I'm sorry, sir, but we have no patient here by that name," Cassie replied.

"I was just called by Dr. Hess informing me that she was here," Edric growled again.

The woman didn't seem intimidated at all.

"I'm sorry, sir, but I will go and check with him. I am sure you are mistaken," she replied, standing up and heading to the back.

"Forget formalities," Edric growled and followed the nurse.

She turned to see three huge men following her.

"Sir, I must ask you to stay up front," she replied. "I could lose my job if you come back here."

"You just did lose your job!" Edric roared angrily. "Do you know who I am?"

"Unless you own this hospital, then I am going to have to ask you to leave, sir," Cassie replied.

"I do own this hospital!" Edric roared again.

All heads turned to Edric, and the wolves in the room fell to their knees. They couldn't help it. Their Alpha was pushing his power to the limit.

Dr. Hess hurried from Jillian's room, the force of the Alpha's power making him stagger.

"Alpha," he gasped out, "ease up, would you?"

Edric released his grip, and everyone sighed, the humans in the room wondering what had just happened.

"Where is she?" Edric growled.

"In your room."

"I want her fired," Edric replied, pointing at Cassie.

"Done. Now come on, we have some things we need to discuss."

"But Doctor," Cassie said, running up to him. "I was doing my job. I don't know this man. He could be a mass murderer for all I know."

"Cassie, this man, is King Edric Ventin, and he owns this hospital." Dr. Hess pointed out.

"Oh, well, how was I supposed to know? He just comes storming in here acting like he owns the place."

"Which he does," Dr. Hess pointed out. "You are dismissed," he told her.

Warren and Orson watched the whole exchange, amused looks on their faces.

Dr. Hess turned to Warren and Orson. "You can go into Jillian's room. There is a nice old couple in there; they brought Jillian in. I need to talk to the Alpha."

"I want to speak with that couple also," Edric said.

"You can, but in a few minutes. I have some news for you." He looked worried.

"Very well," Edric replied and followed Dr. Hess to his office, Warren, and Orson going into Jillian's room.

Dr. Hess closed his door as soon as Edric entered.

"What's going on, doc?" Edric asked, seeing how worried he was.

"I have some news for you."

"Is Jillian dying?"

"Not yet."

"What do you mean?"

"She's pregnant again, Alpha."

The Alpha's face lit up. "So, that is why she is sick."

"Yes."

"You look worried," Edric said.

"I am. Jillian's body is fighting this pregnancy, just like the last one. She is human, and I am sure she is carrying a werewolf baby inside her."

"You don't think the baby is human?"

"More than likely not, considering who she is mated to," Dr. Hess told Edric, "and it is making the Luna seriously ill. Her body is trying to get rid of the baby, hence all the throwing up and her being so weak."

"What can we do?"

"Well, two choices, she aborts the baby," that one made Edric wince.

"Or?" Edric asked.

"She is kept on anti-nausea medicine and I.V.'s for the whole term of her pregnancy."

"Not good choices, either one," Edric sighed.

"I know; I am sorry, Edric. I don't know why her body is doing this, but I am sure it is because she is human, as I said."

Edric sighed. "There is nothing else we can do?"

"Not that I know of. We can discuss it with Jillian when she wakes up."

Edric nodded and followed Dr. Hess out the door. Edric was sick with worry. He couldn't lose his Luna. Tears came to his eyes as he opened the door to her room. All eyes were on him, except Jillian's, whose were closed, her face pale against the pillow. His heart surged in his chest. He would do anything for her, and if it meant aborting the baby so she could live, so be it.

Chapter 34

Edric approached the bed, and everyone left the room to give them privacy. He pulled up a chair and sat down by her, taking her cold hand.

"My love," he murmured. "I am so, so sorry. Sorry that you were so scared of me that you ran away, and sorry that you are going through this. I hope you will forgive me for my foolishness. I cannot live without you, Jillian; I can't. It would kill me if you left me."

He felt her squeeze his hand, and she opened her eyes.

"Hi," he said softly, watching her.

"Hi," she whispered.

"I am so sorry," he said.

"I know, and I am sorry I ran."

"Will you forgive me for my anger?"

"I will," she said.

"Why did you run?"

"You scared me," she whispered. "So I left. I planned on calling you later, but then the car ended up in the pond, and a nice couple took me in; I got sick, and here I am."

Edric frowned. "I would never harm you, Jillian, ever. I love you with my entire being. I was angry at Jessy, and my wolf was fighting to get out. I hated her with every ounce of my being. She was rotten through and through. I am truly sorry, love. I am just glad that Helen and Albert found you."

"They are very nice wolves."

"Yes, they are. I have met with Albert a few times."

"They need help, though."

"With what?"

"They can't pay their bills; they aren't making enough of a living off their hay."

"I'll see what I can do about that, but there is something we need to talk about first."

"I'm pregnant again, aren't I."

"Yes, you are, and it worries me."

"Oh? I thought you would be happy."

"I am ecstatic, but the doctor said this baby does not like your body. That is why you are so sick. You are carrying a werewolf more than likely, and your body is rejecting him or her."

"Oh," Jillian said softly. "What can I do?"

"Two options, and I don't like either one."

"What are they?"

"Dr. Hess suggested an abortion."

"No, no way, no matter what," Jillian said, "please don't make me do that."

"I won't, but the other option isn't great either."

"What?"

"You have to be hooked up to I.V.'s and be on bed rest your whole pregnancy."

Jillian frowned. "You're right; that's not a great option either, but better than the other. I wish there were another option."

"I don't know why you couldn't go about your daily life until you felt like you needed I.V.s'," Edric said. "I can't imagine you being sick your whole pregnancy. Isn't the first few months the worst?"

"It is, but what am I going to tell my parents? They will kill me when they find out."

"We could always get married now, then pretend it's a honeymoon baby, you know like we were talking about before when you lost the other one," he said.

"But if I am puking my guts up during the ceremony, won't my parents be a bit suspicious?"

Edric chuckled. "We can tell them it's the flu."

"Yes, and my mom is going to believe that one when I keep throwing up every day for several days."

"I don't know," Edric shrugged, "what do you want to do then?"

"Will you call Carla and have her come in? And my parents? I am sure they are sick with worry."

"I will; how are you feeling right now?"

"I'm okay, just a bit weak from throwing up so much. Will you thank Helen and Albert for me?"

"How did you meet up with them in the first place?" Edric asked curiously.

"When I left here, I went to the mall; then I left town. I was scared and determined that whoever was after me wouldn't find me, so I planned to leave town for a while. Not that it was a very smart plan since I didn't have any money," she sighed. "I'm sorry that I worried you."

Edric sat on the bed and pulled Jillian onto his lap. "I love you, Luna, and yes, I was worried sick about you. Please don't ever leave again. I promise I will try and control my anger better, too, okay? But I had to deal with that scum, and my wolf wanted to tear into her and get rid of her. Will you forgive me for being so angry?"

Jillian nodded. "Yes, I forgive you. It's just been tough staying sane with all that is going on. I'm tired of having my life in danger, Edric."

"Will you still marry me, though?" he asked her, pulling a ring from his pocket. "I know it's not the romantic proposal you wanted, but Jillian, I want you; I can't live without you; you are my life."

He watched her as tears formed in her eyes. "Do you want me to marry you, even with this whole mess?" she asked him.

"Of course I do. There is no one else in this world I would rather marry."

"I will marry you then," she whispered.

He kissed her and put the ring on her finger, a single solitaire diamond, at least three carats. Tears fell down her face as she looked at the magnificent ring.

"I love you, my Luna," he said, kissing her tears away.

"I love you, I just wish,"

"Wish what love?" he asked her gently.

"I wish this would all end. That whoever is after us would be caught, and we could have our happily ever after."

Edric nodded in understanding. "I know love, and I want to catch the person behind all of this as much as you do, more so even now. We are trying, I promise."

"Did you get anything out of Jessy?"

"No, she was more scared of whoever sent her to kidnap you than me, and I am the Alpha."

"You ended up killing her."

"I did. She has been a major thorn in my side, and she wouldn't answer my questions. I lost it and killed her. I am sorry. Sorry for getting angry, but not sorry for ending her miserable life."

Jillian touched Edric's stubbled face. "You are forgiven."

"I love you more than you will ever know, Jillian Everett. You are my life. I cannot live without you; please promise me you won't ever leave again? If we argue, let's talk through it, okay?"

Jillian nodded. "Okay."

The door opened then, and Jillian's parents walked in, Carla behind them.

Jillian looked at Edric, and he tapped his head. She nodded, understanding.

Jillian's mom came over to the bed. Edric placed Jillian gently down and stood back.

"Mom, Dad," Jillian said sheepishly.

"Honey, what happened?" her mom asked.

"I got mad at Edric and ran away."

"Oh," her mom said, "but why are you in here? Carla wasn't sure."

"I was throwing up all night, so a nice couple who picked me up brought me in."

"You aren't pregnant, are you?" Jillian's mom asked her.

Jillian looked at Edric; he shrugged as if saying, 'this is all yours.'

Jillian sighed. "Yes, mom, I am."

"Oh my gosh!" she squealed, and leaning down, she hugged Jillian tightly. "I'm going to be a grandma!"

Jillian's dad chuckled and came to hug Jillian. "Congratulations."

"You aren't mad?" Jillian asked in surprise.

"Oh, come on, Jillian, we don't live in the 18th century," her mom said. "We were pretty sure that you two were not acting as innocent as you were pretending to be."

Jillian shook her head as Edric chuckled.

"Besides, who could resist someone who looked like him?" Jillian's mom pointed out, looking at Edric.

"Very true," Jillian agreed. Edric *was* smoking hot.

"Hey," Jillian's dad protested.

Jillian's mom smacked his shoulder. "I love you, honey, but I mean, come on, Edric should be a model or something. Even I get hot flashes around him."

Jillian busted out laughing, and Edric grinned.

"So, you don't need me after all?" Carla asked.

"Yes," Jillian replied, "stay; I want you to help plan a shotgun wedding."

"I hope I am included in that," Jillian's mom said.

"Of course, mom. I just figured the sooner, the better, you know, before I start showing."

"How far along are you anyway?" her mom asked.

"Not sure," Jillian shrugged, "but not very far along. A week maybe."

"And you are sick already? You poor thing," Jillian's mom said. "But at least we have a few months before you start showing. How long will you be in here?"

"I'm not sure. My body really doesn't like me being pregnant, so it might be a few weeks before I can go home."

Her mom nodded. "I remember when I was pregnant. I was sick the whole nine months."

"Really?"

"Really. I was on bed rest for the last two and hooked up to I.V.'s to keep me hydrated."

"So, I am having a girl then?" I asked her.

She chuckled. "That is possible. But each pregnancy is different."

Jillian yawned then.

"You look exhausted honey; we will let you sleep and come check back in tomorrow, okay?"

Jillian nodded, hugged both of her parents, and they headed out the door.

"Can Albert and Helen come in?" Jillian asked Edric.

"Sure."

He went to the door and ushered them back in. Warren and Orson were keeping guard in the hall. They both gave a thumbs up to Edric, who nodded at them.

"Albert, Helen," Jillian smiled at them as they walked in.

They leaned down to hug her.

"You look better already," Helen commented.

"Thank you, and thank you so much for bringing me in and staying by my side."

"Our Luna, who knew," Albert chuckled.

"So dear, are you pregnant?" Helen asked.

"I am, and I would like you both to be the Godparents if that is okay."

Helen gasped, covering her mouth as tears came to her eyes. "Of course, we would be honored."

"Good. Edric also wants to talk to you about helping you out with your fields," Jillian then said, looking at Edric.

"Yes, of course," Edric said, "come out in the hall; we can discuss things while Jillian rests."

The couple nodded, and after smiling at Jillian, they left the room.

Jillian sighed. Well, that had been easy, her parents taking her pregnancy a whole lot better than she thought they would. She figured they would have been angry. But now she had their support; her pregnancy would be a lot easier, as long as she could make herself not be nauseated. Jillian thought for a moment and then smiled, putting her hand onto her stomach. If she could heal others, why not herself? Her hand lit up blue as she sent healing vibes into herself. Her body was instantly energized; the lingering nausea was gone. "Cool," she muttered, amazed at how powerful she was, and wondered again, why? And how?

Chapter 35

Jillian leaned over and picked up the phone. She had to tell Kim her news.

"Hello?" Kim answered.

"Hi Kim," Jillian said sheepishly.

"Oh, my gosh, woman! Are you okay? I heard you went missing!"

"Of course, you did, want to come to the hospital and see me? I have a lot to tell you."

"You're in the hospital again?"

"Yes," Jillian laughed. "But I'll be okay; what day is it anyway? I've lost track of all time."

Kim laughed. "It's Saturday night."

"Wasn't the prom tonight?" Jillian asked her.

"Yes, but I didn't go."

"Why not?"

"Ruben and I were too worried about you. I am so glad you are okay, though."

"So, can you come and see me tomorrow?"

"Of course," Kim said.

"Good, I have a lot to catch up on with you."

"I know," Kim said. "By the way, the principal said that Maroon 5 was going to be performing at the school on Monday."

"No way, already?"

"Yeah, they moved up the date for some reason."

"Sweet, so I will see you tomorrow?"

"Of course."

"Until then," Jillian said, then hung up.

The door opened again, and Edric walked back in alone.

"Scoot over," he said to Jillian.

She did as he asked, and he gathered her into his arms, reached above him to shut off the light, and after covering them both up, he said, "Goodnight, my love."

Jillian sighed. She was glad he was there. "Goodnight, Edric. I love you."

"I love you, my Luna, for better or for worse," he whispered.

It was one of the first nights Jillian had slept soundly, and when she woke back up, Edric was there, still holding her, watching her.

"Why don't we share a bed more often?" she asked him.

He chuckled. "That was your choice, and we aren't married yet."

"Oh, because that has stopped you from anything," she teased, pointing at her stomach.

He busted out laughing. "I love you, my Luna."

"I love you too, Alpha," she grinned.

"Hey, am I invited to the party?" Kim asked, poking her head in the door.

Edric grinned and sat up. "Come on in. I'll go get us some breakfast," he said, and getting out of bed, he kissed Jillian then left the room.

Kim pulled up a chair, "So, spill," she grinned.

Jillian grinned. "You would not believe what has been going on."

She told Kim all that had happened from the last time they had seen each other, which had been when Ruben had almost been run over.

Kim kept gasping and wowing over everything, and when Jillian finally took a breath, Kim just shook her head. "Wow, woman, no wonder you haven't been to school, and you're pregnant? That is awesome," she grinned.

"Yes and no. That is why I am in here; my body does not like being pregnant."

"Whose does?" Kim grinned.

"True," Jillian said.

"So, when can you bust out of this place?"

"Not sure. I think the doctor wants to make sure I'm not going to keep puking my guts up first."

"You look okay."

"Right now, I feel great," Jillian nodded. She hadn't had any more nausea since she had healed her stomach, interestingly enough, and she didn't mind not being sick.

Edric walked in the door then with some food.

"That smells heavenly," Jillian said.

"No nausea this morning?" Edric asked her.

"Nope, I feel great."

"Interesting," he mused, setting the food on her lap. "I guess that is good. But we probably should see if you can keep your food down before you celebrate."

"Very true," Jillian agreed, biting into a breakfast sandwich. "So, Edric, Maroon 5 is going to be at the school Monday. Can I go to the concert?" Jillian asked him.

He frowned. "I don't want you back at school."

"But I want to go to their concert, please?"

Edric shook his head in disbelief. "That is the only reason you want to go?"

"Partly," Jillian grinned.

"Oh, brother," he said. "No flirting with the lead singer."

"I won't," Jillian promised. "Besides, you are so much hotter than Adam Levine."

"Good answer," he chuckled, "and yes, you may go, as long as your guards go with you."

Jillian nodded with a smile. "Of course, thank you."

"No problem, my Luna," he told her. He liked making her happy and loved to see her beautiful smile.

Kim smiled at her friend. "Well, girl, I hate to go, but Ruben wants to spend the day together if that's okay?"

"Of course, get out of here," Jillian grinned at her. "I'll see you at school tomorrow."

Kim hugged Jillian and then left the room.

Jillian looked at Edric, who was watching her curiously.

"What?" she asked.

"You came in here last night sicker than sick, and this morning you are acting like you are just fine. What is going on?"

Jillian smiled. "Well, you might have to see it to believe it."

Jillian let her hand glow blue, and he watched in awe as she touched her stomach.

"Amazing," he whispered. "You healed yourself."

"I did."

"You are incredible, Luna."

"Thanks, Alpha; I think you are pretty great also."

"I have a friend," Edric started. "I was going to call him today and have him come and visit us. I think you will like him. He is a unique character. I think he would be impressed at the powers you are showing."

"Sounds nice, so, when can I go home?" Jillian asked him, not caring that he wanted to invite his friend to stay. She just wanted to get out of the hospital.

He chuckled. "Well, let me visit with Dr. Hess, and we will see, okay?" he stood and, leaning down to her, kissed her. "I'll be back in a few, okay?"

She nodded and watched him walk out. She sighed and looked at the ring on her finger. She hadn't even shown it to Kim or her parents; she was sure they would be happy for her.

Dr. Hess walked into the room a few minutes later with Edric. "Well, Luna, the Alpha, was telling me that you are feeling better, but I would like to keep you here for one more day before I send you home. I know your body heals well, and I want to see if you can handle this pregnancy. I am most curious about it."

"Okay," Jillian told him.

"What, no argument?" he chuckled.

"No argument. You know what is best for me."

"What did you do with the real Jillian?" he teased her.

She laughed. "Thanks, Doc, glad you love me so much."

Edric smiled. "Think you are up for a walk, my love?" he asked her. "There is a nice courtyard outside."

"If I can change," she said, looking at the nightgown she was still in.

"I'll have Carla bring you some clothes," he said as he sat down.

"I'll check on you later, Luna," Dr. Hess said, then walked out.

"Edric, do you have any idea who might be after us?" Jillian asked him then.

"No. We think it might be rogues, but someone is leading them, and we need to find out who."

"Do you think we are okay getting married? That we will be safe to do so?"

"I know so. We have plenty of guards, and I can call in the whole pack if I need to."

"You probably want them all at the wedding anyway, yes?"

Edric chuckled. "No, my love, I am over 50,000 or more wolves. I was only going to invite those who are important to me."

"And what of all the other Alpha's?" she asked him. She was sure that several other Alpha's were scattered around the country. "They will come also. As I am their King, they are required to show up."

"Oh."

"Why?"

"I was kind of hoping it would just be my parents and us."

He sat by her and pulled her onto his lap.

"If that is what you want, my Luna, but I would like to invite them. It would be good for them to meet their Queen."

"I will be, won't I," she whispered.

He chuckled. "Yes, my love, you already are. We will just make it official on our wedding day."

Carla knocked and walked into the room then with some clothes for Jillian.

"Feeling better, Luna?"

"Much better; thanks for everything you have been doing." "No problem, here's your clothes," she said, handing them over.

"Thank you again," Jillian replied. She then looked at the saline drip attached to her, pulled it out, then hopped off the bed.

"I don't need that," she said as she headed to the bathroom. "Someone is feeling better this morning," Carla laughed.

Jillian took a quick shower, put on her clothes, and walked out. Edric was there, but Carla was now gone.

"Come, my love, let's take that walk."

Jillian nodded and took Edric's hand. He led her out the door where Orson and Wes were standing guard, then down the hall and outside. Edric was right; the courtyard was very beautiful. It was full of plants and had a small fountain in the middle with coins at the bottom.

"The coins get donated to the hospital," Edric told her, pulling one from his pocket and handing it to her. "Make a wish." "Why?"

"To see if it will come true."

She smiled and put her arms around him. "All of my wishes have come true because I have you."

He smiled down at his Luna. "I would have to say the same thing, my Luna. I love you."

"I love you," she said and kissed him.

Jillian realized she hardly knew a thing about her Alpha and wanted to get to know him better.

"Tell me about your parents," Jillian asked him.

"I would rather not talk about them right now," he frowned. "I want to talk about something more pleasant."

"Okay, what?"

"Tell me of your travels."

So, she did; she told him of her favorite places and why she liked those places. He sat, enthralled, seeing her face light up as she talked.

A few hours later, he pulled her to her feet. "Come on, my Luna, let's head inside and I will go and get you some lunch."

"That would be nice," she told him. "Thank you for listening to me tell you all about my life."

"I love hearing about your life. You are a well-traveled young lady."

"You make me sound like a child," she frowned.

He kissed her softly as they got to their room. "You are anything but a child, believe me," he whispered against her lips.

"Thanks, I think."

When Jillian woke up the following day, Kim walked in with a fresh pair of clothes. "Come on, girly, get up; we have school and a concert," she grinned.

Jillian laughed and pushed Edric from the bed.

"Hey, I was comfortable," he complained good-naturedly.

"Too bad, I have a concert to go to," Jillian said.

Edric shook his head. "Promise me no touching him, or flirting, or.."

"Yes, dad," Jillian said, rolling her eyes and making Kim snort with laughter.

Edric kissed Jillian on the forehead as she got up and then sent her to the bathroom, and then after a quick shower and a quick breakfast, Jillian was headed out the door with Orson and Wes. Emerson was there to drive them. He would drop Jillian and Kim off at the school and take the Alpha home.

Jillian and Kim acted just like typical teenage girls as they ran into the high school, giggling.

"Watch her closely," Edric told Orson and Wes.

The men nodded and headed after the girls.

As soon as Jillian walked into the school, the hallway became silent, and everyone bore their necks to Jillian.

She nodded at everyone as she walked to her locker.

"Man, it is so good to be back," Jillian sighed, pulling a few books from her locker. "I feel like I have missed out on life," she added.

"You have," Kim grinned, and seeing Ruben headed to her, the girls parted ways, and Jillian headed to her first class. Jillian was so behind on work; she wondered if she would even graduate.

When she walked in, the teacher bowed his head to her, then said, "Well, well, Luna, nice of you to grace us with your presence."

"Sorry, sir, it was a rough week last week," she admitted.

"So I heard. But are you back for the rest of the year?"

"I think so, I hope so."

"Good, you have a lot of work to catch up on if you want to graduate."

"I know," she nodded.

The teacher then opened a desk drawer and pulled out a stack of papers, handing them to her. "You have a month to hand all this back in."

"Thank you, sir," Jillian said, and stuffing it into her backpack, she headed to her seat.

The students all nodded at her as she sat down, then they sat down after her.

The teacher went over the lesson for the day, and Jillian sighed in happiness. It was so nice to have a normal day.

As Jillian headed to her other classes before lunch, the girls were all giggling and grooming themselves for Maroon 5, who was performing right after lunch. It was no surprise that they were acting the way they were since the Alpha was off the market; why not go after another handsome unmated werewolf and his band.

Ruben and Kim met Jillian in the lunchroom for lunch just a bit later, Jillian sitting down with her food, then the other students and teachers sitting down while Orson and Wes kept a watchful eye on their Luna.

"So, anything exciting happen while I was gone?" Jillian asked Kim and Ruben.

"Nope, not a thing. It has been totally boring," Ruben said.

"Except for all the rumors flying around about why you were gone," Kim said.

"Why didn't you tell me this yesterday so I could have prepared myself?" Jillian asked her friend.

"Sorry," Kim shrugged but didn't look really sorry.

"So, what are the rumors?" Jillian asked.

"Car accidents, pregnancy, kidnapping, you name it," Ruben said.

"It's all true, though," Jillian told him.

He spit out some milk he had been drinking. "All of it?"

"All of it."

"Woah," Ruben whispered. "So you are pregnant?" he whispered. Jillian nodded.

"That's cool," Ruben said. "But all of that is so crazy, and Kim never tells me anything," he complained.

"That's because I am a good friend," Kim replied, "and I am not going to spread rumors or tell anyone what is going on with our Luna unless I have her permission."

"Thanks, Kim, that means a lot," Jillian smiled at her.

"So spill," Ruben told her, "What happened? You were kidnapped? Jillian nodded, "Yes, by one of the Alpha's harem girls."

"No way," he said, looking shocked. "Seriously?"

"Seriously."

"What did she want?"

"To kill me."

"Wow, Luna, your life is never boring," he chuckled.

"Yes, you could say that," she agreed.

"What happened to her then?" Ruben asked.

So, for the rest of the lunch hour, Jillian whispered to her friends what had happened, even though she knew that the other students could hear her. But Jillian didn't care; then it would squash all the rumors floating around.

Just as the three of them finished their lunch, the principal walked in. "Okay, students, Maroon 5 is set up in the theatre if you will all head there in an orderly manner after your Luna," he said.

"Okay then, what are we waiting for," Jillian smiled and stood, Orson and Wes right behind her.

The principal was already there when Jillian walked in with her guards and told Jillian that she would be sitting in the middle of the front row. Then he nodded at Wes and Orson to sit next to Jillian on either side, making Kim and Ruben sit next to Wes on the left side.

"Hey," Jillian protested. "How am I supposed to enjoy the concert if my best friend is not by me?" she asked Orson, who chuckled.

"This is how the Alpha wants it, Luna," he pointed out.

"I don't care, Orson. I want my friend to sit by me. You aren't going to get up and scream and act all girly when Adam Levine gets on the stage, so move," she told him.

Wes laughed. "You heard her; you had better move."

"No way. I won't go against our Alpha's wishes."

"Then I am going to sit on the side with my friends," Jillian said, standing up to move next to Kim and Ruben.

Orson sighed like he was suffering. "Fine, I will sit next to Kim, but no funny stuff."

"I'm not going to throw my underwear at him, Orson," Jillian said cheekily, making Wes snort with laughter.

"Oh, I will," Kim grinned, sitting by Jillian as Wes and Orson moved to sit on either side of the three friends.

"You had better not," Ruben glared at his mate.

Kim just laughed. "I am kidding, love; I won't do that, not while you are looking anyway," she said, making Jillian laugh.

The other students filed in, all talking excitedly. The row right behind Jillian was left clear for her safety, but she didn't mind.

After all the students and teachers were seated, the principal got up onto the stage. "Students, teachers, I am glad that Maroon 5 was able to take time out of their busy schedule to perform for us today. Luna, if you would also thank our Alpha for sponsoring Maroon 5."

Jillian nodded at him.

"Very well, without further ado, Maroon 5!" the principal shouted and stepped off the stage.

Most girls got to their feet as Adam Levine and his band came to the stage.

Everyone started cheering, and the girls started screaming and crying before they even started to perform.

"Well, I guess you all love us," Adam chuckled to the audience. "It's nice to be here," he said, then looking at Jillian, he bowed his head to her. She smiled back at him, but she stayed in her seat. She knew the Alpha would not be pleased if she was yelling and screaming like the other girls. Kim was even on her feet while Ruben gave his mate dirty looks.

Ruben then looked at Jillian and shook his head. She just shrugged and said, "She's your mate."

Adam then began to sing. Jillian loved their songs. He started with his newest song, and Jillian found herself tearing up. Adam watched Jillian as he sang, and after he ended his first song, he asked her to come onto the stage with him.

Kim gasped. "No fair," she said.

Orson frowned. "I think not."

"I'll be fine," Jillian whispered and headed up to the stage.

Adam walked over to her and took her hands in his. "I heard about all the things you have been going through. You are one tough Luna, and I respect you, so I wrote a song for you."

Jillian blushed bright red as Adam nodded at his band to start playing.

He began to sing, and Jillian began to cry. Stupid pregnancy hormones.

As he finished, he kissed Jillian's cheek. "We admire you," he said, "I am glad you are our Luna."

"Thank you," she whispered and turned to see a very angry Edric standing just below her in front of the seats.

Oops. She walked off the stage amid screams and cheers. Orson and Wes were on their feet, standing next to Edric. He sat down and pulled Jillian down next to him.

"What are you doing here?" Jillian whispered to him.

"I heard that you were enjoying this concert too much," he frowned, "case in point," he said to her, pointing to the stage where Adam, who was watching them, nodded at the Alpha.

"He was being kind," Jillian whispered as Adam started a new song.

"He was flirting with my Luna," Edric growled.

"You are too overprotective," Jillian whispered in his ear.

Edric kissed her cheek. "So you say. I am only protecting what is mine," he responded.

As Adam finished another song, a pair of panties landed on the stage. Adam picked them up and said. "I hope these are new."

The students laughed. He then turned to his drummer. "I think these are your color, Matt," he teased.

Everyone busted out laughing. The drummer took the panties, held them up to his face, and said, "what do you think?"

"They are totally you," Adam nodded.

"Good, I'll let my dog wear them; she's almost potty trained," he grinned.

Even Edric laughed at that one. Adam turned back to the audience. "For my next song, I want to dedicate it to all of you students and to tell you, follow your dreams."

Everyone cheered, and Adam began to sing again. Edric tucked an arm about Jillian, and she snuggled into his shoulder. He sighed, glad she wasn't mad at him for showing up. Orson had mind-linked him about how Adam was flirting with Jillian, and he was going to put a stop to it. No one, not even someone famous, would or could flirt with his Luna, or they would pay dearly.

After the concert, the band left the stage, but not before Adam said, "Alpha, Luna, I would be honored if you would join me backstage."

"No fair," Kim hissed to Jillian.

"Hand me your phone; I'll get a picture of him," Jillian said.

"We are not going back there," Edric replied.

"Yes, we are," Jillian replied. "It would be rude to refuse."

"Luna," Edric growled.

"Alpha, don't you growl at me," Jillian told him. "Besides, you will be right there with me, so stop it."

Orson held back a laugh. The Luna sure was feisty; she was such a good match for Edric.

"Fine, but five minutes," Edric gave in.

"Thank you," Jillian said, kissing his cheek, taking Kim's phone with her.

The band was cooling down and sitting in some comfortable chairs.

"Luna, Alpha," Adam smiled, standing and exposing his neck to them. "I am glad you came back here. I wanted to thank you for inviting me to perform. I haven't been here in ages."

Edric nodded at him.

"So, I heard that you wanted me to perform at your wedding?" Adam asked, looking at Jillian.

"I would like that if you have time," Jillian said.

"For you, Luna, I have all the time in the world," Adam grinned.

Edric growled.

"Alpha, I apologize," Adam said, baring his neck to Edric. "I am not flirting, I promise. I just want to let your Luna know that I am honored to perform for both of you. It's a rare occasion to do such a thing. When is your wedding anyway?"

Jillian looked up at Edric. "Whenever the Luna wants it," Edric replied.

"This weekend," Jillian said.

Edric looked at her in surprise. "Are you sure?"

"Why not? I don't want it to be overboard, and we don't need a lot of people there."

"What, no ten million dollar wedding?" Edric teased her.

"Have I even asked you for anything?" she asked him.

"No, come to think of it, well, except your art supplies."

"Very well then, a ten million dollar wedding is out."

"I assume this will be at your palace, Alpha?" Adam asked him.

"Yes," Edric nodded.

"Would you like a photo with me too?" Adam asked.

"No, she is not," Edric said.

Jillian rolled her eyes, making Adam grin. "Yes, I am. Kim wanted a picture, remember?"

"You have a feisty Luna," Adam chuckled.

"You have no idea," Edric replied dryly.

Jillian took a picture of Adam, then took Edric's phone and took a selfie with Adam, then stuck her tongue out at her Alpha, making Adam laugh again.

Edric looked down at his Luna, shaking his head. She was something else, his Luna, but he wouldn't trade her for the world.

Chapter 36

As soon as Jillian walked from the backstage, Kim accosted her.

"So, how is he? Is he as nice as he seems?"

"He is really nice," Jillian replied, handing over Kim's phone. Kim looked at the photos. "Man, he is so hot, even more so in person," she sighed.

"Excuse me, mate here," Ruben replied, coming up beside Kim.

She turned to him. "Sorry, love, it's just that Adam is so drool-worthy, those muscles and all those tattoos."

"Hey, I have muscles," Ruben protested.

"I know," Kim said, kissing her mate.

"I can get tattoos if you want," Ruben then said.

"No, you wouldn't look good with them," Kim shrugged.

Ruben looked at her. "Really? But you lust after that man because he does?"

"It's different," Kim shrugged.

Ruben looked at Jillian. "Luna, explain to me why it is different."

Jillian shrugged. "I don't know. I couldn't see Edric with tattoos either, but Adam pulls it off."

"But you aren't lusting after him," Ruben pointed out.

"Yes, she was," Edric frowned down at Jillian.

"Hey, he is a hot man," Jillian grinned, but then she looked up at Edric. "But you are hotter."

He smiled. "Glad to hear that, Luna. I was going to go tell Adam to leave and never come back."

"So, am I hotter than him?" Ruben asked Kim.

Kim flushed, and Ruben growled at her.

Jillian pulled Kim to her and whispered, "You had better tell him he is hotter, or he is going to have a conniption."

"Okay, okay, you are hotter. Are you happy now?" Kim said, kissing Ruben.

"That's better," Ruben said, "and yes, I am happy now."

Jillian was about to tease her friend when the lights suddenly went down, and they heard a shout of extreme pain.

Jillian looked at Kim and Ruben. "Stay here." She then hopped up onto the stage, Edric right by her. They went behind the curtains to see Adam kneeling on the floor by Matt.

He looked up at his Alpha and Luna. "He was unplugging the electric guitar, and for some reason, it shocked him, he's unconscious, and I can't hear him breathing," Adam said, worried.

"I'll call for an ambulance," Edric said, pulling out his phone and walking out in front of the curtains while Jillian knelt by the man. She felt for a pulse. "That is not good." She then looked at Adam. "Do you know CPR?"

He shook his head no. Jillian nodded and bent her head, starting mouth to mouth and then chest compressions, but Matt wasn't responding. His lips were beginning to turn blue. She had to do something, or he would die. "Adam, you must swear on your life what you are about to see stays here, okay?"

Adam looked at her curiously. "What do you mean?"

Jillian looked at him. "Do you swear?"

"I swear," he nodded, curious as to what she was about to do. Then he found out. Jillian's hands began to glow blue as she placed her hands on Matt's chest. Adam watched in fascination as the blue spread over Matt's body, and suddenly he gasped in gulps of air.

Edric walked back behind the curtains just in time to see Jillian collapse. He caught her easily, and she looked up at him, smiling weakly.

"What did you do?" he asked her.

"Our Luna just saved my friend's life," Adam said in awe.

"An ambulance is on the way," Edric informed Adam and the rest of the band, who had just arrived back from loading equipment onto the bus. They sat down by their friend, who was trying to sit up. Adam pushed him back down. "Stay there, Matt; help is on the way."

"But I feel fine," he complained, trying to sit up again. "What happened?" he then asked, looking at Adam.

"I think the guitar had a short in the cord or something, it shocked the hell out of you, and you went down," Adam frowned.

Adam then stood and walked over to the guitar in question. He squatted down by it and frowned. "The cord has been sliced."

Edric frowned and set Jillian gently into a chair after ensuring she was okay; he knelt by Adam.

"Someone was trying to kill you?" Edric asked.

"I don't know why," Adam said. "We don't have any enemies, not that I know of."

Adam stood up. "That worries me. Who would do such a thing?"

"That is a good question," Edric frowned and turned to the principal, who was hovering in the wings.

"Do you have cameras backstage?"

The principal shook his head. "No, Alpha, we have never been able to afford them, and I didn't really think they were needed either."

"Well, as of now, you are getting cameras."

The man nodded just as the paramedics showed up. The two men saw Jillian sitting in a chair and nodded at her. "Don't tell me you are causing trouble again, Luna?" one of them teased.

"Not me this time," she said, pointing at Matt, who was still on the floor.

The two men knelt by him and started checking him out.

Two policemen then showed up as Edric had called them also. They knelt by the sliced cord that Edric showed them. After turning off the power for a moment, they unplugged the guitar and took it and the wire in as evidence.

"Why would anyone try to hurt or kill him?" Jillian asked Edric as the paramedics loaded Matt onto a stretcher. The rest of the band followed them off the stage and out the door, but Adam turned back and bowed his head to his Luna. "Thank you, Luna; I will never forget what you did. If you ever need anything, let me know." He then headed out after his men.

"You should have waited for the paramedics to show up," Edric frowned at Jillian.

"He wouldn't have lived, Edric. He needed to be saved." She stood up then and swayed just a bit. He caught her and swept her into his arms. "You are weak," he accused.

"I just healed a man, and I am pregnant," she pointed out.

That brought a deep frown to Edric's face. "I am taking you in to have the doctor look at you and make sure that the baby is okay."

"I will be fine; I just need some rest."

"No, I am taking you in," he insisted and walked down the stairs with Jillian in his arms.

Kim and Ruben were still there, a look of concern on both their faces.

"What happened?" Kim asked, noticing Jillian in Edric's arms.

"One of the band members got hurt, and Jillian saved him," Edric growled, unhappy.

"You saved him?" Kim asked, in awe.

"Mouth to mouth," Jillian replied.

"I am so jealous; oh wait, it wasn't Adam, though, was it."

"Kimberly," Ruben growled at her.

Edric started walking out the door with Jillian, Orson, and Wes stepping up to them.

"Is she okay?" Orson asked.

"I am taking her in to the hospital to make sure she is," Edric replied.

"I am fine," Jillian protested.

"No, you are not. You are going to be checked out, my love," Edric said, kissing her forehead as he tucked her into the limo. Edric then looked at Kimberly and Ruben. "Go home. If Jillian is fine, I am taking her home after she's been checked out, and she is going to rest."

"Yes, Alpha," they both said and headed away. Edric got into the limo by Jillian and tucked her against him, making her lay her head on his shoulder.

"Is she okay?" Emerson asked as he pulled the limo out of the parking lot.

"No, she healed one of the band back there and then collapsed on me," Edric frowned down at Jillian, but she had her eyes closed, feigning sleep so he couldn't cuss her out. "She is doing too much. I knew I shouldn't have let her come back to school today."

"And tick her off?" Emerson chuckled from the front seat. "Let her live her life, Edric. She is still young, remember?"

"But she is pregnant. I don't want her, or the baby harmed."

"She is one of the strongest women I know, Alpha; look at all she has gone through since she met you, and look at what she can do. She is incredible. She saved some of her classmates, my mate, Ruben, and now one of Adam's band members. You can't tell me she isn't amazing."

Edric sighed, looking down at his Luna. "I just want to keep her safe."

"You can without smothering her," Emerson pointed out.

"But she keeps getting hurt," Edric pointed out to him.

"You could always lock her in her room until we catch whoever is after you two," Orson suggested.

"Oh yes, like that would work out so well," Edric said drily. "No. But what I don't understand is why someone tried to kill one of Adam's band?"

"Unless they were after the Luna, knowing she was going backstage," Orson suggested.

Edric growled. "If they were,"

"I can sniff them out," his wolf spoke up. *"We need to end this, Edric; it has gone on long enough."*

Edric agreed it was getting beyond ridiculous. Jillian couldn't even do anything without her life being threatened someway and somehow. He sighed with frustration. "I don't know what to do. We have no suspects at all, and things aren't getting better. I am getting really sick of this."

The other men nodded in agreeance.

Edric looked down at Jillian, who was actually asleep now. "I think I have a plan."

His two guards looked at him curiously. "I will tell all of you when we get home. I want to talk to Warren about it. I think I know a way to draw out whoever is after us."

"Does it involve kicking some serious ass?" Orson grinned.

"Of course," Edric replied, grinning at his guard.

"Good, count me in."

"Me too," Wes nodded. "It is time to bring this reign of terror to an end."

Chapter 37

Jillian was deemed okay and fit to go home at the hospital, but Dr. Hess told her to rest. "If I need to put you on bed rest the rest of your pregnancy, I will do it, just to keep you safe," he threatened. "No, no, I will behave," Jillian promised him.

"Good, how is the nausea?"

"I'm fine."

"Glad to hear it."

Dr. Hess looked at Edric, who was hovering. "She will be fine Alpha, like I said, make her rest."

"Can I go back to school tomorrow?" Jillian asked.

"No, most definitely not," Edric told her.

"But I will never graduate. I have already missed too much."

"Too bad because you are taking online schooling from now on, Luna."

Jillian sighed. She knew better than to argue with him. "Fine, I will, but on one condition."

"What?"

"I want Kim to come over and help tutor me."

"Of course, love, anything for you, as long as I can keep you home and safe."

"Slave driver," she teased him.

Dr. Hess chuckled as he walked out.

"I'll show you, slave driver," Edric told Jillian as he picked her up into his arms and started carrying her out the door.

She squealed, making him laugh.

"Put me down, you brute," she said, but she was laughing.

"No way, not until you take back what you said," Edric grinned.

"Nope, never."

"Very well, then, I will have to punish you when we get home."

"I'm terrified, truly," Jillian said, straight-faced.

That made Edric bust out laughing. He kissed his Luna as he set her into the limo.

"I love you, my Luna," he chuckled, sliding in by her.

She stuck her tongue out at him.

"Bring that tongue here," Edric said, pulling her to him and kissing her soundly.

"We're home," Emerson chuckled a few minutes later, looking back at his Alpha and Luna, who were still kissing.

They pulled apart, grinning foolishly.

Warren was there to open the door of the limo.

"Luna, Alpha," he nodded.

"Warren, my friend," Edric grinned. "Just the man I want to see. I want to meet you and the others in my study. I have a plan to draw out the one after us."

Warren nodded. "Very good. I'll meet you there." He then headed back inside.

"Can I go get my parents?" Jillian asked, "they will want to know."

"Yes, that is fine; I was going to have them a part of this anyway."

"You don't think they will get hurt, do you?" Jillian asked as they headed inside.

"No, hopefully, not anyway. I am hoping that this doesn't resort to violence."

"And what if there is, and you go all wolf in front of my parents?"

Edric chuckled. "We will address that later if it happens."

Jillian nodded and walked into the study with him. Warren brought Jillian's parents in a moment later, followed by Emerson, Orson, Wes, and Carla.

"Warren said you have a plan to draw out the one responsible for hurting Jillian," her father said.

"Yes, and I need your help," Edric said.

"Gladly," Jillian's father replied.

"Good. Jillian wants a wedding, a shotgun wedding as she called it," he smiled softly at her. "I want to have the wedding also this weekend."

"Oh my, that doesn't give us much time to prepare," Jillian's mom said.

"No, and I am sorry, Mrs. Everett, but I think that this is the only way we are going to draw out our enemy."

"By having a wedding?" Jillian's father asked, "but how? And you haven't even put a ring on her finger yet."

Jillian showed her hand to her dad. "Actually, dad, he did."

Jillian's mom grinned. "Oh, sweetie, it is beautiful. You have good taste, your Highness."

"I know," he said, pulling Jillian to him and kissing her on the head. "I want to have the wedding soon so we can draw out who is trying to harm us."

"So, you are using our wedding as a trap?" Jillian asked. "That's not very romantic."

Edric smiled. "I know, love, it's not, but we need to catch who is after you. I want this to end; this has gone on long enough."

"So, we have five days to plan a wedding, got it," Jillian said.

"Make it simple, love," Edric told her. "We don't want something huge and fancy, especially if things go awry and things get destroyed."

Jillian sighed. "Dang, and I was going to have ice sculptures, a ten thousand dollar cake, and a diamond wedding dress."

Carla laughed. "Why do I get the feeling that you are lying?"

"Because she is," Edric chuckled. "Jillian's not that type of girl."

"Says you," Jillian replied.

"Love, if that is what you want, then you shall have it," Edric told her, "but it could be destroyed."

"Are you planning on having the police here?" Jillian's dad asked him.

"I am, but undercover."

"Good. We need this to end. My daughter's life is valuable, and I want this over with; it has gone on way too long."

"I agree, Henry," Edric nodded. "So, Jillian, sit down with your mother and Carla tomorrow and plan something that can be put together by this weekend. The rest of you can help me plan how to trap this guy, and Mr. Everett, sir, I will have you sit out this one. You can walk Jillian down the aisle, and let's hope that is all you need to do."

"I am okay with that," he nodded.

"Jillian, why don't you go rest?" Edric suggested, "I will have dinner sent up to you."

Jillian nodded; she *was* tired. Healing people really took it out of her.

"I'll go help Carla with dinner," Jillian's mother said.

Jillian headed to her room, planning on getting a bit of a nap, but as she sat down on the bed, Carla walked in. "Sorry, Luna, but Kim is on the phone."

"Oh, thanks, Carla," Jillian told her.

Jillian picked up the phone off the bedside table. "Hey, friend."

"Hey, yourself."

"What, do you have something to tell me?"

"Well, when we got home, I started to feel a bit sick."

"Are you pregnant?"

"Yes!" Kim screeched.

Jillian laughed. "Congrats. Now we can be fat and pregnant together."

"I know, right?" Kim laughed. "I am so excited; Ruben is over the moon. He has always wanted to be a dad."

"I'm happy for you both; now I have some news for you. Want to be my maid of honor for my wedding this weekend?"

Kim screamed, and Jillian held the phone away from her ear, but she was smiling.

"Yes, of course, and did you say this weekend?"

"Yes."

"Wow, that is really soon."

"I know, but Edric wants to use our wedding as a trap to catch whoever is after us."

"Good idea," Kim said, "and I get to be a part of it; that is so cool."

"Yes, so cool."

"So, what can I do to help?"

"I don't know. My mom and Carla are helping to plan it, but you can also. The more, the merrier."

"Sweet, so when can I come over?"

"Now, if you want, I'm banned from going back to school. Edric insists I do all my schoolwork online," Jillian sighed.

"That sucks, but at least I can come and see you."

"Yes, and you can help me with schoolwork."

"Sounds like a plan; see you in a few."

Jillian got off the bed, feeling fine and grateful that her body recovered quickly. She wondered how come she was the way she was. Her parents were ordinary, so why was she so special? She knew that Dr. Hess was looking into her family history, so maybe she would have to call and ask him. She decided it was the perfect time to do so while waiting on Kim.

Jillian dialed the hospital and asked to speak with the doctor, and told the nurse who she was.

"Of course, Luna, let me get him."

Moments later, he was on the phone. "Luna, are you okay?"

"I'm okay, Dr. Hess. Do you have a moment?"

"I do; what's up?"

"I have a question about my family history. You were looking into it for Edric."

"Yes, well," he sighed. "I did, and I have some news for you. I was going to tell you earlier, but I didn't have time; I hope you forgive me."

"Why?"

"Your family history."

"And?"

"I got searching into wolf history and found out why you can heal so quickly. It runs in your family."

"Really," Jillian gasped, "but my parents are so ordinary."

"That's the thing, Jillian; you aren't going to like what I have to say."

"Uh, oh."

"I would rather come over there and tell you in person."

"Okay."

"I get off in an hour, and then I will be by to see you."

"Okay, you are worrying me, doc."

"I know, but well, you will understand when I get there. See you in a bit."

He then hung up.

Jillian frowned. "Crap, what is going on?"

She sighed and headed down to the front door, knowing that Kim would be there soon.

Edric was just coming out of the office with his men when he spotted Jillian. He saw her frown.

"Jillian, what's wrong?"

"Dr. Hess is coming to see me."

"Oh?"

"He has some news."

"I don't like the sound of that."

"Me either. He didn't want to tell me over the phone."

"That is not good."

"It's not about my health, though; it's about my family history."

Edric sighed. "That's not so bad."

"So you say. He sounded worried."

"Oh. When will he be here?"

"Within the hour."

"Okay, let me know when he is here. I am headed outside to set up a security system for our wedding. I want to make sure whoever is after us doesn't make it past the backyard."

"Okay," Jillian nodded.

Edric kissed her. "What are you doing right now?"

"I'm going to eat, and Kim is coming over."

"Okay, I'll be outside if you need me," he said and headed away.

The doorbell sounded then, and Jillian smiled as she opened the door. But it turned to a frown. "Dr. Hess, you are here already?"

"Yes, I had the other doctor finish my shift. I really need to talk to you and Edric."

"I am right here," Edric replied, walking up to them.

"Good."

"In my office," Edric replied.

The three of them headed there, and Edric closed the door.

The doctor sat down slowly. "I just found out most of this today, and I didn't have time to tell you earlier," he said. "Edric, you wanted me to look into Jillian's family history."

"Yes."

"It took me a while. I had some obstacles and some threats."

"Threats?" Edric growled.

"Yes, someone didn't want me to find out about Jillian's family."

"Why?" Edric asked.

"Because, Jillian, I don't know how to put this, so I'll rip off the Band-aid and tell you straight up. You were switched at birth. Your parents that you think are your parents? They are not your birth parents. Your real parents are dead, and the child your real parents thought was theirs was killed along with them."

Jillian gasped in shock, and Edric went pale.

"So, what are you saying, Doc?" Edric frowned.

"I don't think that whoever has been harming Jillian is after you, Edric. Whoever it is, only wants Jillian. They know who she is."

Chapter 38

Jillian felt like she was suffocating. Someone had killed her birth parents? And the baby that they thought was her? Who was this person?

Edric sat down by her. "Jillian, take a deep breath, love."

She nodded and did as told. "My other parents," she whispered, "I wonder if they know."

"I think we need to have a visit with them," Edric told her.

"But what if they are totally clueless? What if they think I really am theirs?"

"Then, we have a lot of explaining to do, but we need to tell them that you aren't their real daughter."

"Do we have to?" Jillian whispered. "It would break their hearts."

"What we need to find out is who switched Jillian because whoever it was, saved her life," Dr. Hess said.

Edric nodded. "Yes, they did, but who would switch her, especially right after Jillian's mother had her? Did Jillian show tendencies to her gift already? Or did the person know that the gift ran in the family and knew they had to save her?"

Dr. Hess nodded. "I bet it's the latter. I doubt Jillian could heal herself at such a young age."

"But I could heal myself when I was young," Jillian whispered.

Edric looked at her in surprise.

"What do you mean?"

"I remember when I was only about three years old. I fell from a tree and broke my leg. I knew my parents would be extremely upset, especially when they had told me to stay out of the tree. But my leg healed almost instantly. I didn't think anything of it, and I thought it was normal."

"But it's not," Dr. Hess said. "So, you never told anyone that you could heal quickly?"

"No, I never did. I just figured it was normal, like I said, until one day when I was about ten, and my friend Addison fell off her bike and broke her arm. I thought it would heal, just like I did, but it didn't, and she had to go to the hospital and get a cast. I thought it was weird. I asked her why she didn't instantly heal like I did, and she thought I was nuts. She said no one could just instantly heal; that wasn't possible."

"Did you tell your parents?"

"No, I never did, especially when I saw others with broken bones. I figured I was an anomaly and that if I said anything, I would be teased, and my parents would be angry."

"Interesting," Edric muttered.

"So you have had this gift for many years then," Dr. Hess said, intrigued.

"Maybe since Jillian turned 18, more abilities are showing up," Edric said. "She can heal now others now, and she can see the future."

"But I have been able to see the future since I was younger also," Jillian pointed out.

Edric nodded. "That's right, you did tell me that, plus your powers as a Luna are strengthening."

"And someone knows that the Luna is powerful and wants to get rid of her," Dr. Hess said.

"But why?" Jillian asked. "You would think whoever it was would want to save me, not destroy me."

"That is a good question, my love," Edric frowned.

"She is going to need even more protection," Dr. Hess said.

"As are you," Jillian told Edric. "Whoever is after me will eventually come after you also."

"I can protect myself," he told Jillian.

"Dr. Hess, what about you? If you were getting threats, your life will be in more danger now that you told us what you did," Jillian said.

He nodded. "But, I have work."

"I will hire you on here until this is over," Edric told him. "You can keep an eye on Jillian, make sure she is doing okay with her pregnancy."

The doctor nodded. "Okay, I'll just need to call the hospital and let them know I am needed for an emergency out of town for a few days. But I will need to go and get some clothes."

"I will send one of my men to your place Doc," Edric said. "I don't want you leaving here. I am afraid that someone probably knows that you are here already, and is waiting for you to leave so they can get to you."

Dr. Hess nodded. "You are probably right. Okay, I will stay."

"Emerson is about your size; he can lend you some clothes for tomorrow," Edric told him.

"Very well, say, I haven't eaten yet, is there some food I can grab?"

"We haven't eaten either," Edric said. "But I need to go check on the men in the backyard. You two go and eat, and I will meet you in the dining hall."

The three left the room, and as they did, Jillian heard, "It's about time you came out of there."

"Hey Kim, sorry, but the doctor had some things to tell me," Jillian smiled at her friend.

"Oh, is it about the baby?"

"Kind of," Jillian said. "Have you eaten?"

"I did, but it didn't stay down."

"Of course not. Want some crackers or something?"

"No, I'd rather have real food."

"I can have Emerson pick you up some anti-nausea medicine when he goes to get my things," Dr. Hess said.

"So, you are pregnant also, Kim?" Edric asked, amused.

"Yes, and Ruben is having a conniption that I am here. As a matter of fact, he is outside. He told me I couldn't stay long, that I need my rest."

Jillian laughed. "Go tell him to come in, don't leave the poor man out there."

"I'll go get him," Edric replied. He headed out the front door as the two girls and the doctor headed to the dining hall.

Jillian's parents were there eating, as was Carla.

"Hey, we couldn't wait for you," her mom said. "We were hungry."

"That's okay, mom. I was visiting with the doctor and Edric."

"Oh, hello, doctor," my mom said.

"Good evening Mrs. Everett. I was just here visiting with your daughter about how to take care of herself during her pregnancy."

"Oh, that is nice. Please, join us for dinner."

He nodded and sat down by Jillian's mom. Jillian sat down, and then Kim sat by her.

"I love food, but I hate it right now," Kim sighed, looking at the food on the table.

Jillian helped herself to some and smiled. "Understandable."

"Are you pregnant too?" Jillian's mom asked Kim.

"I am," she sighed dramatically.

"I am happy for you. It will be good for Jillian to have a friend who can suffer with her," her mom teased.

"Your mom knows?" Kim asked Jillian.

"Yeah, it's not like I could hide it from her, especially soon," she said, rubbing her stomach.

"Does she know about you being pregnant for only six months?" she whispered into Jillian's ear.

Jillian shook her head. "Not yet."

Jillian felt a kiss on her cheek then and smiled up at Edric. "Orson suggested we put an alarm in the backyard in case of intruders," Edric said, sitting down and helping himself to some food, Ruben sitting down by Kim. "Edric invited me in," Ruben said.

"Good," Jillian smiled at him.

"It might be a good idea," Jillian's dad said, commenting on what Edric had said.

"I was thinking the same thing," Edric nodded. "That is why I finally got hold of and invited my good friend Hayden to help me set it up. He knows how to set up systems, so they are undetectable."

"Oh, that is nice," Jillian's mom said. "You must trust him."

"I do. He was a friend of my father's also," he mused.

"So, he's old then?" Kim asked him.

Edric shook his head. "Not that old, but yes, older than I am."

"He must be ancient then," Jillian remarked, smirking.

Edric looked at her, ready to let her have it, when he saw her smirking at him.

"You, young lady, are in for it."

"You threatened me earlier too," Jillian said, "and you didn't follow through, so I'm not too worried."

Kim snorted into the juice she was drinking.

"You had better not be threatening my daughter," Jillian's father frowned.

"Oh, lighten up, dad," Jillian said. "He was just teasing."

"Yes, something that you obviously don't do," Jillian's mom told him.

"Hey, I'm not that big of a fuddy-duddy."

Jillian busted out laughing. "Oh, dad, you are so funny."

Even Edric was grinning.

"Hey, can we join the party?" Orson asked, walking into the room with Wes.

"Hey, you two, what's the verdict?" Edric asked them.

"I think we definitely need the help of Hayden," Orson commented.

"Did you say, Hayden?" Warren asked, walking into the room.

Edric nodded.

"I never did like that man," he muttered.

"That's because he can whoop your a..," Orson said, looking at Jillian, then changing his word, "butt."

"Ha, ha," Warren replied, sitting down to eat.

Jillian finished eating and stood up, yawning. "Want to spend the night you two?" she asked Kim and Ruben.

"Can we?" Kim grinned. "I've always wanted to stay here."

"You have?" Ruben asked, "that's news to me."

Edric chuckled.

"Hopefully not as a hussy either," Ruben added.

Jillian frowned, as did Edric.

"What is he talking about, Jillian?" her dad asked.

"It's nothing, dad, something in the past, don't worry about it."

"Let's head up to bed also, shall we?" Nadine asked Henry.

He nodded his head and stood up.

Edric looked at Jillian, who was headed to the door.

"Jillian, did you want to speak with your parents before bed?"

She turned around. "I would rather not; I need to gather my thoughts first," Jillian replied.

"What's going on, Jillian?" her dad asked.

"I'm tired, dad. Can we talk tomorrow?" she asked him

"Very well, but first thing in the morning, I want to talk."

"Of course," she said, and after waiting for Kim and Ruben, she led them up the stairs and to a spare room.

"You can borrow my clothes for the night," Jillian told Kim.

"No way. You are so much tinier than I am," Kim protested.

"Whatever, friend," Jillian grinned.

"Can I borrow your clothes too?" Ruben teased.

Kim smacked his arm. "You are so weird."

"That's why you love me," he grinned as they headed into their room.

"Goodnight, Jillian," Kim grinned and shut the door.

Jillian headed to her room but then thought better of it. She was tired, but she was also restless, so she went back down the stairs and headed out to the backyard.

The back lawn was lit up with moonlight, and Jillian sighed as she sat down in a porch swing. What would she tell her parents about who she was or that she wasn't really theirs? How do you tell someone that?

"Luna," Jillian heard then. She looked up to see a large man standing in front of her. His eyes glowed blue as he watched her.

"Do I know you?" Jillian asked him, feeling the odd sensation that she did from somewhere.

"You might. My name is Hayden. Might I sit by you?"

She nodded, and he sat down. She could feel heat and a raw power emanating from him.

"Do you feel that?" he asked her.

"Feel what?" she asked.

He chuckled. "Your spirit speaks with mine."

"Why?"

"Because you and I, dear, are alike."

"What do you mean?" she asked him curiously.

"What do you remember of your childhood?" he asked her, changing the subject.

"Just the usual. I had good parents, but we moved a lot."

"Did you ever wonder why you moved so much?"

"It was because of my dad's work."

"Are you sure it wasn't to protect you?" he asked her.

She looked at him, and it seemed to her that his eyes were searching her soul.

"Why would they do that?"

"Because of who you are."

"But my parents don't know who I am."

"Don't they?" he asked her.

"But," she said.

He just smiled. "Weren't you ever curious as to why when you made new friends that your parents moved you?"

"But why?"

"Because they were afraid of you being found."

"But that is impossible."

"Is it now," he chuckled.

Jillian frowned. Did her parents really know who she was? And if so, why didn't they say anything?

"To protect you," Hayden told her.

"You can hear my thoughts?" Jillian asked, frowning.

"I can; they are yelling at me," he smiled.

"Who are you?" she whispered.

"That, my dear, is a good question, one that might have to wait until tomorrow to answer," he said, just as Edric walked out the door.

"Ah, my friend, I wondered where you had gone to," Edric smiled at Hayden.

"Yes, I was visiting with your lovely Luna," Hayden told Edric. "She is quite special."

"Yes, that I know," Edric replied, pulling Jillian to her feet and tucking her against him.

"More special than even you realize, Edric."

"Are you getting sentimental on me, old man?" Edric teased him.

Hayden chuckled. "Perhaps. Well, why don't we retire for the night? I know you have had an eventful day, Luna," he said and headed inside.

Jillian looked up at Edric as they headed back into the house.

"Who is he?"

"Even I am not sure," Edric replied as they headed to their room. "But I know that he is one of a kind, kind of like you, my love," he said.

"His eyes glow."

"Do they now," Edric chuckled, helping to undress Jillian for bed. He then tucked her in and climbed in by her.

"Will you tell me more about him?" she asked.

"Tomorrow, my love," he said and then kissed her into oblivion.

Chapter 39

When Jillian woke up, a warm arm was across her belly.

"Good morning, my love," Edric whispered in her ear. "How are you feeling today?"

"I'm okay," she said, rolling over so she could see him.

"Good," he said, scooting down the bed so he could kiss her stomach.

She blushed and pushed him away. "I need to talk with Hayden and my parents."

"Yes, that we do," Edric sighed, getting out of bed. Jillian admired his physique as he got up.

"I know you like what you see, and don't tell me you've seen bigger," he teased her as he headed to get dressed.

"How do you know?" she countered back.

He walked back to her and bent over her. "Oh really, and pray tell, who have you been admiring?" he asked her, grinning wickedly.

"No one," she squeaked as he climbed back onto the bed and started to tickle her.

"Tell me," he said as she laughed.

"Never," she gasped out.

"If you don't tell me, I will just have to get it out of you another way," he said, attacking her lips.

A knock sounded on the door then. "Alpha."

It was Hayden.

"We'll be right there," Alpha laughed and, hopping off the bed, headed to the bathroom. Jillian got up, grinning as she got dressed, and then she opened the door. Hayden nodded at her. "Good morning Luna."

"Good morning Hayden. Did you need to speak with us?"

"I do," he nodded.

"Do I need my parents also?"

"Not yet; we will speak with them later," he said.

Jillian nodded, and she headed down the hall with him, Edric following close behind.

The three of them headed into Edric's office, and Edric closed the door.

Jillian sat down on the couch, but Edric and Hayden stayed standing.

"Out with it, friend; what is going on?" Edric asked him.

He sighed. "You might not be happy with me."

"Oh?"

"I did something long ago," he looked at Jillian and smiled sadly, "but it was to save her life."

"You are the one who switched Jillian at birth," Edric realized.

"Yes, I did, but I knew she was special, and I knew that her life was in danger, so I snuck into the hospital and switched her with the daughter of Henry and Nadine," he sighed, looking at Jillian, "It was their real daughter that was killed, and your real parents, Jillian."

"But why?" Jillian asked softly.

"There is a great evil out there; they do not like people who are like you and me," he said sadly. "I am quite impressed at your skills, for as young as you are, you are very powerful, and that," he then frowned, "is why I am here. Your life is in incredible danger."

"We know," Edric frowned. "Dr. Hess told us."

"Yes, good Dr. Hess," he said, shaking his head.

"Hayden, what is going on?" Edric asked him.

"Dr. Hess left last night to run and get some things from home; he didn't make it back."

Jillian gasped. "He was murdered?"

Hayden nodded. "I am sorry. Whoever was threatening him carried out that threat."

"Why was I not informed?" Edric snarled.

"You were sleeping, because you needed it," Hayden pointed out.

Jillian felt sick to her stomach, and not because of her pregnancy.

Edric's wolf growled. *"We need to stop them Edric, before Jillian is killed."*

Edric looked at his friend Hayden. "We are getting married this weekend."

"I know, that is why you called me. I will help you as much as I can. I just hope it is enough."

A knock sounded on the door then.

"Come in," Edric said.

Kim peeked her head in. "Sorry to interrupt, I was wondering if Jillian was ready for breakfast? We pregnant girls need to eat."

Edric frowned. "Sorry, love," he said, pulling Jillian to her feet. "Are you hungry?"

"Starving," she said.

"Go eat; we can discuss this later," he told her.

She nodded and headed out the door with Kim.

"So, how are you feeling this morning?" Jillian asked her friend as they headed to the dining room.

"Better, you?"

"Great, I think."

"What's wrong?"

"Just too much going on," Jillian sighed.

"I hope that things can settle down soon," Kim said.

"If only," Jillian replied, walking into the room.

Her parents were eating already, as were Warren, Orson, and Wes.

"Luna," they said.

She nodded at them and sat down.

"Luna," her father said, shaking his head.

"Oh, come on, father, quit playing dumb," Jillian spit out. "You know exactly what that is."

He frowned. "No, please enlighten me, daughter."

She stood up. "No, why don't you, father, or should I call you Henry. Why didn't you even say anything to me? Why didn't you tell me who you were?" she began to cry.

"I think we need to talk," Jillian's mom said, nodding at her husband.

"Yes, let's," he said.

Kim sat at the table in shock. What was going on? Orson and Wes exchanged a glance, and Warren looked amused.

Jillian walked out of the room, her parents following her and into the office where Edric and Hayden were still visiting.

"Hayden," Henry said, walking into the room.

"Henry," Hayden responded.

"So, you know each other," Jillian accused.

"Jillian, perhaps you should sit down," her supposed mother said.

"No, I will not sit; I want you to tell me why you lied to me my whole life? Why didn't you say anything?" she cried.

"I am so sorry, honey, but we had to protect you," Nadine said. "We had to save your life."

"At the sacrifice of our own daughter," Henry spit out angrily, glaring at Hayden.

"Your daughter was doomed from the start Henry. She would not have lived long, and you know it."

Nadine began to cry. "But she was ours."

"Yes, and I am sorry, Nadine, but Jillian's life was so important. I am sorry, I really am, for making you choose, but Jillian was worth saving."

"So you said," Henry said, "and we don't regret raising her, but we need to know exactly why she is so important. You promised to tell us when the time came."

"Yes," Hayden sighed, "I did."

Hayden looked at Jillian, who looked like she was in shock.

Edric walked to her and pulled her up to him, holding her.

"Well?" Henry asked him.

"Jillian is more important than I am; that is why I sent you here," Hayden said, looking at Henry and Nadine, "so that Jillian could meet Edric. He is the only one who can protect her."

"So, it wasn't just my parents moving here because my dad had work?" Jillian asked.

"No, I sent all of you here," Hayden said.

"Yes, and then Henry dug up my ancestors' graves," Edric frowned.

"Yes, sorry about that. But it is here that we can finally catch whoever is after Jillian."

"But no one has harmed me before," Jillian said.

"That is because I have stopped them," Hayden informed her.

"You saved her from harm her whole life?" Edric asked.

"Yes, that is why I was not around much Alpha, I was keeping her safe."

"I see," Edric nodded.

"So, why is she so important?" Henry asked.

"Because she is going to unite all the werewolves around the world."

"You knew all along that Edric was a werewolf?" Jillian asked Henry.

Henry shrugged. "I did, but I couldn't let on now, could I."

Jillian sighed. "Liars surround me."

"Sorry, honey," Nadine said. "We were only trying to protect you."

"I know, and I thank you for that and for trying to give me a normal life. I really did love having you as parents," Jillian admitted, hugging Nadine.

"We would still like to be your parents if that is okay," she said.

"I would like that," Jillian agreed.

Hayden frowned. "Well, now that that is taken care of, we need to get rid of the person after Jillian."

"Do you know who it is?" Edric asked.

"No, but it is someone you know, that much I do know," Hayden frowned.

Edric frowned. "That is not good. So we can't trust anyone."

"No, not a soul. What I have told you must not leave this room," Hayden nodded, "or all of you could die."

Chapter 40

Jillian didn't know what to do. Who did they know that would want her dead? And why would she be the one to save all the werewolves? She wasn't that wonderful. It sounded way too complicated, and she wanted to run and hide, but she was a Luna; she wasn't supposed to do that, right?

A knock sounded on the door then, and Nadine answered it.

"Hi, I'm wondering if Jillian is okay?" Kim asked, looking worried.

"You can come in, Kim," Jillian said, still in Edric's arms. She stepped back to talk to Kim.

"So, what just happened back there?" Kim asked.

"A big misunderstanding," Jillian sighed.

"So, your parents really are your parents?" Kim asked.

"Yes," Jillian nodded. "I was just acting hormonal," she lied.

"Yes, that is going to happen," Kim nodded.

"Plus, I had to ask them to forgive me for the way I acted earlier."

"You are forgiven, of course," Nadine smiled at Jillian. "So, our meal was interrupted, and I know you haven't eaten, Jillian. Shall we go back and eat?"

Jillian nodded. "Yes, let's."

Her mom tucked an arm about her waist and headed back to the dining hall.

Orson, Wes, and Warren were just finishing up when they walked back in.

"Is everything okay?" Orson asked Jillian.

"Yes, sorry, pregnancy hormones. I was just angry at my mom."

"So, she really is your mom then?" he teased.

"Yes," Jillian shrugged. "I was just angry over some stupid things."

Orson nodded. "Alpha, since Hayden is here, let's work on the backyard perimeter."

Edric nodded. "Good idea. Let me eat first; you three head out with Hayden and get started."

The men nodded and left the room as Edric sat down. Carla walked back in a moment later with warm food.

"Here you are," she said, placing it on the table. "I figured you would be coming back."

"Thanks, Carla," Jillian smiled at her.

"Why don't we girls go to the sunroom and start planning your wedding?" Carla suggested after they had eaten, and Edric had headed outside.

"I think that's a great idea," Jillian agreed. She then looked at Kim. "Where is Ruben? I noticed he's not attached to your side today."

"School," she chuckled. "He can't miss anymore, or he won't graduate, so I sent him this morning."

"He was okay with leaving you here?"

"He was, knowing that I would be well taken care of if I got sick. Where is the doctor this morning anyway?"

Jillian frowned. "He had to leave last night."

She didn't want to tell Kim that he had been killed.

"So Ruben will be by after school then?" Jillian asked her friend.

"Yes, then we'll head home."

"You can stay another night if you want," Jillian told her. "No, that's okay; I miss my own bed and my own clothes," she said, looking down at the clothes she had on from the day before. "Your clothes are too small for me," she pointed out to Jillian.

"Sorry about that."

"No problem, but if that's okay, I'll go home when Ruben gets here."

"Of course, friend," Jillian smiled at her, and they headed to the sunroom.

Carla went to get a notebook so they could start planning a wedding.

"Let's make this simple," Jillian told the ladies. "I don't need something extravagant, although that would be nice," she sighed, "but where we only have a few days, we had better make it simple."

"So, where are we getting your dress?" Kim asked her.

"Edric is sending in a tailor," Carla spoke up. "He doesn't want Jillian out shopping in case she is harmed again, and it might get ruined if we end up having a war because whoever is after Jillian might be there."

"Do you think that they are going to start something with all the wolves that will be there?" Kim asked.

She then looked at Nadine. "Oops, sorry, Mrs. Everett, you probably don't know about werewolves, do you?" Kimberly asked. Nadine grinned. "I have known about all of you my whole life."

Kim's jaw dropped. "Jillian, did you know that she knew?"

"No, I just found out today, actually. It was kind of a shock."

"I bet," Kim laughed. "So where were we, oh yes, a dress."

"I was kind of hoping to pick out my own dress."

"You can, Luna," Carla promised. "But it needs to be simple so that it can be done within a few days."

"What, no diamonds sewn into the gown?" Jillian grinned.

"I can't even see you with that," Nadine said. "It's just not you."

"I know," Jillian agreed. "I like simple, but not too simple."

"Show some skin, girl," Kim grinned at Jillian.

"Now girls," Nadine shook her head, "we don't need the other wolves drooling over the Alpha's bride, do we?"

"Sure spoil my fun," Jillian grinned at Nadine. "Fine, but I still want a say in my dress and what it looks like."

"The tailor will be here around 3:00 to measure you and show you some patterns," Carla informed Jillian.

"Now, how about a cake?" she then said. "I can make it if it's not too difficult."

"I have always wanted this certain cake," Jillian admitted. "Can I have your phone to show you?"

Carla handed it over so Jillian could pull up a picture of the cake; she then passed it back to Carla.

"Oh, that is nice, and yes, I can do that."

It was four tiers, with lacework frosting and fresh rose petals on it.

"That is lovely," her mom said.

"I think so, and it's not too hard to do, at least I hope not," Jillian said.

"How about food?" Carla then said. "Edric wanted it catered so I wouldn't have to do it all."

"That's fine, but we need to make sure the caterers go through a thorough background check and are checked at the door for weapons," Jillian pointed out.

"I don't think the Alpha thought of that one," Carla smirked and then nodded. "He didn't, and he will make sure of it."

Jillian sighed.

"You want to have a mind link, I know," Carla smiled at her, "but sometimes it would be nice not to have one."

"Yes, like the time right after Ruben and I had just met, and I snuck out one night to go to a party, and I didn't tell him," Kimberly laughed.

"I take it he found out anyway?" Jillian asked her.

"Yep, especially when the cops busted the party, and he had to come and get me."

Jillian laughed. "I could see you doing that."

"It was fun while it lasted," Kim shrugged, a smile on her face.

"So, a menu, what to serve?" Jillian turned to Carla.

"Do you want elegant or simple?" Carla asked her.

"More on the elegant side if we are to have other Alpha's here."

"Very well; I will have a menu sent over from the local caterers by tonight."

Jillian nodded, and then they decided on what flowers and what florist and who would make her bouquet.

By the time they were winding down, Ruben had walked in the door to get Kim. She stood up and kissed him. He patted her stomach. "How have you been doing today?"

"I've been okay, actually," she smiled. "I've had a nice day."

"Good," he smiled. "Can I steal you away?"

He frowned then. "I guess not; the Alpha wants me in the backyard."

He kissed Kim and headed out the door.

"Might I interrupt your party?" came a voice then. The girls looked up to see Adam and his band walk in.

"Adam, what are you doing here?" Jillian asked him.

"The Alpha invited us to stay, and since we are playing at your wedding," he shrugged, "I thought, why not? I have always wanted to stay in a palace."

"Oh, that's great."

"He did tell me not to flirt with you, though," he chuckled. "As if that would stop me."

Jillian laughed. "You do know that he is my mate, yes?"

Adam nodded. "Yes, I know Luna; I was just kidding. So what do you have to eat around here? I am starving."

"I'll take them to the kitchen," Kim volunteered, looking starry-eyed at Adam.

"Matt, how are you feeling?" Jillian asked him, joining them as they headed to the kitchen, Carla, on their heels to make sure they had plenty to eat.

"Good, thanks to you," he grinned at her. "I owe you everything Luna," he said and kissed her hand. "What can I do to repay you? You name it; I will do it."

"How about you keep your hands off of her?" Edric said, walking into the kitchen and frowning at him.

How did he do that? Jillian wondered. He always knew when another man touched her. She wished she could do the same when another woman touched her man.

Matt backed away. "Sorry, Alpha, I am just indebted to the Luna. She saved my life."

"Yes, I know at the expense of her health," he growled.

"I am fine, you big bully," Jillian said to him, making the men chuckle.

"You are pregnant, Luna," Edric said, "and saving people is not good on you or our baby."

"You are pregnant? Damn," Matt muttered. "I am sorry, Luna, for compromising your health."

"Don't think anything of it," Jillian told him, glaring at Edric. "I am fine, and so is the baby. Now, why don't you men eat while I go have a chat with my soon-to-be husband."

The guys grinned at her as she pushed Edric out the door and down the hall to his office. She closed the door behind her, and he pulled her into his arms, kissing her soundly. "I don't like it when others flirt with you."

"I am yours, Edric; how many times do I have to tell you that?"

"I would like to hurt them when they look at you the way they do."

"Stop it," she frowned up at him. "You are acting way too jealous. I know I am your mate, but give them a break. They are men, men lust after women; it is the nature of things."

He growled. "I don't like it."

"You can't stop it," Jillian told him, "besides, it's not like the men are the only ones drooling. Kim is in there lusting after Adam."

"She had better not be; Ruben will be furious."

"Just like the men lust after us, women do the same thing to men."

"You had better not be eyeing him," Edric frowned deeply.

"I can look, Edric; you did plenty of looking and touching before I met you, so don't go there," she pointed out to him.

He sighed. "Yes, it is true until I met you."

"No, not true. You still kept them here, even after you kidnapped me, remember?"

He sighed. "Jillian, that is in the past; I made some stupid mistakes, okay? Please, don't bring that up again."

"I'm just saying, you tell us girls, not to lust after men when it's okay for you to lust after women?" she asked, getting angry, tears forming in her eyes.

"I said no such thing, and I am sorry for ever having women here; I truly am," he told her, pulling her tight to him. "I hope you will forgive me one day."

Jillian sniffled. "I will; it's just these stupid pregnancy hormones; they are making me moody."

Edric smiled down at his mate. "I understand, love, just try not to take your anger out on me, okay?"

She nodded. "I'll try not to, as long as you do the same."

"You have my word, my love. He kissed her softly. "Now, what were you girls doing besides feeding the band?"

"Talking boring wedding stuff. Can I come outside and see what you are doing?"

Edric nodded. "Of course, love. You can see the security we are setting up to keep intruders out."

"Okay," Jillian smiled at her mate. He took her hand and led her out of his study and outside. Warren, Wes, Orson, Hayden, and Ruben were visiting when they walked out.

"Well, Alpha, Luna, it seems that we have done the best we can," Hayden told them, pointing to a laser system that lined the edges of the backyard. "It is set up so it will keep out unwanted guests."

"Does it hurt when it touches the skin?" Jillian asked.

"It hurts like the dickens," Wes chuckled, showing her a burn on his arm. "If I weren't a wolf, it would have cut me through."

"Ouch," Jillian said. "Do you want me to heal you?"

"No," Edric frowned. "You have healed enough people for now, Jillian; you need to rest."

"He is right," Hayden replied. "You need to protect yourself and your little one."

"He knows what he is talking about, Jillian," Edric told her. "I want you to rest."

"Besides," Wes grinned, "I think a scar is kind of cool."

"Of course you would," Jillian teased him.

"Alpha, do you want certain songs from us?" Adam asked them as he and his men headed outside.

"No, just whatever is popular," he told Adam.

"Luna, how about you?"

"Your newest songs," she told him.

"You mean, Girls Like You?" he grinned at her.

"Yes, I really like that one."

"You should; it is about you," Matt chuckled.

"Too bad you're getting married to the King of the Alpha's," Adam grinned at Jillian.

"Yes, it's truly awful," she sighed, making the men laugh.

"Ruben, I think I need to go home; I don't feel well," Kim said, heading out to them.

"Of course, love," he told her and picking her up into his arms, he started to head inside with her.

"Bye Kim, see you tomorrow?" Jillian asked.

"Yes, after school," she said as they disappeared inside.

"I think it is time we go eat," Edric said, looking at his men and Jillian.

They nodded.

"Might I speak with Jillian before you do?" Hayden asked Edric.

"Yes, but don't stay out long; she needs food and rest."

Hayden nodded and motioned Jillian to sit on the swing.

He sat down by her once again.

"What is it?" she asked him.

"I am sure you have some questions for me."

"I do."

"Go ahead."

"What do you mean by me bringing all the wolves together?"

"You are a very powerful young lady. You have no idea how powerful you are."

"How come you saved me? Why would someone want me dead?"

Hayden sighed. "There is a very evil wolf out there, leading a group of rogues that would love to see you dead."

"But why?"

"Because they are descendants of the ones who killed the High King and Queen, and they see the same potential in you."

"Tell me about my parents."

"They were grand people. Very kind and very great. They made your Alpha look like a tyrant," he chuckled.

"So, my father was an Alpha?" she whispered.

"Yes, the Highest of High."

"But, Edric, he is the king."

"He is also the son of the Beta to your parents."

"But how come he didn't tell me?"

"Because he wouldn't have known that his father was *your* father's Beta. Besides, he was only seven at the time."

"Oh."

"What happened to Edric's father?"

"He was killed while serving your parents."

"But how?"

Hayden sighed. "Your mother had just given birth to you and was still in the hospital when an ancient and evil wolf found out who you were, and your potential."

"But, I was only a baby."

"Yes, but you were powerful, and he could sense it. So he sent his men to kill your parents. I could not save them; I knew that the evil one was on his way. I could only save you, so I begged Nadine and Henry to trade their dying baby with you. Their little one didn't have long to live; she was born without a valve in her heart; it was only a matter of hours or days before she was gone, so Henry and Nadine agreed. A few hours later, the men destroyed the nursery, killing their child and your parents. Edric's father tried to save your parents but died also. I will never forgive myself for letting them die, but I knew that they would forgive me, knowing that I had saved you."

"Why couldn't you have saved my parents, though?" Jillian asked, tears streaming down her face.

"Because little one, I was not strong enough to do so. I wish with all of my heart I could bring them back for you; I wish I could have saved them, but this man was so evil, no one could stand up to him."

Jillian gasped then, remembering how she had been told that the Great King and Queen had been killed along with their baby in the nursery.

"Hayden."

"Yes, Luna, you are their daughter. The one that everyone thought was the great Luna Princess was not her. You are her."

"So, what happened to the one who killed my parents?"

"He is dead, but he has many followers, and one of them is after you."

"Kelson, was he one of them?"

"He was but one of them. He was jealous, but he was also working under the new evil one."

"But you don't know who."

"No, they are blocking me out, and that worries me. I am greatly worried about you, Jillian. Your life is so precious, and I can't do a thing about stopping the evil one; it will be up to you."

"But how?"

"You will need to have your wolf help you."

"What?" Jillian asked, then fainted from shock.

Chapter 41

When Jillian woke up, she was in her bed, and Edric was by her, watching her.

"What happened?" she asked him.

"You fainted. Hayden said it was from lack of food, that I need to feed you more; you are eating for two, he reminded me." Edric smiled at her. "I have food here for you if you are hungry."

"I am," she admitted and wondered why Hayden didn't tell Edric why she had really fainted.

"Edric, can you mind link with Hayden like you do with the others?"

"No, he is more like you, which bothers me because I swear that man is keeping secrets from me."

He helped Jillian sit up and handed her a plate of food. "What were you two talking about?"

"My real parents," Jillian whispered as she began to eat.

"He knew them, didn't he."

"Yes," she nodded, "and so did your parents."

"My parents?" he looked confused. "How did my parents know your parents?"

"Your father was my father's Beta."

Edric swore. He looked at Jillian. "You have got to be kidding me," he whispered.

"No," Jillian said, shaking her head.

"That means your father was the High Alpha King."

"Yes."

Edric let out a deep sigh. "No wonder so many are after you. You are the next in line for the throne. But everyone thought you were dead."

"Hayden said he switched me at birth to save me, remember?"

"I do. I didn't realize he switched out the princess though, no wonder your adoptive parents moved so much," he whistled in awe. He was sitting next to the High Queen, unbelievable.

"Edric, you hold the title of King now. Why?"

Edric looked at her and smiled softly. "I only hold the title until someone, the rightful heir, takes my place, and that is you, my love."

"But I am not a wolf."

"But you are a healer and a seer, which makes you even more valuable."

"But we are getting married, which makes you the High King," Jillian insisted.

Edric kissed her. "I love you, my sweet, High Queen," he chuckled. "And yes, I suppose it does make me the true High King once we are wed."

"How did you go from being a Beta to an Alpha?" she asked him as she ate.

"After your father and my father died, there wasn't anyone to take their place. I was a Beta at the age of seven and scared spitless. That is when Hayden stepped in and guided me."

"So, who was Alpha while you were growing up?"

Edric frowned. "A distant cousin of your parents. He was the only one who was related. He was an evil man, and when I turned 18, I challenged him for the spot of Alpha and won."

"How?"

"I killed him. That is the only way one can take the spot from another Alpha."

"Oh," Jillian said, handing Edric her plate so he could set it on the nightstand.

"You aren't upset about me killing your cousin?"

"Why would I be? You said he was evil."

"Very evil. He wanted all humans wiped from the earth or changed into a werewolf."

"Is that possible? Changing humans?"

"Not that I know of. Legends have it wrong when they say a bite from a werewolf will make you one. That is not how it works. Werewolves exist because their parents had them, and it was in their blood, just as their parents and their grandparents before them."

Edric pulled Jillian to sit on his lap. "No wonder Hayden took such an interest in you. He knew who you were."

"Yes, and I think that is why I fainted. I was in shock."

Edric chuckled. "I can see why. That is a lot to take in. But rest assured, my love, I will be by your side every step of the way."

"I know, and Edric, please don't tell anyone. If word leaks out who I am..."

"Yes, my love, it would be horrible."

"Promise not even to tell your men?"

"Of course, love, I won't say a word."

He then pulled off her clothes, lay by her, and kissed her stomach. Then he started talking. "Hey, little one in there. I can't wait to see you; you are going to be some great wolf pup, I know because you have an incredible mother."

Jillian giggled.

Edric looked at her. "Hey, I am being serious here."

"Oh, please continue," she laughed.

"Your mother is a handful too, just to let you know," Edric continued. "But I love her with all of my soul."

Jillian smiled at Edric as he pulled her into his arms. "I love you too, High King," she whispered.

He kissed her softly. "Goodnight, my High Queen, in four days, you and I will be wed, and we will live happily ever after."

When Jillian got up the following day, Edric was gone. She sighed as she got up but smiled, remembering Edric talking to their baby the night before. He really was a sweet man, and she was glad she would marry him.

Jillian got dressed and then went to eat breakfast. The hall was quiet, and she ended up eating alone. She wondered if Kim was at school or if she was having morning sickness, and then she wondered if Edric would be mad if she went; yes, he probably would be. Her life was in even greater danger now, and she hadn't even told Edric that Hayden said she had a wolf in her. It made sense, she supposed, since her parents had been wolves, but how come her wolf hadn't shown itself yet? Did she even want to be a wolf? She wasn't so sure. It would be scary, especially shifting for the first time. She frowned, wondering how to bring out her wolf or if Hayden had been feeding her a story. But he hadn't lied to her yet, had he? Maybe she would have to have another visit with him.

Jillian finished eating and was heading from the dining hall when Adam and his men walked in. "Luna," he nodded to her.

"Good morning Adam."

"We were wondering if we could practice in the backyard after we eat?" he asked her.

"I don't see why not? There is plenty of room out there."

"Think the Alpha could get us a stage?"

"I am sure he could," Jillian told him. "I'll go find him and ask."

"You can't mind link?" Adam asked her in confusion.

"I'm mostly human, Adam; I don't have that capability."

"Even though you have been marked?"

"Even though I have been marked."

"That is crazy."

"It's okay, though; then, the Alpha doesn't know everything running through my head."

"Yes, that would be okay, I suppose," Adam chuckled. "So, what are you up to today?"

"Not sure yet."

"You can come and watch us practice."

"I'll get back with you on that," she said and walked out.

Jillian headed outside, but the backyard was quiet also. Where was everyone?

"Jillian," she heard and turned around. Nadine was headed to her. True, she was still her mom, but it seemed weird knowing that she wasn't really her mom.

"Hey mom, where is everyone?"

"Edric and the others went to town to get some more security systems for the house. Someone stepped past the barrier last night even though it was on."

"Wow, did it kill them?"

"There's not a body, but there was blood. Edric is pretty upset."

"Yes, I could see him being so. What are they going to do to stop whoever it is?"

"I don't know, honey, but it is best if you stay inside today. If whoever it is, is still out there, I don't want them trying to come for you."

"Okay, I was just out here trying to find out where everyone was."

Nadine nodded and tucked an arm about Jillian's waist, leading her back into the house. As they stepped inside, Jillian heard an unearthly howl. She turned back around, but Nadine ushered her inside. "Go to the office. It is safe there."

"What was that?"

"I think a wolf just tried to cross the barrier," she frowned and ushered Jillian into the office. "I'll call and let Edric know."

"Where are the other guards?"

"They are headed to the noise. Stay here, please," she said and closed the door behind Jillian.

Jillian sighed and sat in the office chair. Who had crossed the barrier? It obviously hurt them, whoever it was. She hoped it wasn't Adam or one of his band members. That wouldn't be good.

Jillian heard another howling and jumped. Then she watched as five giant wolves ran around the mansion's front; Edric was among them. She felt safer and let out a sigh of relief. Obviously, whoever had tried to get past the barrier had made Edric concerned enough that he had returned. She wished then that she could be out there. She wondered what it would be like to run free like that and shift without thought. Would she ever be able to? Would her wolf even wake up so she could?

"*Hello, I am right here, and yes, I have been waiting for a long time for you to acknowledge me,*" came a voice.

Jillian about fell out of her chair.

"*Who are you?*" Jillian asked.

"*I'm your wolf, duh. My name is Aria, and it's about time you talked to me; I mean, hello, I've been here since you were born.*"

"*How did I not know this?*"

"*I was that little voice in the back of your mind all these years,*" she chuckled.

"*So, I have a wolf, after all.*"

"*Um, yeah,*" Aria laughed. "*Want to let me take over so I can show you how pretty I am?*"

"*Oh, hell, no,*" Jillian said.

Aria chuckled. "*Okay, okay, we can wait, but your life is going to be in more danger the longer you wait to shift.*"

"*Does it hurt to shift?*" Jillian asked.

"*The first time, yes, but it's not that bad. Besides, I heard you thinking about wanting to be out there with the other wolves; I don't blame you. It is pretty freaking awesome to be a wolf,*" Aria chuckled.

"*So you say, but I'm scared.*"

"*Oh, please, girl. You, scared? You are the High Queen, a healer, and a seer; no one or nothing should scare you.*"

"*But I'm only 18; I think I have that right.*"

"*Okay, okay, you are young still. But with my help, I will make you strong. Hayden will help us also. He is a good man.*"

"I gathered that. So now that you are here with me, does that mean that I can mind link with Edric?"

Aria chuckled. *"I thought you didn't want to."*

"I don't really, not right now anyway."

"Good, because if anyone finds out right now that you can shift, you might end up dead really fast and really soon."

"But how do I keep Edric out of my head so he doesn't know you are there? Because if he finds out, and he accidentally lets someone else know, that could be bad."

"I will hide again, at least until after the wedding, and then you can break him the news."

"So, he won't know until then?"

"Nope, my lips and mind are sealed."

"Okay," Jillian sighed. *"Won't he be surprised?"*

"Yes, yes, he will be," Aria laughed and faded into the background once again.

The door opened then, and Edric walked in. He walked over to Jillian and picked her up out of the chair, holding her close to him.

"When Nadine told us that a wolf had crossed the barriers, I was extremely worried and hurried back here. Are you okay?"

"I'm fine," Jillian assured him.

"Good," he sighed.

"Who was it?"

"We don't know. Whoever it was, was gone before we came back."

"Why are they testing the barrier?"

"I don't know, but it worries me. That is why we are going to strengthen it."

"What do you mean?"

"Hayden is going to rewire it and make it so if any wolf touches it, they will be gravely injured or die."

"What if one of us touches it?" Jillian asked him, worried.

"We won't. The lasers are bright enough that any one of us should know to stay away from it."

"Why are they so determined to get past? Why not come through the front door if they want me."

Edric frowned. "Because there are guards all around the front, and now the back. I am not taking any chances, and because of that, I want our wedding moved up."

"Moved up? it's only four days away as it is."

"Yes, but I want it to be tomorrow. I have already informed the other Alpha's."

"What about my dress? Which, by the way, I never saw the tailor yesterday."

"Yes, about that," Edric frowned. "She was kidnapped on her way here."

"What? Why didn't you tell me?"

"Because I didn't want you to worry."

"Where is she? Is she okay?"

"I have the police looking for her."

"But why kidnap her?"

"Because she was coming here."

Jillian's eyes teared up. "I feel so bad. First, Dr. Hess, and now the tailor. When is it going to stop Edric?"

Edric kissed her forehead. "I am hoping tomorrow. We are going to get married, and hopefully, bring out whoever is after you."

"And if they don't show up?"

"I can guarantee you that they will."

"I'm worried, Edric."

"So am I love, so am I."

Chapter 42

Hayden walked into the office then and nodded at the two of them. "Edric, a word?"

Edric nodded. "Stay here. I want to make sure it is safe before you come outside," he told Jillian.

"Okay."

"Good, they're gone," Aria chuckled as the door closed behind the men.

"Aria, I am worried. If someone is trying to test the barriers, that means they are determined to come and get me."

"Oh, posh, girl. You can take any one of them down if Edric would let you."

"What do you mean?"

"I mean, once you shift, you will be unstoppable."

"Oh. You are probably right. Edric will probably try and be too overprotective, though, when he sees I can shift to a wolf."

"You had better believe it; that is why you and I aren't saying a word until after the wedding."

"We will be attacked tomorrow, though."

"Of course, we will be. It is too much of a temptation not to attack. The one after you doesn't care who he kills, as long as he can get to you."

"I wonder how many people are on his side?"

"Too many, more than likely."

"I wonder if I will be strong enough to fight tomorrow. If I have never shifted before, where can I practice shifting? If Edric heard me, well, all hell would break loose," Jillian said.

Aria chuckled. *"You had better believe it. Wolves have excellent hearing. I'm sorry to tell you, but you will have to wait until tomorrow to shift. But where you are a healer, you should be able to shift easier."*

"I wonder if my mother could heal."

"Yes, you are just like her, but more powerful, especially when you get angry. Your mother couldn't bring people to their knees like you can."

"I can do that, can't I," Jillian chuckled. *"Just wait until everyone finds out about you."*

"I know, it will be so awesome," Aria agreed.

Jillian sighed then. *"I wish that I could have the wedding of my dreams tomorrow. But no, I will be forced into wearing something I know I will hate, plus no cake, no decorations, no bouquet."*

"Girl, you are marrying the hottest man alive, and you are worried about your dress? Get over yourself," Aria chuckled. *"You are a High Queen, not some teenage girl who isn't getting her way."*

"But I am a teenage girl not getting her way," Jillian pouted.

"Oh, please, girl. Suck it up. I am sure Edric would give you the wedding of your dreams after this is over."

"You are right, he probably would, and yes, I need to suck it up."

"Good girl. I can hear Edric."

And then Aria was gone again.

Edric walked back in, and walking to Jillian, he picked her up and then set her onto his lap, kissing her fervently. "I love you, sweet Luna of mine."

"I love you too." She looked at him. "You are worried."

"Very."

"We can put off our wedding if you want."

"No, I want to marry you, my sweet Luna, and I know it's not going to be your dream wedding, but I want us wed. I want others to know that you are mine and mine alone."

"Don't they already know that?" she grinned.

"Well, I suppose so, but I know we can catch whoever is after you if we hold a wedding."

"I know," she sighed, leaning her head against his chest. He rubbed her back. "How are you feeling?"

"Okay."

He kissed her softly, then stroked her belly. He sighed. "We are going to make good parents; you know that?"

"I hope so."

"I know so," he said, kissing her again. He then gently put her on her feet. "I need to make sure the other Alpha's are on their way. I'll see you for dinner."

She nodded and watched him walk out.

"*He's worried about me*," Jillian said.

"*No duh, we are carrying his baby, the heir to the throne.*"

"*Yes, I suppose we are*," Jillian sighed.

"*You're going to be fine; everything will work out, you know that.*"

"*I know; I just hope Edric isn't upset at me when he finds out I am a wolf.*"

"*He will be thrilled, believe me,*" Aria chuckled.

Chapter 43

Everyone called it an early night. It would be a long day the next day, and if Hayden and Edric were right, they would be attacked.

Jillian cuddled up against Edric in bed.

"I'm worried about tomorrow Edric."

"I also love, but I know we are going to end this whole thing tomorrow, finally."

"You are sure of that."

"Of course, I am. Who is going to resist coming and destroying our wedding? I just hope we at least get to say our vows," he chuckled.

"I do, too," she sighed.

"Don't be too worried, love. I have an army for tomorrow. We will be okay, and I will be right by you if and when something happens, okay?"

"Okay, love," Jillian sighed. "Do you think Hayden will help stop them?"

"I am sure he will help."

"I wonder why he isn't a wolf."

"He's like you, my love, which is interesting to me. Especially since your parents are werewolves."

"I guess I am an anomaly," Jillian told him.

"That you are my love, but it doesn't matter; I love you just the way you are."

"Oh, really."

"Oh yes," he chuckled, pulling her on top of him.

"Show me," she whispered.

"My pleasure."

Jillian fell asleep in Edric's arms, but then a dream started, and Jillian knew it would be bad. She woke up screaming. Edric pulled her into his arms. "Shh, I am here, love. You had a dream again?"

She nodded into his shoulder.

"Want to tell me about it?"

"Tomorrow," she whispered. "There will be so many of them, more than you thought, attacking us."

"Will we win?"

"I don't know," she whispered, "all I saw was blood and destruction."

"Do you know who is the one leading the rogues?"

"No," she lied. She had seen who it was, and she was in absolute shock; it couldn't be them, but her dreams never lied. One thing was for sure; she would make sure she protected her Alpha; that was the most important thing. She couldn't let him die.

Edric whispered encouraging words in her ears until she finally fell asleep.

The morning came too soon, and when Jillian got up, Edric was gone again. She sighed; of course, he wouldn't stick around on their wedding day.

Aria chuckled. "*Come on, girl; it is going to be a big day for us.*"

"*Yes, yes, it is,*" Jillian agreed. "*I wonder what color you are?*"

"*Hmm, not sure, but I know I will be beautiful.*"

"*I am sure you will be.*"

"*I can't believe the one over the rogues is him,*" Aria then said.

"*You can see my dreams?*"

"*Of course. I am a part of you, so what you see, I see.*"

"*Wow, and I know, it's crazy, right? But I couldn't tell Edric; he would be devastated.*"

"*You are right; he will be. But you will need to be extra cautious.*"

"*I will be, especially knowing who it is.*"

Jillian then headed into the bathroom, did her daily routine, and dressed into a skirt and blouse before heading down to breakfast. The palace was busy as she walked down the hall. Several men were wandering about; all of them bore their necks to her as she passed. They must be the other Alpha's, Jillian thought.

"*They are and here to protect you*," Aria said.

"*I feel honored.*"

"*You should be; it's not every day that the whole nation's Alphas gather.*"

Jillian headed to the kitchen and found it full of people getting ready for the wedding. They all stopped and bore their necks to her.

"Luna, it is a pleasure to meet you," a tall and beautiful woman with a chef's jacket on said, bowing to her. "I am Scarlett, your caterer."

"Nice to meet you, Scarlett."

"We were just about to start cooking for your wedding. Would you like some samples?"

"I would," Jillian replied, "but breakfast first."

"Right here," Den replied from the middle of the crowd. He handed her a plate loaded with all kinds of protein. "You need your strength on your wedding day," he winked at her. She blushed at his innuendo, making him chuckle.

"Thanks, Den," Jillian said and headed into the dining hall.

Edric was there finishing his breakfast. He covered his eyes when she walked in.

"Edric, what are you doing?" she asked him.

"I heard it's bad luck to see the bride on the wedding day before the wedding," he chuckled.

She walked over to him and pulled his hand away. "You are funny, and I am not worried."

"Good," he said, kissing her. "How are you feeling?"

"Okay, I guess."

"I brought in more men. After your dream last night, I don't want to take any chances."

"Thank you, Edric."

"Anytime, my love." He sighed. "I will be glad when this day is over. Not that I can't wait to get married," he started.

"I know what you mean, Edric, and I agree. I want this whole mess over with."

He looked at her curiously. She looked worried but also happy and something else.

"Jillian, what are you hiding from me?" Edric asked her.

"What do you mean?"

"You are hiding something, I can tell."

"Edric, can I tell you at our wedding?"

"Is it something I am going to be upset about?"

"Yes, and no," Jillian said.

"Jillian."

"Edric, you need to trust me. It is our wedding day; we need to be happy and not argue, okay?" she batted her eyes at him, making him chuckle.

"If I find out it is something important," he then threatened.

"Edric, I love you, but trust me."

"That is my line," he chuckled.

"Alpha, the stage is set up outside for the band," Emerson said, walking into the room.

"Good. Go tell Adam they can practice now."

"Where is Hayden?" Jillian asked as Emerson walked out.

"He is making sure last-minute details are taken care of."

"Oh, I wanted to talk to him."

"That's fine; I'll send him inside to visit, but stay out of the backyard."

"Why?"

"I want you safe inside, where there are several Alpha's who will make sure you are protected."

"And you? What will you be doing?"

"I will be inside for part of the day. But I need to make sure everything is set for this afternoon."

"Who is marrying us?"

"Hayden."

"Okay, and where are Nadine and Henry?"

"Jillian, they are still your parents."

"I know, but it's weird, calling them that."

"You need to, for now, and they are out in the backyard helping."

"Oh. But you aren't worried about their safety?"

"No."

"Why not?"

"Because the person responsible for all of this is not after your parents."

"He's right, you know," Hayden said, walking into the room. "Alpha, we might need to move the wedding up."

"Why?"

"A storm is going to be moving in this afternoon." "Of course, it is," Edric sighed. "How much time do we have?"

"About four hours."

"That's not much time."

"No, it's not."

Edric looked at Jillian, then at Hayden. "Okay. Tell the caterers to speed things up and for the others in the backyard to get things set up quickly."

Hayden nodded and walked out.

"He can predict weather too?" Jillian asked.

"That man can do about anything, I swear he can," Edric chuckled.

Nadine walked into the room. "Hayden said a storm would be moving in?"

"Yes."

"Then we had better get you and the bride ready, yes?" she grinned.

"I suppose we do," Edric grinned and stood. He then helped Jillian up. "Come, my love, it is our big day, and it is time to go and get ready for it."

"But I don't have a dress."

"Check your room," he smiled, kissed her, and then walked out.

"Come on, daughter of mine," Nadine smiled. "Let's get you looking like a bride."

Jillian nodded and headed out the door and up to her room. Kimberly was there, wearing a beautiful dark blue gown. "You never said what colors you wanted for me to wear, but I thought it would match your bouquet."

"I get a bouquet?" Jillian asked.

"It's right here, Luna," Carla stepped forward to hand it to her. It was beautiful. There were blue roses tucked in the middle of white roses and a single red rose in the middle.

"Edric said the white is for purity," Carla and Kimberly both snickered, as Nadine said, "Blue is for the blue of your beautiful eyes, and the red is for his eternal love."

Jillian started to cry. "Stupid pregnancy hormones," she muttered, making the women laugh.

"Now come on, girl, let's get you ready," Kimberly said, pushing Jillian into a chair.

Carla had makeup, Nadine had a curling iron, and the two ladies got to work.

A while later, they stepped back and admired their handiwork. "Amazing," Carla breathed out.

"You look so beautiful," Nadine said, wiping at tears.

"And she doesn't even have her dress on," Kimberly grinned, bringing out a bag. She unzipped it and pulled out the most stunning dress Jillian had ever seen. It was beautiful, with diamonds in the bodice, sleeveless, and flared from the hips down, ending in a beautiful but short train.

"Are those real diamonds?" Jillian whispered, touching the dress reverently.

"They are," Carla nodded, "and how the Alpha pulled it off, I don't know."

"He chose this for me?" Jillian's eyes started to water.

"Now, Luna, no crying and ruining your makeup," Kimberly laughed, "and yes, he chose it for you."

Jillian stood, and the women helped her into it, then they tied, zipped, and buttoned her in. It fit perfectly. Carla then put some slippers on her feet. "That way, you aren't tripping down the stairs," she grinned.

"Oh my goodness," Nadine cried. "You are so exquisite. Wait until Edric sees you."

"Can I go look now?" Jillian asked.

"Not quite," Carla said, and walking over to a box on the bed, she opened it and pulled out a crown. "This, your Highness is your crown," she placed it onto Jillian's head. The three women began to cry. "Now you can go look," Carla whispered.

Jillian headed into the bathroom and gasped at her reflection. She didn't even recognize herself; she was so beautiful. Her hair was curled and piled onto her head under the crown, but a few curls surrounded her face. The makeup was light but made her look ethereal. She almost didn't recognize herself.

"*You go, girl,*" Aria chuckled. "*Won't Edric be panting when he sees you.*"

"*I think so,*" Jillian smiled.

"Wait, we forgot the necklace and earrings," Nadine said. Then she headed back into the bedroom and opened a box. Jillian gasped. Inside sat a sapphire necklace on a gold chain, with sapphire earrings.

"Those were mine; I wore those on my wedding day," Nadine whispered, tears in her eyes. "And you are supposed to have something borrowed and something blue."

She helped Jillian put them on, and then she handed Jillian her bouquet. "Your father is ready to walk you down the aisle."

"I am ready also," Jillian whispered, even though she was shaking. She was so nervous. Nervous about getting married and anxious about the outcome of the day.

Chapter 44

Jillian took a deep breath and headed out the door behind the other women. Ruben met Kimberly at the top of the stairs and kissed her. He then bowed gallantly to Jillian. "You look stunning, your Highness."

"Thank you, Ruben."

"Jillian," Henry said, stepping up to her, wiping at his eyes. "You look so beautiful."

"Thanks, Dad," she smiled at him. He took her arm in his and kissed her cheek. "Are you ready?"

"I think so," Jillian told him. Nadine headed down the stairs so she could go sit down outside, and then Ruben walked down the stairs, Kimberly on his arm. Jillian then followed with Henry.

Jillian took a deep breath as they headed down the hall and to the door that entered the backyard.

Adam was playing some soft music, which she didn't know was possible on an electric guitar, but it sounded nice. Then he started playing the wedding march.

"Are you ready, daughter?" Henry asked her.

"As ready as I will ever be."

Ruben and Kimberly headed outside, and then it was Jillian's turn to step outside. When she walked out, she hardly noticed the yard beautifully decorated and all of the people who were now standing and bowing their heads to her. All she could see was the most incredibly handsome man standing under an arch in a black tux, a matching crown on his head. He saw her step out and head to him. Jillian was an absolute vision. He had never seen anyone so incredible, and she was all his.

She stepped up to Edric, kissed Henry on the cheek, and then put her hand in Edric's hand.

He had tears in his eyes. "You look exquisite," he whispered to her.

"You look rather debonair yourself," she smiled at him.

"You both look stunning," Hayden smiled at them. Everyone took their seats but Kimberly, who stood by Jillian, and Warren, who stood by Edric as his best man.

"Welcome friends and family to this most joyous occasion," Hayden smiled. "You are about to witness a monumental occasion. For today I am going to wed the High Queen to the High King."

Everyone gasped; this was the High Queen and King? How was that possible?

"You see, I have a confession," Hayden smiled at Jillian and Edric. "Everyone thought that the royal princess was killed with her parents, but she was not. I saved her from such a fate and present her to you today, "High Luna Queen Jillian."

Everyone dropped to their knees; even Edric, Jillian's sweet Edric, bowed to her.

"Queen, King, it is time we marry you," Hayden chuckled as everyone got up a moment later and retook their seats. Edric stood up and grasped Jillian's hand in his, winking at her.

"I am going to spare you the long-drawn-out ceremony because of the storm moving in," he said, looking at Jillian. She knew what he meant—a storm not only from the clouds but from those wishing to attack them.

"High Alpha King, Edric Ventin, do you take High Luna Queen Jillian to be your bride?"

"I do," he said proudly.

"And do you, High Luna Queen Jillian Everett, take High Alpha King Edric Ventin to be your husband."

"I do," she smiled as tears fell down her face.

"Very good. I pronounce you man and wife, High Queen and High King."

Everyone cheered, but then Kimberly gasped as Warren stepped out from behind Edric, snuck behind Hayden, and walking up behind Jillian; he pulled out a long dagger and held it to her stomach.

"Nice ceremony, you two," he grinned evilly.

Edric's jaw dropped. He looked at Jillian. "Jillian, your dream, did you know?"

Tears came to her eyes as she nodded.

"Why didn't you say something?"

"Because I knew that I could take care of him," she told him.

"What do you mean?" he asked her.

"Hey, I have your Luna here and am going to kill her," Warren pointed out.

"Why, Warren? What did I do to you?" Edric asked his Beta, shock clearly written on his face.

"Well, first of all, you had Kelson killed, which was okay, by the way, because then I could take over the rogues."

"You are leading the rogues?" Edric growled.

"Yes, I am."

"But why? You are my Beta."

"So? I deserve to be King."

Warren nodded then, and several guests shifted into wolves. "Lovely Jillian, it is sad that you and your child won't live, but I really don't care."

"You are the one who has been after me this whole time?" Jillian asked, but it made sense, of course. The house being bugged, the car accidents, of course, he would have known where she was at all times.

"Of course, I was the one after you, and it was so easy too. My father, and then me chasing after you, your whole life, but Hayden always stopped us," he said, shaking his head. "Then I heard what was going on here with the Alpha and Kelson. Kelson and I were good friends, cousins actually, and then after he tried to become Alpha but lost, I stepped in as Beta; it was perfect. Get revenge on the Alpha for my cousin, but then imagine my delight when Edric found out you were his mate," he chuckled. "I was after you my whole life, and here you show up, just like that. It was perfect. My grandfather killed your parents and who they thought was you, but he was wrong, and now, here I am, to kill you and the Alpha. It is a dream come true," he chuckled evilly.

"Your grandfather killed my parents?" Jillian gasped.

"Yes, he did, and good riddance. They were too good, too pure, and too powerful, and my grandfather didn't like that." "What did I ever do to you?" Edric asked him, his heart heavy as he watched Warren hold the love of his life hostage. His guards were surrounding Warren without him noticing, but would they be able to save Jillian?

"You took my spot," Warren shrugged. "My grandfather and father wanted to be Alpha, and I should have been made Alpha also, which soon, I will be, but first, King, you are going to watch your Queen die, and you can't do a thing about it."

"Jillian," Edric whispered.

"I love you," Jillian cried.

"How sweet, time to die," Warren said, raising his knife to drive it into Jillian's stomach.

"*Time to shift*," Aria chuckled. "*And show this loser what we are made of.*"

Jillian suddenly dropped to the ground and became the most beautiful white wolf anyone had ever seen, her beautiful dress shredded to pieces as she shifted, but she didn't care. All she cared about was getting the man who had hurt her and was now trying to kill her. She turned to Warren and ripped his throat out. He didn't even have time to shift; he was so surprised. He dropped to the ground, dead, and all the Alpha's cheered, then turned into their wolves; it was time to have some fun.

"*Sweet,*" Aria chuckled. "*That was fun; let's do it some more.*"

"Jillian, you are a wolf?" Edric asked as he shifted.

"Sorry I didn't tell you, I have only known for two days," Jillian thought to him.

His wolf chuckled. *"Sweet."*

Edric felt a wolf jump on his back then, and he turned to fight him off. Several wolves surrounded Jillian, trying to protect her. *"No, I can defend myself,"* she told them. *"Go fight, defend the crown!"*

"Yes, your Highness," they all chorused and took off running to join the fight.

Aria chuckled as she bit someone's neck and threw them aside. *"More,"* Aria laughed as she headed into the middle of the fight.

Edric ran up to her. *"Jillian, stay out of this; I don't want you hurt."*

"Are you kidding?" Aria laughed and bit into another wolf, making it fall to the ground. *"Let me fight; I have the right to do so,"* Jillian replied and took off running, chasing after another wolf who was trying to go after Hayden. Jillian jumped onto the wolf and tore it apart.

Hayden bowed to her. "Thank you, your Highness, should I make it rain? It might slow them down."

She nodded at him, and he clapped his hands. It sounded like thunder.

"Sweet," Aria chuckled as it started to rain.

"You know, I can teach you how to do this, too," Hayden thought to her. *"You are more powerful than me."*

"Another day perhaps," Jillian said, chasing off after another wolf.

She suddenly felt herself being tackled and watched as two wolves sailed over her head. She rolled over to see Edric on top of her. She licked his face, making him chuckle.

The two rogue wolves stopped and turned, ready to attack the King and Queen.

"You take the right; I'll take the left," Raul told Aria.

"*You got it,*" she laughed, and the two leaped together at the wolves. Two mighty beings, more significant than the other wolves. One gray, one white.

Soon, the two wolves were dead, and Jillian headed to the laser barriers. She could see Emerson getting too close to the lasers. He suddenly pushed a wolf, and the wolf fell across the lasers and was cut in half.

"*Ouch, that's not going to heal,*" Aria chuckled as she joined Emerson.

A large wolf was trying to get to Emerson's neck, but Aria bit his leg, taking a massive chunk out of it. The wolf fell to the ground, and Emerson finished him off.

"*Thank you, your Highness,*" Emerson said, running to take another wolf down.

"*I am getting sick of this,*" Jillian told Aria. "*We need to put a stop to it.*"

"*I agree,*" Aria said, as one of the Alpha's fell across the lasers and was sliced in two.

"*Maybe that wasn't a smart idea to put that in,*" Aria said.

"*I agree, time to shut it off.*"

"*We're too far away from the breaker,*" Aria told her, and then they watched in horror as Edric was pushed closer to the laser.

He was busy defending himself from two wolves and didn't realize how close he was.

"*Edric, the lasers!*" Jillian cried out.

But he couldn't do anything about it. The two wolves were pushing him closer and closer, and no one was nearby to help him.

"*How are we going to stop them?*" Aria asked in a panic.

"*Watch me,*" Jillian stated and then shifted to her human form. She was ticked, really ticked. How dare those rogues try and kill her Alpha. As she shifted, she was dressed in an ethereal white dress. Her body and her eyes glowed blue, and those who were next to her dropped to the ground because they couldn't handle the power that was pouring from her.

"If Hayden can make it rain, I can make it lightning and thunder!" Jillian shouted, and gathering a lightning ball into her hands, she shot it at the breaker box, making it explode, just as Edric fell across the lasers.

He was sure he would die and grimaced as he hit the ground, but nothing happened. He had hit solid ground. He sighed in relief, and with renewed vigor, he took down both wolves trying to attack him.

"That is enough!" Jillian roared, making the ground shake. All the fighting stopped. They looked to their High Queen, who was glowing blue. The wolves whimpered at her power, and all of them dropped to the ground. Henry, Nadine, and the caterer hiding inside could even feel the power coming from her.

"Stop this now, or all of you who supported Warren will die!" she warned them, making them all whimper in pain. "Rogues, give up now!" she roared.

No one could move; she had such a hold on them; even Edric had difficulty moving. Hayden, who had just fried a wolf, was also on his knees, impressed that Jillian had power over him.

"Well, what is your answer?" Jillian growled at the rogues.

"*We surrender*," came the response.

"Good answer," she said and released them. All the wolves panted with relief, and those who were surrendering came to her in human form, kneeling before her. They would not mess with the High Queen anymore. They didn't want to die.

"Any Alpha that is capable, take these men," Jillian demanded of them. The Alpha's nodded and shifted into their human forms. There were several naked men suddenly, but Jillian didn't notice; all she saw was her love, her King, headed to her in all his naked glory. He walked up to her and bowed before her.

"My Queen," he choked out.

"My King," she responded, pulling him to his feet.

"Have I told you lately how amazing you are?"

She kissed him. "I know, and so are you; you are looking especially hot right now," she teased.

"You saved us, my Queen, and made the rogues surrender. I am proud of you," he said, ignoring her comment.

"Thank you, my King."

"My Queen," Emerson said, walking up to her and dropping to his knees. "Permission to transport the prisoners to a holding cell. We have one in the basement."

"Permission granted, Emerson, but not alone, take others with you, so they don't think of escaping."

He nodded and, jumping up; he headed away with the prisoners; there were about twenty of them left, the others were dead.

"My Queen," Kimberly approached her, kneeling at her feet. "I can't believe you are a wolf."

"I know, right?" Jillian laughed, pulling her friend to her feet and hugging her tightly. "I am glad you are okay."

"I am too. You saved us, and might I say, you can kick some serious ass."

Edric chuckled as Orson handed him a suit that he had brought from the house.

"Hmm, too bad you have to cover up such sexiness," Jillian told him as he put on his clothes.

He grinned. "Later, my love," he promised.

Jillian looked around the yard then, shaking her head. It looked like a tornado had hit. There were dead wolves everywhere, even the pool had wolves in it, and the water was a bright red from all of the blood. The chairs set up were now destroyed, along with the arch and all of the flowers.

Edric pulled her close to him. "I am sorry our wedding day was ruined."

"Are you kidding? That was the most excitement I have ever had in my life," Jillian grinned, making Aria chuckle.

"Besides, we still have food and cake," Jillian told him.

"Yes, yes, we do," Edric agreed. "I'll have the men help clean up this mess."

The wolves that were there for the wedding were now all dressed, and all of them headed to her, then fell to their knees.

"Your Great Highness," one of the Alpha's said, "We all swear fealty to you for as long as all of us live."

"Thank you, all of you," Jillian smiled at them. "Thank you for being here and defending us. Now, what do you say about having a party? I need to celebrate my marriage to an incredible man."

"And an incredible lady," Edric smiled and kissed her cheek.

"Since the backyard is ruined, let's head inside," Jillian suggested.

"That might be a problem since you fried the electricity," Carla told her, walking up to her; she bore her neck to Jillian while she smiled.

"I did fry the electricity, didn't I, but I don't regret it. I had to save my Alpha."

"I do appreciate that," Edric replied. "Why don't we have our reception out front? There is plenty of grass; we can set up tables and chairs out there."

"Good idea," Jillian grinned at him, "and we can clean up this mess later," she told him, waving her hand at the backyard.

Orson and Wes walked over to her then, and both dropped to their knees.

"High Queen," Orson said. "We would like to stay as your personal guards if we might."

"Why would you think otherwise?" Jillian asked him.

"Because the rumor going among the wolves is that all of them want to guard you."

Edric chuckled. "Do you think our High Queen needs that much protection?" he asked, pointing to the destroyed backyard. Everyone chuckled.

"No, I suppose not, but Wes and I would be honored if we could stay as your guards," Orson told her.

"Of course, Orson, I would be pleased to have you as our guards."

"Yes, your Highness," he said, then he and Wes got up to stand behind the royal couple, starting their new jobs as High Royalty Guards.

"Jillian, I mean, your Highness," Nadine said, walking up to her, Henry by her side, holding Jillian's crown. "This was in the mess in the backyard."

"And yours also, Alpha," Henry said, holding Edric's crown.

Jillian took hers, and Edric took his. "Well, High Queen, what do you say? Think we can have our happily ever after's now?" Edric asked, putting the crown on his head.

"I believe we just might," Jillian replied, putting her's on her head.

"*How about chasing some tail later,*" he thought to her and winked.

She blushed. "*Bring it on, my sexy Alpha King.*"

He chuckled. "*Oh, I will, believe me.*"

He tucked an arm about her waist. "Come, my Queen, let's go and cut our wedding cake."

"I have a wedding cake? How did you pull that one off?" she asked.

"It's just like the one you wanted, and you can thank Carla and Den," he smiled as they headed to the front of the palace, everyone following behind them.

"I am sorry that I destroyed that beautiful dress you got for me," Jillian told him.

"*I don't mind at all, especially when I saw your wolf come out. That was a whole lot sexier than anything I have ever seen,*" he thought to her, making her blush.

"*See, I told you I would be beautiful,*" Aria chuckled, "*and Raul agrees.*"

Jillian kissed her husband as they walked out front. "I love you, my High Alpha King."

"I love you, my High Luna Queen," he responded.

She looked around then. "Where did Hayden go?"

Edric chuckled. "He told me to tell you that he was not needed here. That he wouldn't be able to teach you a thing, so he is headed back home."

"I didn't get to say goodbye."

"But you can, remember?" he said, pointing at her head.

She smiled, "*Yes, that is nice, as long as you don't see all the things I have in here.*"

"*Why not? I want to know what goes on in that sexy mind of yours, especially when you are thinking of me.*"

She grinned and thought of something, and he actually blushed.

"Are you sure you want to be in my head?" she laughed.

"Even more so now," he chuckled, laying an incredible kiss on her lips.

"All right, you two, knock it off and come and cut the cake," Henry teased. "I'm hungry."

Jillian and Edric laughed. She was glad her adopted dad was finally warming up to Edric.

"*My great Luna Queen,*" Hayden sounded in her head then. "*I know you will be an incredible queen. Just stay true to yourself, and don't change for anyone.*"

"*I won't, Hayden, and thank you for everything.*"

"*No, thank you, sweet Jillian. You saved us all. You are truly your mother's daughter and then some. You would have shown her up any day.*"

Jillian teared up, and Edric looked at her.

She just smiled at him. "Hayden," she replied.

"He is a good man," Edric said.

"Yes, but you are a perfect man," Jillian replied; then, taking her husband's hand, they walked to the table that had their cake set on it. It was just as beautiful as she had imagined.

"Thank you, Carla and Den," she told them.

They bowed their heads to her. "Anything for you, High Queen," Carla smiled.

"Anything at all," Edric added, looking lovingly at his Luna. He was the luckiest man alive, and Jillian felt the same way about him.

Adam and his band, who miraculously didn't lose their equipment, set up in the front yard and began to play.

"High King, High Queen," Adam bowed to them, "I dedicate this song, borrowed from Kodaline to you," he said, "***You are the One.***"

Jillian knew that song; she loved that song. Edric pulled her into his arms. "This song was made for us."

"It is," she agreed. "Because you are my only one."

"As you are mine," he said and kissed her deeply, sealing his love for her.

Epilogue

"Push, Luna, push," Carla told her. She was in Edric and Jillian's room; Jillian was on the bed and in labor. Her friend Kimberly was there, as was Nadine, and Dr. Benson, who had been made their doctor since Dr. Hess was gone.

"Just a few more pushes, Luna, I can see the head," Dr. Benson told her.

Edric was standing by her side, gripping Jillian's hand. "You can do it, love," he told her, leaning down and kissing her cheek.

"Here it comes," Dr. Benson said. He pulled a little and out popped the baby.

"It's a boy," Dr. Benson said proudly.

"We have a boy?" Edric asked, tears in his eyes.

"Hold on," Dr. Benson said, "push Luna, one more time," he told her, handing off the little boy to Carla.

"Here's another one," he chuckled as another baby popped out.

"Twins?" Jillian cried.

"Twins," Dr. Benson said, "This one is a girl."

Jillian looked up at Edric, who was crying. "Twins, my love," he said reverently. Jillian smiled at him, tears in her eyes, as she watched her sweet husband cry with joy.

"What are you going to name them?" Kimberly asked as the umbilical cords were cut, and the babies were placed on Jillian's chest.

"I think the boy should be Rodrick Hayden Ventin," Edric replied, "named after my father and our great friend."

Jillian nodded. "Yes, Hayden would love that, and for the girl, I would like to name her Eliza Nadine Ventin, after my High Queen-mother and my mother that raised me."

Nadine began to cry, as did Kimberly.

"Thank you, sweet daughter of mine," Nadine whispered.

Edric picked up Rodrick, who looked at him with beautiful blue eyes.

"They are going to be a handful if they take after their mother," he teased, snuggling the warm little body against him.

Jillian tucked Eliza against her. "Are you kidding? They are going to be perfect children, just like their mother," she grinned at him.

"Yes, you are quite perfect," Edric agreed and then kissed her until the babies started to cry.

Nadine laughed. "Well, we all know who is going to rule the palace now."

"You had better believe it," Jillian laughed and kissed her little girl. Edric handed Rodrick to Jillian so she could feed the babies. Everyone left the room to give her privacy, except for Edric, who sat down by her. "I am a father," he whispered, looking at his children in awe.

"You are going to be a perfect one, too," Jillian told him.

He leaned in and kissed her. "And you, my High Queen, are going to be an incredible mother, as long as you don't spoil them rotten."

"That's what grandparents are for," Jillian smiled. "We need to call Helen and Albert and let them know the good news."

"After you heal, my love," he told her.

"I already am healed; I am good like that," she winked at him.

"Yes, yes, you are good like that," he growled at her, then his wolf howled with joy.

Aria howled back, and the rest of the household answered back in howls, Long Live The Royal Family!

Printed in Great Britain
by Amazon

16089718R00228